Tammy McDonald

A Slender Thread

TRACIE PETERSON

A Slender Thread

BETHANY HOUSE PUBLISHERS
MINNEAPOLIS, MINNESOTA 55438

Published by Bethany House Publishers
A Ministry of Bethany Fellowship International
11400 Hampshire Avenue South
Minneapolis, Minnesota 55438
ISBN: 0-7394-1061-X

Printed in the United States of America

In loving memory of my grandmother
Georgia Williams

"Many women do noble things,
but you surpass them all.
Charm is deceptive, and beauty is fleeting;
but a woman who fears the LORD is to be praised."
Proverbs 31:29-30

Books by Tracie Peterson

Controlling Interests
Entangled
Framed
A Slender Thread

WESTWARD CHRONICLES

A Shelter of Hope
Hidden in a Whisper
A Veiled Reflection

RIBBONS OF STEEL*

Distant Dreams
A Hope Beyond
A Promise for Tomorrow

RIBBONS WEST*

Westward the Dream
Separate Roads
Ties That Bind

*with Judith Pella

TRACIE PETERSON is an award-winning speaker and writer who has authored over thirty-five books, both historical and contemporary fiction. Her latest book, *Ties That Bind,* follows the history of America's railroads and is co-written with Judith Pella. Tracie and her family make their home in Kansas.

Visit Tracie's Web site at: http://members.aol.com/tjpbooks

"Let a man set his heart only on doing the will of God and he is instantly set free! No one can hinder him. It is only when we introduce our own will into our relation to God that we get into trouble. When we weave into the pattern of our lives threads of our own desires we instantly become subject to hindrances from the outside."

A.W. TOZER

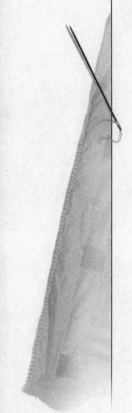

PART ONE

textures and colors

Chapter 1

Ashley Mitchell Issacs looked at her mother from across the room. It amazed Ashley that her mother had maintained her youthful beauty after all this time. Though nearly fifty years old, she appeared flawlessly young. From the stylish cut of her brown hair to the elegant gold jewelry around her neck and dangling from her ears, Rachelle Barrister could only be described as stunning.

"She looks wonderful in Christian Dior" came a voice from Ashley's side.

Turning, Ashley faced her sister Brook. The mirror image of her identical twin had a comforting effect on Ashley. "When did you get here?" she asked, hugging Brook tightly.

"Oh, about ten minutes ago. I got waylaid by Erica and Deirdre as I came in."

Ashley nodded knowingly. As one of five sisters, she knew very well how that could happen. She herself had been caught off guard by their middle sister, Connie.

"Did you drive here alone?" Brook questioned, glancing around. "Didn't Jack and the boys come?"

"No, Jack just couldn't do it. He was lucky to get time away from the hospital to spend with the kids while I came here. The boys are still in school, after all, and we didn't want to disrupt them." Ashley didn't add that she wished she'd insisted her husband and sons accompany her. The day promised to be a large-scale ordeal, and Ashley needed them to keep her calm. "So I flew in by myself, rented a car, and drove here from Kansas City."

"Me too," Brook admitted. "Too bad we didn't think to coordinate our trips." Smiling, she stepped back to assess her sister's dress. "I see we still think alike."

Ashley laughed softly and noted the matching Calvin Klein dress that Brook wore. "I wondered if we'd show up wearing the same thing. I mean, with me living in Denver and you in New York, I thought there might be some chance we'd have found our own creative outlets."

"We've always had our own creative outlets," Brook replied, "but I kind of like the way we seem to gravitate toward the same styles for really important moments in life."

Ashley frowned. "I suppose this is an important moment."

"Probably more important for our mother than for us," Deirdre Mitchell Woodward said, joining her sisters. She gave Ashley a hug and stepped back, smiling. Four years her sisters' junior, Deirdre shared many of the twins' characteristics and facial features. All three had nut-brown hair, compliments of their mother, and the dark brown Mitchell eyes. They were all about the same medium height and slender frame, with exception to the fact that Brook, a model in New York, kept herself a good twenty pounds lighter.

"Every appearance is important to Rachelle," Erica, the baby of the family, joined in. Her dark auburn curls betrayed her recent trip to the salon.

"I like your hair," Ashley declared, giving Erica a quick hug. "It suits you very nicely."

"Yes, I like it a lot," Brook agreed.

"What about mine?" The voice came from behind them, and all four sisters turned to find Connie, the middle child of the family, starkly changed from the last time they'd seen her. Her hair, now bleached to blond and cut in a boyish shortness, seemed well suited for the sister who had spent a lifetime going out of her way to be different.

Ashley nodded, determined to show no sign of disapproval or shock. Connie could be so funny about the way people responded to her. "I think it's very nice. I meant to tell you that earlier," Ashley added, though she thought it made Connie look rather hard and unapproachable.

"Where's Grammy?" Erica asked, glancing around the room.

Ashley realized she'd lost track of her grandmother. Mattie Mitchell had been a mother to all five of the girls—in fact, if it hadn't been for her, probably none of them would have been here on this most austere of days.

"She's probably just talking to someone before we get this ordeal started," Ashley said, still not able to locate where Mattie had slipped off to.

"Are you going to stay at the farm?" Connie asked Ashley.

"I suppose so," she replied. "Are you?"

Connie nodded. "I figured Grammy would want it that way—you know, have us all under one roof again."

"It has been a while," Erica admitted.

"I'd say so," Deirdre replied. "I figure it's been at least three years since we were all together. It was that Fourth of July celebration when Morgan was just two years old."

"How is my little niece?" Ashley questioned. She and Deirdre were the only ones who had married and produced children. Brook was busy with her career, and Connie had never seemed to settle down to just one guy. Erica, on the other hand, appeared precariously close to being engaged to a wonderful young man named Sean Foster.

"Morgan is fine. I left her home with Dave. He agreed with me that this was no place for kids. After all, she hasn't a clue who Rachelle is."

"Jack and I felt the same way about John and Zach. I'm sure they'd have a ball at the farm, but for this . . ." Ashley let her words trail off. She looked at her mother again—almost against her will. "A funeral is no place for children."

The five sisters walked collectively to where their mother's casket was on display. Ashley sighed and privately wished that Jack and the boys had been there with her. She hated being away from them, even for a few days. All she could think of was how she was missing the boys coming home from school, listening to their stories, tucking them into bed at night. She missed Jack's reassuring touch and smile, and she absolutely despised the fact that she had to trade time with those she really loved for someone she didn't care about at all.

Rachelle Barrister, her own mother, was dead. Ashley felt guilty as she realized that this fact elicited nothing more in the way of emotions than anger and frustration.

Seeing Mattie approach, Ashley tried to forget the anger she held against her mother. Mattie didn't deserve to deal with that today, and Ashley knew full well that her grandmother was trying desperately to cope with her own pain. The loss of a child, even a very absent child, could never be easy.

"We need to take our seats," Mattie said, reaching out to put her arm around the closest of her two granddaughters. Deirdre and Brook received her embrace with warmth and love.

"Oh, Grammy, how are you holding up?" Brook questioned first.

"I'm doing all right," the older woman replied.

But Ashley could see the regret and longing in her grandmother's eyes. A simple glance toward the coffin revealed her emotion. Mattie felt responsible for Rachelle's absence in the lives of her daughters, and Ashley knew this without Mattie speaking a word.

The organist began playing a soft medley of hymns. Ashley had spent some twenty years attending this small Kansas church, but she didn't recognize the woman now seated at the organ. Times changed. People grew up and moved away and people died. Died without caring about reconciling the past. Died without knowing what the future might hold.

"Come on, girls," Mattie said, motioning them toward the front row of pews. "It's time to pay our last respects."

Ashley took a seat beside her grandmother, while Brook sat on the other side of her. It seemed ridiculous to pretend to care about the woman in the casket. She had never been much more than an image in a photograph. *How does one pay their last respects, Ashley* wondered silently, *when there was no respect in the first place?*

Chapter 2

For as long as Deirdre could recall, the church had looked much the same. The single narrow aisle down the center of the building led straight through the sanctuary to the slightly elevated pulpit. Positioned at the base of the stage, a twelve-foot wooden rail marked the place where people could come and kneel in prayer. Deirdre had accepted Jesus as her Savior at that altar railing. She had seen her sisters do likewise. It was here that Mattie came regularly to lay her various burdens at the feet of Jesus. And now it was the place where Rachelle Barrister's casket had been so artfully displayed.

Deirdre nervously crossed her legs, then uncrossed them. Folding her hands in her lap, she was determined not to think about her mother's lifeless body in the casket at the front of the church. Rachelle meant nothing to her. She was little more than a stranger, and in her absence, Mattie had been the only mother any of them had ever known or wanted.

Deirdre knew it was Rachelle's desertion that made her cling so protectively to her relationship with her own daughter, Morgan. She had wanted to bring Morgan with her to Grammy's but realized that Dave's suggestion of keeping her in Kansas City made more sense. His folks were only five and a half hours away in St. Louis. Besides, they loved nothing more than to come and spend time with their only grandchild.

Deirdre had finally agreed, knowing that Morgan would probably have more fun, and this way she would also not have her kindergarten attendance disrupted. But Deirdre needed her daughter. Even if she was only five years old, Deirdre found a source of strength in Morgan's presence. Motherhood had been fiercely important to Deirdre. She wanted children more than anything else, and when she'd been blessed to have Morgan, she immediately began to plan for her child's future. Maybe that was why it was so hard to imagine her own mother giving birth to five children only to desert them all. Grammy had tried many times to explain—even excuse Rachelle—but somehow it had never rung true for Deirdre, who would rather die than be separated permanently from her daughter.

When Rachelle had run away and married Gary Gable at age sixteen, she found herself almost immediately pregnant with twins. Abortion wasn't legal at that time, and even if it had been, Rachelle had held to the beliefs of her upbringing that a human life was indeed a human life—whether she wanted it to be or not. Rachelle gave birth to her daughters, then quickly found herself overwhelmed with them. Hoping to save her young marriage, Rachelle had begged Mattie to take Brook and Ashley before hurrying off to try to reconcile with her husband.

But it was a marriage hardly worth saving, as far as Deirdre was concerned. How could a mother who chose her husband over her children and a father who couldn't have cared less that they even existed be selfless enough to make a marriage work? It had begun to disintegrate almost from the start—and why not? They were both too young. He was into drugs and drinking and she was simply looking for a male figure to fill the void left by her father's death.

When Connie was born, everyone who knew the young couple realized Connie wasn't Gary's child. Thus, getting rid of Connie and relegating her to Mattie had been an easy choice. Two years later, however, with the hope that their marriage was finally on the right track, Rachelle had given birth to Deirdre. She was to be their love child. They were going to raise Deirdre and focus their attention and time on her, and they were going to do things right. Never mind that Mattie was back in Council Grove, Kansas, raising three little girls all under the age of five.

Deirdre often found herself feeling guilty about her position.

Her sisters knew that Rachelle had purposefully gotten pregnant with Deirdre—the only one of the five she had planned. Her sisters also knew that while their mother had decided on a new life with Deirdre as her child, they were given little consideration. Deirdre felt horrible for that, but it wasn't like she'd had anything to do with it. Besides, it didn't work out the way Rachelle had planned anyway.

Things might have gone all right, had Gary Gable not found another love. Heroin became his full-time mistress. And by the time Rachelle found out how much money Gary was putting into his heroin addiction, she had learned to her horror that she was pregnant again, despite being on birth-control pills. Realizing the babies would be born barely nine months apart, Rachelle considered abortion to be a reasonable way out.

But then Gary had died from an overdose, and Rachelle had been too stupefied to do anything. Within months of Erica's birth, however, other people had taken Rachelle in hand and the life they had plotted out for her had nothing to do with children. Once again, Rachelle made the trek to Mattie's farm and left yet two more children with her mother. Only this time she assured Mattie there would be no more. She'd had her tubes tied to prevent further pregnancy and was leaving the area for good. Then, to Mattie's surprise, she laid out adoption papers with the promise that if Mattie didn't take her daughters, Rachelle would put them into a state agency.

Deirdre sometimes wondered if her mother would have really taken her children to the agency, but there was no way of knowing the answer. Mattie had apparently thought it a big enough threat that she took on the responsibility of two more children without further consideration.

Glancing down the row at her grandmother, Deirdre thought Mattie Mitchell deserved some kind of award for her sacrifice. *I wouldn't be here if not for her. I wouldn't know love or security or even how to care for Morgan, if not for Grammy.*

Deirdre glanced forward and forced herself to reconsider Rachelle. *I don't even know you. I have no memory of anything personal or real with* _you. You are nothing more than an image—a thought. A very fleeting thought._

As she settled into the pew, Ashley thought about the pain and suffering Rachelle had caused. Ashley convinced herself that it didn't matter, however. She was only really here for Mattie. Mattie, the only mother Ashley had ever known. The only mother she would ever need.

But if that's true, she thought, _then why do I have such a feeling of disappointment?_ It was almost as if she felt cheated and let down. But why? Why should she care that Rachelle was gone, when she'd never been there in the first place? Why should Ashley even give it a second thought?

She is your mother, a voice in her head reminded.

But in name only, Ashley argued with herself. _She left us with Grammy and rarely ever bothered to even find out how we were doing. She chose her life and we weren't a part of it._

Despite Ashley's attempts to eliminate Rachelle's image from her life, she knew quite well that her mother had always been an unseen presence. Ashley had purposefully scrutinized Rachelle's shortcomings and had tallied them in a mental list, determined to be nothing at all like her mother.

Ashley had married a handsome professional man, settled into an upper-class community, and given birth to two boys. She was the epitome of a successful woman. A superwoman—at least her own version of one. But behind it all, she sadly had to admit, she had been driven by Rachelle's image.

As bad a mother as Rachelle had been, Ashley had worked in the opposite direction in order to be noted for her capabilities and graciousness in the role. She never complained when the PTO called her the night before to request four dozen cookies for a class party. Instead, she would always brush off the oversight and ask if four dozen would be enough. Then, should the mere mention be made of buying cookies at the store, Ashley would nix the idea, proclaiming it no trouble at all to bake them herself. She was just as bad when it came to working with the social groups she and Jack had chosen for their pastimes.

Frowning, she bit her lip. *Rachelle has made me who I am . . . I was driven by a desire to be nothing like her.* As she pondered the revelation, it slowly revealed the reason behind her disappointment. Ashley supposed she would have liked to have had her mother acknowledge her accomplishments.

If just once she would have come to see the boys, Ashley thought sadly. Just once. Just to see what they looked like . . . if they favored her. If only Rachelle would have taken time away from the world she'd created for herself in order to partake of the world she'd left behind.

I could have forgiven her then, Ashley reasoned. *If she would have come to me . . . even then . . . I could have forgiven her the lost years.*

Brook, too, was troubled by thoughts of the years she'd spent hoping for some kind of acknowledgment from her mother. Her anxiety had caused her to throw up twice before even getting as far as the church, and she couldn't help but wonder if she'd be able to keep from running to the rest room to relieve herself before the funeral was completed.

She hated her nervous stomach. Hated that she felt light-headed and faint anytime something became overly traumatic. Her friends teased her that if living in New York City didn't keep her in a per-petual state of anxiety, then why should simple things like dating or going home to family cause her to lose her lunch?

But it wasn't a simple thing to return home. Mattie was too per-ceptive and Ashley could read her like a book. Deirdre, Erica, and Connie were less capable of knowing her innermost thoughts, but they weren't averse to trying to figure them out. Privacy was a luxury in a large family.

Flexing her fingers, Brook laced them together and sat ner-vously, awaiting the eulogy. She didn't want to think about the woman in the coffin. She didn't want the others to know how it hurt her to realize she was never going to know Rachelle Barrister—her own mother.

It's just that she never wanted us, Brook thought, staring at an arrangement of apricot roses. *She didn't want a family—she wanted a career. If she had ever shown us the slightest reason to believe she was acting in our best interest instead of her own* . . .

Brook sighed and pushed aside those thoughts, as she did all the other unpleasant feelings . . . feelings of betrayal and frustration and bitterness. Rachelle's betrayal had fueled Brook's need for revenge, a need to prove her own beauty and ability. During long flights and endless modeling sessions, when everyone from photographers to agents had made passes at her, Brook's desire to show up Rachelle kept her motivated.

She crossed her legs and relaced her fingers. Why did it have to be this way? What purpose was there in the events of her life? Gram had said that all things happened for a reason—that coincidences didn't exist. If that were true, then how could Brook explain her life—the choices—the mistakes? Without the hope of trying to attract Rachelle's attention, what purpose did she have in going back to a world she had come to despise?

As if reading her mind, Ashley leaned over and whispered, "I feel so lost."

Brook met her sister's ashen-faced expression. "Me too."

"I think I have been trying to one-up Rachelle. Isn't that awful? It's just finally sinking in. I wanted to show her how great I'd turned out—how I did it all without her. And now she's gone and she probably never knew and furthermore, never cared."

"I know how you feel," Brook whispered back.

Ashley's gaze was direct. "Really?"

"I hate to admit it, but I'm seeing a side of myself that I have ignored for a long, long time. And I fear I might find myself more devastated over Rachelle's death than I ever expected to be."

"I was just thinking that. I would never, ever have expected it."

"Never," Brook muttered, shaking her head. "We might as well have never existed as far as Rachelle was concerned, yet here she is in the middle of our lives, having a control we vowed she would never have."

Ashley's voice fell silent and Brook caught a rustling sound behind her. Turning to look, she couldn't help being stunned to meet the sober expression of Harry Jensen. He gave her the briefest nod before squeezing Mattie's shoulders in a supportive manner. Mattie turned, and Brook saw the way her face lit up to find her life-long neighbor sitting behind her. After Harry's parents had died and he'd inherited the farm adjoining the Mitchell land, he and Mattie had become like mother and son. Mattie and her husband, Edgar, had been good friends with Harry's parents. In fact, Edgar and Harry's father, Jacob, had been the best of friends. They might as well have been blood family for the way they took care of each other. And in the same way, Brook knew that Harry had come here to support Mattie in her hour of need. Mindless of how it might affect anyone else.

Taking a deep breath, Brook turned back around. "Don't look now," she whispered to Ashley, "but Harry's here."

Her sister's stoic expression never changed. "Where?"

"Right behind you."

Brook glanced at Ashley, wondering if it still hurt her to see him. Ashley and Harry had been a certainty that Brook would have put money on. They seemed perfect together and yet . . . Rachelle. That was the reason Ashley and Harry didn't work out. Rachelle stood in their way. Ashley, too, had had to make a different life for herself. A life her mother might take notice of and be intimidated by.

Ashley might have been happy with Harry, Brook couldn't help but think. *And I might have been happy too—happy and content to live in Kansas and marry a sweet farmer like Harry rather than getting entangled with the fast-paced life I live now.*

Brook glanced back at him and found him studying the funeral agenda. Ruggedly handsome in well-defined features, Harry wore the years well. Only five years older than she and Ashley, Harry maintained a boyish charm that had captivated most of the girls when they'd been growing up. Brook couldn't help but wonder if Harry felt nervous about being here. After all, he had loved Ashley quite deeply. Her rejection of him nearly ten years ago had stunned everyone in the family. Brook could only imagine how much it had stunned Harry. Since that time, Brook knew her sister had gone out of her way to avoid seeing Harry—even when she returned to the farm to see Mattie. Brook looked over to Ashley and squeezed her hand. The day promised to be quite trying.

The pastor, a lean man in his fifties with piercing blue eyes and wavy brown hair, stepped up to the podium. Brook drew a deep breath and forced herself to look forward. She felt her stomach churn nervously. *I only have to get through the next few hours and then all of this will be behind me,* she promised herself. But would it really be behind her? Could she honestly relegate Rachelle to the past?

"I'm pleased to have the Mitchell girls back in our congregation, but sad that it should have to be on an occasion such as this," Pastor Paul Wallace said. "I know this is a difficult day for all of you. I know, too, that you face many mixed emotions in dealing with Rachelle's death. For this reason, I will open us in prayer and then proceed in the manner outlined for me by Mattie."

The girls bowed their heads and Brook was only slightly surprised when Ashley reached for her hand. It seemed only natural that Brook reach for Deirdre's, and she felt a sense of completion when Deirdre reached for Erica's and Erica did likewise with Connie.

"Father, this day is among the most difficult for any person to endure. A loved one has passed away and the loss that is felt comes to us in different ways. We ask that you would oversee this day and the days to come. We thank you for your mercy and honor you this day as the all-knowing God who directs our steps. In Jesus' name, amen."

Brook felt her sisters release their hold and instantly wished that she could somehow get it back.

"Rachelle Mitchell Gable, better known as Rachelle Barrister, was born right here in Council Grove, Kansas. She lived her childhood here and later married and moved away. She gave birth to five daughters; they survive her."

Survive her. What a perfect expression, Brook thought. That is exactly what we did.
We survived her desertion. We survived her absence. We survived her.

The pastor looked up and met their faces. Brook thought he looked very sympathetic and compassionate. And why not? He'd been the pastor of this church for the last twenty-some years. He'd watched them grow up and leave home and more than once he'd counseled them in times of need.

He smiled benevolently. "Mattie asked me to be less formal, to not dwell on the obvious. We all know the details of Rachelle's life. We could spend the entire day listing her accomplishments, but that would serve you poorly and it would hardly help Rachelle. This family has endured much pain and I know the way hasn't always been easy. But there is a strength you have in each other—a strength that makes you more than merely survivors of Rachelle Barrister—it makes you family."

Connie heard the words but found it difficult to focus on the meaning. She glanced at her watch as covertly as she could manage and noted that less than ten minutes had passed. It seemed like an eternity. She shifted uncomfortably, feeling her straight navy skirt bind as she moved. This was the last place in the world she wanted to be.

Connie didn't know if she could buy into the pastor's words on family. She knew that he hoped to bring them together—probably for Mattie more than anyone. After all, Mattie was the one still living here in Council Grove, Kansas. No doubt Mattie had to face the questions of her neighbors and friends. *"Where did your girls get themselves off to?" "When are they coming home?"* Connie supposed it was hard for some folks to understand the need to break away from the farm—to live a life where the memories couldn't hurt you.

Connie almost laughed out loud at that thought. *Is there such a place?* If there was, Connie had never found it. Memories still haunted—still wounded—even when you lived a hundred miles away.

The eulogy continued, but Connie hardly even heard the words.

She hadn't come here to listen to her mother's praises being sung, neither had she come here to get some psychological or theological lecture on how she should find strength in her family. She knew all of that already. The only trouble was, she never felt very much a part of the family. Being the middle child of five had its grave disadvantages, and Connie had endured every one of them. And while she couldn't change her birth order, she could manage her feelings toward the mother she had never known.

It seemed odd to feel so unfamiliar with her own mother, but Connie knew that if given a chance to speak their minds, her sisters would no doubt agree with her. Mattie said they could know Rachelle, at least in part, because they had each other and even Mattie to find comparisons in. But no matter how hard Connie tried to find her mother in others, it never made up for the fact that she had never been there in the first place.

Against her will, Connie remembered feeling outcast by her friends. They were both in awe of her mother and in contempt of Connie's position. *"Why isn't your mother ever home? Where is she?"* They would ask her these and other taunting questions. *"If your mother loved you, she would take you to live with her."*

Even now the wound felt raw. Then another, even more painful memory came to mind. Connie had once tried to telephone Rachelle, only to be intercepted by her mother's personal secretary. The woman had assured Connie that Rachelle would probably have loved to talk to Connie, but that now wasn't a good time. There was never a good time, Connie quickly came to understand.

"Rachelle may be gone from this earth," Pastor Paul was saying, "but she has left a legacy that will remain for generations to come. A legacy comprised of flesh and blood. This legacy is you." He said the words so simply, yet Connie felt almost startled by them.

"God, too, has given us a legacy. An inheritance from Father to child. He offers us eternal life—salvation through His Son, Jesus. A free gift that we have but to accept in order to obtain. We are His children—His family. No one person is more important than the other.

"Scripture likens it to the parts of a body, all of which are necessary to support the whole. Just as Scripture points out that one part of the body can't say to another part, 'You aren't important. You aren't needed,' neither should we say those words to one another."

But I don't feel important or needed, Connie thought to herself. She folded her arms against her chest as if to shield herself from being hurt by the words. Talk is cheap. Wasn't that the old adage? Put your money where your mouth is. Of course, she knew the pastor couldn't give her what she needed. She doubted very seriously that what she needed could ever be provided.

Pastor Paul seemed to be concluding his service, and for this reason alone, Connie forced the dreary thoughts away from her mind.

"I want you to remember today that nothing Rachelle Barrister has done matters anymore. She is gone and there is nothing more she can do or say to change her life. But just as clearly as this is true, it is also true that you are still alive. You are here and you have a choice to make." He stepped down from the podium and went to stand at the end of Rachelle's coffin.

"Rachelle made mistakes—poor judgments—and often very hurtful decisions. But she will never make another. You, on the other hand, are alive and free to determine how you will deal with this situation."

Connie bowed her head ever so slightly. She couldn't handle the intensity of the pastor's words. She knew her life was a mess. She didn't need him to remind her of it.

I won't listen. I will think of anything but what he's saying. I will think of home.

"Sometimes we get a second chance." The pastor's voice pierced her thoughts.

"Sometimes we don't," she nearly murmured aloud. She felt as if a band were tightening around her chest. It caused her to draw her arms even closer, tensing against the feeling of pressure.

"Sometimes we lose our way."

I won't listen. She wanted to put her hands over her ears.

"But sometimes—just when we least expect it," he said very softly, "we find it again."

Connie forced herself to remain seated. It would be over in just a few minutes, and then she would never again have to listen to anything so unnerving. She made a mental rundown of anything and everything that came to mind. She spelled the months of the year backward and then tried to remember the entire Declaration of Independence, which she'd had to memorize in high school.

And then it was over. Pastor Paul was praying, and before she knew it they were standing and thanking him for a lovely service. Connie edged away from where Mattie and her sisters shared their thoughts with the gentle pastor. She wanted no part of this.

"Running away?" a deep, husky voice questioned.

The words startled Connie and she jumped. Looking up, she found Harry Jensen staring at her rather quizzically.

"Connie, are you okay?" he asked as she continued to look at him.

"Yes," she said. "I'm perfectly fine."

"You look as white as a sheet."

"It's been a hard day," she admitted. "And seeing you is . . . well . . . a surprise."

He smiled. "Why is that? You had to know I'd be here for Mattie."

Connie nodded. "I suppose I could have figured that. I'm surprised you recognized me, though. It's been a long time since I saw you and . . . well, I've changed a lot in that time."

"Not so much," Harry said, smiling. "The hair is a little dramatic, but it's still the same pretty face."

Connie felt her cheeks grow hot. No doubt Harry would note her blush and realize his comment was the cause. She turned away rather abruptly and said, "Gram seems to be holding up pretty well."

"She's a strong woman," Harry replied. "She has to be."

Connie turned back. "What's that supposed to mean?" She knew her suspicious, even guilt-ridden nature was getting the best of her, but there seemed to be a challenge in Harry's words.

"It means just what I said," Harry replied. "She has to be strong. Life's dealt her some harsh blows—the death of her husband and son when they were both so young and vital, and now the death of her only other child."

"She's not the only one who's had to be strong," Connie said, knowing how selfish the words sounded. She thought to take them back but knew it would do little good. She hadn't wanted to alienate Harry—not really. Not any more than she wanted to alienate anyone else. She simply didn't want to deal with the pain, and sometimes putting people away from her before they could hurt her was the best thing she could do.

Chapter 3

Mattie watched each of her girls carefully. In so many ways they were no different from the children she'd raised. The twins stayed close, usually consoling each other in unspoken ways. A touch here, a glance there. It was their way—a bond that no one had ever been able to come between. Erica and Deirdre were standing together, their whispered thoughts exchanged as they carefully observed the others. Ever the peacemaker of the family, Deirdre kept a kind of silent vigil over the group. Mattie had seen her do this since she had been quite small. She always seemed to observe the family, watching for trouble, heading it off before it got out of control.

And while Deirdre was the self-appointed peacemaker, Erica, barely nine months younger, was the happy-go-lucky sort that just seemed to take life as it came. Babies of the family were often that way, Mattie had observed over the years. They wore hand-me-down clothes and found themselves passed around among the other siblings while exhausted mothers—or grandmothers, in this case—struggled to meet some newly mandated deadline.

Then there was Connie. Connie had always been a bit more difficult than the rest, Mattie remembered with a smile. But Connie had been the one most like Rachelle. Rachelle with her wild, independent streak. Rachelle with her penchant for danger and adventure.

Thinking of her only daughter caused Mattie more pain than she cared to admit. She made her way to the casket, happy that everyone had preoccupied themselves with someone else. She needed a few moments alone.

The woman in the casket hardly resembled the lively teenager

Mattie had raised. Gently, Mattie touched her daughter's cold hand. *Oh, Rachelle . . . my daughter.* Tears came to Mattie's eyes and her previously squared, strong shoulders slumped forward in sorrow.

I failed you, my little one. I failed you. I wish I could somehow live life all over again and do things right. When your Daddy and little Robbie died in that car accident, I should have known the pain would be devastating to you. I should have found a better way to help you deal with your grief. Maybe if I had, you wouldn't have run away. You wouldn't have gone searching the world for a love that always existed for you at home.

Mattie regretted the past, holding a painful notion that somewhere along the way she had been an inadequate mother. When her beloved Edgar and son, Robbie, had died on an icy highway, Mattie had felt the bottom go out of her world. Left alone with a farm and a twelve-year-old daughter, Mattie had done the best job she could do. Sadly, it hadn't been enough.

Rachelle had withdrawn inside herself, and Mattie had been too preoccupied with seeing to their finances and other needs to give her the attention she needed. *But I tried,* Mattie reasoned. *I tried to talk to you, Rachelle. I tried to make you realize the accident wasn't your fault.* But Rachelle had always bore a guilt that Mattie knew would never be easily dissolved. Edgar had been on his way to pick up Rachelle from school when the car slid off the ice-covered road and over an embankment. The twelve-year-old had never been able to get past the idea that she had been the cause of her father's death.

"I wanted so much more for you," Mattie whispered. She knew that if anyone would have overheard her, they'd never have understood. Rachelle Barrister had everything money could buy. What more could Mattie have desired? But there was so much more.

"The cars are ready to take us to the cemetery," Pastor Wallace said softly.

Mattie turned and smiled. "You did a wonderful job. I'm sure the graveside service will be just as lovely."

"Probably a bit more crowded," Harry said, coming to stand beside Mattie. "I think you did well to limit the church service."

Mattie nodded. "Such madness. I suppose we can't put it off."

"I'll be right beside you," Harry promised.

Mattie looked up at the young man who had become like a son to her. They had needed each other, and with nothing more than a scenic lake and acres of farmland between them, it had been only natural for them to share their loneliness. Not only were their farms joined, their lives were joined as well. Harry had become just as important to Mattie as any of the girls.

Taking a deep breath, Mattie looked to Harry for direction. "I guess I'm ready."

Harry jumped back as photographers snapped pictures and forced microphones in front of his face. Behind him, Mattie and the others were trying to emerge from the church, but the press was making it almost impossible. The death of world-renowned actress Rachelle Barrister was the type of affair the media craved, especially in light of the cause of her death, an overdose of sleeping pills. Accidental or on purpose, no one could be sure, but the actress had been en route to a remote location in Alaska where she was filming her latest movie. When the plane landed and her personal secretary, Mavis Lane, attempted to wake the sleeping actress, disaster unfolded and a world tragedy was born.

Turning, Harry took hold of Mattie's arm. "This looks like it will be quite an ordeal," he said, leaning close to her ear. "I'll get you out of here the best way I can."

"Sorry about this, Harry," Mattie replied.

Harry pushed forward, hoping that Mattie's granddaughters would have the good sense to follow at a close pace. "Look, they don't want to talk to you, so just back off!" he declared to the press.

"Please, Mrs. Mitchell, could you just answer a few questions?"

"Mrs. Mitchell, can you tell us how you feel now that your daughter has died?"

"Will you be going to California to settle Ms. Barrister's affairs?"

The questions were haphazardly called out as the photographers angled their cameras and snapped pictures as quickly as they could.

Harry maneuvered between two television reporters, pushing a little harder than he had to in order to get Mattie to the awaiting limosine.

"Mrs. Mitchell! Mrs. Mitchell!"

The cries were rather unsettling to Harry, who wasn't accustomed to such rudeness. How could these people live with themselves? They were intruding on a private moment, a moment of mourning for a mother who had just lost her child. Didn't they realize what they were doing to her—to the others?

He reached the funeral home limousine and opened the door. He practically had to shove Mattie inside as one particularly brave reporter reached out to take hold of her arm. When Mattie yelped painfully, Harry pushed the man away.

"Leave them alone!" he demanded.

Ashley and Brook were holding on to each other, while Connie was sandwiched between Deirdre and Erica. Harry pushed his way back through the reporters to help the girls to the limo.

"Get in," he ordered, glancing only momentarily longer at Ashley than any of the others. He saw her look away rather quickly and wondered if it would always be that way between them.

Ashley and Brook quickly allowed Harry to help them up into the car. Deirdre was waylaid as a reporter stuck a microphone in her face, while Erica and Connie were pushed away from her in a sudden surge of the crowd. Harry quickly moved to Erica and Connie, helping them into the car as the reporters demanded answers from Deirdre.

"What's your name? Which daughter are you?"

"Deirdre Woodward," she replied, seeming almost mesmerized by the sudden onslaught.

"How has the death of your mother affected you?" another questioned.

Harry had forced his way back through the group at this point. "It's made her camera shy," he said sarcastically and pulled Deirdre close to him.

"Are you her husband?" a bearded man questioned before sticking a camera inches away from Harry's face. He snapped the picture, then waited for an answer.

Harry grimaced and struggled to half drag, half carry Deirdre to the limo. "Just a few more feet," he told her.

Finally they reached the car, where reporters were still trying to get answers to their questions from the others. Harry had reached the limit of his patience. He pushed two men and one woman aside and shoved Deirdre into the backseat. Closing the door, he turned and said, "No more!"

Heading to the front passenger side, Harry got in amid protests from the media people. *They're vultures and they want to feed on our bones,* he thought.

"Are you still sure you want to go to the cemetery?" he called back to the women.

"I think we have to," Mattie replied. "We'll just have to stick together. Is everyone all right?"

"Fine," they answered in unison.

"What about you, Deirdre?" Mattie asked.

"I'm okay, Grammy. Harry got me out of there in the nick of time. Maybe they could make a movie of this madness. You know, one of those really awful made-for-TV movies," Deirdre suggested with a laugh. "I thought for sure I'd be eaten alive back there. You make a great hero, Harry."

Harry turned around, a slight grin on his face. His expression faltered as he surveyed the women. They looked so frightened and shaken that he wanted nothing more than to insist they head back to the farm.

"If I have to play that scene too many more times," he finally said, "I'm not sure I'll be nearly so civil. I might turn into the bad guy without any trouble at all."

Ashley looked at him, her eyes full of expression. "You could never be the bad guy, Harry."

Her words pierced his heart. He wasn't still in love with her, but in her way, Harry knew she was taking responsibility for the way she'd left him—nearly at the altar. They'd never talked about it. Not once in ten years. Harry had never demanded an explanation and Ashley had never offered one. He figured at first that she'd called off their engagement because she was afraid to commit, but when she'd married the soon-to-be doctor from Denver only a few months later, Harry couldn't help but feel he deserved a few answers. But he went on waiting and wanting those answers and, for a time, wanting Ashley as well.

He felt a bit of relief in the fact that he could now look at Ashley and feel nothing more than he felt for any of the other Mitchell girls. Oh, his memories were perhaps more bittersweet, but at least he didn't feel as though his heart might break at the mere sight of her. That was especially important now that he was engaged to Sarah Hooper and planning to get married in the fall.

He turned back around and said nothing. There really was nothing to say. Everyone in the car knew that Ashley's words held a double meaning. There was no sense in making an issue of it. Perhaps it was her way of settling the past once and for all.

Chapter 4

The graveside service proved to be the three-ring circus that everyone feared, but after the hoopla faded and the last "amen" was offered, there was, in Deirdre Woodward's mind, little left to do but return to the comfort of the farm.

Of course, the media had it figured otherwise, but the local law enforcement was good to offer help and soon the family returned to their various vehicles at the church. Deirdre had driven to Council Grove from Kansas City, taking Erica with her and picking up Connie in Topeka. The three sisters probably had more in common with each other than with Ashley and Brook, but Deirdre had always figured that to be due to the twin bond shared by their elder sisters.

She and Erica shared a similar bond. They had always been close as youngsters, and when Deirdre had married and moved to Kansas City, Erica soon followed. It seemed only natural, and it fit well with Erica's desire to play flute in a large philharmonic orchestra.

Deirdre had been happy for Erica's company, especially when Dave had to stay late at the office. Dave Woodward worked as a successful law partner with one of Kansas City's more prestigious firms. Being a junior partner, his job often kept him downtown well into the evening, but he had promised Deirdre the sacrifice would be worth it in the long run. Deirdre hoped so. It seemed they never had a moment for each other and lately Dave had been awfully preoccupied with one particular case.

"Have you ever in your life seen such a mess?" Erica questioned as she climbed into the front seat. Connie had opted to ride with Harry and Mattie, and that left just Erica to make the trip back to the farm with Deirdre.

"Rachelle would have loved it," Deirdre replied, starting the car.

"No doubt." Erica looked out the window at the open country-side. "I suppose there will be a big dinner."

"Yes, Gram told me the ladies of the church were at the house preparing it while we were at the funeral," Deirdre admitted. She turned off the highway onto a gravel road and followed the dust left by Harry's pickup truck.

"Everything's really greened up nicely," Deirdre said as she gazed off to her left.

"I remember springtime down here. You could smell it almost before you could see it," Erica said, closing her eyes. "I remember the smells almost more than anything else."

Deirdre laughed. "Sometimes those smells weren't too good, but I know what you mean. Nothing—absolutely nothing—smells like freshly turned dirt."

"I guess they'll never take the farm girl out of us," Erica replied, opening her eyes. "Sometimes I feel like such a hick for liking the simple things. Sean's family has money and they find my laid-back country tastes to be quaint, but certainly not anything worth boasting about."

Deirdre knew exactly what Erica meant. She found herself in a constant battle over fashionable taste and reminiscent charms. Dave didn't seem to mind her love of Grammy's quilts, but he drew the line at having country knickknacks around the house. He preferred a kind of Art Deco modernistic design for the living room, dining room, and kitchen—the areas where visitors were sure to venture.

Looking back at the landscape around them, Deirdre felt her heart ache with a kind of longing. She hadn't expected to miss the prairie or the smells or the colors. There arose in her soul a sense of searching, a needful desire to go back home. Funny, in all her pre-vious visits, she'd never felt it quite so strongly. Perhaps it was Rachelle's death or maybe it was the conflict and strife in her own life, but whatever it was, Deirdre felt as though she couldn't get to the farm fast enough. Somehow she knew the farm and Grammy would help fill the empty places in her heart.

She smiled at the memory of spending day after day in the garden with Grammy. Grammy had taught the girls to plant vegetable gardens and to harvest fruit from the various trees and bushes in the area. Canning lessons came after that, as well as sewing, knitting, crocheting, and embroidery. Gram had a desire for all her girls to be self-sufficient.

"We had it pretty good here," Deirdre said.

"We didn't think so at the time," Erica replied, laughing. "I remember how we could all hardly wait to get out of this little no-nothing town, as we used to call it."

"I kind of miss the serenity."

"You'd die of boredom within a week," Erica teased.

Deirdre laughed. "Maybe, maybe not. Sometimes I think I would much rather raise Morgan in this kind of an environment. Five years old can be a magical time on the farm. Don't you remember how wonderful it was having your own horse and dozens of cats and dogs to play with? Morgan keeps pestering me for a puppy, but with Dave planning our anniversary trip to Hawaii, I just don't think it would be a smart way to start the summer."

"But that's a couple of months away. You could get the puppy now and then let Morgan bring it with her when she stays here with Grammy. That way she'd have something to keep her company. She is still staying with Grammy, isn't she?"

Deirdre shrugged. "I haven't had a chance to talk to Grammy about it since this whole mess happened with Rachelle. I don't imagine she'll want us to change our plans, but I am going to look for a quiet opportunity to talk to her."

"Are we still going to stay the rest of the week?" Erica questioned. "I mean, I have the time off from work, so it's not a problem for me."

"Dave's mom and dad said they'd come and stay with Morgan, so I don't see it as a problem. I figure Grammy will need the company."

Erica nodded. "I just hope nothing goes wrong. We haven't been together like this in years."

Deirdre turned onto the long lane that led across Mitchell land to the house where they'd all grown up. A feeling of nostalgia washed over her. She was coming home—they were all coming home—and strange though it might seem, Rachelle had brought them all here.

Pulling her car up alongside Harry's old beat-up pickup, Deirdre turned off the engine. Harry was already helping Mattie and Connie from the truck. Connie laughed about something and Mattie waved to a woman on the front porch.

"Help me convince Harry to stay for the dinner," Mattie told Deirdre as she joined the group. "There will be more than enough food. You know how these things go, Harry."

"Besides," Deirdre teased, "six females and no man to pick on, what fun would that be?"

Harry grinned. "It's that last part that has me worried."

"Nonsense," Mattie declared. "Come on, Erica, Connie—let's go inside and recollect our thoughts. This day has done its best to completely scramble my brain, but I'm bound and determined to enjoy my time with you girls."

Deirdre stared at Harry. "You should stay," she reiterated, watching Brook and Ashley head up the front porch steps behind her grandmother. "I know we'd all like to have you here."

"I guess I might as well. The press will probably have the end of the driveway blocked by the time I can get the truck turned around."

"Let them sit and wait," Deirdre replied. "Just spend the day with us."

Inside the house, the aromas of meatloaf and fried chicken wafted through the air like invisible advertisements for the meal to come. Harry took off his tweed suit coat and loosened his tie.

"Why don't you just lose that altogether?" Connie suggested. Then before Harry could protest, she reached up and finished pulling the tie apart. "You look so uncomfortable."

Harry grinned. "That's because I am uncomfortable."

Connie nodded and tossed the tie over her arm, then reached out to take Harry's coat. "I'll put these things in the hall closet."

She turned to walk away, but Harry wanted to say something about their conversation in the church. He hadn't meant to upset her, but it was obvious that he had.

"Connie, I'm sorry if I intruded earlier."

"I know you didn't mean to be anything but helpful. I was just having a particularly bad moment."

"I kind of figured that. You looked like you might pass out any minute. That's the only reason I came to check up on you."

"The only reason?" Connie questioned, seeming to regain her composure.

"You seemed so alone," Harry admitted. "I didn't want you to feel like that—especially at something like a funeral."

"I am alone, Harry. But you don't need to let that bother you. It's just the way my life has always been."

"Oh, Connie, get over it," Deirdre commented as she came into the hall. "You aren't alone. We're all in this together."

Connie looked as though she might say something, then changed her mind. Looking down at the floor, she murmured, "I didn't expect you to understand. I think I'll go see if Grammy needs help."

"She's still the insecure one, eh?" Harry watched Connie disappear down the hall.

Deirdre shrugged. "She's been giving us that same song and dance since she was little and found out she had a different father than the rest of us. Who cares, is what I say. So she had a different father. It's not like any of us knew our father or had him in our lives. She acts as though she was the only one to endure such a tragedy."

Harry leaned back against the wall and crossed his arms. "Sounds like you're all still trying to shake the past."

"It's a tough past to shake," Deirdre said, frowning. "You knew your mom and dad, Harry. You had a lifetime of memories with them and an honest-to-goodness relationship. We can't say that of our folks. Our mother had us, got rid of us, and moved on to something else. And in the meantime, she buried our father and never told us much about him."

Harry shifted uncomfortably and tried to think of something to say, but Deirdre quickly changed the subject. "The food smells great, don't you think?"

"Yes," Harry admitted. "It does."

"I think these funeral rituals are kind of silly. The dead folks don't know you've done anything nice for them anyway. Funerals are rather a waste of time—and money."

"Funerals are for the living," Harry quickly threw in. "The dead don't care. They're dead."

"Exactly my point. They've gone, and whether to heaven or hell or wherever else you think they might be, they aren't here eating Mrs. Wallace's famous pineapple upside-down cake."

"But those folks are here for Mattie—and you and your sisters," Harry said softly. "Mattie probably feels a great deal of comfort in their being here. I know she feels comforted because you're here."

Deirdre softened at this, her expression thoughtful. "I hope she'll be all right when we leave. You do think she'll get through this okay, don't you?"

It was Harry's turn to shrug. "Mattie's a strong woman, but losing Rachelle this way is going to be hard on her."

"Why any harder this time than the other times Rachelle walked out of her life?"

"Because with the other times, there was always the chance that she would walk back in. That can't happen this time," Harry replied.

"I hadn't really thought of it that way," Deirdre replied. "I suppose you have a point."

"I know I do," Harry said. "Mattie's closing an era of her life. Her children are gone, as well as her husband. You girls are all she has left."

"I'm sorry, Harry," Deirdre said softly. "I know I've been rather selfish. The others would probably say the same thing."

"It's easy for us to get wrapped up in our own lives," Harry said with a smile.

Deirdre nodded. "Grammy means the world to me, and I know she's important to you as well. I've always appreciated that you bought up her extra land when she felt the need to sell. She's a very special lady—I think we can all agree on that."

"She's been a strong foundation for this family. But even foundations can only bear so much weight."

Deirdre watched Harry walk away. She felt a burning in her heart at the words he'd just spoken. She knew Mattie needed them, and the guilt she felt only made matters worse.

"Are you okay?" Erica questioned, coming up from behind her.

Deirdre turned to face her younger sister, realizing what an intricate role Erica played in her life. "Harry was just reminding me how hard all of this will be on Grammy."

Erica looked at the floor. "She really loved Rachelle."

"Yes, and maybe that's why I'm feeling so bad. I've made it very clear to Gram that Rachelle meant nothing to me. I'm sure that hurt her feelings."

"We've all said things like that. She knows we have a difficult time in understanding the past. She's been a wonderful mother to us, but she can't expect us to love Rachelle vicariously through her."

"Still, we should probably spend extra time down here now that Rachelle has died. I mean, at least for a while. I know it's harder for Brook and Ashley, but even Connie wouldn't have to go too far out of her way to spend a weekend here every so often."

"None of us are really that far away," Erica admitted.

"Harry reminded me that even though Grammy is strong, we shouldn't take that for granted. Yet I know I have," Deirdre said, shaking her head. "I've just always needed Grammy so much, it's hard for me to remember that she needs me—us. I don't like to think of her being lonely."

"I guess I've been far too wrapped up in my own worries."

Deirdre hugged her sister close and sighed. "We've both been rather shortsighted. We thought this day was for Rachelle . . . but in truth, it's for Grammy."

Chapter 5

At age thirty, Ashley figured she was as grown-up as she was going to get. But somehow coming back to Grammy's made her feel like a little girl again. She forgot about her ten-year marriage to Jack, a general practitioner, and she even set aside thoughts of her two boys—John, age nine, and Zachary, seven.

Standing in the center of the bedroom she'd known as her own for a lifetime, Ashley let out an audible sigh. The marbled blue wallpaper, the white ceiling and molding trim, and the wispy white sheers at the windows instantly took her back to her teens. Again she sighed.

"I had the same reaction when I saw my room," Brook said from the door.

Turning to find a mirrored image of her own face, Ashley smiled. "It's both creepy and comforting at the same time."

"Kind of like time stood still, eh?"

"Something like that. I mean, I know I was here just three years ago, but Jack was with me and the boys were so young I was constantly running after them. I guess I just didn't pay that much attention."

Brook nodded. "It's been only two years for me, but it feels the same each time I come home. I walk through the front door, smell the baking bread and the apple wood fires, and I can't help but be transported back to childhood. It makes me feel young again. Almost carefree."

"We aren't that old," Ashley protested and began unpacking her suitcase.

"You aren't, but I am," Brook countered.

Ashley laughed at this. "We're the same age—or have you forgotten?"

Brook came around the end of the solid cherry sleigh bed and sat down to lovingly touch the double-wedding-ring quilt top. "In my line of work, I'm old."

"You're in your prime," Ashley said jokingly.

"Right," Brook replied, "if I want to model for nursing home commercials."

Ashley smiled, but she knew her sister's age was a critical factor in her line of work. She also knew Brook's paranoia over her rapidly ticking biological clock. Many women feared that clock's increasing pace because they longed for children. Brook feared it because she had no idea what to do with her life after modeling.

Picking up a stack of clothes, Ashley moved to the armoire and opened the drawers. The rich scent of lavender assaulted her nose. Grammy was ever faithful in keeping the rooms aired out and the drawers smelling fresh.

"I wish the world didn't fix such attention on looks and age," Ashley said, placing her things in the drawer. "It seems like nothing else matters anymore. Appearance is everything."

"Why would *you* say that?" Brook questioned. "You have your family and a husband who loves you. You live in a gorgeous house in a fashionable neighborhood—"

"My point exactly," Ashley cut in, slipping out of her black dress. She looked at the long-sleeved creation for a moment and shook her head. "I didn't know if people wore black to funerals anymore, but since they do in the movies, I figured it was only fitting." She set the dress aside and pulled on a cotton sweater and jeans. "I'm just so glad to have that funeral behind me. I didn't want to come in the first place, but I knew Grammy would expect it."

"You would have wanted to be here for Grammy whether she expected it or not," Brook said quite seriously. "Face it, whether we like it or not, we are who we are."

Ashley couldn't deny her sister's statement. "It's just so hard to give Rachelle any presence in my life. She doesn't deserve to be a part of us, and yet here she is, right in the middle of everything. And for the sake of appearances—we're here in the middle as well."

"You keep mentioning appearance. What was it you were saying about the world only valuing looks and age? How does that figure in your world?"

"It's simple enough," Ashley said, hanging her dress in the armoire. "Success in my world depends on having the right sized family, participating in the most politically correct charities, wearing the current fashions, and living in the best neighborhoods. It means little things like agreeing to a certain order of exterior Christmas decorations for your house. Or that you won't wear fur or drive certain cars. It means that your children will play soccer but not Little League Baseball, and that you'll never buy anything but real leather when purchasing shoes."

Brook laughed and shook her head, her dark hair falling just below her shoulders. "And I thought my world was preordered."

Ashley finished unpacking and slipped the suitcase to the side of the armoire. "Don't get me wrong, Brook, I wouldn't trade what I have with anyone else. I love my family and cherish my house—it's just that sometimes I wonder if I've given up my freedom."

"I know I have. I'm in bondage to the proper beauty products and clothing designers. I have no say over my life or my schedule—my manager sees to all of that, and she's a rigid taskmaster. I go where they send me. I dress in what they give me, and I walk and talk as they tell me to, all while they snap their pictures and sell their products." Brook leaned against the footboard, a rather distant look in her eyes. "I don't know what I'll do when it's gone. I've never had to make my own decisions. I mean, I went to college and landed this career right off the bat. Ever since, people have been taking care of me."

Ashley shook her head. "No, Brook. You've been taking care of yourself, and you'll go on taking care of yourself until you decide otherwise. You've always been that way. I realize you have all those people between you and everyone else, but that's just your way of having a safety net."

"Hey, are you two going to hide in here all night?" Erica questioned from the doorway.

"I was just unpacking," Ashley said, giving Brook one final lingering glance. She knew her twin was deeply troubled and wished nothing more than to be able to ease her mind. However, she knew it wasn't a matter Brook would like shared with everyone else.

"And I was just complaining," Brook said, getting up off the bed. "So how have you been, Erica?"

Erica frowned. "Just peachy. I've been sending audition tapes out to every major orchestra on the East Coast, but so far no one needs another flutist. Sometimes I think my big break will never come and I'll have to settle for a career in fast food."

"You still playing with the community orchestra?" Ashley asked.

Erica nodded. "Yeah. I suppose I should be grateful that they want me."

Brook stretched and shoved her hands into her jeans pockets. "What about your love life?"

"What about yours?" Erica countered. They all grinned, easily recognizing the uncomfortable subject. Relationships came hard to this group of sisters, and no one liked to admit to the fear they faced in dealing with other people—especially men.

Erica finally let out a nervous little laugh. "Well, the truth is, Sean wants me to give up the idea of going elsewhere to play and stay in Kansas City and marry him."

"Do you love him?" Ashley questioned.

"Yes," Erica said reassuringly, "I do. I'm just not sure how I can fit him and my music into the same life."

"So here you all are," Deirdre and Connie said in unison. They came into the bedroom and for a moment everyone fell silent.

"Just like old times, eh?" Ashley finally said. She couldn't help but feel the hands of time slip away as she looked into the faces of her sisters. Oh, they had all aged and changed their hair and style of dress, but somehow they were just the same as they had always been.

"Seems like I never left," Connie said, looking around the room. "I don't know how Grammy keeps up with this place. Everything looks like it did when we lived at home."

"I know," Brook said. "My room looks virtually untouched. It's as if I only went to town for a day rather than left the state for years."

"I think Grammy works too hard," Ashley commented, sitting down at the end of her bed. "I mean, I know what goes into keeping a house this size. It isn't easy at my age, and I have a housekeeper. Grammy has no one but herself now."

"She ought to sell the place." Connie paused, as if feeling guilty for voicing what they were all thinking. "Harry's bought up all but sixty acres of the original homestead. With the house and remaining sixty acres, Grammy could probably get a good price—especially with it positioned on the lake like it is."

"A good price isn't what Grammy's after," Deirdre said, lightly fingering the white sheers bordering Ashley's window. "Grammy keeps this place for us."

"No doubt about that," Connie agreed. "She thinks the farm will keep us coming back."

"As if we wouldn't come back for Grammy herself," Ashley threw in, knowing even as she did that her own trips back to the farm were few and far between.

Connie frowned. "I think Grammy keeps the farm to keep her tied to the past. I mean, this is the place she came to live as a bride. She and our grandfather probably had some wonderful times here."

"She had some bad times here as well," Brook said rather dryly.

"True," Connie agreed. "But the farm is the only link she has to most of her memories—good or bad."

Ashley watched her sisters as they discussed the reasons for their grandmother's devotion to the old homestead. She thought how odd they all looked. Connie with her short bleached hair, looking as different from the rest of them as was humanly possible. Erica had permed her hair and colored it a beautiful shade of auburn, but even that didn't have her looking so very different from her brown-haired siblings. The one feature they all shared were those wonderful brown Mitchell eyes. A birthright passed down from their mother—the only thing she'd bothered to leave of herself.

"Did we lose you, Ashley?" Deirdre questioned.

"I guess I'm just tired. The funeral took more out of me than I thought," Ashley replied. "What did I miss?"

"Not much. I guess we were just hoping that maybe this time we could encourage Grammy to think about moving."

"I don't think that would be a wise idea," Ashley replied, casting a quick look to her twin. They were so very close—they always had been. And often it seemed that when something happened to one, it happened in some fashion to the other. Even now Ashley could sense her sister's feelings on the matter and continued with her thoughts, knowing that Brook would agree. "Grammy has just buried Rachelle. She loved her, even as she loves us. I don't think asking her to give up the farm would be kind or considerate of her needs."

"I guess I hadn't thought of it that way," Connie said.

"Me either," Deirdre admitted.

"It's just that Grammy has her needs too," Ashley said, smiling as she studied the room. "If she keeps the farm in order to remember the past, then I say let her. What's the harm in it? If the gardening and yard and even the house itself get to be too much, Harry will let us know."

"And if it keeps her tied to the future, with the hope that we'll keep coming back," Erica offered, "what harm is there in that? Personally, I like knowing the place is here and that Grammy has kept my room just as I left it. There's a certain comfort in that."

They all nodded. There was comfort in that, Ashley thought. Some things should never change, and the comfort of the Mitchell farm was one of those things. Ashley had only to conjure up images from days gone by, happy times when she and her sisters had spent lazy summer afternoons by the lake. Days when the only real worry was whether or not it would rain and ruin their picnics or swimming fun.

We were all so innocent then, Ashley thought. *Innocent and hopeful.* She almost laughed out loud. *I'm not without hope now. It's just that life has gotten to be so very complicated and fast paced. I have so many routines that seem to revolve around me, and if I'm not there for them, they simply fall apart.*

"I'm glad Grammy has the farm," she whispered absentmindedly. "I'm even more glad that she allows me the privilege of calling it home."

Chapter 6

Mattie Mitchell looked up from the churned soil of her flower bed to find Harry coming up the stone path from the boat dock. A large lake adjoined the two farm properties, and long ago both families had put in boat docks for the purpose of taking shortcuts across the lake for visits. Mattie no longer had a boat for such activities, but Harry used an old rowboat to keep up his exercise and visits. He had told her that rowing gave him time to think, and Mattie understood perfectly. Sometimes life refused to give a person time to think—unless they took it outright and forced time to wait.

Mattie smiled and waved. With the girls all sleeping in, Harry was welcome company for the early morning hour. Ambling up the path, Harry looked for all the world to be a man without purpose or worry. Mattie liked that about him. He seemed to take life in stride and not get overly worked up about a problem until it absolutely had to be addressed. He'd taken after his father that way, and he was a perfect addition to this delicious spring day—the day after Mattie had buried her only daughter.

"Why, Harry, don't tell me you rowed over here." She patted the dirt firmly around the newly planted rosebush, then dusted her hands.

"All right, I won't tell you," Harry said with a grin. "I see I've caught you on your knees again."

Mattie laughed. "Prayin' and plantin' are the reasons God created knees, or so my mother used to say." She slowly started to get up from the ground and instantly Harry was at her side, helping to ease her burden. With her seventieth birthday not so many years in the future, Mattie had long ago begun to feel the effects of her age. Her knees ached from the constant kneeling required in planting her beloved flowers, and her fingers easily stiffened from the cold, damp soil. Harry had suggested on more than one occasion that she buy a good pair of gardening gloves, but Mattie loved the feel of the soil and so held off on that idea. Gloves, like many other things, were just unnecessary window dressing as far as Mattie was concerned.

"I tried to call. . . ."

"Oh, the girls unplugged the line. Some of the newspaper people kept calling, and they thought pulling the plug might discourage them."

"After seeing the way they acted at the cemetery, I doubt anything could discourage them. Hopefully they'll just pack up and go home now that the funeral's over." He shoved his hands into his pockets and leaned back on the heels of his cowboy boots. Harry's denim jeans were well worn and faded, as was the plaid flannel shirt on which he'd rolled up the sleeves. Even at thirty-five he'd retained a certain amount of boyish charm, like an overgrown teen looking for a baseball game instead of a man with a field to plow.

Mattie looked beyond him, down the path to the lake that joined their properties. "With the breeze blowing up the way it is, I wouldn't have expected you to brave the water today."

"The exercise does me good—besides, it wasn't that bad." Harry glanced around as a stiff April wind picked that moment to prove him wrong. "I wanted to check up on you. Yesterday was pretty exhausting."

Mattie couldn't agree more. "The only good thing was having the girls back home. The house positively rang with noise until the wee hours of the morning. It was marvelous."

"I'm sure it was just the thing you needed," Harry said, pulling down his ball cap to keep it from blowing off his head.

"March went out like a lion and April decided to imitate it," Mattie said, laughing at the wind. "That storm on the first was a doozy. Of course, you remember the old proverb, 'If it thunders on

April Fool's Day, you have good crops of corn and hay.'"

"Wouldn't hurt my feelings none," Harry replied.

Mattie nodded and for a moment she said nothing more, relishing instead the way the wind felt against her skin—the way it smelled of new grass and freshly plowed fields. She couldn't imagine a time closer to heaven on earth than springtime in Kansas.

"Why don't we go on up to the house. I put on a pot of coffee before coming down here this morning. I figured by the time I made it back into the house, the girls might even be up and around."

"Coffee sounds good," Harry admitted. "Your sour cream coffee cake would sound even better."

"There's some of that too," she said, knowing how much he liked it. She knew, too, how much he appreciated their conversations and time together.

"You sure the girls won't mind my being here?"

"I can't imagine why. They seemed to enjoy your company yesterday. Besides, they know you spend a good deal of time over here." Mattie gathered up her tools. "Just let me get things put away and we'll go on up."

All of her life, Mattie had adhered strictly to the instructions of her parents: Never start a job and leave it for someone else to finish. Never leave your neighbor in need. Never leave your tools out with the plan to come back to a job undone. Of course, there were other rules, little sensible rules that had helped Mattie's quality of life to remain remarkably high, but those were three of the more important ones.

Pausing by a white wooden garden bench, Mattie lifted the seat to reveal the perfect place to stow her tools. The bench had been made extra long to accommodate the full length of the hoe and rake that were usually stored there.

"Looks like it's holding up pretty good," Harry said as he put the tools inside.

"It'll outlast the both of us, Harry," Mattie said with motherly affection. "The creator knew what he was doing when he fashioned it."

Harry chuckled. "Nah, he just followed instructions and squeaked by with a B-plus on the project."

"It's held up well, along with the other two you made for me. Now I can have my tools close to where I need them most—not in some storage shed half a mile away."

Harry nodded as the wind picked up again. Mattie noted that he gave up trying to keep his cap secure and instead stuffed it into his back pocket and let the breeze blow through his hair. Kansas was well known for its hearty breezes, and today seemed to be no exception. It was little wonder that the vast prairie farmlands were dotted with windmills. Mattie could remember her beloved Edgar saying that windmills should be assigned the honor of official state symbol.

"I see you have that north bed weeded and replanted," Harry said as they made their way up to the house.

"The ground is warming up fast," Mattie admitted. "But you already know that. How're the fields coming along?"

Harry beamed proudly. "I've got it plowed up, thanks to that new tandem disc I bought myself for Christmas last year. I'm ready to put in the corn as soon as I'm convinced the weather's going to stay warm."

"I wouldn't be surprised if you could start planting in the next week or two. The spring's been unseasonably warm, and I haven't heard any talk of it changing. 'Course," she said, pulling open the screen door, "I wouldn't want you to risk a crop on my say-so."

The door creaked as she opened it wide. Mattie thought it gave the house character, although Harry had offered a hundred times to oil it and see if he couldn't make it a little more quiet. Mattie loved her farmhouse with all its idiosyncrasies and faults. She didn't mind the kitchen sink dripping with a steady rhythm that mimicked the grandfather clock in the hall. Neither did she mind the way the wind whistled in the chimney. They were little personality features that made the Mitchell farm something personable—something more than just an old house with new additions.

They walked through the sun porch to the kitchen door, and as soon as Mattie opened it, the warm scented air hit them full in the face. Cinnamon, nutmeg, and the aroma of freshly baked cake made a delicious welcoming committee.

"Smells good in here," Harry said, tossing his cap aside. "You must have just made that coffee cake this morning."

Mattie washed the dirt from her hands and went to the coffee maker. "I figured you might come around. I bet Sarah Hooper has something to do with my lack of company lately, though." Harry blushed and Mattie laughed. "So you've cast me aside for a younger woman, eh?"

"You know how it is to plan a wedding. I suggested to Sarah we just elope, but she has in mind to invite half the county."

"Only half? I figured since that girl waited so long to pick a husband, she'd invite all of the county and good portions of those surrounding us."

Mattie saw the way Harry fidgeted at her words. He reminded her of a little boy forced to recite from memory a Bible verse he didn't know. Harry always looked rather uncomfortable when discussing his fall wedding. It wasn't that he didn't seem to care greatly for Sarah, but the entire matter just seemed to take a toll on his peace of mind. Pouring a cup of coffee into a thick white porcelain mug, Mattie almost felt sorry for the grown man. He seemed so completely out of touch with the things that women deemed important in their lives. He had no sisters and his mother had been a farmer's wife, and while that didn't mean that Thelma Jensen didn't think and reason as a woman, she was by her own choice a confirmed tomboy. It was Thelma who had ridden in rodeos as a teenager and who thought nothing of donning a pair of overalls to join her husband in roofing the barn.

Of course, there were Mattie's girls. But Harry had been a good five years older than the twins and as much as ten years older than Erica, the baby of the family. Once the girls were old enough to be interesting, Harry was off to college or so closely wrapped up in the farm that he seldom had time for anything else. Mattie supposed his experience didn't allow for much of an education in what women were truly like. Maybe that was why he and Ashley hadn't been able to stay together.

"The winter wheat looks good," Harry offered as a means to change the subject. "After the heavy snow coverage we had this winter, I wouldn't be surprised if it didn't turn out to be a bumper crop."

"I love the color of it when it's about ankle high," Mattie said, bringing the cake to the table. She cut a generous slice for Harry and a smaller one for herself. "It's such a bright emerald color and the fields look so soft you just want to run barefooted through it."

"I'd appreciate it if you didn't do that to my wheat," Harry chided. He took the offered plate and fork and immediately dug into the treat. "Mmm, good as always."

"You know, I could teach you to make it."

Harry looked at her almost indignantly. "Are you trying to get rid of me?"

"Never," replied Mattie with the slightest shake of her head. "I cherish the company. But, you know, Sarah will probably want to keep you close to home. At least these first few years. I suppose I could just share the recipe with her."

Harry's expression changed again, and this time he looked almost perplexed. "I suppose."

"What is it, Harry?" Mattie asked in a motherly fashion. "Every time I mention the wedding or Sarah, you look like you just swallowed a June bug. Are you getting cold feet?"

"I don't know if it's cold feet or not, but I guess that's as good a thing to call it as any," he admitted. He took a long drink of the steaming coffee before continuing. "I guess it's just all a bit overwhelming. I've got my mind on getting the crops in and she's throwing brochures about trips to the Bahamas in my face."

"I take it you don't want to go to the Bahamas?"

He shrugged. "I guess it doesn't matter. You know me. I don't mind traveling a bit—in fact, I enjoy it a great deal. I guess I just didn't expect to be flying off that far away."

"Poor Harry."

"Aw, don't go throwing pity at me, Mattie. I'll be fine," he said casually, as though the matter meant nothing to him. He finished off the cake and waved her away when Mattie offered him seconds. "Nah, I have to get going. I didn't realize it was getting so late."

"Trying to duck out before you have to deal with us?" Connie asked as she bounded into the room.

She had tied a pink robe around her, and without her makeup and perfectly styled hair, Mattie thought she looked like a teenager again. "I was beginning to wonder if you girls were going to sleep away the entire day."

"Oh, Grammy, it's only eight-thirty. Even I wouldn't be up if it weren't for the way my internal clock runs. I guess it's part of being a gym teacher. I'm trained to the clock." She plopped down on a kitchen chair and smiled at Harry. "So how are the affairs of the Kansas farmer these days? Wheat selling for a good price? Drought worries cleared up?"

Harry gave her a kind of lopsided smile. "You know farming as well as most."

"That bad, huh?"

"Now, Harry, you know full well that things have perked up a bit," Mattie threw in as she poured Connie a cup of coffee.

"What's perked up?" Deirdre asked, yawning sleepily.

"Well, it certainly isn't you," Connie teased. "We were just discussing the future of farming in Kansas."

Deirdre yawned again and took a seat beside Connie. "Dave says the days of individual farms are pretty much passé. Corporations are buying up farmland and making business ventures out of it. Did you know that Arabs own a good portion of land in Kansas?"

"I can't say that it surprises me," Harry admitted. "And you're right. Individual farms are having a tough go these days."

"So why do you do it?" Deirdre questioned.

"That's easy. I love it. I can't imagine doing anything else," Harry admitted.

"I thought I heard voices," Erica said, bounding into the room fully dressed and ready for the day. "I thought maybe we'd been overrun by the media." She kissed Mattie on the cheek and poured her own coffee.

Mattie liked the comfortable way everyone just sort of gathered in the kitchen. She reached into the cupboard and brought out more plates for the coffee cake just as Brook joined the festivities.

"What's that about the media?" Brook asked, then added, "Morning, Grammy."

"Morning," Mattie said, returning to the table with the plates. "Erica was just commenting on the noise of our breakfast gathering. Thought we'd been overrun by those media folks."

"I haven't seen that much commotion in Council Grove since the year Ashley and Brook graduated," Deirdre teased.

"You mean that ruckus the Grover boys started?" Harry questioned, raising his eyebrows.

"The boys were only half the problem. The Grover girls were just as rowdy," Brook said with a grin.

"They took after their mother," Mattie added, enjoying the memory every bit as much as her granddaughters.

"I always thought she was their sister," Harry admitted.

"Orneriness just seemed to run naturally in that family," Mattie said. "They were good folk. Good as they come, but my, oh my, they could think up more rowdiness."

"I never knew you could get that many steers inside a jail cell," Deirdre said, her laughter becoming contagious. "Who would have guessed it would bring television crews from Topeka?"

Erica giggled, then laughed out loud. "I remember how they took that one steer's picture and their cousin made a Wanted poster out of it."

"We had . . . those things . . . all over town," Mattie said, laughing so hard she could barely get the words out. "They turned up in... the strangest places." She had tears in her eyes now. "For weeks afterward."

"A talented group, those Grovers."

By now all of them were laughing so hard that no one noticed Ashley watching from the doorway.

"What's so funny?" she asked.

Mattie dried her eyes and smiled. "Life," she replied. Though she had buried her daughter the day before, Mattie was thankful she could enjoy these moments of laughter with her granddaughters.

Ashley eyed the group suspiciously, as if they were holding out on her, then nodded. "I suppose that should be our family motto—life is funny."

Mattie nodded, smiling. "Far better than the alternative."

Chapter 7

Against the backdrop of the setting sun, the lake looked like shimmering glass. Overhead, a flock of ducks broke the silence as they squawked noisily. The sound faded, however, as they made their way to the far side of the one-hundred-acre lake. There, the undisturbed marshlands made the perfect place for their habitats.

The day had really been very pleasant, at least physically. The humidity was low and the skies were a powdery blue with wispy white lace for clouds. Emotionally, Ashley thought the day to be most trying, but she tried not to let it ruin the time she had left on the farm. Denver awaited her, and by the weekend she would return to meticulously ordered schedules and demanding social obligations. But for now, Grammy's farm offered her a much needed respite.

"This is so refreshing," Brook said, leaning back on her hands. Her long, slender legs were positioned in front of her.

"You look awfully thin, Brook. Are you sure you're eating okay?"

Brook looked at Ashley with a frown. "Are you afraid I have some eating disorder?"

"I just know what a focus weight can be in your career. I don't want to see you getting into one of those bingeing and purging situations."

"Well, sometimes I do throw up," Brook admitted. "But not on purpose. If I get all stressed out, my body reacts that way. But I swear to you that I'm not doing anything on purpose. I think my high level of energy and activity keep the calories from going to fat."

"I'm probably just as busy as you are," Ashley said with a hint of a smile. "And while I know it's not the same kind of busyness, I feel I am probably just as much on the run as you are. But I have to watch everything I eat."

Ashley stared out across the lake, knowing that the shoreline on the opposite side belonged to Harry. "It was strange seeing him again," she said without needing to give Brook any explanation.

"He could tell us apart right away. Just like the old days," Brook countered. "Even though we were dressed alike at the funeral, he came right up and called me by name. I didn't say much at all, and still he knew."

"Of course he knew. You don't have that haggard look of running after children," Ashley said. She gave a nervous sort of laugh that wasn't at all in keeping with her reserved nature.

"Does it bother you?" Brook questioned, tossing her dark hair over her shoulder as she studied her sister for a response.

"Not like I thought it might," Ashley replied. "But it does bother me in some ways."

"Such as?"

Ashley shrugged and rubbed her hands against her bare arms. With the sun continuing its descent, the evening was turning chilly. "I suppose it bothers me in the sense that it takes me back in time. And that bothers me because it shows me how much time I've let slip away from me. There's so much I still want to do with my life."

Brook nodded. "I know what you mean. I suppose Grammy would say, 'Landsakes, child, you're only thirty.' But thirty is marriage and family and mortgages and trying to plan vacations around school schedules. And I have none of that."

"Yes, it is," Ashley agreed. "But it's more than that. Or at least it should be." Her voice faded for a moment before she continued. "And unfortunately, there never seem to be enough hours in the day. Sometimes I just wish everything would come to a grinding halt. Like right now. There's no place I need to be. Nothing I need to be doing. I can sit here all night if I want to, and no one will be the worse for it."

"So how do we capture this slow pacing for our otherwise out-of-control lives? After all, we have to go home sometime. And as I recall, we were both rather anxious to get away from all this peace and quiet when we were younger."

"I'm not sorry I left," Ashley stated thoughtfully. "And I can't say that I would ever want to come back to this on a permanent basis. It's just that sometimes I think I've bitten off more than I can chew."

"But you are happy, aren't you?" Brook sat up and eyed Ashley as though her answer carried great weight.

"I think so. But sometimes I wonder . . ." Ashley said. She could never have lied to Brook even if she had wanted to, but it wasn't a lie to admit that she was confused by her own existence.

Brook crossed her legs and leaned forward. With elbows on her knees and her hands cradling her own face, she looked very much like a lost little girl. Ashley wondered if Brook was more miserable than she let on. She knew Brook would tell her the truth if she asked, but a part of Ashley wondered if she really wanted to know. The fact was, Ashley felt confident she already knew. Brook had told her how worried she was for her future and how confused she was about what her choices might be. Ashley didn't really need to ask.

"I am happy," Ashley finally said. "I know what I have. I know what I can count on and what I can't. I've adjusted to Jack's schedule and to the social life we're expected to participate in. I have my sons, and they make me very happy."

"But . . . " Brook prompted, not even bothering to look at Ashley.

"I don't know, and that's the honest truth." Ashley shook her head. "Sometimes, like yesterday when I first saw Harry, I can't help but wonder if I've missed the boat altogether. Then again, there's the realization that so much of what I've done has been accomplished in order to prove something to Rachelle. I feel so stupid. I guess just thinking about it causes me to feel discontent and . . . and almost fearful for my future."

"Do you have a reason to fear?"

"No. Not really." Ashley sighed. "I know this sounds so silly, but I guess it's almost a feeling of waiting for the other shoe to drop."

Brook nodded. "Yes. That's it exactly."

"You know what I'm talking about?"

Brook turned ever so slightly and raised her head. "We've known the good of life, and we're afraid someone or something might come along and take it from us. Harry has never stepped outside of his area of comfort to risk everything for something new. But we have. We know what it is to start from scratch, and now that we've built ourselves a comfortable life, we fear that we could just as easily lose it."

"But I can understand *you* feeling that way," Ashley said, hoping Brook wouldn't take offense. "Your career hinges on public opinion and approval. You do have some uncomfortable decisions to make because of what you do for a living. But I shouldn't feel this way. I have stability. A family. A home. I even love my church, although I'm sure Grammy would say I'm more of a pew-warmer Christian than an everyday one."

Brook laughed. "Grammy is so dear. But I worry about her."

Ashley nodded. "So do I. I mean, look at all of this. She's taken such loving care of the grounds. I know Harry mows the larger portions, but Grammy is the one who plants and tends it. I remember when we were little girls and she taught us to plant a vegetable garden."

Smiling, Brook added to the memory. "She made us put stakes in the ground at each end of the garden and then she'd tie a string to each stake and that way she could keep straight rows."

"She said life was the same way. We needed to focus on the stakes God puts out for us and make our rows straight in accordance."

Brook nodded. " 'Christians have a tough row to hoe,' she'd tell us. I had imagined that when we grew up we'd have to be hoeing all the time. Either when we tended a garden or when we shared our faith."

Ashley laughed. "Remember how we'd drag the corner of that hoe along the dirt, just under the string? We were so meticulous in our labor. We watched that string every step of the way in order to make sure our furrows were straighter than anyone else's."

"I do remember," Brook said, and her voice had that faraway sound that matched Ashley's thoughts.

"Grammy always had us planting, weeding, or picking one thing or another. I used to hate it, but now I'm glad for the training we had. Sometimes her stories and examples are so clear in my life," Ashley admitted. "Still, I think she'd be disappointed in me if she had to spend much time in my world."

"Me too," Brook replied. "My world has very little in common with Grammy's teachings. People are harsh and ruthless. They care very little for each other. Everything has its price—yet nothing seems to matter much."

"What about love, Brook? Haven't you managed to meet anyone who strikes your fancy?" Ashley watched as Brook turned to gaze back out over the water.

"My fancy has very little to do with it. I've met some really nice men in the past years. But just when things start to progress beyond the place where we introduce ourselves and share a few dates, well, I get too uptight. I try not to let the past influence me, but I can't seem to shake it."

"Because of Rachelle?"

Brook nodded. "I'm so hesitant—so afraid to get close to anyone. It's just hard for me to trust."

"But you don't want to go through life alone, do you?"

"Not particularly, but neither do I want to be hurt."

"Life hurts. That's just the way it is."

"But it shouldn't have to hurt that much," Brook said softly. "Every time I start to think about someone—seriously think about them—I remember the pain I felt when I was a little girl. Do you remember when we still shared the same room, the one I have now?"

Ashley nodded and Brook continued. "We were four years old the last time Rachelle came home to see us. I remember we were asleep in our room and Rachelle started arguing with Grammy and it woke me up. You were still asleep, but I went to the door and opened it up just enough to hear their words. Rachelle was telling Grammy how we were a burden, how she didn't want to be bothered with motherhood and all its problems. That if Grammy didn't want us, she'd put us up for adoption. Grammy told her she couldn't possibly mean what she was saying, but Rachelle assured her that she did.

"Then she said something I don't think I'll ever forget. She told Grammy that if she could have found a way to rid herself of us before we were born, she would never have had a single one of us."

"I remember," Ashley said, her brow knitting together. "I only pretended to be asleep. Once you opened the door, I heard everything."

Brook looked at her strangely. "You didn't tell me you were awake."

"It hurt too much. I almost felt like if we didn't talk about it, it wasn't true. I kept thinking I'd misunderstood her. That I didn't know what all the words meant."

"I know. I remember now that the word 'abortion' was mentioned, but at four years old, I had no idea what that meant. But when I got older I knew, and I remembered." Brook bit at her lower lip. "It hurt knowing she hated me enough to wish me dead. And I just can't deal with that kind of pain again. I keep imagining giving my heart to someone only to have the love die and hear him say to me that if he could only have found a way to avoid ever having known me, he would have."

"Better to not love anyone than to have someone come to hate you, is that it?" Ashley asked.

"I guess so."

"But you know that isn't valid, Brook. You're missing more this way, and Rachelle's hatred is the reason. Don't give her that kind of power in your life. She doesn't deserve it."

"I know you're right," Brook agreed. "Of all the ways we are alike, I wish being able to trust my heart was one of them."

"It didn't come easy. I guess I kept thinking of Grammy and how if she could love me, somebody else could love me too. Then when things didn't work out with Harry, I knew it was mostly because I didn't want them to work out. I didn't want to stay here in Kansas. I didn't want to be a farmer's wife. But it wasn't because I didn't want to be someone's wife. I think you have to look at this aside from Rachelle. Grammy and I love you, and so do the others. I know we're family and should love each other, but Rachelle should have loved us too. That just shows that the love you have from me and the others is genuine. We could have chosen to hate, just as Rachelle did."

"I suppose I never thought of it that way. Grammy could have just as easily said no to adopting us. She could have refused to love us because of how Rachelle acted."

Ashley nodded. The first stars of the evening were just appearing against the darkening sky. She couldn't help but remember their childhood wishes placed upon the first star of the evening. *I wish true love for Brook,* she thought silently as her gaze fixed on that first star. *I wish love and happiness and contentment for her.*

Ashley lowered her gaze and met Brook's brooding expression. "I found the wishing star," she said, reaching out to take hold of her sister's hand. "And I wished for you to find true love."

Brook grinned. "You aren't supposed to tell your wish to anyone else."

"But you aren't just anyone else; you're a part of me."

Brook nodded and squeezed her sister's hand. "Then that wish is for us both."

"Supper is nearly ready," Mattie said, turning to observe Deirdre shredding a carrot stick into a beautifully prepared salad. "Mmm, that looks tasty."

"I think so too," Deirdre replied. "I love to add color to food. It sounds silly, but somehow it just looks more appetizing with a few orange flecks."

Mattie laughed. "Well, we're visual folk. Why else do you suppose I spend so much time in the yard?"

Deirdre nodded. "The flower gardens will no doubt be just as glorious as ever. I love the early flowers. They look so sturdy and plush. Crocuses always look as though they can endure anything."

"They usually can. One of the prettiest sights I ever saw was purple crocuses peeking their heads above a dusting of snow." Mattie wiped her hands on a dish towel. "Shall we have an evening supper down by the lake?"

"I think that sounds wonderful, but I could go ask the others if you like," Deirdre said, ever conscious of everyone else's desires. Mattie had watched her go through life trying hard to keep everyone pleased and happy, always playing mediator when the occasion arose.

"No, if you think it sounds good," Mattie replied, "then I think it sounds good too. I'll turn on the gazebo and dock lights." She went to the back door and flipped a switch. Through the screening of the porch she could make out the shadowy forms of Brook and Ashley on the walkway.

"Looks like Ashley and Brook are already enjoying the evening," Mattie commented. She went back to the counter and began slicing leftover ham. "This will make great sandwiches." Deirdre nodded and went to pull condiments out of the refrigerator. "So are you and Dave still planning the trip to Hawaii?" Mattie questioned.

"Yes. That is, if he wins his case. His law firm is deeply embroiled in some sort of big dispute. They are representing a car manufacturer or someone like that. Anyway, Dave has all this responsibility and it's taking most of his time. But God willing," Deirdre said, giving Mattie a big smile, "our sixth wedding anniversary will get time too. We plan to fly out the first week of June. Are you sure you still want to watch Morgan?"

"Absolutely! She and I will have as much fun as a great-grandmother and five-year-old can have."

"She'll keep you hopping, that's for sure."

"I'll teach her how to plant flowers and weed the garden. Just like I did with you," Mattie replied.

"And if she tells you that she's bored, will you make her go pick up rocks in the yard?" Deirdre questioned.

Mattie chuckled. "You can count on it." Picking up rocks in the yard had been one of her devices of breaking the kids' habit of commenting on being bored. *"Life has all sorts of things for you to do,"* she would tell them, *"even if it's nothing more than picking up rocks."* It usually only took one or two times of that chore to help the girls focus their attention on making their own fun or finding entertainment elsewhere. Of course, sometimes their choices were poorly thought out, but they learned to practice their creativity nevertheless.

"I know Morgan will love it here," Deirdre said, placing all the condiments on one of Mattie's trays.

"Will she miss her friends?" Mattie asked, taking out another tray for the ham and chips.

"There aren't too many other kids nearby. One little girl lives a couple of houses down, but most of the people in our neighborhood are older. I suppose that's the trouble with living above your means," Deirdre said with a bit of a laugh. "All our friends are being sensible and living in lower-cost neighborhoods, but Dave and I both wanted something really special."

"And is that how you feel about what you have?"

Deirdre sobered. "I think so. I love my house. It's everything I ever dreamed of owning. It's such a far cry from that two-bedroom cracker box Dave and I lived in after we were first married."

"I thought that house was charming," Mattie said, remembering the quaint little ranch-style home.

"Well, charming wasn't exactly on my list of definitions. But this house is definitely charming and wonderful, and I couldn't be happier."

Mattie grinned. "You sound very content."

"I am," Deirdre admitted. "Dave has a good job. Morgan is in kindergarten, where she finally has friends to play with. I even go out once a week with my girlfriends and have a bit of fun for myself."

"Really? What do you do?"

Deirdre looked a bit hesitant. "We go to the casino. But before you say anything against it, just know that we do it only for fun. I take an allotted amount of money and never spend past that. Sometimes I win and sometimes I lose, but it's nothing more than a game."

"Did I say it was?" Mattie asked, knowing that she had always spoken against gambling in any form.

"Well, I just remember how you always put it down and told us our money and time were better spent elsewhere."

"So you were at least listening," Mattie said, rather amused.

Deirdre smiled. "I was listening. I just wasn't sure it could be all that bad."

"Well, I suppose you know best for yourself," Mattie said, adding bread and silverware to her tray.

Just then Ashley and Brook came in through the screened porch. "Oh, good," Mattie declared. "You're just in time to help."

Chapter 8

The next morning the skies rumbled with thunder. Mattie awoke slowly, and upon realizing the tone set for the day, she snuggled deep into the comfort of her quilts. She didn't mind the rain. Her gardens loved the watering and nothing fed them so well as rainwater. She didn't even mind that she'd have to stay indoors. She had her quilting and crocheting, not to mention just visiting with her granddaughters. Smiling at the thought of them all spending the day inside, Mattie threw back the covers and sat on the edge of the bed.

"I'm getting old," she murmured at the aching in her hips and lower back. "Sometimes it doesn't seem like I should be this old, then other days I feel like an eternity has been spent on this earth." She got to her feet and stretched.

Lightning flashed, drawing Mattie's attention to the window. She went to stand and watch the storm move in. You could never tell what you might get with a Kansas spring storm. Tornadoes, lightning, hail—it was all part of living in the Sunflower State. In the distance a line of heavy black clouds churned with the rumbling of the thunder. It looked like heavy rain, maybe even a little wind and hail. Mattie prayed there wouldn't be anything more severe.

Going to her vanity, Mattie sat down and began to brush her short gray hair, each stroke bringing back a memory. How many times had she brushed and styled the girls' hair when they were little? How many times had she done the same for Rachelle?

Rachelle. Mattie could still see her child lying so still and silent in the coffin. *Why did you leave me without letting me know if you'd made your peace with God?* she silently questioned. Mattie feared the answer was found in the probable fact that Rachelle hadn't found any peace with her Creator. But no mother liked to contemplate her child spending an eternity separated from God and those who loved her.

"I wish the girls could have loved you," Mattie murmured. "I wish you could have loved them. They are so like you. Especially Connie. Sometimes I look at her and I see you." Mattie ignored the tears that fell. All she had ever wanted was to be was a wife and mother. It was all she had wanted to be good at . . . and it was the one thing she had failed at.

Well, in truth, she hadn't had much of a chance with Edgar and Robbie. They were a part of her life for such a short time. But Rachelle had remained, and Mattie's inability to instill in the child a sense of belonging and contentment weighed heavy on her heart.

Mattie dried her eyes and stared at her reflection in the mirror. The woman staring back had known great grief, and no one understood the pain of separation she was feeling. Rachelle might have been one of the most sought-after actresses in the world. She might have dined with kings and queens and danced with presidents and other world leaders, but she would forever be Mattie's little girl.

———————————

"Sorry I'm so late," Mattie announced, coming into the kitchen to find Connie on the telephone rapidly jotting something down on paper. The clock pointed to eight-forty, a time of day when Mattie was usually pausing to take a break in her chores rather than just getting out of bed. She glanced to the kitchen window. At least the rain had stopped.

Deirdre stood over the stove, fork in hand, bacon sizzling on the stove. "Sleep late and there's always someone trying to move in on your territory," Mattie teased, reaching for her apron.

"Now, you just put that apron back and sit down. I wanted to bring this to you in bed, but since you're here, I'll just set you a place at the table."

Mattie laughed as Erica popped in from the screened porch with a daffodil in a small vase. Raindrops still clung to the yellow petals. "Oh no!" Erica declared. "You aren't supposed to be in here. You're spoiling our surprise."

"So I heard," Mattie said, watching as the vivacious redhead carefully placed the vase on the table. She had pulled her hair into a ponytail, and the curls bounced and danced as she turned to retrieve something else from the counter. Mattie thought how much like a teenager Erica seemed. So youthful and happy. So unscathed.

Erica brought a glass of orange juice to the table just as Deirdre announced breakfast was ready. To Mattie's surprise, she placed a white china plate in front of her. Four strips of bacon were joined by thick slices of tomato and two pieces of lightly buttered toast. It was Mattie's favorite breakfast.

"You remembered," she said, feeling almost emotional about the moment. How silly that something so simple could move her so deeply.

"Who could forget?" Deirdre replied. "You are the only one I've ever seen eat tomato for breakfast."

"Then you just didn't pay much attention to the rest of the world," Mattie said with a smile.

At this, they all heard Connie hang up the phone. "You aren't going to believe this," Connie said, bringing a piece of paper to Mattie. "This man wants to buy some quilt you have. He's offering twenty thousand dollars. I had to ask him three times to make sure I had the amount right."

"Twenty?" Erica questioned, adding, "Thousand?"

"That's right. He wants some quilt Grammy showed off last year at the fair. He called it 'Piece Work,'" Connie said, looking at her note.

"Could a quilt really be worth that much money?" Deirdre questioned.

Mattie laughed. "I suppose so. Although to me it's worth much more."

"More?" Connie questioned. "How so?"

"He's talking about a quilt I made and entered into competition last year. I'll show it to you if you'd like. It won several competitions locally, then went on to win other competitions nationally. Pretty soon I found folks asking to buy it, photograph it, and show it. I just got it back, in fact, from an art gallery in Texas."

Connie sat down at the table as though the wind had been knocked out of her. "I've never heard about any of this."

"Me either," Deirdre admitted. "Do you get many calls?"

Mattie took a bite of the sandwich she'd made and shrugged. "Some," she finally managed to say.

"But what's so special about this quilt?" Erica asked.

"A lot went into it," Mattie replied. "I spent hundreds of hours on the hand quilting alone."

"When can we see it?" Deirdre asked.

"Just as soon as I finish this great breakfast."

The girls hung around the kitchen almost nervously as Mattie completed her meal. She had nearly asked Deirdre to make her a bowl of oatmeal, but seeing the anxious looks on their faces, Mattie figured she'd just grab a snack later if she needed more food.

Pushing her plate back, Mattie got to her feet and smoothed down her soft denim skirt. After methodically washing her hands at the kitchen sink, she turned and smiled. "All right. Come with me."

She led the girls out of the kitchen and into the hallway toward the south wing of the house. Here her own bedroom and a small den were located, as well as a large sewing room. Opening the doors, Mattie flipped on the light and stood back. "Well, there it is."

On the interior wall she had mounted the quilt for display. Each of the girls gasped at the sight of it.

"Oh, Grammy!" Erica said in reverence for what her grandmother had accomplished. "This is wonderful."

"I've never seen anything like it," Deirdre replied. "Look at all those tiny stitches."

"It's incredible," Connie admitted, coming close to touch it. She reached out, then stopped, remembering Grammy's admonitions for clean hands when handling her sewing projects. Looking down at her fingers, Connie glanced up to meet Mattie's watchful eye.

"It's okay," Mattie assured her. "If you want to touch it, go ahead."

"Hey, where is everybody?" Ashley called from the kitchen.

Mattie leaned out the door. "We're back here in the sewing room."

In a few moments, Ashley and Brook made their entrance.

"What's going on—oh wow!" Ashley's tone said it all.

"That's really beautiful, Grammy," Brook said, giving Mattie a kiss on the cheek. "When did you make this?"

"She finished it last year," Connie interjected. "And someone wants to pay her twenty grand for it."

Mattie smiled at Brook's and Ashley's looks of disbelief. She went to the quilt and studied it for a moment. The quilt's background was a soft white, and in every available space Mattie had intricately hand-quilted designs to enrich the piece. She had basically taken six individual squares, each square measuring 30" x 30", and sewn them together. The entire quilt measured 60" x 90". But it was those individual squares that added the color and ornamentation for the work. Within each one were six perfectly matched circles, intertwined in an array of colors and materials. At the small center where all the circles met, there was just enough room for Mattie to embroider the initial of each girl's name. The last square was given an *M* for Mitchell. And around each gathering of circles, Mattie had appliquéd material in a ribbon-like effect to frame each square.

"I've never seen anything like it," Ashley commented.

"Nor will you again," Mattie replied. "If you look closely, you can see that each of the circles contains materials saved from outfits I made for you girls when you were younger. That's why this quilt is special to me."

"So you don't plan to sell it?" Connie questioned.

"No," Mattie answered flatly.

"You aren't even considering it?" Brook asked. "I mean, twenty thousand is a lot of money."

"I don't need it. Your grandfather had plenty of insurance when he died. I've never had to worry about money." She turned away from the quilt to study the girls. "I couldn't sell it. It's too much a part of me—of you. No, this quilt will stay in the family."

She turned back to the quilt. "See here? This square is for Ashley. There is an *A* in the center and the rings are made from something special that each one of you wore. See the blue circle in each square?" They nodded. "That's from Ashley's sixth-grade graduation dress. This green circle is for Brook. And here is her square," Mattie said, pointing out the square with an embroidered *B*. "Each girl has a square with her initials, but each is joined to the others within the connected circles."

"But what about the sixth square?" Erica asked. "Is that you? There's an *M* there."

Mattie smiled. "That's for Mitchell."

The girls fell silent as they continued to study the work. Mattie felt an overwhelming love for each of them as she continued. "The circles show how we are all joined together—no beginning, no ending. Just like the love we have for one another. It's a blend of all of us, and I spent four years laboring in love to create it. I couldn't even think of selling it."

"What will you do with it?" Connie asked, appearing almost startled that she'd spoken the words out loud.

"I suppose I'll use it. I'll wrap myself up in the memories and cherish the love I've known with each of you. On those days when I feel sorry for myself because you haven't come to visit or call," Mattie said with a grin, "I'll take it up and tuck it around me and tell myself what a silly old woman I am for doubting that you care."

Mattie realized she hadn't meant to say exactly those words. She certainly didn't want to lay a guilt trip on her granddaughters. But the words were true. She missed them more than she could put into human language. She comforted herself with things that reminded her of them. That was one of the reasons she left their rooms exactly as they had always been.

Feeling almost ashamed of her words, Mattie turned to leave. She paused at the door, however, and looked back at them. "Family is important, girls. We were given to each other for a reason. Rachelle is gone and in fact was never really a part of your lives," Mattie said softly. "But the rest of us are still here, and you girls are what remain of her—and of me. It may be a slender thread, but it connects us nevertheless."

Chapter 9

After three days at Grammy's, Connie finally managed to make it down to the lake for a leisurely time of meditation. She sat on the end of the dock, lazily touching her toes to the water and contemplating her surroundings. The lake felt icy and even though the afternoon had warmed up nicely, Connie knew it would be at least June before the lake would be warm enough for swimming.

She relished the quiet afforded her. Her sisters were off somewhere engaged in conversation, and Connie desired nothing more than a moment to pull back from everything and study life at face value.

How strange it felt to be home again. She never seemed to get over the feeling that embraced her each time she pulled up the long lane to the farm. As much as she hated to admit it, this was the only place in the world where Connie felt truly happy. And Connie had tried it all.

Teaching physical education allowed her most of the summer off, as well as nice chunks of time in the winter. She had traveled throughout the world—skied, parachuted, mountain climbed, and in general, tried anything she thought might satisfy her yearnings. But it was always Grammy's farm that made her feel at rest.

Closing her eyes, Connie could see herself driving through town, heading out west on Highway 56. She remembered the feeling of anxiety—a good anxiety—that made her heart pound in anticipation just like a child at Christmas. Then the gravel road turnoff came and she would head her car down the rural lane where fields of newly plowed dirt filled the air with a sweet, pungent odor. The trees were dressed out in the palest of green leaves, and vegetation alongside the narrow lane was starting to show life anew.

Then a beautiful white house set atop a gently sloping hill came into view. Gram and "her girls" had terraced the walk down from the house with small self-constructed walls of native limestone. Atop each of these were tiny gardens of herbs and flowers, giving the front yard a well-manicured appearance.

All around the house were trees, a rarity on the prairies of Kansas. Willows, oaks, elms, and cottonwood dotted the landscape surrounding the house and lake, their thick and hearty limbs shading the Mitchell farm from the harsh Kansas sun. And then there were Grammy's beloved fruit trees and flowering dogwoods and redbuds. Beyond the perimeters of the yard and lake area, rich Kansas soil was plowed for planting or already green with winter wheat. It was all glorious, and to Connie it was what came to mind when she thought of happiness and safety.

A rhythmic splash in the water caused her to open her eyes. Approaching from the west, Harry Jensen rowed his boat in a steady pace that brought him closer and closer to Connie's sanctuary.

"Hello, Harry," Connie said, giving a little wave. She would have just as soon been left alone, but Harry's sudden appearance rather pleased her.

"Hi, Connie," he said, reaching the dock. He tied off the boat and threw a brown paper sack onto the dock before climbing up. "How have you been?"

Connie shrugged and glanced down at her shoddy attire. She'd taken no care with her appearance, and now with Harry here, she felt almost self-conscious of the old college sweat shirt and well-worn jeans. "I'm okay."

"I brought you ladies a smoked turkey." He motioned to the sack and picked it up. "Mattie loves them."

"I do too," Connie said, unable to keep from grinning. "I'm a nut for barbecued and smoked meats."

Harry came to the side where Connie sat. "Mind if I join you for a minute?"

"Not at all." She waited until he'd stretched out on the dock beside her. His dusty jeans and threadbare work shirt helped to put her at ease. After all, this was just Harry. He was nearly a member of the family. She took a deep breath. "So how have you been? I mean, after all these years?"

Harry took off his ball cap and wiped his forehead. "Not bad, I guess. Certainly not bad enough to complain about it. How about you? You don't look anything like the girl I remember."

Connie took that as a compliment and smiled. "I thought a change was in order."

"Why? There was nothing wrong with the way you looked before."

"In your opinion, maybe, but to me there was a great deal to be desired."

"How so?" Harry asked, seeming genuinely interested.

"I always felt I looked too much like everyone else," Connie replied. "I mean, not in the same way Brook and Ashley look alike, but I just felt I got lost in the shuffle. No one ever noticed me. It's hard to explain, but I wanted to find a way to be different, and at the same time—fit in. I hated being just one of the Mitchell girls, especially when I didn't feel like one of them. But I also hate it now when people stare at me like I'm some sort of freak. I just bleached my hair and cut it—it's not like I put in a nose ring or anything. Yesterday when I went to the store for Grammy, I must have had everyone in the place staring at me."

"Well, you do look different. Not that folks around here don't ever dye their hair."

"But that's no call to be rude. They could have just minded their own business. I didn't ask for the extra attention."

Harry chuckled. "That's a bit like painting the tractor pink, then getting mad when folks notice."

Connie grinned. "Well, I suppose you have a point. But with all the people showing up for Rachelle's funeral, I can't imagine why they'd worry about me."

"I think folks probably recognized you, but knew you weren't the way they remembered you. Maybe folks just wondered what had gotten into you."

Connie frowned. Harry had always been one to speak his mind. "Well, enough about me. What about you? I hear you're getting married to Sarah Hooper in the fall."

"That's the plan," Harry replied, revealing no interest in elaborating further.

Connie watched him look out over the lake. His jaw was set in a firm way that suggested she had touched a nerve. And his eyes, although accented by tiny laugh lines at the corners, were fixed and brooding. She couldn't help but wonder why he seemed so serious all of a sudden. Had the talk of marriage somehow put a kink in their conversation? She thought of Ashley and how close he had once been to her. Maybe that was the problem.

Their conversation lagged while the gentle lapping sound of the water against the dock and shore made a melodic symphony. Overhead, a bevy of robins, blue jays, and orioles joined in as they called to their mates from the trees. Gram called it "nature's music." Connie smiled as she remembered Grammy trying to get her to stop and listen.

"You can hear things growing," Grammy had told her, *"but first you have to be quiet and listen."*

She thought in that moment that Gram had been right. She could almost hear things growing around her. If nothing else, she could hear Harry's rhythmic breathing and somehow that seemed just as natural as the sound of the water. Harry was so much a part of the land and the farm. It seemed only right that he spend his life here.

"So how have you found things?" Harry finally asked. "Has the farm changed much since your last visit?"

"Not that much," Connie admitted. "Grammy hasn't changed much either. She still looks too young to have all of us for granddaughters."

Harry smiled again, and the shadowy look in his eyes seemed to pass away. "Mattie is eternally young. I think keeping busy has kept her that way."

"Probably so."

"And what about your sisters? Have they changed much?"

"Ashley is too perfect. Brook, too famous. Deirdre is too preoccupied trying to please everyone, and Erica is too busy trying to become a world-class flute player."

"And what are you?" Harry asked, fixing his gaze on her face.

"I'm too out of place," Connie said sadly.

"How so?"

He seemed genuinely interested, and because Connie felt strangely comfortable with this old family friend, she decided to answer him. "I suppose I've never fit in this family. I wanted to. But there were many strikes against me. I'm a middle child, and not only that, but the middle child of all girls. It's bad enough to be the middle of three kids, but I'm the middle of five. At least with three, the middle child usually ends up on someone else's side—she has an ally at least part of the time. But the middle child of five is just stuck. She has two siblings older and two siblings younger and they cling to each other in a way that ostracizes that middle person.

"And to make it worse, my older two siblings are twins and the younger two might as well be. And they all share the same father, while my father was an unknown figure—the momentary indiscretion of a rocky marriage."

"That was hardly your fault," Harry said softly.

"Maybe not," Connie admitted, "but it isolates me in a way that no one else shares."

"Seems to me you all have special qualities that make you unique. I wouldn't give too much credit to blaming life's problems on being a middle child. You could have just as easily been first born or last, and then what would you blame?"

Connie felt a sense of indignation. "So you're saying I'm being silly—maybe even stupid?"

Harry seemed unconcerned by her harsh tone. "I'm saying a person can waste a lot of their time looking for something or someone to blame for their miseries. Why not stop worrying about who or what's to blame and just get on with your life? Accept responsibility for what belongs to you, and don't worry about the stuff that doesn't."

"You make it sound so simple."

"Does it have to be hard?" Harry asked softly.

Connie shrugged. "It seems like it always is." She met his compassionate gaze and turned away. Why did he have to be so patient—so nice?

"So do you have someone special in your life?" Harry asked, changing the subject.

Connie grimaced. She hadn't wanted to discuss her love life with her own family, much less Harry Jensen. He'd never understand the choices she'd made—neither would Mattie or her sisters. How could she explain that she just didn't feel the same way they did? She couldn't begin to think about permanently settling down in marriage before knowing that she completely understood the person she was marrying.

"So?" Harry pressed. "Is there some special guy?"

"There've been special guys," Connie replied, still not wanting to give up too much information.

"What about now?"

Connie drew a deep breath. "I'm seeing someone." She neglected to add that this particular someone was living in her apartment back in Topeka. She hadn't found the nerve to even be honest with Deirdre and Erica on the ride down to Mattie's.

"So what does he do?" Harry questioned.

Connie grew very uncomfortable. "Why the third degree? Why are you so interested in me all of a sudden?"

Harry laughed, leaving her completely unnerved. "First it was a problem because no one noticed you, then you get uptight because folks at the grocery store stared at you. Then you feel that no one cares, and now when I show some interest in your life, you act as though it's the most intrusive attack ever made on you. Come on, Connie. Make up your mind."

"You always were one for getting right to the heart of things," Connie said, trying hard not to notice how his eyes crinkled at the corners when he laughed. "I remember how it was."

"Remember what?" Harry seemed genuinely curious.

His soft-spoken manner caused a spark of electricity to run up Connie's spine. She looked away quickly. "I remember you giving me a hard time. I always thought you were very bossy and way too serious."

"And I thought you were just a ragamuffin tagalong," Harry replied, the joy of the memory clear in his tone. "I remember how you used to spy on Ashley and me."

"Somebody needed to," Connie said, smiling in spite of herself. She looked up to find Harry blushing. "See, you remember."

"That's beside the point. We behaved well enough."

"Probably because you knew you had an audience."

"Remember when I taught you how to pitch a softball?" Harry questioned, changing the subject.

Connie did remember, figuring she had probably developed her love of sports because of Harry's gentle, patient instruction. "You were a good teacher," she said, allowing herself to meet his gaze. His eyes seemed to break through her façade of strength. The feeling was both startling and terrifying.

"I'll bet you're a great teacher," he encouraged, his voice soft.

"I try to be. I try to remember the things you taught me." She smiled up at him. The time Harry had spent with her as a kid had always been special, for she had basked in his praise and longed for his approval.

Suddenly uncomfortable with the feelings her memories evoked, Connie no longer wanted to remember the past or any of the pleasant moments she'd shared with Harry.

"I'm really surprised you remember any of it," Harry said, not seeming to notice her discomfort. "Half the time I wasn't even sure you were listening."

Connie felt the tension evaporate as she took offense. "I listen when people care enough to talk to me and not lecture."

"Why is it when someone fails to agree with you or bothers to ask difficult questions," Harry began, "you automatically title it a lecture? I think most of the time people are downright afraid to talk to you for fear you'll misunderstand their motives."

"Oh, never mind," she said, getting to her feet. "I don't expect you to understand."

Harry stood as well and picked up the turkey. "Don't expect me to or don't want me to?"

Connie put her hands on her hips and stared at his grinning face. "You are insufferable, Mr. Jensen."

His grin broadened into a full smile. "And you are stronger and more capable than you give yourself credit for. Probably the reason more people don't get close to you is that you intimidate them with your strength."

Connie recognized the compliment but refused to give in to flattery. Instead, she protected herself by buffering herself against his gentle spirit. "But I don't intimidate you, do I?"

"No, intimidate would definitely be the wrong word."

He had taken her completely off guard. "What would be the right word?" Connie asked, softening her tone.

"Hmm," Harry murmured thoughtfully. "I'll have to get back to you on that one."

Chapter 10

"Sean, listen," Erica said irritably into the telephone receiver. "No, just listen to me!"

She felt a total sense of frustration as the man continued to plead his case. "Look, I have to go," she finally said. "I'll call you tomorrow." She hung up before he could protest her words.

In the living room she could hear her sisters' animated chatter. They were discussing something to do with Brook's most recent trip to British Columbia, and Erica had no desire to get in on the fun. Sneaking down the south hall, she slipped up the stairs as quietly as she could and made for the haven of her bedroom.

They called it the Ivy Room because the wallpaper held a delicate ivy pattern in various shades of green against a white backdrop. The curtains at the window were a dark hunter green with white sheers, and all of the trim had been painted white, while the closet and entry doors had been painted the same shade as the curtains.

To break the green and white monotones, Erica had chosen bright ginghams with white ruffles for her bed pillows, and Grammy had designed her a wonderful eight-pointed star quilt in white and rose.

Erica loved the effect and often wondered why she hadn't tried to recreate the design in her own apartment back in Kansas City. But down deep inside, she knew why. This room belonged at Grammy's. It simply wouldn't fit anywhere else.

"May I come in?" Grammy asked as she entered the room.

Erica realized too late that she'd failed to close the door behind her. "I guess so," she said, knowing her voice betrayed her emotions.

"Want to talk about it?"

Erica smiled. "Not really. It wouldn't do much good."

"I couldn't help but overhear some of your conversation. I take it your young man is pressuring you to marry him," Grammy said, taking a seat in a white wicker rocker. Her short, layered hair, frosted with gray and white, made a fitting frame for her aging features. But no matter how many years etched themselves in Grammy's face, her blue eyes were bright and alert, never missing a single detail of life.

Erica gave up trying to keep anything from her grandmother. The woman had an intuitive nature that seemed capable of ferreting out even the tiniest bit of information. With a sigh, she sat down on the edge of her bed and leaned her chin down on the brass railing of the footpiece. "Sean doesn't understand my goals."

Grammy smiled. "Music?"

Erica nodded. "I've sent out audition tapes to several eastern orchestras, and he's furious with me. He wants me to stay in Kansas City and marry him and have lots of children and teach music to other people."

"He expects you to give up the orchestra? Surely he knows how important playing the flute is to you."

"I thought so," Erica replied, lifting her head with a shrug. "But I guess he doesn't. Maybe no one understands like you do. You know how this has been my passion since I was a little girl. You're the one who paid for my lessons and drove me to practice."

"I've also reaped the benefits of listening to you play."

"Well, Sean sees my passion for music as a competition for my love."

"It does take up a great deal of your time, Erica. I remember how you'd spend long hours practicing to get one piece right. Remember when your first-chair position was challenged in high school? You practiced so much we were all sick and tired of 'The Dance of the Blessed Spirits.'"

Erica giggled. "But it needed to be perfect. That snotty Justine had her new open-holed flute and her fancy private lessons from a real college professor."

"And the more you practiced, the worse it got," Grammy reminded her.

Erica could remember it as if it were yesterday. "I stood right over there," she said, pointing to the window. "My music stand was positioned to get the best lighting from the lamp and from the sunlight. I played and played and it just didn't feel right. No matter how hard I tried, I just kept messing up."

"And then I made you quit."

"Not before I was ready to throw my flute across the room," Erica said, shaking her head. "I was about to send it sailing through the bedroom window."

"So I made you pack it up and stop practicing."

"That was the hardest moment of my life. The competition was the very next day."

"But you were ready. You knew the notes, but you'd lost sight of the music," Grammy said.

Erica nodded. "I remember telling you that you couldn't possibly understand how important that first-chair position was to me. I cried and cried and you still wouldn't let me practice. You told me I'd either do my very best and remain as first chair, or I would do my very best and become the second chair." Erica could remember the words distinctly. "Then you told me that if the music was really my love, it would show in my tryouts. If not, I was in the wrong place and needed to know it."

"But you were in the right place," Grammy said with a loving smile. "And you kept your first-chair position."

"And you were right about making me stop. I've kept with that practice ever since. When things get too stressful and I'm hitting more wrong notes than right ones, I make myself stop and do something else. Sometimes I just go jogging, sometimes I shop—but taking a break always does the trick. Sometimes I'm just as glad to run away."

"Is that what you're doing now? Running away from Sean and his proposal?"

Erica got up and walked to the window. She shoved her hands into the pockets of her jeans and sighed. "I guess I am. Rachelle's funeral seemed like the perfect way to escape dealing with him. I know that sounds terrible. But at the same time that I was running away from Sean, I felt like I was running to my family."

"I understand," Grammy said softly. "But just like music had to be your focus rather than the position you held in the band, the love of your family should be the focus rather than the event that brought you here. You feel comforted coming home because you know you are loved unconditionally. We won't berate you for choosing an orchestra that takes you far away, although we'll miss you and wish you were closer."

"I do feel comforted here. Sometimes I feel so childish. Like everyone else grew up, but I didn't. I'll always be a baby in their eyes. The kid sister. Yet as bossy as they can be, I wouldn't trade them."

"Just remember, Erica," Grammy said, getting to her feet, "jobs will come and go. So, too, will passions. Your music is important, but family is more so. Maybe that's what Sean recognizes and wants to share with you."

"But my music is so much a part of me that it's often impossible to tell where I end and it begins. My music transports me beyond the emptiness and loneliness I feel."

"Maybe Sean is jealous," Grammy replied, pausing to gently touch Erica's cheek. "Maybe he wishes you would let him have that place in your life. Maybe he would like to fill your emptiness and take away those lonely moments."

Erica knew she was right. "I just don't know how to make it all work. I'm making so many mistakes."

"Then quit trying so hard. Remember, you won first chair even though I made you stop practicing. You knew the music, but you were losing the heart of it. Maybe you're losing the heart of this as well. Maybe you're afraid to trust Sean to be to you all that music has been."

Erica wrapped her arms around Grammy's shoulders. She smelled like cinnamon and nutmeg—no doubt left over from the coffee cake she'd baked that morning. Erica loved the fragrance and hugged her just a little longer than she might have under other circumstances. "Thank you for loving me," she whispered.

Grammy stroked her head gently. "Thank you for loving me."

Erica pulled away and sniffed back tears. "I'm so glad we have each other."

"Me too." Grammy went to the door and paused. "Sometimes life hands us surprises, like flowers coming back up a second year when you thought they were good for only one season. Maybe God will hand you a surprise in this situation as well. Just don't run so far away that you aren't around to see it when it comes." She smiled and slipped away.

"Am I interrupting?" Deirdre questioned not a minute after Mattie had stepped from the room.

"Not at all," Erica replied. "Grammy and I just had a conversation about Sean. Say, did you get ahold of Dave and Morgan?"

Deirdre came in and dropped into the wicker rocker. "Finally. Dave had taken her out for pizza and to play. They were just getting back. Sounded like they had a really good time. Dave sent his mom and dad to the theatre to give them the night off, so everyone's doing just fine."

"Sometimes I envy you," Erica said, leaning against the wall. "You have your life so perfectly ordered."

"Don't bet on it," Deirdre laughed. "If I've learned one thing, it's that life has no perfect order. There's always something to come along and zap you just when you least expect it. Take Rachelle, for instance. Who would have thought she'd be dead at such a young age?"

"I wonder if she killed herself," Erica said absentmindedly.

"I guess we'll never know. Either way, she's gone. Not that she was ever here for us anyway."

"I know you told me not to bother," Erica confessed, "but I kept trying to get a call through to her. I just kept thinking that maybe if I reached out to her, she'd be inclined to reach back."

"People aren't always going to respond that way," her sister chided. "Just because you have a good heart doesn't mean everyone in the world does. Rachelle's heart was ice. She wasn't about to let it thaw for even a minute."

"Maybe she was afraid."

"Afraid? Of us?" Deirdre questioned. "I can think of a lot of things in this world to be afraid of, but us?"

Erica shrugged. "Why not? We're the one audience she couldn't sell. We're the ones who refused to buy into her hype."

"She's the one who walked out on us," Deirdre said, shaking her head. "We weren't to blame."

"Maybe that's what made it so impossible for her. She would have had to face up to her mistakes and see herself the way we do. That would have been enough to keep me away, had I been Rachelle."

"Well, it wouldn't have been for me. I have a daughter," Deirdre replied. "Nothing could separate me from her. Nothing. And I'm not talking physical distance. She has to go to school, Dave and I will take our trips, and I had to come here. No, I'm talking about true separation. I'm talking about the heart."

Erica nodded. "I know. I am too. I think Rachelle was afraid to love us. I think the price was too high and she was terrified of what it might mean to her if she let us in. Now she's dead, so I guess we'll never know."

Sadly, Erica realized the truth in her own words. She had always hoped for one of those sappy reunions where she and her sisters could lovingly embrace their mother and find true happiness as a family. *I've always been a dreamer,* she told herself. She just always assumed everyone else was too.

"Erica, don't let it get to you," Deirdre said, getting to her feet. "I'm sure that wherever Rachelle is, she's not giving us a second thought."

"But what if she is?" Erica questioned.

"Then it's her loss."

Chapter *11*

"Grammy?" Ashley called as she peeked into the sewing room. She figured it to be the one place she could count on finding her grandmother on a rainy day. Sure enough, Mattie was hunched over her sewing machine, trying to thread it.

"I'm in here, Ash," she replied, appearing to finally accomplish her goal. "Just thought with the rain and all I'd get a little sewing done. Come on in." She patted a cushioned chair nearby. "Come talk with me."

For as long as Ashley could remember, Grammy had kept a chair beside the sewing machine. She had told the girls over and over that just because she was sewing did not mean she wasn't available for them. In fact, Grammy had so often been sewing clothes for one girl or the other that the talking sessions usually turned into fitting sessions as well.

"What are you working on?" Ashley asked, admiring the Piece Work quilt before joining her grandmother. The amount of work Grammy had put into the quilt was incredible. Lovingly, Ashley touched her own square, tracing the embroidered letter *A*.

"I'm just putting together some curtains for the back door," Grammy replied.

"This quilt is absolutely incredible, Grammy. I can't imagine the time you put into it. The work is so intricate—especially the hand quilting."

Grammy stopped her work and looked up, just as Ashley turned. She smiled appreciatively. "I'm glad you like it. I figure it's something that will be in the family for a long time to come."

Ashley nodded. "I know I'd be proud to have it in my own. I just can't imagine using it. I suppose for special occasions it would be all right. I know the other quilts you've made for me have been built to last."

Mattie chuckled softly. "What good is something that's merely ornamental? Pretty things are seldom appreciated as much as useful ones."

"I suppose that's true. Still, things like this are important. There will never be another Piece Work quilt made by Mattie Mitchell with exactly this material and with these precise stitches."

"That's true," Mattie replied. "But the same is true of each of my pieces. Each one is a part of my heart—a labor of love, if you will." She paused to gaze into Ashley's eyes. "I have a feeling you didn't come in here to talk about sewing and quilts, though. Why don't you come here and tell me what this is about?"

Ashley nodded and glanced to the window. Outside the heavy gray skies poured rain, making what she'd come to say a little harder. "I have to leave on Saturday morning," she finally said, taking the seat beside Grammy.

"Yes, I know. You mentioned that when you first came. I know you're anxious to be with your family again," Mattie said, her sharp eyes focusing on Ashley's face. "But something is troubling you. What is it?"

Ashley smiled, noting her grandmother's intuitive nature. "I was kind of hoping maybe you would come home with me. I mean, I hate to think about you here by yourself. Especially with this sadness over Rachelle."

Grammy leaned over and patted Ashley's hand. "You needn't worry about me falling apart, if that's it. I've dealt with this kind of loss before. I can deal with it again. I suppose my biggest sorrow is in not knowing if Rachelle made peace with God. I'd like to believe she did—it's not like she didn't know the way."

"But you have to want to make peace," Ashley replied. "Some folks don't think they need God. They feel He's just out there somewhere making a disinterested observation of all creation."

"Then they're mistaken," Mattie replied. "We know the difference and, even though she ignored it, so did Rachelle."

"Well, for your sake, Grammy, I hope she found her way back to God and the overdose was just a mistake."

"I hope so too," Mattie replied. "Her life was lived in strife—never a moment of rest or peace."

"Well, I think it might do *you* good to get away for a while. You could come stay with us in Denver and just relax. We could even go up to the cabin at Estes once it warms up."

"I'd almost forgotten you had bought yourself a place in the mountains. I'll bet the boys just love that."

"They do," Ashley admitted. "You would too."

Mattie shook her head. "It's planting time here. If I don't stay and tend things, I won't have much of a garden."

"But you could just stay all summer with us and not have a garden this year. I worry about you, Gram. I don't like to think of you rambling around all alone in this big house with no one to talk to."

"I have Harry and my church ladies. Pastor Wallace and his wife come see me at least twice a month. And the telephone works—at least usually," she said with a smile. "Besides, Morgan is coming the first week of June. She'll be here for a few weeks and I've already got great plans for showing her the kind of summer you girls used to enjoy. You know, you could always bring the boys and come spend time here too."

Ashley nodded. "I've thought of that, but the boys have so many summer activities planned. They're going to camps and spending time with some of their cousins in California. They've looked forward to this all winter, and I can't take that from them."

"I understand." Mattie leaned forward, taking both of Ashley's hands in her own. "I'll be just fine. Don't worry about me. God planned all of this out before the beginning of time. I believe firmly that there is a purpose, even to this. But what I do worry about is you and your sisters. You've all grown so distant. Even you and Brook seem separate—like there's some sort of wall between you. Oh, it's nothing like I see between you and the others, but it's there."

"I don't think I know what you're talking about," Ashley said. She and Brook had shared quite a bit of time together on this trip as usual, and Grammy's words didn't completely make sense.

"It's only natural that you all go your separate ways, have families of your own. You can't stay Kansas farm girls in pigtails and pedal pushers forever." She smiled and gave Ashley's hands a squeeze. "I just don't want you to let time and other business come between the closeness you've always shared with each other. Why, there was a time when Brook couldn't take a breath without you exhaling it for her."

Ashley knew exactly what her grandmother meant. "We're still close, Grammy. Please don't worry. Brook has a different life from mine, but we still call each other and check up on each other. Why, she knew the minute I went into labor with each of the boys, and that time I hurt my ankle, she was on the phone before I could even call Jack to come home and help me to the doctor."

"What about your other sisters? Connie feels that no one cares about her. Does anyone ever call her?"

"I call at least once a month, but it's like pulling teeth to get much of a conversation out of her. She's the one who puts up walls. She's always been that way."

"Maybe so, but that shouldn't stop you from tearing them down. If you and your sisters tried extra hard with her, you could probably pull down those walls faster than she could put them up. After all, she's just one person."

Ashley stiffened. She'd tried to understand and befriend Connie most all of her life. The hard truth of the matter was that for all Connie's grumbling, she didn't want a closeness with Ashley or anyone else. It suited her to be estranged from everyone. Still, Ashley didn't want to leave the farm with Grammy thinking she was at odds with Connie.

"I'll keep trying, Grammy," she promised. "Just don't expect a miracle."

Mattie laughed. "Child, I always expect miracles. It's the only way to get through life."

Ashley got to her feet again and found herself drawn to the quilt. "You know, you're always asking us what we want from the farm when you die. I'd like Piece Work. I think it's the finest work you've ever done, and it would always serve to remind me of how you worked all your life to join us together as a family." She looked back at her grandmother and smiled. "But even better, I'd rather you just live forever and that way there won't be any need to divvy anything up."

"Well, I don't plan to live forever," Mattie said, moving to stand beside Ashley. "At least not on this earth. That's why it's so important for me to get things in order while I'm here. I want to stand before God with a clear conscience. I want to know that I did my best."

"You have, Grammy," Ashley said, hugging the older woman close. "No one could have done more."

"I'd like to believe that," Mattie replied, wiping a tear from her eye as they pulled apart. "But everyone makes mistakes. I'm no different. I've made my share, and all I can hope is that God's mercy will work them out in the long run."

———

Mattie joined her granddaughters in the living room, happy for the time they could share. Someone had thoughtfully started a fire to ward off the chill brought on by the rain, and a collection of light classical pieces played softly on the stereo system. It made an ideal setting for a quiet afternoon.

Easing back into her favorite chair, Mattie reached into a nearby sewing box and took up a quilt square she had begun piecing. She loved to work with her hands—she always had. It was not simply the creativity of what she was doing; the work relaxed her and eased the tension and stress of the day. Gardening was the same way. It refreshed her to nurture life and to focus on something other than the miseries that strayed into her otherwise orderly world. The quiet time also gave her pause to pray.

With the funeral now said and done and most of the hoopla settled, Mattie realized the girls would soon be going home. It saddened her to think the house would again be silent and empty. She tried not to imagine how it would feel to wake up and know there was no one there to care for or visit with. She thought of Ashley's offer to go to Denver. She could always do that and just plan to be back in time to care for Morgan the first week in June.

As if on cue, Brook turned to Mattie and said, "I'll be leaving early Saturday. I want to give myself plenty of time to get to Kansas City. My flight is at two."

"I'll be sorry to see you go," Mattie said, trying not to sound morose. "It's been such a pleasure to have you all here. I'm almost glad you girls left your husbands and kids at home. Almost. I would have loved seeing them, however." She put her work down and stilled her hands. "It's been like old times with the five of you here."

"I've certainly enjoyed getting to talk with everyone," Ashley admitted, "but I have so much work waiting for me at home. My schedule just seems to get more and more complicated."

"Oh, you have it easy, Ashley," Erica said, almost snapping at her sister.

Erica had been edgy all day, and it showed clearly in her attitude now. Mattie couldn't help but wonder if her feelings about Sean were causing her additional pressure.

"I beg your pardon?" Ashley's voice sounded defensive.

"You don't have to report to a regular job. You get to be your own boss. I had to have permission to even be here," Erica replied.

"So what?" Brook jumped in to defend Ashley. "You're doing what you want to do. Why shouldn't Ashley live her life the way she chooses?"

"Ashley's just trying to make Mother of the Year," Erica said, looking to Deirdre for some kind of support.

"It does seem that way," Deirdre commented. "I'm a mother, too, but I don't let my schedule run me like you do. By your own admission you keep pushing toward perfection, and then you get frustrated and unhappy when it eludes you."

"I'm happy doing what I'm doing," Ashley protested. "I wasn't complaining, I was merely commenting on being very busy."

"You're still trying to outdo Rachelle," Erica said rather bitterly. "You and Brook have always played this game to one-up our mother."

Brook looked rather guilty. "I'm not trying to one-up anyone. I'm making a living, nothing more."

"Oh, don't give us that, Brook," Connie said, jumping into the fracas. "The only reason you got into modeling was because of Rachelle. You wanted to prove you could be just as successful."

"I do it because I'm good at it," Brook declared defensively.

"And I married and had a family," Ashley added, "because I found more value in that than chasing after a career."

"Oh, and I suppose you think family means nothing to the rest of us," Erica countered.

Ashley threw an apologetic look at Brook before saying, "If the shoe fits—"

"That's hardly called for, Ashley," Deirdre threw in. "We all have our responsibilities. I have my family and social duties. I do charity work and help out at the church, but it's no reason to hold someone else's life in contempt. Erica often comes to share in things with Dave and Morgan and me. Can't we just agree to disagree about what matters most to each of us? In my opinion, Christians should-n't deal with each other so harshly. Grammy didn't raise us that way."

"Oh yes," Connie said to Deirdre before Ashley could reply, "let us not forget your piety and religious servanthood. Leave it to you to throw religion in our faces."

"Girls! Listen to yourselves. You're taking the tensions of Rachelle's death and funeral out on one another," Mattie finally said. "You should be drawing strength and support from each other. Your unique differences make you special and they also help to give you opportunities to bless each other. You should also focus on the similarities—the fact that you are sisters and share the same memories. This should draw you together!"

"We've learned how to be independent and find strength in ourselves as well," Connie said softly. "Everyone has gone their own way, Grammy. We can't be there for each other in the way you're talking about."

"That's not true." Mattie shook her head in denial. "You can be there as much as you choose to be there. You've all done well on your own, but I believe that is due to the foundation you had to begin with. You had each other and you knew that no matter where you went in life, there were four other people you were intricately tied to. Five, if you count me—and I hope you do."

"But, Gram, I think you are clinging to old-fashioned notions," Connie stated firmly. "Today's family can't live life like they did when you were a girl. Families today are far more mobile and spread out. There are more responsibilities for the average person. Besides, I've always been odd man out in this group. My father is different from theirs, and they've always been close because they were born either together or a matter of months apart. For all intents and purposes, I am alone."

"By your own choosing," Ashley suddenly added. "I think you wear your position in this family like some medal of honor. Did it ever dawn on you that your feelings of separation are all your own doing?"

"That's not true!" Connie declared. "You had Brook, and Deirdre and Erica had each other. I had no one. Not one of you wanted me in your world."

"I've had enough!" Mattie exclaimed, putting her things aside. "I won't sit here and listen to you bicker. You'll have to work it out for yourselves. I've tried to help you see the importance of family and of faith in God. I've tried to compensate for Rachelle, but instead, I find myself competing with her in my desire to instill positive values in you five girls. I guess with this kind of attitude, you are more like your mother than you would believe."

With that, Mattie headed to the stillness of her bedroom. She had barely made it through the door, however, when she felt an overwhelming urge to kneel in prayer. Gripping the carved post of the bed Edgar had made for them decades ago, Mattie knelt on the soft rag rug and began to pray. Her heart was in greater turmoil than it had been in years. She saw her family falling apart, shredded in pieces by anger, bitterness, and regret.

"Father, you know I've tried to show them the right way. I've tried to help them to see that family is more than being raised under one roof—to one set of parents. I've tried to teach them about love—about you, but their hearts are so wounded. Only you can heal them. Only you can give them hope again."

A knock at her door brought Mattie back to her feet. "Come in," she called.

Deirdre opened the door just enough to look inside. "Are you all right?"

Mattie could have guessed that it would be her little peacemaker. Deirdre had spent a lifetime trying to ease the tensions in the family. "I'm fine," she told her granddaughter. "Do you want to come in?"

Deirdre nodded and slipped inside and closed the door. "Grammy, we're all so sorry for fighting. It's like you said—the tension of the last few days, dealing with Rachelle's death and the media circus . . . well, it's just made us a bit crabby. We really do care about one another."

"I know you do," Mattie replied, taking a seat on her bed. "It's just that sometimes I think you take for granted that you'll always be here. That the pain you forge today can somehow be melted away tomorrow. But, Deirdre, there aren't always tomorrows to deal with."

Her granddaughter nodded. "Like with Mom."

Mattie smiled. The girls seldom referred to Rachelle as "Mom." "Yes, it's exactly like that. I don't know if Rachelle meant to take her life or not. It might have been nothing more than an accident, but either way she's gone now. She couldn't have made up for the past even if she'd have remained alive. But at least alive she could have created a new future. Now she can't even do that."

Deirdre sat beside Mattie. "I just don't want you to fret, Grammy. We know how important it is to remain close. We love one another, even with all our quirks and problems. We can't help fighting sometimes, but we always make up."

"But there may come a day when you don't get a chance to make up," Mattie said quite seriously. "That's why the Bible admonishes us not to let the sun go down on our anger. There isn't always a tomorrow in which to fix things. You have to remember that."

"I will, Grammy," Deirdre said, leaning over to hug Mattie close. "Connie and Erica and I will be leaving on Saturday too. I just wanted to let you know. I sure wish you'd consider coming home with us. It's not that far away and I could bring you back when it's time for Dave and me to go on our trip."

"Ashley already invited me to go to Denver. I'll be fine, I promise you," Mattie said reassuringly. She held Deirdre's hand for a moment and relished the memory of another time when that hand had been much smaller.

"You'd probably better get on back out there," Mattie said softly. "They'll all be wondering if you soothed my worries away."

Deirdre smiled. "You know us pretty well."

"Some things stay the same. Your temperament has always been to worry about everyone's feelings. You've always been the least selfish of my girls."

Deirdre laughed. "Oh, I can be selfish. For instance, it wouldn't hurt my feelings at all if you decided to give me Piece Work. I fell in love with that quilt from the first moment. I'd be selfish enough to take it home and keep it all my days."

Mattie shook her head. "You aren't the first one to suggest such a thing."

"I didn't figure I was," Deirdre admitted. "Just remember that I like it too—and don't go selling it off to strangers."

"I can promise you I won't do that," Mattie assured. "It has a special place in this family—just like each of you do. I hope you won't forget that you will always have a special, reserved spot in my heart. A place I keep just for you."

Deirdre nodded and gently reached up to touch Mattie's cheek. "Despite what anyone else feels, and yet I'm sure I speak for all of us, Grammy, you were always more than we could ever hope for in a mother. You were always there for us, always faithful. It would have been nice to know our mother and father, but you were everything we needed."

Mattie felt tears come to her eyes. Deirdre's affirmation felt like words from God himself.

Chapter 12

Mattie got off the phone and went immediately to where the girls had gathered in the kitchen for a snack.

"That was Mavis Lane, your mother's secretary," she offered as she joined her granddaughters.

"What in the world did she want?" Erica questioned.

"Apparently there are specific funds to help with the funeral expenses. There are also some papers, letters, and other things that Mavis is boxing up to send to me here. She thought it might be things we'd want to have right away. Also, there are some insurance policies with me as the beneficiary. She didn't say what they were worth, but apparently I need to see to them." She paused, seeing she had everyone's full attention. "I may be the beneficiary, but as far as I'm concerned everything of hers belongs to you." All heads turned at this. "I had a small policy on Rachelle from the time she was a child and it easily covered her funeral expenses, so I have no need for anything more."

Deirdre put down her magazine and shook her head. "There won't be a lot of money—will there?"

Mattie shrugged. "I can't say. Rachelle had a lot of debt, according to Mavis, but her properties will be sold off to cover that. The estate will probably take years to settle in full. The insurance policies she had are free and clear of the estate."

"I never thought to inherit anything from her," Erica said softly. "I'm not sure I want anything from her."

"I know I don't." Ashley's voice sounded bitter, almost angry. "She can't buy my affection."

"I don't think anyone is suggesting that," Connie commented.

"She did leave it in your name, Grammy," Brook added. "I doubt she meant for us to have it."

Mattie saw the hurtful look on their faces and longed to make things right for them. She had once tried to help them see that letting go of Rachelle and the past was the only way they could go forward with their lives, but each one had her reasons for carrying their grudges.

Erica got up from the table and grabbed a soda out of the refrigerator. Taking the can back to the table, she took her place beside Deirdre. Mattie smiled at their grouping. It was very nearly a traditional matter and some things never changed. Ashley and Brook were within easy distance to share a conversation, while Connie had placed herself at the far end of the table and Deirdre and Erica had taken chairs opposite the twins.

"You know, I'm reminded of the day Rachelle came home with Ashley and Brook," Mattie said, hoping that by sharing a link to their past, they might not feel so angry. At least not with one another.

"She was sixteen and so skinny and dirty. She'd run away the year before, and I hadn't heard so much as a word from her. Then one day she just shows up pushing a stroller with two tiny bundles. She came back into my life as suddenly as she'd gone out from it," Mattie said, leaning back in the chair. "She was nothing like the defiant child who'd left me. This Rachelle was quiet, almost frighteningly so. She wore a ring on her finger and told me that she'd married, but she wouldn't say who her husband was or where he was.

"She put Ashley in my arms and told me her name. Then she did the same with Brook. When I asked why she'd picked those names, she shrugged and said, 'In the hospital nursery their beds had little signs that said Mitchell Baby Girl A and Mitchell Baby Girl B.' So she went with alphabetical A's and B's for her babies' names. I asked her about them having the last name of Mitchell, if she had married, but even this didn't seem to phase her. She simply declared that she had kept her last name and that she had demanded her children also keep it."

"Why would she do that?" Brook questioned aloud. "I mean, if she hated everything here so much, why would she keep the Mitchell name?"

"She didn't keep it for long," Connie said snidely. "I mean, no one in the world knows her under that name. She's Barrister to them."

Mattie shook her head. "I don't know why she did it. She never said. It might have been because she had such a fear of losing people."

"What do you mean?" Ashley questioned, shifting to draw her legs up under her.

"Rachelle never got over losing her father and brother," Mattie said thoughtfully. "I always figured that she refused to give you your father's name because she was afraid he'd up and die on her too. Which, of course, is what happened."

"That must have really been upsetting," Erica said, shaking her head. "I never thought of how it would have made her feel."

"Well, given the losses in her life, I think Rachelle tried to buffer herself from any more pain. I think she had figured it would be easier to have everyone hate her and think her unloving than to love them and lose them. Of course, she made up for that loss through her acting, where the rest of the world praised and loved her."

"Still, it should have mattered that the people who could have given her a great deal of love were the very people she drove away," Deirdre suggested.

"When Rachelle was twelve and her father died, she blamed herself. If you'll remember, it was shortly before Christmas and she had to stay late to practice for a special play they were to give on the day before winter break began. Her father and brother were on their way to pick her up when they hit the ice and were killed."

"We've heard this before," Ashley said uncomfortably.

Mattie nodded. "Yes, I know. I'm only telling you this because of something that happened later. Rachelle had an assignment at school. She was to write a theme on her family. Instead, she made the assignment a declaration of why fathers were unnecessary in the lives of children. I can still see her little-girl handwriting, always so neat and concise. She wrote, 'I don't think it's good to have a father. Fathers just work and get tired and have to go rest. They go away a lot and sometimes they never come back. I don't need a father, and I'm glad that mine went away.'"

"How could she say that?" Brook questioned in disbelief.

"How can you say what you do about Rachelle?" Mattie countered. "Pain makes people say and do things that are ugly and hurtful. Rachelle was just trying to deal with her pain, as you are trying to deal with yours."

"But she had a father at least for part of her life," Ashley said softly. "We were never allowed that privilege."

"I know," Mattie said sadly. "I wish I could have made it different for you. I suppose it matters very little that your father was of the undesirable sort who dabbled in crime and drug trafficking."

"That's what Rachelle told you," Connie said angrily. "For all we know he could have been the governor of Kansas."

Mattie shook her head. "No, I had a lawyer square everything away when I adopted you girls. Your father was a drug addict named Gary Gable. He died from an overdose, just like your mother. End of the story. Except that with you all still alive, it really isn't the end."

"He wasn't my father," Connie interjected. "At least not if what Rachelle told you was true. In my case, I don't even have a name to associate with that honored position. My father was one of Rachelle's one-night stands and I was simply a mistake." The bitterness in her voice was clearly evident.

Mattie shook her head. "Rachelle made more mistakes than any of us care to remember, but you are not one of them, Connie."

"I wish I could believe that."

Mattie's heart nearly broke for the pain in Connie's voice. "Then do," Mattie said firmly. "God makes life, not mistakes. Please understand me—I'm not excusing Rachelle's actions or even her inaction. I only brought up the issue of the accident because it forever changed the little girl I knew."

"I'm sure it was hard for Rachelle to live with the accident," Erica offered to her sisters. "I mean, we can't be without compassion."

"Why not?" Connie questioned. "She was."

"But just listen to yourself," Erica replied. "Listen to all of us. We're so bitter and angry. Are we going to stay that way the rest of our lives?"

"I'm only bitter when I have to think about her," Ashley said. "When I go home to my family, I will bury Rachelle both literally and figuratively. She won't figure into my future."

"You're being awfully negative, aren't you? I mean, I realize Rachelle left a lot undone, but does she really deserve your hatred?" Mattie questioned.

"Yes." Connie's matter-of-fact statement caused her sisters to turn in unison. They stared at her for a moment as if she'd spoken some horrible, unspeakable thing, then turned to Mattie and nodded.

"I don't know how you can love her after all she did to you," Brook finally stated in a soft, reserved manner. "You were wounded every bit as much as we were. She doesn't deserve a thing from us— certainly not love."

"I have to agree with Brook," Ashley said, nodding her head ever so slightly. "You taught us that love was a special gift."

"That's true, but I didn't say you should be stingy about giving it," Mattie countered. "Do you really see anything positive to be gained in my taking up your cause and hating Rachelle?"

Ashley looked away uncomfortably. "You always said, 'What goes around comes around.' Rachelle refused to think of anyone but herself. Not us. Not you. Not even God."

Mattie felt tears come to her eyes. The thought of having failed to bring Rachelle to salvation ate at her like a caustic acid. "But you're her daughter," Mattie said. "You're all her daughters. As much as you would all like to deny that or pick it apart for your own purposes, the woman gave you life. You share some of her looks, her temperament . . . and you share me. I don't like what Rachelle became or how she lived her life or that she left you behind—but to hate Rachelle and everything about her would also mean I'd have to hate you. Wouldn't it?"

They all fell silent at this and looked away to avoid Mattie's inquiring gaze. Mattie could only pray they would somehow hear her. Despite their beliefs that they could leave Rachelle behind when they went back to their perfectly ordered lives, Mattie knew better.

"Look, it's getting late and I'm tired," Connie said, getting up. "Guess I'll see you all tomorrow."

"I'm going to turn in too," Deirdre said. "If I oversleep, somebody just come wake me up."

"Good night, Grammy," Brook said, placing a light kiss on Mattie's forehead.

One by one, they moved off toward the oak staircase, disappearing into the shadows of the hallway. Mattie could hear them first on the steps, then their footfalls in the hallway upstairs. They weren't at all enthusiastic or speedy. Their voices weren't raised in animated laughter as they had been on that first day back home. She had given them something to consider. Something that had haunted her for quite some time. They almost seemed to desire her hatred for their mother, as if they needed Mattie to swear a total and complete allegiance to them, condemning Rachelle to the utter recesses of her memories. They couldn't bear that Mattie still loved Rachelle— because they couldn't love Rachelle.

But they *were* Rachelle, at least to Mattie. They were little pieces of a child who went away and never really returned. They were the heart and soul and life's blood of a love she'd shared with Edgar so many years ago. They were the continuation of the Mitchell name and bloodline, and they were all that Mattie had left on this earth.

Chapter 13

Friday dawned clear and beautiful. It looked as if the world had been washed and everything had come out fresh and crisp. The colors were invigorating, as was the warmth of the springtime air.

Connie had decided with great purpose and effort to make peace with her sisters, for Mattie's sake. She knew the day before had created great turmoil, and even though she felt they were all justified in their feelings, she hated that they'd hurt Mattie's feelings.

The girls had decided earlier in the week to plan a special picnic down by the lake for their Friday luncheon. Deirdre and Ashley were in charge of food, while Brook and Erica talked Mattie into venturing into town so that Connie could decorate for the party.

"I'm sure glad the rain moved on," Deirdre said, bringing a platter of sandwiches. "Oh, Connie, this looks just great!"

Connie smiled. She'd done what she could with what few decorations they had been able to buy in town. Crepe paper streamers decorated the lakeside gazebo and colorful napkins, plates, and tablecloth made up for the lack of Mattie's blooming garden.

"I wish Grammy's flowers were out," Connie commented. "It would have made things perfect."

"I think you did a good job in spite of that handicap," Deirdre said. The honking of a car horn brought their attention. "Grammy's back! Come on, let's go get the rest of the food so that when Brook and Erica bring her down, we'll be ready!"

The luncheon was a huge success. Mattie seemed pleased to have her girls all in such good spirits. They ate and laughed and lounged down by the lake until the light began to fade from the sky and the lemony hue of sunset turned a startling pink, lavender, and orange.

"I miss these times," Brook said softly. "I seldom get the chance to enjoy sunsets anymore. Although, when I was up in British Columbia earlier this year, I saw some wonderful sunsets."

"We were in Key West over spring break," Connie offered, "and would go down to the dock and watch the sunset. It was magnificent, but it had nothing on a good old-fashioned Kansas sunset."

"I didn't know you went to Key West," Erica commented.

"Me either," Deirdre joined in. "Who did you go with?"

"Why did I have to go with anyone?" Connie questioned rather defensively.

"Well, you did say 'we,'" Ashley pointed out, nibbling on a brownie. She thought Connie looked rather embarrassed, but she couldn't imagine why.

"I just went with friends, okay?" She got up and started to clear away the dishes.

"Hey, no one meant to upset you," Deirdre said, reaching out to touch Connie's arm.

Connie nodded. "I know. I guess I'm just dreading tomorrow."

"Dreading it?" Mattie questioned.

Connie put the plates down and shrugged. "I just have a lot of unsettled business. Then, too, I'll have to deal with the kids on Monday after they've abused a substitute for a whole week. They're always harder to get back into the swing of things after that."

"I think we all have our reasons for dreading tomorrow," Deirdre finally said. "None of us want to leave you, Grammy."

Mattie smiled. "I hate seeing you all go, but the sooner you go, the sooner you can return."

As she looked at each one, Ashley noted the expression on her face. Her grandmother took great pride in each of them, even with their flaws. She loved them unconditionally and unquestionably . . . just as she had loved her daughter, Rachelle.

Ashley looked out over the lake and suddenly it came to her that no matter what John or Zach might ever do, she would love them. She would fight to the death for either one of them, no matter how bad they acted—no matter what poor choices they made. Why hadn't she thought of that before? Why hadn't she equated the love she felt for her children with the love Mattie felt for Rachelle?

"We'd better get this stuff inside, or else go up and turn on the lights," Mattie suggested. "Otherwise, we'll soon not be able to see a thing."

The girls quickly agreed and helped carry the dishes and leftover food up to the house. With her sisters occupied in the kitchen, Ashley slipped into the living room to call home. Her thoughts of the boys made her miss them and Jack more than ever. Worries over her sisters and Mattie had dimmed her longings for home, but with so many of those issues set aside, Ashley wanted more than ever to return to her family.

Punching in the number, Ashley waited as the phone began to ring, anxious to talk with her boys and then Jack. Jack would understand her concerns about Brook. Jack would understand her feelings of inadequacy when it came to being there for Mattie. And Jack would help her to forget about Harry's soft-spoken voice and gentle manners.

Thinking of Harry almost startled her. Why had that come to mind? Harry meant nothing to her. At least nothing in the sense of what he had once meant. Why now, out of the clear blue, did the thought of him make her so uncomfortable?

The phone continued to ring.

It wasn't that Harry meant anything to her, Ashley decided. She wasn't in love with him, nor did she even give a second thought to such matters. But his easygoing nature was almost unnerving. In the wake of Harry, Jack seemed aggressive and bossy and maybe even a touch insincere. Yet Ashley knew that wasn't the way she saw Jack. At least that wasn't how she'd seen him in the past. And it certainly wasn't how she wanted to see him now. Where were all these thoughts coming from?

The answering machine clicked on. "Hello, you've reached the home of Dr. and Mrs. Issacs. At the sound of the tone, please leave your name and telephone number and we'll return the call. If this is a medical emergency . . ." Ashley hung up the receiver. It was nearly eight o'clock. Where could they be?

Thinking they might be at Jack's mother's house, Ashley picked up the telephone again and redialed. This time, her mother-in-law answered the phone on the second ring.

"Ann, this is Ashley. I tried to call home but no one answered. I just wondered if Jack and the boys were with you."

"Oh, hello, Ashley. Yes, the boys are spending the night with me. Jack had an emergency with a patient and had to go to the hospital. He figured he might be out all night and asked me to keep the boys. If you want to talk to them, I'm sure they're still awake."

"That would be great, Ann. Thank you." Ashley waited for a moment and was finally rewarded with the sound of her youngest son's voice.

"Hi, Mommy. When are you coming home?" Zach questioned.

"Hello, Zachy," she said with a smile. "I'll be home tomorrow. How are you? Are you being good for Grandma?"

"Yup. She gave us cookies and milk for a bedtime snack." There was a momentary pause. "Are you bringing me a present?"

Ashley laughed. "If you be good, I'll bring you something. I love you, sweet boy. Now let me talk to John."

The exchange with John was similar to what she'd had with Zach. "I wish you were home now," John added.

"I wish I were too," Ashley replied, knowing she was rather mixed on her feelings of the matter. "Actually, I really wish you and Daddy and Zach were here with me."

"Daddy's at the hospital," John informed her as if Grandma might have forgotten. "He got a phone call and told us we had to stay with Grandma."

"Yes, I know. But he'll be back soon. You behave for Grandma."

"I will," John promised. "I love you, Mommy."

"I love you, John." Ashley felt the warmth of his words spread throughout her body. She longed to be able to hold both her boys close and to kiss them good-night.

"Did you want me to have Jack call you?" Ann questioned as she came back on the line.

"No, that's okay," Ashley replied. "We're an hour ahead of you and he probably won't be home anytime soon. That's usually the way these things go. Just tell him I called and that my plans to return tomorrow are still on schedule."

"I'll tell him." Ann paused, then added, "I saw the funeral on television."

"Yes," Ashley replied. "It was a regular three-ring circus. The media was very intrusive, but we managed to escape, thanks to Harry."

"Harry?"

Ashley instantly bristled. She hadn't intended to bring Harry into the conversation. She couldn't even really understand why he was in her thoughts at all. "Harry Jensen, my grandmother's neighbor. He's been like a son to Grammy and he helped us get home from the cemetery when the reporters were so difficult."

"Is that the same Harry you were once engaged to?"

Ashley thought she denoted disapproval in her mother-in-law's voice but decided against worrying about it. "Yes, that'd be the one. He helps Gram all the time now, what with all us girls living elsewhere. Anyway, thanks again for seeing to the boys, Ann. I know I don't have to worry if they're with you," Ashley said. "I'll talk to you soon."

She hung up the phone and stared at it for several moments. She really wanted to talk to Jack, and the void left her feeling rather out of sorts. Why did he have to be tied up tonight of all nights?

Ashley decided not to dwell on it and headed upstairs in order to take a quick shower. There was no sense in being bothered by something that would no longer have any influence on her after tomorrow. Harry would go back to his farm. Mattie would make her quilts and plant her flowers, and Ashley would fulfill her duties as a wife and mother. It all seemed rather planned out and certain.

Nearing the bathroom, Ashley heard the unmistakable sound of Brook being sick. She knocked lightly on the door and announced her presence. "Brook, can I help at all?"

A pale-faced Brook opened the door and shook her head. "I'm all right. It's just nerves."

"Have you had a doctor check it out?" Ashley questioned.

Brook nodded. "Yes, and I have half a dozen prescriptions to take in order to help me combat life. But I don't want to be dependent on such things."

"Still, maybe it would help you to feel better in the long run. Maybe you could take something just long enough to get your feet back under you."

Brook shook her head. "Don't worry about it. I'll be fine. Did you get ahold of Jack?"

"No, he's off with a patient and his mother is taking care of the boys."

"I'll bet they'll be glad to have you home."

Ashley murmured rather absentmindedly, "Yes, I suppose you're right."

"What is it, Ash? Is something wrong?" Brook asked intuitively.

"I don't know." Ashley felt the return of her empty longing. "I kept thinking about Harry tonight, for some reason. I mean, not all night. Just when I called home. I don't know why he's on my mind. I'm certainly not in love with him and I don't feel that I have any reason to be concerned with his feelings for me."

"Maybe you need closure."

"What do you mean?"

Brook shrugged. "You never really explained yourself to Harry. You know, in leaving him and breaking the engagement. You never asked him to forgive you. Maybe you should go over to his place and tell him what really happened."

"You think so?" Ashley questioned. "Just show up, just like that? What about his fiancée? What if she were there?"

"Ashley, listen to yourself. You're a married woman. An old friend of the family. What are you worried about?"

"I just don't want to cause him any more trouble. I think I've done enough of that."

"Ashley, you and Harry broke up over ten years ago. Just go talk to him. You'll never really feel you've put this thing to rest until you do. You'll probably laugh about it once you explain, and he'll feel exactly the same way. You were both young and immature. Chalk it up to experience and leave this place as friends."

Brook's advice made sense. "All right," Ashley said, nodding. "Just don't tell everyone else where I went. I don't want anyone getting the wrong idea."

Ten minutes later, Ashley shut off her car engine and stared at Harry's old farmhouse. The place was nearly as familiar to her as Grammy's farm. The old screened-in porch with its solid square pillars at the corners beckoned to her, assuring her that she was welcomed. When the porch light came on, Ashley knew she couldn't put off her purpose any longer.

Getting out of the car, she went up the porch steps just as Harry opened the door. He looked surprised to see her.

"Hello, Harry," she said, then drew a deep breath. "If you have a minute, I was hoping we could talk."

He nodded and opened the screen door. "Come on in, Ashley."

She walked into the house, surprised to find that very little had changed since she'd last been here. Photographs of Harry and his family still hung on the wall, along with a couple of cheap reproduction oil paintings that depicted Kansas prairie scenes. An old crocheted throw of browns and tans lay across the back of the well-worn floral-print sofa. She smiled, finding comfort in the familiarity.

"It looks the same," she finally said.

"Guess no one could accuse me of following fads," Harry countered. He motioned for her to sit and Ashley did so. "You want something to drink?"

"What do you have?"

"I made some coffee earlier. It's probably a little strong now—"

"Sounds fine."

He disappeared into the kitchen and soon returned with two mugs. Ashley smiled when she noted that he'd put cream in her coffee without asking. She sampled it and nodded. "It's perfect."

She waited until he'd taken a seat on the sofa before beginning. "I know it's probably silly for me to be here, but I kept thinking that I should come." She forced herself to meet his curious stare. "Harry, I've never been able to work up the nerve to talk to you about us. About what I did. But now I know I have to put the past to rest." He said nothing, so she continued.

"I treated you badly, and I've always been sorry. I just never found a way to tell you or to explain myself. I thought I really loved you, and in my childish way, I know I did. You were good and kind and sensible and secure. You were everything that I wanted in a husband—except . . ." she trailed off into silence, wondering how to put into words the selfishness of the woman she had been back then.

She took a drink and shook her head. "I couldn't stay here. I couldn't bear the idea of staying in Kansas and being a farmer's wife. It wasn't you, Harry. It was me." She looked at him, hoping to emphasize the truth. "I hated Rachelle for what she had done to me—what she had done to all of us. I wanted to prove to her that I could be ten times the woman she was. I wanted a visible, impressive life that would jump out and be evidence of my ability to be better than Rachelle Barrister."

She put down the coffee and got to her feet. Pacing seemed to make the words easier to say. "I married Jack because I knew he'd become a very public figure. He had drive and motivation to become not only a doctor but a wealthy and famous one. He wanted a showplace and a wife to host his parties and to bring fame and notoriety upon him. And I wanted that too. I didn't really love him when I married him, and I know he didn't love me, but we learned to love each other and as some of the things of this world faded in importance, we realized how much we had come to care about each other. Suddenly Rachelle didn't seem to overshadow everything I did. The boys came along and Jack began to change. He adores his children." She stopped pacing and smiled. "He's a good father and a wonderful husband, and I love him with all of my heart."

Sitting back down, Ashley faced the silent man she'd wounded. "I ran away from you, Harry. I ran away for a lot of reasons, but the biggest was because I knew I couldn't give you what you wanted from me. I couldn't give you my heart. It wasn't because you didn't deserve love and hadn't shown me the very best of your affections, it was because my heart was so encased in ice that I couldn't share it with you. I had to come here and tell you how sorry I am for the pain I caused. I should have just been honest with you from the start, but I couldn't even be honest with myself."

"I know," Harry said softly. He stared at his coffee cup and seemed to consider her words for a moment. "I guess I always knew, but then one day Mattie had a long talk with me. She explained that you were too young and that the scars Rachelle had given you were not going to be easily overcome. She helped me to see that I had very little to do with your decision."

"Do you hate me?" Ashley asked. She dreaded the answer.

Harry looked up and smiled. "No. I don't hate you. I didn't hate you then. Frankly, I know now that neither of us was ready for marriage. It would have been a big mistake."

Ashley breathed a sigh of relief. "I know it would have been. You deserved someone a whole lot better than me. I hope Sarah will be that for you. I hope she deserves your love."

Harry shook his head and looked back at the coffee mug. "Don't say anything to Mattie, but I'm not sure I'm going to go through with it."

"Not go through with marrying Sarah? Why?"

"I'm just feeling funny about it. Like maybe it's a mistake."

Ashley felt rather stunned by his declaration. "But why, Harry?"

He looked at her, and the intensity of his gaze nearly made Ashley turn away. "Because I'm not sure I love her—not the way I should."

Ashley nodded. If anyone could understand the meaning of his words, it was Ashley. "I won't say anything," she promised. "Grammy would tell you to take it to God, so I guess that's the suggestion I'm making as well. We were friends for a long time, Harry. I'd hate to see you hurt, especially after what I did."

"All's forgiven," he said quite soberly. "That *is* why you came here, isn't it?"

Ashley nodded. "I guess it is. I don't know why it seemed so important just now, but I think it's probably because of some things Grammy has been saying about not knowing how long any of us have on earth. Of learning to forgive and forget mistakes and to let go of the past."

"As with Rachelle?" he questioned.

His words struck a chord that resonated within her, for Ashley knew she wasn't ready to let go of her anger toward her mother. "I imagine I'll be working on that for some time."

"The woman definitely left her mark on the world," Harry replied.

"She left her mark on me as well," Ashley admitted. "She left it on all of us."

———————

The next morning the Mitchell farm was alive with activities. Breakfast was bittersweet as Mattie faced her grandchildren's departure with mixed emotions. They had their own lives. They had to go back to their families and jobs, but she would miss them so very much.

"Grammy," Connie began when breakfast was nearly half over, "do you suppose I could someday have your quilt?"

Her sisters immediately focused their attention on Connie. They all seemed to understand only too well which quilt Connie had requested.

"What makes you think you should have it?" Erica asked. "I'm just as crazy about it as you are. I wouldn't mind having it myself."

"You aren't the only one," Deirdre threw in. "I already told Grammy that for myself."

Mattie found herself immediately caught up in an onslaught of questions and requests. "Girls!" she pleaded. "Don't start arguing now. Not when you're getting ready to leave."

"Connie started this," Brook said seriously. "If anyone should have that quilt, I would think it should go to the oldest child and be passed down from there."

"That's not fair," Erica said, pushing back from the table. "I've spent my entire life getting hand-me-downs from this family. Why shouldn't I be entitled to be first in something?"

"Oh, please," Ashley replied, throwing down her napkin. "You've been spoiled all your life. We've all pampered you at one time or another."

Mattie was astounded at the harshness of the tone and words that continued. Unable to listen to any more of their insults, Mattie slammed down her favorite glass pitcher, shattering it against the table. She hadn't meant to be so dramatic, but when it drew everyone's attention, she no longer cared about the results.

"I had hoped that you girls would have worked out some of your differences in light of putting your mother to rest. Obviously, I was wrong. You have no idea the pain it causes me to see you at each other's throats. My quilt is immaterial. It was made as an act of love, but you clearly don't understand that."

More angry at them than she had ever been, Mattie shook her head. "You're going to have to clean up the mess you've made of your lives." She went to the kitchen door and looked back at their remorseful expressions. "Just don't expect me to be in the middle of it."

She took herself off to the front porch, aware of the tomblike silence in the kitchen. *Good,* she thought. *Maybe they'll learn the importance of kindness and consideration. Maybe they'll finally see themselves and their actions for what they are.*

Mattie was gravely disappointed, however, when she returned to the house to find the kitchen cleaned up but the girls barely speaking. While they tried for appearances' sake to deal with one another in a civil manner, Mattie could see the tension in their expressions. Why couldn't they let go of their anger and sorrow? Why couldn't they find strength in one another instead of anger and resentment?

"I hope it won't take another funeral to bring you all back home," Mattie told them honestly. The four separate stacks of luggage at the bottom of her staircase spoke volumes to Mattie.

"I'm sorry for the trouble, Grammy," Connie said, the first to bid her good-bye. She had obviously been crying, for Mattie could see the smudges where she'd wiped at her mascara.

"We didn't mean to get so angry," Erica said when her turn came to hug Mattie.

"We have a lot to work on," Ashley admitted. She and Brook seemed to be the only ones who were at ease with each other.

"Girls, you're all so important to me," Mattie finally said. "I don't expect you to always agree with each other. I know you'll have your differences from time to time, but I don't want you to forget how intricately connected we are to one another."

"Like the quilt?" Ashley questioned with a smile.

"Yes," Mattie replied, "like the quilt. I never meant it to be the cause of dividing you even more. I made it as a symbol of our unity and love. You're a part of one another and together you make up the whole. But divided and separated, you stand alone."

The girls eyed her seriously, and even though they were all grown-up, Mattie couldn't help but remember them as little girls. They would always be her girls—vulnerable and precious.

"Our lives are inseparably connected," she said, reaching out to touch each one. "Joined together for a reason by the Master. It isn't important to remember those who didn't love you." She paused. "What counts is remembering those who do."

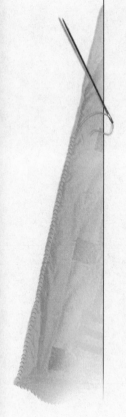

PART TWO

bits and pieces

$$Chapter\ 14$$

At twenty-six, Deirdre Woodward felt she pretty much had the world by the tail. Her husband, Dave, was a successful Kansas City attorney and her golden-haired daughter, Morgan, was happily completing her kindergarten year in school. There was even talk of having another baby, and Deirdre thought she might try to get pregnant on their anniversary trip to Hawaii. A child would be a pleasant reminder of the trip, and since they were scheduled to head out at the end of the first week of June, that would allow her to give birth in March. A spring baby sounded like the best of all possible planning. The weather would just be getting warm, yet Morgan would still be in school. In fact, she'd be in first grade, so school would be an all-day event—unlike today, which had Deirdre running from her afternoon of fun with her girlfriends to the school to pick up Morgan from kindergarten.

Deirdre glanced at her watch and grimaced. She had overstayed her time at the casino, but by taking a few side streets a little faster than the posted limit, she knew she could make up the time.

Hitting a red light and seeing no way out but to run it or stop, Deirdre did the sensible thing and stopped. She checked the rearview mirror to see if her hair and makeup looked all right, and finding them so, she returned her attention to the road. But her mind refused to stay on the job at hand, returning instead to her time at the casino.

"I shouldn't have placed that last bet," she said aloud, frowning at the reminder that she'd broken her own private pledge to spend nothing more than what she allotted ahead of time. Today, for the first time, she had hit up the ATM machine for extra money, and because of that mistake, she was down by some three hundred dollars.

Traffic began moving again, but Deirdre couldn't stop thinking about what she'd done. She had vowed that she would never be like those other poor fools who didn't know when to quit. People who ended up spending that week's grocery money for one last chance at the slots or the blackjack table. But now she found herself in the same sort of situation.

But it felt so right, she argued to herself. *I was sure I would win, and then I'd have all kinds of extra money for Hawaii.* Instead, she was left wondering how she was possibly going to cover her household expenses for the next week. Dave was always generous with money, giving her a healthy allowance to buy pretty much whatever she needed. But lately she'd been spending a lot. Most of it was in preparation for the trip, but there had been other things as well. She'd refurbished part of the living room and bought new china. And the things she'd selected had come from stores with steeper prices than most. Then there was all the money she'd insisted they pour into their landscaping project for the backyard. She sighed and turned onto a side street.

"I'll just tell him I hit a sale and couldn't help myself," Deirdre muttered and wheeled her car into the drive of Morgan's private school.

Morgan danced out to the car, swinging a book bag in one hand and her sweater in the other. She turned and gave a shy wave to a group of girls sitting on the steps of Heritage School before climbing into the car.

"Hello, sweetie," Deirdre said, helping to secure the seat belt around her petite daughter's waist. "How was school today?"

Morgan shrugged. "It was okay. I had to read in a real book. It had hard words and everything."

"Read? Really?" Deirdre had only spent time working with Morgan on primers that contained a half dozen small words at most. "What was the book about?"

"It was a story about a dog and a cat and how they got lost. I read it real good, Mommy. Teacher said I might be gifted. What's gifted mean?"

Deirdre smiled and merged into the busy afternoon traffic. "It means you're special, which we already knew."

Morgan continued to give her mother details of the day while Deirdre let her mind wander back to her financial problems. It was only three hundred dollars. She had jewelry worth more than that. Maybe she could just pawn a piece until Dave gave her next week's allowance. That would work! She could pawn the antique necklace her mother-in-law had given her for Christmas. It was worth at least three hundred dollars. And because it was so ugly, Deirdre never wore it. No one would even miss it.

She pulled into their driveway and stared for a moment at the modest two-story brick house as the garage door opened slowly. She loved her house. Loved the elite neighborhood too. She felt safe here, and in spite of her thoughtless mistake at the casino, she was determined to have a good evening.

Parking the car, she helped Morgan gather her things and headed into the house. "Change out of your uniform before you go off to play," she admonished her daughter. Morgan had a habit of forgetting and had ruined more than one jumper by climbing one of the flowering redbud trees in the backyard.

"Can we get a dog?" Morgan asked instead of acknowledging her mother's command.

Deirdre stared at her child for a moment. Huge brown eyes seemed to zero in on her heartstrings. "You know we can't get a dog right now, Morgan. In a few weeks, Daddy and I are going on a long trip and you are going to stay with Grammy Mitchell. A dog would get too lonely while we were away. Besides, who would feed him while we were gone?"

Morgan seemed to consider this for a moment. "I could take him with me to Grammy's."

Deirdre shook her head. "Grammy told me her cat just had kittens. I don't think she'd like having a dog around. We'll think about getting a puppy after we get back."

"But—"

"Morgan, don't argue with me," Deirdre said, trying to sound firm. Truth be told, she wouldn't mind having a dog around. She'd grown up with all sorts of pets and had always said she'd have a lot of dogs and cats when she had a place of her own. Now, with her daughter looking at her so mournfully, Deirdre felt consumed with nostalgia and guilt. Ever the peacemaker, she smiled. "We'll work it out. Don't worry. I promise you one way or another, we'll get a pet before summer is up."

Morgan smiled. "Okay, but it has to be a really good one."

Deirdre nodded and watched her daughter scamper upstairs. "Remember to put your dirty clothes in the hamper."

With Morgan taken care of, at least momentarily, Deirdre went to the kitchen and began preparations for dinner. Dave was working such crazy hours lately that she never knew exactly what to fix. He liked steak and liked it pretty rare, so that was something she could throw on at the last minute. But as for things to go along with it, well, she'd very nearly given up trying to have anything too elaborate. Sometimes she'd fix one of those boxed rice dishes, then reheat it if Dave came in long after she and Morgan had eaten their meal. Other times, it was just as easy to throw some vegetables in the Crockpot and hope they wouldn't mush up too much.

Three hundred dollars.

The number popped into her thoughts and she couldn't believe she'd actually lost that much money. She was used to playing with no more than twenty. Usually she could make five or ten dollars and come out ahead. One time she even managed to hit a jackpot on the slots and win a hundred dollars. Shaking her head, Deirdre tried to reason that in another few weeks she'd be away from the casino for over a month. That was eighty dollars right there that she would save. Of course, she and Dave would be spending over eight hundred dollars a week on their Hawaiian accommodations, so it really didn't even out at all. But one way or another, she'd work it out. It was just this one time, after all.

At seven o'clock an exhausted Dave walked in and eyed the dining room table with a sort of suspicious questioning.

"We haven't eaten, if that's what you were wondering," Deirdre announced as she came to greet him. "We really wanted to wait for you." She saw the weariness in his eyes but nevertheless pressed close to him and kissed his lips lightly. "How was your day?"

"Awful," he admitted. "The case is dragging on a lot longer than it needed to."

Deirdre frowned. "It won't interfere with our plans, will it?"

Dave stiffened. "That's really all you care about it, isn't it?"

Deirdre was hurt that he'd taken such a tone with her. She had believed him to be every bit as enthusiastic about this anniversary trip as she was. "I didn't mean it that way," she offered. "I'm sorry if it sounded selfish."

Dave nudged past her. "Don't worry about it. I'm just out of sorts."

"Daddy!" Morgan exclaimed, bounding into the room.

Dave actually smiled. "Hello, princess. My, don't you look pretty."

"Mommy told me to change my uniform, and I wanted to wear this dress."

Deirdre looked up to find Morgan in a stylish green plaid play dress. Grammy would probably say it was sinful the way she spent money on Morgan, but Deirdre liked her looking nice. The play dress carried a designer label, but then, so did most everything else in the Woodward home.

"Well, what do you say about you and me going into the living room and reading a storybook until Mommy calls us for dinner?" Dave said. He glanced up over Morgan's shoulder to flash an apologetic smile to Deirdre.

"I can read to you," Morgan declared. "I read a book all by myself today at school."

"Is that true?" Dave said in complete amazement and looked

again to Deirdre.

"That's what she told me," Deirdre admitted. "Along with her teacher's notion that she might be gifted."

Dave smiled wearily and nodded. "Well, Miss Morgan, I will indeed let you help me with the reading."

Deirdre relaxed and smiled. All was well again. Dave would combat his fatigue and trials of the day by letting Morgan's sweetness soothe him.

But for all of Deirdre's hopes that they might share a peaceful family evening, it was not to be. Not even fifteen minutes after Dave had settled down with Morgan, the telephone rang. Dave took the call in his office and when he returned, he acted sullen, even angry.

"Bad news?" Deirdre questioned as she called the family to dinner.

Dave took his place at the table and refused to even look at his wife. "I don't want to talk about it."

Deirdre couldn't imagine what the phone call had been about. Dave was usually so easygoing and capable of handling surprises. If the call were in regard to a case and something had gone wrong, as things sometimes did, Deirdre would have expected him to be concerned, even distracted. But never had she seen him downright angry. It wasn't like him to take things out on her and Morgan.

The rest of the evening passed in tense silence. Even Morgan seemed to realize that it would be a mistake to misbehave. She didn't even argue when Deirdre announced it was time for a bath and bed.

Deirdre tried several times to talk to Dave, but to no avail. The first time had been after dinner, but he'd muttered something about needing to distance himself from the office. The next time, she'd asked him if there was anything at all he wanted to discuss. This time he snapped at her to leave him alone, then turned on the television and settled into his favorite chair.

She was at a complete loss as to what to do. Dave had never been like this. Usually he was more than happy to explain the daily traumas of one case or another. He'd even told her most of the details of the case he was currently on, but that had been in the early days of the trial. It seemed a man had been severely injured in an accident and was suing the car manufacturer for faulty equipment. Dave's law firm was representing the manufacturer and had felt, at least in the beginning, that the case was pretty much open-and-shut. Apparently that situation had changed.

Deirdre helped Morgan get into her nightgown, then combed out her long hair. This was their nightly routine and Deirdre loved it. "Let's say our prayers," she said after laying down the brush.

Morgan popped up on her knees and folded her hands. "Thank you, God, for my nice day. Don't let me have any bad dreams and please make my daddy happy again. Amen."

"Amen," Deirdre murmured before tucking her daughter under the covers.

Downstairs, Deirdre found Dave still spacing out in front of the television. The show that played was something she knew he detested, yet there he sat, absorbed in the soft electric glow of network Technicolor.

"Dave?"

"What?"

"Can we talk?" She hesitated at touching his shoulder, even though she longed to reach out to him.

"There's nothing to talk about. Now get off my back," he retorted angrily.

"Look," she started in, "I'm not on your back. I just wondered if there was some way I could help."

He slowly turned to eye her. "Stop spending so much money. Stop complaining about my long nights at work, and stop asking me stupid questions. That's how you can help."

Deirdre knew the shock must have registered on her face, but she couldn't hide the emotion she felt. Instead she hurried from the room and sought sanctuary in the kitchen. Leaning against the counter, she bit at her quivering lip. In their six years of marriage,

Dave had never once talked to her in such a manner.

She felt tears well up in her eyes. *Why is he shutting me out?* she asked herself over and over. *Is it because of the money? He said stop spending so much money. Does he know about the ATM today?*

Her guilt overcame the desire she felt to make peace with her husband.

Before she could think any further, the telephone rang. Knowing this would be yet another irritant to Dave, she quickly picked it up after the first ring. If it turned out to be someone from his office, Deirdre vowed to herself that she would just tell them Dave was out of the house.

"Hello?" she asked almost breathlessly.

"Hi, it's Erica."

"Oh, hello," Deirdre said, glad for her sister's call. "How are you?"

"About the same. I'm just so discouraged. I still haven't heard anything from any of the orchestras back East, and it's really starting to bug me."

"Waiting is always the hardest part, especially when everything is out of your control," Deirdre said. Then she thought about her mistake at the casino. Maybe she could ask Erica for the money—just a short-term loan. She could have the money back to her in a week— two at the most.

"I really enjoyed our time at Grammy's," Erica said, moving the conversation along. "I can't believe it's been nearly a month since we were there. Seems like just yesterday."

"You're still planning to come down with me when I take Morgan, aren't you?"

"As far as I know. I don't have to work Memorial Day weekend, so there isn't any reason at this point why I can't go. Sean offered to drive us. Do you want me to have him do that?"

Deirdre frowned. "Well, I suppose he could. I hadn't really thought it would be anyone but us."

"It doesn't need to be. I'll just tell Sean no."

"I think I'd prefer it that way."

"I guess I would too. In spite of the way we tend to snip at each other," Erica said softly, "I wish we could all be together again. It's sad that it took a funeral to get us all together, but it was so nice to have time with Ashley and Brook and even Connie. Plus, being on the farm just kind of took me back in time. We really had it sweet there. Wish we could have seen that before we all rushed off to start our own lives elsewhere."

"We saw it," Deirdre replied. "But sweet wasn't what we were after. We wanted adventure and something new and bold. We didn't think about Grammy or the rest of the family."

"I think Grammy's right," Erica added. "I think we are all interconnected. We might be spread out to the four corners of the earth, but we're still family and we have a strong bond. We need to be there for each other."

Erica's words seemed to present the perfect opportunity for Deirdre to ask for the money.

"Oh no," Erica said in exasperation. "Someone's at my front door. Do you want to hold on for a minute?"

"Sure. Go ahead and see who it is," Deirdre said, trying to think of the perfect way to approach Erica for the loan.

Erica came back to the phone after several minutes of silence. "Sorry, but I'm going to have to go. Sean just showed up. I'll probably talk to you tomorrow."

Deirdre realized her opportunity had passed. "Okay. I'll talk to you later."

She hung up the phone and sighed. It looked like the pawnshop would be her best bet for getting the money back into their checking account before Dave questioned its disappearance.

Chapter 15

The final few weeks of school for Denver Christian Academy were filled with celebrations and picnic outings. Ashley had made more sack lunches in the past few days than she had for the rest of the school year. Zach and John had traveled from one field trip to the next, their level of excitement building as the final close of the school year neared.

Ashley felt anticipation and a sense of relief that the boys were so excited about summer. There were so many plans, in fact, that Ashley had worried that it was simply too much. Athletic camps, trips, and outings of every kind dotted the calendar, and although the boys were an energetic nine and seven, they had things planned out in more detail than many adults might ever have thought to do. Ashley likened it to the strategic positioning of a battle. Each side knew their responsibilities and the ground they would have to cover, and short of taking prisoners and sustaining casualties, she felt certain their summer would be no less effective than a grizzled army general's plans for assault on the enemy.

But with the boys in school and occupied for at least a few more weeks, Ashley hurried to try to get all of her own loose ends tied up. Dressed in a comfortable pair of navy blue slacks with a white-and-navy sweater, Ashley checked her hair and lipstick before grabbing the box on her front passenger seat. She had promised to help with an early graduation party scheduled for that evening at the country club, and inside the box were two hundred party favors she had helped to make.

She deposited the favors at the front desk and hurried to the lounge to meet her friends Willa James and Rhonda Reecer for lunch. The floor hostess motioned Ashley to follow her to where Rhonda and Willa were already seated.

"We ordered for you," Willa stated as though Ashley were always late.

"Thank you! I thought I'd never get here." She took her seat and immediately latched on to a glass of iced tea. "This mine?"

Willa nodded. "Oh good. Here come our salads now. I had them put your dressing on the side, Ashley."

"Sounds like a good idea," Ashley replied, tasting the tea. Frowning at the lack of sweetener, she put it down and made room for the salad.

"I swear, you are never home," Rhonda stated as she immediately began to pick at her food.

"I can't help it," Ashley admitted. "I have a list a mile long to accomplish before the kids get out of school."

"Me too," Willa chimed in. "This time of year is a real killer."

"So what did I miss last week?" Rhonda questioned. She had been away at a women's conference in Colorado Springs and had been unable to make their weekly women's meeting at the country club.

"Not much," Ashley said, spooning a bit of sugar into her tea.

"Have you heard from the lawyer yet as to what your cut of Rachelle's estate will be?" Rhonda asked Ashley in a brazen manner.

Ashley would never have tolerated the question from anyone else, but she seldom kept anything from Rhonda and Willa. "I haven't received any real information. Grammy said the estate is tied up in probate. Frankly, I don't care. I'll just put whatever I get into a college trust fund for the boys."

"What does Jack think about that? Wouldn't he rather you use the money for something to benefit the family now?" Willa questioned.

Ashley shrugged. "I don't know. Jack's been so tied up lately, we haven't really had much of a chance to talk about it. Besides, there may never be any money at all. She had a lot of debt. I guess it went with the life-style."

"I just can't imagine being the daughter of Rachelle Barrister," Rhonda continued. "I mean, I knew it was true, but when I saw you on that news coverage of the funeral, I just about flipped. I mean, there you were—my friend—and you were related to the most popular woman in the world."

Ashley shook her head. "She wasn't popular with me or my sisters, and frankly, I'd just as soon not talk about it anymore. It's been over a month and I'd like it to just fade away."

Rhonda shrugged and ate in silence, while Ashley tried hard to put the memories behind her. Rachelle's death wasn't supposed to be a big deal, yet Ashley couldn't help but dwell on the things she'd learned about herself at the funeral. She still battled with the idea that everything she'd accomplished in her life had been done in order to show up her mother. What kind of person did that make her?

"Did you hear about Cynthia?" Willa asked, leaning forward to avoid being overheard by anyone else. "She's marrying Richard Devader."

"I knew she'd been going out with him, but marriage?" Rhonda questioned in disbelief. "He's got to be at least thirty years her senior."

"I know," Willa said, nodding. "But he's also at least thirty million dollars richer than she is. Money has always been very attractive to Cynthia, and she probably figures that he'll die soon enough and leave her a fortune. At least that's the way I figure it. What about you, Ashley?"

"I suppose you're right," Ashley admitted. She continued eating, hoping that this would discourage anyone from soliciting her further opinion on the matter.

"Of course I'm right. We know Cynthia well enough to know she'd never even look at an old geezer like him if she wasn't going to benefit in a big way. They're supposed to be married sometime next month, and I just know she'll expect us all at the wedding."

"I'm not sure I could sit through an ordeal like that," Rhonda said before Ashley could voice her opinion. "Imagine, marrying only for the money and position someone could give you. Cynthia should be ashamed. Maybe I should speak my mind."

Willa threw her friend an amused look. "Like it would matter to Cynthia. She'd just tell you not to worry your head over the matter and invite you to her new estate once the marriage was in place."

Ashley took a sip of tea and changed the subject. "I thought I'd go shopping again this weekend to find something for the annual dance. I want something completely different from the off-the-rack styles around here."

"Maybe your sister could send you something from New York," Willa offered.

"Like I could fit into any of Brook's clothes. The last time I saw her, I'll bet she was down to a size four."

"Oh, to be a four again," Rhonda said with a sigh.

Willa laughed. "I'd just like to be a four for the first time. I think I probably skipped right over it even when I was child." They laughed together at this.

Ashley glanced at her watch. "Oh no. I didn't realize it was getting so late. I have to run. Have them put this on my bill," she said, waving at the uneaten food. She pushed back from the table and grabbed her purse. "I'll be here to help with the graduation party tonight. Seven o'clock, right?"

"Be here by six-thirty," Willa corrected. "The kids will get here at seven."

Ashley nodded and made a mental calculation as she took up her purse. She made a mad dash for the door before anyone could say anything to halt her progress. She had to make a two-thirty doctor's appointment and still manage to pick up groceries before the boys got home from school. There just weren't enough hours in the day.

Heading north, Ashley tried to concentrate on the interstate instead of the rest of her itinerary for the day. *The maid should be at the house by now,* she thought. *Hopefully, she'll see my note about taking the laundry out of the dryer.* She looked at her watch again and saw that she'd only be a few minutes late. Breathing a sigh of relief, she finally began to relax. Maybe the day would settle down now.

Inside the doctor's office, Ashley waited for thirty minutes before being called back to consult with her gynecologist. A good friend of the family, Janice Nevin smiled and welcomed Ashley.

"I'm sorry you had to wait so long," she said. "I had to make a quick trip to the hospital and deliver twins."

"That's okay," Ashley said nervously. She didn't really mean it, but what could she say given the situation?

"Well, congratulations are definitely in order," Janice told Ashley after she closed the door. "You're pregnant."

Ashley smiled and felt her stomach do a flip. "I was pretty sure about it but just didn't want to say anything to Jack before I had a test done."

"You mean he hasn't suspected?" Janice questioned.

"No. At least I don't think he has. He's been too busy lately."

Janice nodded. "He has had an incredible load. I've seen him up at the hospital four times this week. But why didn't you want to tell him? You *are* happy about this baby, aren't you?"

"You know I am. But because of the miscarriages in the past, I didn't want to get Jack's hopes up until I passed the twelfth week. That seemed to be when the other two went sour."

"So you're figuring yourself to be about three months along?"

"A little over," Ashley admitted.

"Wish I could have looked like you at the end of my first trimester," Janice said with a grin. "I needed maternity clothes the minute I conceived."

Ashley smiled and put her hand on her stomach. It was an action she hadn't allowed herself until just now—now that she knew she was carrying a new life. "This is so wonderful. I can hardly speak."

"Well, you don't have to. I want you to set up an appointment with the receptionist and we'll get your initial blood work and exam out of the way. After that, you probably remember the routine. Eat healthy, exercise, avoid caffeine and cigarette smoke."

The rest of the advice pretty much went in one ear and out the other. *I'm pregnant,* thought Ashley. *I'm going to have another baby!* More than anything in the world she wanted to tell Jack. He would be so happy.

After bidding Janice good-bye and stopping long enough at the receptionist's desk to make her next appointment, Ashley fairly ran for the car. She could barely contain her excitement. She and Jack had been trying for nearly five years to have another child, and after one miscarriage in the early weeks of a pregnancy nearly three years ago and a second miscarriage a year later, she had seemed unable to conceive. But now her long wait was over. She was going to be a mother again. Maybe even have a daughter. She really wanted a daughter.

Ashley maneuvered through traffic, well aware that time was getting away from her. It was nearly three-thirty. The boys would be coming home in about ten minutes and she wouldn't be there to greet them. The housekeeper would see that they were safely looked after, but it wasn't the same. She wanted to be there for them. She also wanted to share her good news with them. She wanted to tell everyone the news!

Jack's clinic was out of her way, but it was well worth the effort to go there before returning home. Ashley tried to picture the look on his face. No matter how overworked he was, he would be thrilled to know about the baby. Maybe it would even help him to slow down and spend more time at home.

After a stressful journey through the very beginnings of rush-hour traffic, Ashley finally managed to pull into the parking lot of Jack's clinic. Four o'clock, she noted, frowning at the time. It had taken twice as long to get here as she had hoped, but there was no sense in bemoaning that fact. It wasn't going to spoil her surprise. On the bright side, Jack would be finished with patients for the day. She could walk right into his office and share the news with him, and maybe he'd even be able to go home with her. Every cloud had its lining, she reminded herself as the tension of the last month seemed to dissipate.

Inside, the private clinic was deserted. Ashley passed the closed receptionist's window and opened the side door to the private employees' entrance.

"Oh, hello, Mrs. Issacs."

Ashley spied the receptionist. "Hi, Shelly. How's it going?"

"We've just about broken every record possible for bad days," the petite brown-haired woman replied. "I've never seen so many emergencies. The good weather must have everyone acting crazy."

Ashley laughed. "Well, maybe things will calm down." She pushed on down the hall, calling over her shoulder, "I'm just going to see Jack. Is he in his office?"

"Should be," Shelly called after her. "All the patients are gone."

Ashley felt the joy of the moment reaching a wonderful climax. They were going to have another baby. It was all too wonderful to imagine. Without even bothering to knock, Ashley flung open Jack's office door with an ear-to-ear grin.

"Have I got news for you!" she declared to her surprised husband.

Chapter 16

Mattie stood back to admire the wealth of buds on her rose-bushes. "This will be the best year ever," she told Harry.

Harry, sweaty and dirty from a hard day in the fields, nodded and took a long drink of the lemonade Mattie had poured for him only moments ago. "Everything is looking real good."

"Another month of fair weather and sunshine and you'll be harvesting your winter wheat crop," Mattie stated matter-of-factly. She came to sit down beside Harry at the small patio table.

"True enough," Harry said, his voice betraying his weariness.

"Harry, why don't you get on home, clean up, and go to bed early?" Mattie suggested. "You've been working yourself too hard."

"Now you're sounding like Sarah," Harry said none too affectionately.

"Well, this time I would have to agree with her. You have been working awfully hard."

"No more than what it takes to keep the farm in order," Harry replied defensively.

"I know that, Harry," Mattie said softly. "I just worry about you."

His expression relaxed. "I know."

The cordless telephone gave a shrill ring. Mattie glanced at her watch. It was about a quarter to six. "Hello?"

"Mattie, it's Jack." His voice was edged with emotion.

"What's the matter, Jack?" Mattie questioned, somehow knowing the news would be bad.

"Ashley's been in a car accident. She's hurt pretty bad. They've taken her to surgery."

"What happened?" Mattie asked, sinking into the nearest chair.

"Uh . . . I'm not completely sure. She was here at my office and then she left in a hurry. It happened on the interstate. She wasn't buckled in and the car flipped several times. Look, I just wondered if you could come out here. Ashley's going to need you when she wakes up. For that matter, I'm going to need you too."

"Of course I'll come," Mattie replied, feeling overwhelmed with emotion. How serious were Ashley's injuries? What kind of surgery were they performing? Her mind flooded with questions.

She promised to call Jack back with the details of the flight, then took down the telephone number for the hospital on a scrap of paper that Harry handed her. Hanging up, she handed back the pencil stub Harry had also given her and shook her head.

"Ashley's been in a car accident. I need to go to Denver."

Harry nodded solemnly. "I'll drive you to the airport."

Mattie looked at him and sighed in relief. "Could you, Harry? That would be wonderful."

"No problem. Why don't you call and see what flights are available, and I'll run home and shower. I can be back in fifteen minutes." He was already getting to his feet.

"I should call the other girls. I doubt anyone can get away as quickly as I can. I know school's not out for Connie, and Erica has a big concert coming up tomorrow night. Brook is in England somewhere and Deirdre is preparing for her trip to Hawaii." Then Mattie thought about her commitment to care for Morgan while Deirdre was away. It was something she'd simply have to deal with later.

She thanked Harry again and hurried into the house as he made his way to the truck. She looked up the telephone number for the airlines and called the first one she came to. There was a flight out of Kansas City in the morning, but nothing that night. Continuing down the list, she called the next number and waited for what seemed an eternity.

Dear Lord, she prayed, *please be with Ashley. I have no way of knowing her needs, but you do. I also ask that you would just work out the details of my trip to*

Denver. You know it's important for me to be there—at least I believe it's important,
so please provide a way.

"Thank you for holding," the operator said pleasantly. "We have
one flight out yet tonight. It's the last one for the night and leaves at
9:45. Can you make that?"

"I'll try," Mattie said. "Book me on it." She gave the woman all
the necessary information, then hung up and raced for her bedroom. Pulling a suitcase out from under the bed, Mattie threw a
hodgepodge collection of clothes into the case, then went to her
sewing room and took several projects up to take with her to Denver.
She would need something to keep her hands busy while she waited
for news of Ashley.

She looked at the pieces in her hands and felt hot tears come to
her eyes. Poor Ashley. She remembered a time when Ashley had
fallen out of a tree down by the lake. Minutes later, Brook fell off
the front porch and both girls sustained broken right arms. It was
uncanny how the twins had a way of getting into similar problems at
the same time.

This caused Mattie to tremble. Brook! What if something like
this happened to her as well? Mattie felt a sense of true frustration.
She knew Brook was in England, but she had no way to reach her.
They were doing photo shoots somewhere on the moors in the
northeast. Brook had had no way of giving Mattie an itinerary and
instead promised to call from time to time as she always did when
she went abroad.

Everyone seemed so far away. Fragmented into pieces and different directions of life. What had happened to her family? Why
couldn't they have all remained close to home? Mattie chided herself
for being silly and wiped her eyes with the back of her hands. _Maybe_
it's because I'm growing old, she thought. _Maybe that's why it troubles me to see them_
so far apart—not only physically, but emotionally as well.

She heard the pickup horn and knew Harry had made it in
record time. She hurried back to her bedroom and stuffed her
handwork into her suitcase, then zipped it closed. The last thing she

took up was her well-worn Bible. This she would put in her purse.

Harry met her at the door and took her suitcase. "This it?" he asked, his hair still dripping water from his shower.

"Yes," Mattie answered, looking around the room. "Oh, I forgot to call Jack with the flight information, and I still need to call the girls. Let me at least call Erica or Connie." She went to the telephone and picked up the receiver. "That way they can tell the others and even call Jack for me."

Harry nodded and waited at the open door.

"Erica?" Mattie said as she heard her granddaughter's voice.

"Hi, Grammy. I was just on my way out the door. Dress rehearsal for tomorrow night, you know."

"I understand. Look, I'm getting ready to head to the Kansas City airport with Harry. Ashley's been in an accident and Jack has asked me to come to Denver."

"Is it bad?" Erica asked.

"Bad enough that she's in surgery. Look, I don't know what all is wrong, but I'm going out there."

"I can't leave," Erica said, as though Mattie wouldn't already realize this.

"I know, sweetie. Don't worry about it. If Ashley gets worse, I'll call. But I need you to contact Deirdre and Connie. Can you do that after your practice or maybe right before?"

"Sure. I'll take care of it."

"Would you also call Jack and give him this flight information? I don't know if Harry can get me to the airport in time, but we're going to try. Either way, I want Jack to know where to send someone to pick me up." Mattie didn't wait for Erica's response but hurriedly gave her the flight number and time of arrival, as well as the telephone number for the hospital.

"I'll be praying," Erica said before hanging up.

This came as a pleasant surprise to Mattie. "Pray for Harry and me as well. We may have to do some flying of our own, but it's in God's hands. If I'm supposed to make that flight, God will make a way."

"If you can't go out until morning, you can always stay the night with me," Erica offered. "My guest room is ready and waiting."

"I'll keep that in mind."

Hanging up the telephone, Mattie grabbed her sweater and nodded to Harry. "Let's go. It's going to be tight—the flight is at 9:45."

Harry grimaced and looked at his watch. "We're going to need a minor miracle to make it."

Mattie smiled. "We'd best get to praying, then."

It was a little past one A.M. when Brook looked down at her watch for the fifth time in less than half an hour. She longed for nothing more than her own bed and her quiet little apartment in New York. Instead, she had to wait on her co-workers, most of whom were friends, while they partied. Their hotel was located not far from York, England, and somewhere nearly a dozen or so miles from there, one of the local estate owners had thrown a party.

Brook hadn't wanted to attend the party, but because her manager pointed out that the host was a major player in their trip to England, Brook felt obligated to acquiesce and join in the merrymaking.

The estate was incredible with long rolling lawns of lush green and an intricate stone manor house with no fewer than forty rooms. When inside, Brook had the overwhelming sense of having stepped back in time. The ceilings were nearly thirty feet high and trimmed with the most incredible moldings. She walked from room to room, just gazing upward, studying the beauty.

"Hello," a familiar voice sounded behind her. She turned to find Aaron Munns, one of the assigned photographers.

"Hello yourself," she said, trying hard not to feel ill at ease. Aaron had asked her out on more than one occasion, and each time she'd told him no.

"This place is pretty impressive," Aaron said, sweeping back his brown hair and smiling. "But I think I liked that one palace we used in Italy even better. Do you remember it—the one with all the gold trimming?"

"I'm not sure," Brook replied, trying to conjure the image to mind.

"It was owned by a doctor and his wife. They were there for the entire shoot and kept asking us all questions about why we were doing things certain ways."

Brook smiled. "Yes, I remember it now." The mention of a doctor and his wife caused her to think of Ashley and Jack. Ashley had been on her mind all day and Brook felt a sense of urgency to get in touch with her twin.

"But this is nice," Aaron continued. He smiled and the action lit up his entire face. He was a nice-looking man and he always treated Brook respectably, unlike some of the others. "In fact," he added, "I could stand to spend a few days here. Couldn't you?"

"Yes. Much nicer than traipsing around on the moors in hip waders," Brook said, trying hard to remain interested in the conversation. She had promised Ashley that she would give special effort to keep from turning people away when they tried to befriend her. Especially men.

"You'd be mighty sorry without those pesky old things," Miriam Wells, Brook's manager said without concern that she had just interrupted a private conversation. The five feet four woman was built rather like a lineman for a football team. Stout and thick, she was a force to be reckoned with. "You'd be soaked to the knee before you made it halfway up one of those hills." She turned to Aaron with a shrug. "Who would have thought the moors were so wet?"

"Yeah, but we got some great pictures. I think the client is going to be pleased," Aaron said enthusiastically. "What with the way the skies were all gray and moody and the wind was just strong enough to add to the effect without ruining the shot . . . man, I was psyched."

The room adjacent to theirs broke out in laughter, followed by someone attempting to play a rendition of "Yankee Doodle" on the piano.

"Are you having a good time?" Miriam asked Brook.

"Actually, I'm exhausted. I'd really like nothing more than to go back to my hotel room and get out of these clothes. Do you suppose I could get away with that?"

Miriam frowned, but Aaron immediately jumped in. "I could take you. I was just about to give this up myself. We'll never be missed."

Brook felt herself tense at the thought of being alone with Aaron but said nothing. Instead, she looked at Miriam, who had charge over every area of her life—or so it seemed.

Miriam glanced at her watch. "I suppose it wouldn't hurt to have you get some rest. In fact, I should probably send Andrea and Kristy with you. No sense in having you completely done in for tomorrow's shoot."

"I thought that sickly waif look was in," Aaron teased.

"True," Miriam replied, not seeing any humor in his statement. "Go ahead, Brook. You've put in your appearance. I'll talk to the others and see if they want to leave. If not, you two can go back alone."

Alone. The one word that Brook responded so poorly to. She would be alone with Aaron for a trip that would probably end up lasting twenty or thirty minutes, given the winding back roads they would need to take in order to get back to their hotel.

Miriam sauntered off across the room and into the adjoining one before Brook could say a single word.

"You don't mind riding with me, do you?" Aaron asked. "I promise to behave myself. I won't even ask you to go out with me. Although I do have tickets for a wonderful play in London." He feigned stoic resolve. "But I won't ask you to come with me. Not to the play. Not to a wonderful dinner. Not for a moonlight cruise on the Thames."

Brook smiled and lowered her head. "I've been pretty hard on you, haven't I?"

"Terribly hard on me," he agreed, laughing. "But believe me, it's okay. I've been turned down lots of times."

Brook looked up and caught him looking at her with such a look of sweetness that she couldn't help but laugh as well. "If it helps, you're my favorite photographer."

He shook his head. "It doesn't help at all. Somehow, dating Brook Mitchell and photographing her are just not the same. One is a job—albeit a fun one—but the other would be pure pleasure."

Just then Miriam returned. "Go ahead, you two. The others want to stay."

Brook nodded and looked around for one of the house staff. She had given them her black wool wrap for safekeeping. "Excuse me," she said, slipping past Miriam to where a uniformed man stood attentively just inside the other room.

Her wrap was quickly retrieved and before she knew it she was belted into the front left passenger seat of Aaron's rental car.

"So have you managed to get used to driving on the opposite side of the road?" she questioned.

"I've mastered that," Aaron admitted, "but I haven't mastered dealing with all the traffic. Drivers over here seem crazy." He secured his own belt and started the engine.

Brook tried to relax, but her tension level was high and for just a moment she felt certain that she was going to throw up. Struggling to remain in control of her emotional state, she tried to think of her sister and what she would say when she called home. What time was it in Denver? She calculated it to be seven hours behind and realized it would be nearing six-thirty. She could call from the hotel room and it would still be early enough in the evening so as not to disrupt their sleep.

Aaron turned onto the narrow hedge-lined lane and maneuvered the tiny car down the road. The lights beamed out straight and true, revealing nothing but empty open space ahead.

"Can I ask you something personal?" Aaron questioned out of the clear blue.

Brook swallowed hard. "I suppose. I won't promise to answer it, however."

"Fair enough. It's just that I notice you never drink anymore. You used to party with the best of them. What happened?"

Brook shrugged. "I guess I saw it was taking a harder toll on me than the hours I was putting in on the job. I always woke up the morning after feeling like I had the flu, so I asked myself why a person would subject themselves to that kind of feeling—on purpose."

He laughed. "I know what you mean. I don't drink nearly like I used to. I gave up the drugs too."

Brook stiffened. "You were into drugs?"

"Not heavy. Just smoked pot on occasion. Stuff like that. The hard stuff was too expensive, even though I had ready access to it at most of the parties I attended. I guess I saw too many people head down that path and not come back."

Brook nodded. "It doesn't make sense to do yourself in like that. I figured I would rather have some control over my life. Even if it's only marginal. Miriam has the rest." She smiled and tried to make light of her bondage to her tyrannical manager.

"She drives you pretty hard, doesn't she?" Aaron asked, turning onto a slightly wider road.

"She tells me it's for my own good," Brook replied. "I guess she sees my youth slipping away and wants me to cash in on my looks while they last."

"You'll always look good, Brook. You have your mother's face."

That was the wrong thing to say, but Brook tried not to hold it against Aaron. He couldn't possibly know how that innocent line would make her feel. "Actually," she said, clearing her throat, "I have my sister's face."

"Huh?"

She smiled. "I'm an identical twin. My sister Ashley looks just like me."

"There are two of you? Man, God must have been feeling particularly generous that day," he replied. "Does she model somewhere?"

"No," Brook replied. "She lives with her husband and kids in Denver. She's a happy housewife with a wonderful family."

"You sound like you envy her."

"I think I do," Brook said softly, turning to stare out her darkened window. "She knows what the future holds for her life."

"Watch out!" Aaron called out, swerving hard to the right.

Brook had no time to react. She glanced up in time to see a huge dog dart across the road. Aaron struggled to keep the car on the road, but no sooner had Brook thought them to have escaped unscathed than the car went smashing into a rather large tree at the end of a private drive.

Because of their seat belts, neither one was seriously hurt, but Brook was notably shaken. "Are you okay?" she managed to ask with a shaky voice.

"I'm fine," Aaron muttered. "What about you?"

"I'm okay."

"Are you sure? It's impossible to see," he said, opening his door. "Maybe you should stay put while I go up to that house and get help."

"I'm really okay, Aaron," Brook replied, unfastening her belt and opening her own door. The image of Ashley flashed in her mind and instinctively Brook knew that her twin was in some sort of peril. "But I have to get to a phone," she murmured, knowing that he would never understand.

By three-thirty they were finally back at the hotel. Aaron apologized at least a dozen times and Brook assured him each time that the accident was hardly his fault. She hurried to her room and immediately went to the telephone. Dialing up Ashley's number, Brook felt her sense of urgency build. Something was wrong—she just knew it—and with each ring of the phone she felt it confirmed. When the answering machine came on, she slammed the receiver down and dialed Mattie.

Struggling to keep from being sick, Brook waited impatiently as the ringing began on the other line. Again there was no answer, and now Brook was beginning to panic. She felt her face flush in anxiety and fought the urge to run for the bathroom. She had to know what was going on. She had to talk to Ashley!

Desperately, she pulled her address book out of her purse and looked up Deirdre's number. Dialing, Brook whispered a prayer that her sister would answer the telephone.

"Hello?"

"Dee, it's Brook."

"Oh, Brook," Deirdre said, her voice tenuous.

"Something's happened to Ashley, hasn't it?"

"Yes."

"How bad?"

"Pretty bad, Brook. She was in a car accident. She's in the hospital."

Brook forced herself to ask the next question. "Is she going to die?"

"They don't know at this point. She wasn't wearing a seat belt and the car rolled several times."

"She always wears her seat belt," Brook said, still fighting the sense of shock that was overwhelming her. "Why wouldn't she be wearing one this time?"

"I don't know," Deirdre admitted. "Brook, there's something else. Ashley lost a baby. Apparently she was about three months pregnant."

"I know," Brook whispered. "She mentioned she might be when we were back at Grammy's."

"Well, apparently no one else knew it. Not even Jack."

"Speaking of Jack," Brook said, reaching into her purse for a pen, "how can I reach him?"

Deirdre gave her the telephone number. "I'm sure he'll want to talk to you. Grammy is on her way there already, but I know he'll feel better if you call him."

"I'll do it as soon as I hang up," Brook promised. They concluded their call quickly and Brook immediately redialed.

"Dr. Jack Issacs, please," she told the woman who answered the call.

She waited for several minutes before her call was redirected to the surgical waiting room. Apparently Ashley had needed to go back into surgery for some reason.

"Jack?"

"Who's this?"

"Brook."

"Oh, Brook. I'm so sorry. I called Mattie and never thought to call you."

"It's all right. You couldn't have reached me if you'd tried. I'm in England. Now, what's going on with Ashley?"

His voice broke and she could tell he was crying. "She's in surgery—again."

"So I've been told. What are they doing to her?"

"She was pregnant and lost the baby and they can't get her to stop hemorrhaging. They're doing a hysterectomy. She's going to be devastated."

Brook swallowed hard and brushed away the tears that slid down her cheeks. "Will she be okay?"

"The doctor thinks that once they perform this surgery, she'll be out of the woods. They won't know anything for sure, however, until she regains consciousness. That might be days."

"No!"

"I'm sorry, Brook. I know this is hard for you. Is there someone to be with you?"

"No," she managed to whisper. "But that's all right. I'll try to find out when I can fly home."

"No, don't do that, Brook," Jack replied. "Ashley's situation is going to be critical for the next few hours. Just stay put. I'll call you or you can call me for updates, but I'd rather not have anyone else en route here. Mattie's on her way and that's enough for now."

"But I should be there," Brook said, knowing even as she said the words that there was no way Miriam would allow her to just up and leave the photo shoot. She felt torn in two. "Jack, what happened, anyway?"

There was a long pause before Jack spoke. "She was on her way home from my clinic. I don't know what caused the accident, but she flipped the car several times and because she wasn't wearing her seat belt, she was thrown around until the car came to rest upside down."

"Why wasn't she wearing a seat belt?" Brook questioned, desperately needing to understand why this had happened.

"I don't know." He sounded far away, as if he were having difficulty focusing on their conversation.

"I still think I should be there," Brook said, already flipping through her address book.

"Honestly," Jack reiterated, "it would be better if you didn't come back just now. Give it a few hours and we'll know more. You can't get back here very soon anyway. Stay where you are and just keep checking in. If she's going to die . . ." His voice trailed off.

"She's not going to die!" Brook replied fiercely. "She can't die. She just can't."

Chapter 17

Jack Issacs felt sweat trickle down the back of his neck. The sun had barely cleared the horizon to announce yet another morning, the clock on the wall ticking in agonizing slowness. The heart monitor beside Ashley's hospital bed showed the steady rhythm of his wife's vital signs and gave a dull green glow in the dimly lit room.

She shouldn't be here, he thought for the millionth time. *This never should have happened.* He reached for her small smooth hand and clutched it tightly. She was so cold and lifeless. As a doctor, he knew the details of everything they had done for her. Knew, too, the details of everything the accident had done.

He studied her I.V. bags with a doctor's eye. She had fluids to help sustain her life, a bag of O positive blood, and a self-medicating drip of morphine for the time when she actually regained consciousness and found herself in too much pain.

Jack felt hot tears pour down his cheeks. *This is my fault! This is all my fault. She's hurt and can never have another child, all because of me.*

He let go of her and balled his hands into fists. "I'm so sorry, Ash," he said, his emotions getting the best of him.

He leaned his head against the rail of the bed and felt the cold metal penetrate like a knife. It gradually became more painful, but still he kept his weight rigidly against it. He deserved to hurt. He deserved much worse than what he had. Quietly he sobbed.

The door opened quietly behind him and within a matter of seconds he felt warm hands on his shoulders.

"Jack, you can't do this to yourself," Mattie told him softly. "You shouldn't do this to Ashley, either. Who knows what she can hear?"

Jack composed himself and nodded. "I know you're right. It just hurts so much." He got to his feet and looked Mattie in the eye. "I just can't lose her."

"The doctors all say her prognosis is good. You yourself know all the mechanics and textbook circumstances. The rest is in God's hands, Jack. Have you prayed about this?"

Jack couldn't lie. "I've prayed, but I don't think God is listening."

"Of course He's listening," Mattie chided. "He just doesn't always seem to jump when we demand it. Now, why don't you come have some breakfast with me. I was just going to go get something in the cafeteria."

"No, you go ahead. I want to be here when she wakes up," he said soberly. "I need to be the first one she sees."

Mattie seemed to understand. "All right. I'll be back shortly."

Jack felt both a sense of relief and abandonment as Mattie exited as quickly as she'd come. He was glad she was here with him. His own mother had agreed to stay at home with the boys. No sense in having them up at the hospital where everything would be foreign and nothing would offer them comfort. At least at home they could watch television and play with the things that were familiar to them.

In the bed behind him, Ashley stirred and moaned softly. He turned and found her eyes blinking ever so slowly as if trying to focus, and then she was out again. At least it was something.

Jack went back to the bedside and thought of Mattie's suggestion that he pray. "God, this isn't her fault. We both know that she doesn't deserve to suffer like this."

———

Nearly twenty-four hours and dozens of phone calls to the family later, Ashley regained consciousness. She had come back gradually—staying awake a little longer each time, answering questions as they checked her responses.

"Jack," she whispered his name as the last nurse left the room.

"I'm here, Ash," he told her and went quickly to her side.

She looked awful. Her face was swollen, her right eye blackened from colliding against the steering wheel. Several stitches had been made just above her right eyebrow and left uncovered.

"What happened?" she asked.

Jack had already told her three times about the accident, but as was often the case with victims of this kind of trauma, she didn't remember or retain the knowledge.

"You were in a car accident. Don't you remember?"

Ashley shook her head ever so slightly. "Where?"

"On the interstate—up north."

"North?" she seemed to question, then nodded and repeated the word as if this explained everything.

"The kids?" Her voice became panicked and Jack patted her reassuringly.

"The kids were in school. You were alone."

She nodded and let out a raspy breath. "Am I going to be all right?"

"Yes," Jack said, his voice catching, unable to continue.

Ashley closed her eyes and faded off to sleep. Jack didn't know if it was from sheer exhaustion of fighting to recover or from the morphine that coursed through her body. Either way, he could no longer bear the misery he felt. Sobbing, he sunk into the hard leather chair at her bedside and cried.

"Oh, Ashley. My sweet Ashley."

"You can't keep mourning her, Jack," Mattie told him, leading him to the waiting room. "Ashley's recovery looks good. You have to focus on the hopefulness of this situation."

"She's lost so much," Jack replied. "The baby."

"I know," Mattie said, patting his hand.

"She can't have any more children. That will devastate her."

"She's stronger than you give her credit for."

Jack shook his head. "But maybe I'm not that strong."

Mattie nodded. "Everyone has been focused on Ashley. But you've lost a child as well. Jack, there are no words I can offer that can make that pain go away."

"I just want her back," he murmured.

"She'll be home before you know it."

"I want everything to be like it was," Jack added. "But it will forever be changed."

"Change isn't always bad, Jack. You can both get through this together. I know you love Ashley and she loves you. You have to help each other through this."

"If she'll let me," Jack replied. "If she'll let me."

Deirdre waved good-bye as Morgan trudged up the steps to Heritage School. Another two weeks and they would be out for the summer. Another few days after that and Deirdre would pack Morgan off to Grammy's farm and she and Dave would take a much-needed vacation. At least they would if Ashley's recovery continued and if Dave's legal case was completed.

She frowned at the thought of the case. His job was monopolizing his life, and yet Dave continued to push himself. He seldom talked anymore and he isolated himself from her and Morgan on most occasions. Deirdre had gotten tired of fighting it and finally gave up. She simply steered out of his path and cut him as much slack as she could. She had meals ready in case he wanted to eat but said nothing when he refused them and locked himself in his study.

Reaching into her purse, Deirdre pulled out the black case that held her mother-in-law's necklace. Because of all the problems in her life, she'd forgotten all about pawning the necklace to replace her household money.

She'd arranged an appointment at one of the better pawnshops in town and had decided to make her way there as soon as Morgan was in school for the day. This way, she reasoned, she'd have plenty of time to get to the bank and then go grocery shopping before she needed to be back at the school to pick her daughter up.

Deirdre had planned to have this done before now, but with

Ashley's accident and Dave so preoccupied, she hadn't felt pressed to do it. In another day or so she could ask Dave for the household money and then she would be able to go back and retrieve the necklace. But another day or two wouldn't help her now. She needed money to pay all the small incidental things that should have been paid last week.

Pulling up in front of the pawnshop, she grimaced at how seedy everything looked. She'd been told this was a good place—a safe place to deal—yet it looked ominously threatening and made her skin crawl.

Refusing to give in to her fears, Deirdre made her way into the shop. She placed the black case on the counter and waited while the owner was summoned. A tiny elderly man emerged from the back room to greet her.

"I'm glad to meet you, Mrs. Woodward," he said congenially. "Let's see what you have." He opened the case, then took out a jeweler's loop and held it to his eye. Picking up the necklace with his free hand, he carefully scrutinized the jewels in the necklace. "A most unusual piece," he commented.

Deirdre glanced around nervously. Taking an uneasy breath, she asked, "So what can you loan me on it? I only need it for a couple of days."

He said nothing while he continued examining the piece, leaving Deirdre to wonder if the necklace was nothing more than costume jewelry. Maybe she had been foolish to even bring it here.

Glancing at her watch, she saw that only a few minutes had passed. It felt more like hours. Finally the old man put down the necklace and the loop.

"Five hundred dollars," he said.

"I beg your pardon?" Deirdre was certain she hadn't heard him right.

"The piece is worth much more, of course. But I can only offer you five hundred."

She nodded. "That's enough."

He went to his desk and began taking out papers. "We'll need to fill these out."

Five hundred dollars! Her worries were easily lifted as she considered what she would do. With the extra money she could go to the casino and earn back what she had lost. Surely she wouldn't be that unlucky two times in a row. Her spirits raised. *With the extra two hundred I can play a few hands of blackjack and double it. It won't take long at all to win five hundred dollars,* she thought, even though she'd never won that much money from gambling.

She finished her dealings at the pawnshop, promising to be back by Thursday in order to retrieve the piece. Deirdre returned to her car feeling like a new woman. She had five hundred dollars in her pocket and a confidence that suggested she had already won the casino's jackpot.

From the moment she wheeled into the parking lot to her first steps inside the casino, Deirdre felt her excitement build. She was going to win the money she needed and maybe even more. Wouldn't it be a relief to Dave if she could come home with an extra thousand dollars?

She bought chips and proceeded to the blackjack table knowing that somehow everything would be all right. She had a feeling about this and smiled confidently as the dealer put down the cards. She held at nineteen.

She won the hand and ten dollars and beamed a smile at the dealer. "This time let's make it a little more interesting," she said and made a twenty-five-dollar bet.

The afternoon wore on and all thoughts of buying groceries or going to the bank disappeared. Deirdre lost all track of time, as was the intent of the casino owners. There were no clocks, no windows to tell what time of day it was. Just the bright lights and noisy activities associated with the casino floor. She had downed several sodas and the surge of sugar and caffeine coursed through her system. It only added to her excitement.

"You're sure doing great today, Deirdre," the handsome young dealer told her. "Lady Luck must sure be with you today."

She grinned. "I knew it would be a good day."

From across the room at the slot machines someone was yelling in victory. Clanging bells and lights were going off to indicate another winner.

"Guess I'm not the only one."

The dealer nodded as Deirdre put down a gutsy bet of one hundred dollars. "Let's see just how much luck I have." She laughed as she realized her cards totaled twenty, then frowned as the dealer turned over twenty-one.

"Sorry about that," he said with a sympathetic smile. "Wanna try again?"

She pushed out her chips less enthusiastically this time. "A minor setback. Let's try it again."

But again she lost.

Deirdre took a gulp of the icy soda and steadied her jittery nerves. Just one more hand, she told herself. *One more and I'm sure to be back on track.*

She bet fifty dollars and felt her stomach do a flip. It just had to work!

And it did. She smiled and suddenly all was right with the world. This was going to work out after all. She just knew it.

But it didn't.

By the time Deirdre looked at her watch and realized she was over half an hour late to pick up Morgan, she had lost everything she'd come in with. All five hundred dollars were gone. Just like that.

She dragged herself out to the car and sat in the front seat for several minutes. Feeling the start of some form of panic sweep over her, she shoved the key in the ignition and tried not to think about what had just happened.

Remembering Morgan, she picked up the cellular phone and called the school.

"This is Mrs. Woodward," she said rather mechanically. "I've been having car trouble. I'm sorry for not calling sooner but I couldn't. I'll be there in a few minutes to pick up Morgan."

The secretary sympathized and promised it was not a problem. Deirdre felt guilty for the lie, but she could hardly explain that she'd just spent the afternoon in the casino.

The drive to Heritage School allowed Deirdre more time to reflect on what she'd just done. Was she completely out of control? Was she addicted to it like so many of those poor fools she'd made fun of with her girlfriends?

She thought over her actions. She was gambling alone—in secret. And she had lied to cover her actions, taking money away from her family and even pawning valuable jewelry to cover her losses.

"But I'm not addicted," she told herself. "I just wanted to make that money back and I felt certain I could win."

She pulled up to the school and shut off the car. She knew because of the lateness of the hour she'd have to go inside and explain the situation in more detail. Morgan would no doubt be playing in the principal's office or somewhere nearby.

Burdened by her worry, Deirdre made her way inside. *What am I supposed to do now?* she wondered. I'm down by over eight hundred dollars. That's more than I could ever explain to Dave and certainly more than I'll ever manage to get my hands on through the household money.

"Mrs. Woodward!" the principal called in greeting. "I'm so sorry about your car trouble. What seemed to be the problem?"

Deirdre stared at the woman blankly for a moment. It was time to invent yet another lie. "It was something to do with the radiator. I just don't understand cars." At least that much was true.

Morgan came bounding up to her mother. "I'm hungry!" she announced.

Deirdre smiled with a contentment she didn't feel. "Me too, sweetie. Let's get your things together and go home and fix a snack." Enthusiastically, Morgan raced off to retrieve her things.

"I'm really sorry about this," Deirdre apologized. "The time just got away from me. I thought I could have things under control in time to pick Morgan up."

"No problem," the principal assured her. "I had to be here until five."

"Well, thank you for being so understanding," Deirdre replied as Morgan rejoined them. "I promise it won't happen again."

———————

That evening Dave Woodward maneuvered his car into the garage and turned off the engine. As the automatic garage door closed behind him, Dave wondered how in the world he'd ever make it through the evening. Exhaustion and mental duress drained him so completely that all he wanted to do was hide away in his office and never come out again.

Staring at the door to the house, he sighed. He'd been so harsh with Deirdre and Morgan that morning. He almost hated coming home to try to explain. Especially when there was no real explanation. He couldn't tell them why he had acted the way he had. He couldn't admit to the problems plaguing his mind.

Slowly he got out of the car, dragging his briefcase with him. He felt like throwing the burdensome thing through the garage window, but something inside him caused sanity to prevail. *If I can just get through this case . . . if I can just make everybody happy.* But he knew there was no way to do that. Someone would have to lose and someone would definitely win.

Coming into the house, Dave found a surprising silence. He glanced back out the door, noting that Deirdre's car was parked there alongside his own. Maybe they were upstairs, he thought, deciding to slip into his office quietly before calling attention to the fact that he was home.

In his office, Dave gave the briefcase a toss onto his desk and began to shed his suitcoat and tie. He then walked back down the hall, suspicious of the solitude. He glanced at his watch. It was well before six. He sniffed the air. Deirdre wasn't cooking anything, so maybe he could make it up to them by suggesting dinner out.

"Dee?" he called questioningly.

No answer. The downstairs appeared completely deserted.

Now he was starting to worry. Hurrying up the stairs, he paused by their bedroom door. He had just reached out to turn the knob when he heard Morgan's animated singing. Slipping across the hall to her bedroom, Dave peeked inside.

Dressed in a bright pink outfit, Morgan was entertaining herself by serving tea to a rather worn woolly lamb named Baa Baa and two pristine-looking fashion dolls.

"Got room for one more?" Dave asked, hanging his suit coat and tie on the doorknob.

"Daddy!" Morgan exclaimed, running. She reached her arms out and Dave lifted her into the air. Wrapping her arms around his neck, Morgan pelted him with kisses.

"That's quite a welcome," Dave said, holding his daughter tight. How he loved this little girl. She was light and life and all things special.

"Mommy told me to play quiet and not bother you if you came home before she finished with her bath," Morgan said, pulling back to study her father's face. "Are you still mad?"

Dave shook his head. "No, sweetie. I shouldn't have acted like such a grump this morning. Do you forgive me?"

"Sure, Daddy. We learned in Sunday school that you're s'posed to forgive," Morgan assured him.

"So Mommy is taking a bath?" he questioned. That at least explained why the house was so quiet.

"Yup. She had a bad day. The car got broken and she didn't pick me up until late."

Dave frowned. "The car broke down? Did she say what was wrong?"

Morgan shrugged. "I don't 'member."

"Well, that's okay. Why don't you just serve me up some tea and you can tell me what kind of day you had at school. Then when Mommy gets done, maybe we can go out to eat. Would you like that?"

Morgan clapped her hands. "Can we get hamburgers?"

Dave grinned. "I was thinking of something a little bit nicer. You know, something special to help Mommy since she had such a bad day."

Morgan nodded. "Sure. We can do that." She wiggled out of Dave's arms and pulled on his hand. "Come on. My tea is getting cold."

Dave had only been seated at the tiny table for a few minutes when his robed wife peeked in to check on Morgan.

Her expression was one of pure surprise. "I didn't expect you this early."

Dave nodded. "I know. But after the way I acted this morning, I really felt I owed it to you and Morgan to take you out for a nice night on the town."

Instead of looking happy, Deirdre's expression contorted into one of pure panic. "We can't do that. You said we needed to be careful with money. Remember?"

Dave laughed. "I remember. I was just being a grump and now I want to make it up to you." He got up and walked to where she stood. Her wet hair touched the top of her shoulders and Dave couldn't resist putting his fingers to it. "Why don't you just dry your hair and put on a pretty dress and I'll get Morgan ready. There's a new restaurant over by Oak Park Mall I think would be perfect for tonight."

Deirdre stared at him in disbelief. "I'm still not sure it's a good idea."

Dave pulled her close, causing her to give a yelp of surprise. He tightened his hold on her. "Did you have something else in mind?" he whispered against her cheek.

Morgan giggled. "Are you going to kiss?"

Both parents became rather self-conscious. Dave gave Deirdre a wink. "Later," he whispered before turning to his daughter. "And just what if I am going to kiss Mommy, little Miss Morgan? There's nothing wrong with that."

Morgan became very thoughtful. "Matt Smith says his daddy kissed his mommy on the mouth and now they're going to have another baby. Are we going to have another baby?"

Dave looked at Deirdre with a panicked expression. How was he supposed to handle this one?

Deirdre smiled at his sudden case of nerves. "Would you like for us to have another baby, Morgan?"

The five-year-old seemed to think this over momentarily before bursting into a huge grin. "Yes! That would be even better than getting a puppy."

The tension broke for Dave with that one simple statement. For Morgan it was all issues of puppies versus babies. How he wished life could be so simple for him. Still, he wasn't about to let his worries get him down. Smiling, he looked at his wife.

"So what do you think, Mrs. Woodward? Shall we have a puppy or a baby?"

Deirdre cocked her head to one side. "I'll have to think about it," she said quite seriously. But already Dave could see a bit of twinkle returning to her eyes.

"Well, think about it over dinner. I'm starved." He scooped Morgan up and headed to his daughter's closet. "And if you aren't ready by the time we are, you'll just have to stay here and eat canned soup."

He glanced over his shoulder and found Deirdre smiling. Maybe everything would work out all right after all. Dave couldn't help but sigh. Somehow he had to find a way to protect them. Somehow he had to make things right.

Chapter 18

The school year over, Connie loaded the last of her things into the car and headed home. Her apartment wasn't but two miles from the school, but during that course of time she had come to a final conclusion about the man she was living with.

Ray Baker had been finishing up his degree at the local college when Connie had met him. It was winter break and he was attentive and helpful and said all the right things. And before she knew it, Connie had taken Ray as her lover.

Ray had moved in shortly after the spring semester began. He was happy-go-lucky and made Connie feel good. His temperament suggested that life was just a game and the only way you could fail at it or ruin it was to force yourself to make a move that made you unhappy.

"We call all the shots," he had told her once. "I do what makes me feel good and you should do the same. Remember, you only have one life to live."

But Connie knew that her upbringing suggested otherwise. Gram had said that God was in charge and that life didn't end with physical death; rather, a spiritual one. But believing in Ray's way was easier.

The apartment complex loomed up ahead and Connie felt a strange aching begin. It was right to send Ray packing, but for the life of her she didn't know how she'd fill that void in her life. She had no classes to help with or even to participate in until she began as the assistant weight-lifting coach for a summer school class. Losing Ray would leave her with empty evenings and boring weekends. Maybe she shouldn't ask him to leave. But deep in her heart she knew it was the only way to get back on the right track. She needed to find her way back to the values and life-style she knew were right.

Connie parked the car in her assigned slot and reached over for her box of paraphernalia. Her whistles, lesson plans, pens, papers, and other assorted bits of her life as a physical education teacher were contained in that box. Throwing her purse on top, she made her way up the steps and into the apartment complex.

Internally, she continued to argue with herself. She could just wait until she got back from the farm. She was scheduled to go with Deirdre and Erica next week to take Morgan down to Grammy. And if Gram wasn't back from taking care of Ashley, they all agreed that Connie should stay at the farm and take care of Morgan. Either way, she would be gone anywhere from a few days to several weeks, and Ray would be on his own.

Balancing the box on her hip, Connie unlocked the door and sighed. Answers regarding relationships had never been her strong suit.

"That you, Connie?" Ray's voice called out.

She looked at the clock on the kitchen stove before setting her box on the counter. "Yeah, it's me. What are you doing home at this hour?"

"Packing" came the answer.

Connie froze in place. *Packing?* She nonchalantly walked into the bedroom and found Ray clearing out his side of the closet.

"So what's up?" She tried her best to only sound marginally interested.

Ray's whole face lit up. His blond crew cut seemed to glisten, perhaps from a recent shower. "I'm going to Mexico."

"Oh," she said, nodding. "Vacation?"

"Well, actually, we're going down for the summer. Some buddies and I got together and started talking about the cheap cost of living there, and one thing led to another. We figured we could spend the whole summer down there for what we would have spent for a week in California at a beach house."

"You're probably right," she said, still not fully understanding what was happening. "What's the plan after the summer?"

Ray shrugged. "Who knows. We might angle on down to South America. Just seems like the right time to be moving on."

He was leaving her. Just like that.

Forcing herself to nod again, Connie smiled. "It does seem like the right time, doesn't it?"

Ray grinned. "We're so in tune with each other. I knew you'd understand. We sure have had a good time together, and man, it's saved me a bundle to live here with you instead of trying to live on my own."

"That reminds me," Connie said, walking to her dresser. "You still owe me for last month's phone bill."

Ray nodded and pulled out several twenties. "This should cover that one and next month's as well. I'll try to call you from Mexico sometime. Who knows? Maybe you'll want to come down and see our place once we get set up."

"I doubt that," Connie said, stuffing the bills into the pocket of her shorts. "How soon are you leaving?"

"As soon as I get this stuff together. Joey's picking me up and then we're heading off to get the other guys."

"Sounds like a good plan," Connie said, the smile still pasted on her face.

Ray finished just as a honking sounded outside in the parking lot. He darted to the window and waved. "That's him. Wow! I'm so psyched about this! Thanks again, Connie," he said as he hoisted his duffel bags. "I really enjoyed our time together."

"Yeah," Connie said in a noncommittal manner. They made their way to the door. "Have fun, Ray."

He turned and grinned. "I intend to." He started to leave, then turned around again. "I left the key on the coffee table—oh, and some guy named Kevin called. Said he really needed you to call him back. Sounded kind of lonely." Ray laughed. "Guess that's perfect timing, huh?"

He seemed completely unconcerned that one of Connie's previous boyfriends should call and leave such a message.

"Perfect," she murmured.

Ray leaned over and gave her the briefest of kisses on the lips and he was gone. Connie stood at the open door for several minutes, unsure of what to do.

She closed the door and leaned against it for another few minutes. This was what she wanted anyway, wasn't it? She had planned to ask him to leave, so why did she feel so suddenly abandoned?

A feeling of sadness washed over her and Connie went to the coffee table, where Ray had left his key. She picked it up and fingered it for a moment, then plopped down on the couch to think.

"This is silly," Connie said to herself. "You wanted him gone and now he's gone. So what's the problem?"

The problem was, she wasn't the one to back out of the relationship first. She had always made it a point to break up before her boyfriend could suggest doing the same thing. This had given her the control, and whenever she started to feel sorry for herself because her life was empty or void of a relationship, she simply reminded herself that she had orchestrated the entire matter.

But this time things were different. This time the control had been stripped away and she was left to stand in the wake of someone else's choice. And it was obvious that the choice hadn't been that hard for Ray to make. He didn't seem the least bit upset by their separating and in fact had seemed completely unconcerned. *Didn't I mean anything to him? Was I really nothing more than a cheap place to live until college was finished?* She struggled with her thoughts. Living free and easy—without ties or restraints—certainly wasn't all it was cracked up to be. The guy just walked out of her life without anything more than a "thanks for the good times."

"But that's what you wanted, stupid!" she told herself aloud. She tossed the key back to the table and crossed her arms. "That's the way I want it."

I just need to get busy, she thought. There was plenty to occupy herself with, and in a few days she'd be taking a brief trip and that would change her scenery and give her something else to focus on. Resolving to put the entire matter of Ray behind her, she picked up the phone. She'd call a friend—a girlfriend. They could go out shopping, grab a bite to eat, and maybe even see a movie. She would just get on with her life. It was just that simple.

———————

Ashley stared out the window and sighed. She had been home for only two days, and yet nothing seemed right. She was notably sore from the trauma to her abdominal region, but her recovery had been remarkable. Her doctors credited it to her good health and fit body.

Pity they couldn't have done something to straighten out my mind, Ashley thought. Her body might be knitting itself back together, but her emotional state was precarious at best.

Sitting down cautiously to avoid causing herself any pain, Ashley found herself engulfed in silence. Mattie had returned, albeit reluctantly, to Kansas, and Jack had taken the boys to catch a plane for California, where they would spend time visiting their aunt, uncle, and cousins before soccer camp started. Ashley had cried after the boys were out of sight. She couldn't imagine having them away from her at a time like this. They were all she had now. All she would ever have.

Ashley put her hands to her stomach and blinked back tears. She had lost the baby. Not only that, but there would be no more babies. She kept having nightmares about Jack leaving her because of her inability to bear more children. She squeezed out such thoughts, but no matter how hard she tried to think positively, she felt an overwhelming fear.

Her nightmares weren't just limited to Jack leaving. Sometimes in her dreams she found herself up against his accusations that she had killed their child. He would yell at her and say ugly, hurtful things. Then he would tell her that he wanted her to leave. Putting her hands to her head, she sobbed. The accident had robbed her of so much, and the worst part was that she couldn't remember any of it.

She remembered seeing Willa and Rhonda at the country club—even remembered going to her doctor's appointment and learning about the baby. But after that, nothing fit. She couldn't remember where she'd gone or how she'd ended up on I-25. She couldn't remember the accident or the aftermath. She did remember waking up in the hospital and having Jack and Mattie at her side.

And then she remembered Jack telling her about the baby.

In the stillness of her plush Denver home, Ashley cried quietly for a time. It seemed tears were her constant companion these days. She cried when she woke up to realize the accident wasn't just a bad dream, and she cried when she went to bed—unable to think of facing yet another day.

Realizing that she'd spent nearly all of her energy on tears, she wiped her eyes and tried to regroup her thoughts. Brook had called her every day, sometimes two and three times a day, and Ashley always insisted that she stay where she was and not come to see her. Ashley had lied to Brook, saying that she was fine and that while her heart was broken over the news of the baby, it wasn't the end of the world.

So why did it feel like the end of the world?

Nothing felt right. Nothing was right.

Even the house felt foreign to her. She walked from room to room, slowly trying to regain her energy, but nothing appeared as it had before the accident. The house seemed cold, almost impersonal. She found no comfort there.

Her other sisters had tried to keep close tabs on her condition, and Ashley was grateful for their attentiveness and concern, but she had no desire to see them or to talk to them. She usually would say a few words, then ask them to get any other details from Jack. Sympathizing with her condition, they had all been gracious about it, but Ashley knew she hadn't fooled anyone, especially Brook.

Brook could read her like a book, and Ashley knew if Brook were to come to Colorado, she would see just how emotionally empty Ashley had become.

Gingerly, she eased up out of the chair and made her way into her bedroom. She was tired of wearing a robe and nightgown, but the thought of wearing anything with a waistband made her wince. The incision from the first operation to remove her spleen was healing nicely, but the cut ran down her midsection and would be sensitive to anything tight. The doctor had assured her that she could have plastic surgery later to lessen the scar's ugly puckering, but Ashley hadn't concerned herself with the matter. Nothing could remove the scars inside, so why worry about those on the outside?

Pulling at the ties of her robe, Ashley slipped it off her shoulders, then discarded the nightgown as well. She caught sight of herself in the full-length mirror. Forcing herself to look, Ashley studied the changes in her body. The ugly scarring, the bruises and discoloration. It was like looking at a stranger—a very ugly stranger. No wonder Jack treated her with such kid gloves. He was probably repulsed by her. She touched the area around her right eye. The swelling had gone down and the laceration above her brow had healed. So why did her face seem so different? She shuddered and turned away.

Ashley went through her entire wardrobe before deciding on a loose pair of drawstring slacks and soft knit T-shirt. Stretching her arms upward hurt more than she'd like to admit, but she endured it nevertheless. Easing onto the side of the bed, she managed to work each leg into the pants without pulling too much on her incisions. She secured the tie just enough to keep the pants from sliding back down, then rested from her ordeal.

"I can't just sit around and be an invalid all my life," she announced to the empty room, frustrated not to be able to do all the things she had done before.

She heard the car pull into the drive just outside their bedroom window. Jack was back from the airport. She grimaced, remembering how she looked. How could he stand the sight of her? Since it hurt to raise her arms, it was almost impossible to do anything with her hair. Feeling completely unattractive and responsible for the death of her baby, Ashley couldn't imagine Jack wanting anything to do with her.

"Honey, where are you?" Jack called.

She could hear him moving through the house. "I'm in the bedroom."

He appeared at the door and frowned. "You shouldn't have gotten dressed without someone here to help you."

"I can manage," she answered. "You and all your doctor cronies have told me over and over how miraculously I've healed. So why not let me prove it by getting dressed on my own? It seems the least I can do."

Jack smiled at her and came to kneel down beside her. "I don't want you to overdo it. Yes, you've made great strides in your recovery. Most folks would still be in the hospital. But I want you to rest and take it easy."

"I'm not much good to anyone sitting around on my backside."

Jack shook his head. "That's not true. Oh, Ash, I almost lost you. You can sit here and do nothing the rest of your life, and I'll still feel grateful to have you here."

Ashley looked up at him. He was so attentive, so loving. How could she ever explain her feelings? How could she continue to question his love for her?

"Look," he continued. "I have an idea. Let's go up to Estes. I can care for you and we can take a long weekend for the holidays."

Ashley looked at him to gauge how serious he was about the suggestion. He seemed to be genuinely excited about the prospect, and so she nodded. "If you think I won't be overdoing it."

He laughed. "I won't let you overdo it. Now you tell me what you'll need and I'll pack it all up."

Within two hours they were headed north. Jack had announced the need to stop by his office before they left, and Ashley gave it little thought. In deference to what Ashley had been through, Jack even stayed off I-25 and took the side streets to the clinic. He was helping her in every possible way. If only she could somehow help herself.

Ashley watched the traffic indifferently. She had thought she might be terrified to get back into a car, but there hadn't been any feelings of panic or fear. Her own car had been totaled, and Jack had arranged for it to be hauled off so that she would never have to see it. He had told her a bit about it—how the entire roof had collapsed and the front end had mashed back toward the front seat. She had been wedged between the dash and the front seat, Jack had told her, and because she had forgotten her seat belt, she was lucky to be alive. But was she lucky?

She chased off such thoughts as Jack pulled into the clinic parking lot. For a moment a scene of déjà vu flashed before her eyes. She shook her head. It was silly, she told herself. I've pulled into this parking lot a hundred times. I would naturally remember it. But it seemed to be something more than that.

"You stay put," Jack told her as he got out of the car. "I'll be right back."

She nodded and watched him walk up the drive. "Jack!" she called out almost against her will. Something felt fearfully wrong.

He turned and called to her. "What's the matter?"

"Nothing," she replied.

"I can't hear you, sweetheart," he said, leaning his hands on the hood. "Did you want something?"

Ashley saw him standing there and again that feeling of having lived through the scene washed over her. She shook her head and Jack smiled. He took this as his cue that everything was all right and headed inside.

Licking her dry lips, Ashley struggled for a moment with a flickering memory. *I'm being silly,* she said to herself and eased back against the leather upholstery of Jack's Bronco. Still, no matter how hard she tried to convince herself to relax, the feeling stayed with her. Even after Jack returned.

"Shall we go by way of Highway 36?" he asked, throwing some things into the backseat.

"That sounds good," she whispered.

"I know you like Big Thompson Canyon, but I think all the twisting and turning might rub you sore. Not that Highway 36 is devoid of those places, but it shouldn't be quite as rough." Ashley nodded as he maneuvered the car down the road.

She couldn't think of anything to say, and so she stared out the window at the passing scenery. As they began the climb upward into the Rockies, she tried to focus on the landscape. Wild flowers bloomed along the road, and the sun reflected against the snow-capped mountains like glitter sprinkled there by a child. She thought of a Mother's Day card Zach had picked out for her with just such glitter.

"I wish you would talk to me," Jack said out of the clear blue. She turned and looked at him. "I know you're hurting," he continued. "I just wish you wouldn't shut me out."

Ashley looked away and studied the road ahead. "There's nothing to say. I can't remember the accident, and I don't want to dwell on the aftermath."

"You mean the baby?"

Ashley felt a tightness in her chest. "Yes . . . the baby." She couldn't explain it, but she simply could not bring herself to share her feelings or fears over her loss.

Jack said nothing more until they reached Estes. He was angry, or at least she supposed he was. He didn't really look mad, but he seemed impatient to arrive. Ashley felt bad. He was trying so hard with her and she continued to push him away.

They drove through Estes and took the north bypass, where they turned onto Devil's Gulch Road. Winding through the trees, past McGreggor's Ranch, they finally reached their summer home away from home. Jack turned into the long drive and once he'd circled the path to back in, Ashley had a magnificent view of the towering peaks of Rocky Mountain National Park. The view was inspiring. This had been the reason they had purchased the property from one of Jack's friends. The former owners, an aging doctor and his wife, had decided that warmer climates and lower altitudes were their calling, and because Jack had voiced interest after sharing their hospitality one week several years ago, they had offered their place to Jack and Ashley first.

Waiting for Jack to help her from the elevated Bronco, Ashley remembered the peaceful feeling she'd known when she'd first come here. Would it be possible to feel that way again?

After helping Ashley inside the cabin, Jack retrieved their things and took them to the bedroom, placing them where Ashley could get to them without having to lift anything.

"I think this was one of the best decisions we ever made," Jack said. He emerged from the bedroom with a smile on his face. "I think the mountain air will do you good."

Ashley could still denote a touch of sadness in his voice. Sadness that she had put there. "I hope so," she managed to say.

She glanced around the living room at the sparse furnishings. She had planned to spend most of the summer redecorating and finding special furniture for the place. The knotty pine interior was very rustic, and combined with the native stone fireplace and vaulted ceilings, Ashley had imagined all sorts of neat combinations to accentuate the features.

"What are you thinking about?" Jack asked, coming up from behind her.

"I was just remembering all the work I had planned for the place this summer," Ashley replied. "You know, buying furniture, redecorating, and such."

"So why not go forward with that idea? I can get you a bunch of catalogs and samples and you can sit here and quietly plot and plan to your heart's content. Wouldn't that be fun?"

She turned and looked at him for a moment. He was trying so hard to please her. She nodded. How could she do otherwise?

He reached out to touch her cheek. Without meaning to, Ashley recoiled, and his expression revealed the hurt he felt at her rejection. "I'm sorry, Jack. I'm just so jumpy." She reached out and took hold of his hand and put it up to her face. It didn't feel right, but she wasn't going to say a word.

He smiled again. "I understand. Look, I'm going to run to town and see what I can dig up for you in terms of decorating equipment. I'll pick up the groceries as well—and hey, how about a movie? I could rent a video."

Ashley forced a smile. "Sounds good."

He gathered up his keys and bounded out of the house, whistling a tune. Ashley sighed and made her way to the nearest chair.

"What's wrong with me?" she questioned, ignoring the tenderness in her stomach. She buried her face in her hands and tried to settle her nerves. "I feel like I'm losing my mind."

Unable to cope with the soreness and her emotions, Ashley went to the bedroom and climbed into bed fully clothed. She pulled a pillow over her stomach and held it tight. They had advised this in the hospital, telling her it would help with the pain. It did, but only slightly. The mounded bulge of the pillow only served to remind her of the flatness of her own abdomen. *There should be a baby in there,* she thought sadly. Warm tears trickled down her face and slid into her ears. The discomfort was nothing compared to her aching heart.

She ran her hand over the pillow, pretending for just a moment that she was still pregnant. She remembered the first time she had felt John kick in her womb. She thought of the wild antics Zachary used to perform inside her. She had teased that he would no doubt be an acrobat.

"It's not fair!" she cried out, clutching the pillow tight. "My baby is gone. My baby is dead!" She threw the pillow across the room and curled up on her side. "Oh, God, help me. I can't bear this pain. I just can't."

Chapter 19

At the last minute, Deirdre's plans changed and she found herself driving to Council Grove with Morgan alone. Erica had received a call to fly to Chicago to audition for a position with the Philharmonic, and Connie had come down with the flu. She supposed it was just as well. She was in no mood to make small talk with anyone.

There had been one positive occasion in her life. Dave had suggested they pay Mattie up front for caring for Morgan, and Deirdre had eagerly agreed. She knew Mattie wouldn't take the money, but she thought if she could get her hands on a good chunk of cash, she might be able to make back the money she'd lost at blackjack. When Dave had soberly asked her how much the average babysitter earned, Deirdre had told him it was quite common to pay one hundred dollars a week. Then she quickly pointed out that this was for daytime care only. Twenty-four-hour care would probably be at least double that. Dave had hardly done much more than nod. He pulled five hundred dollars from his wallet.

"Take three hundred out of the ATM," he told her.

Deirdre could hardly believe her luck. The eight hundred she had lost was now back under her control. It was a clear sign to her that God had answered her prayers. She wouldn't take three hundred from the ATM, since she was already trying to figure out how to cover the three hundred she'd taken out weeks before. When Dave received the bank statements, he'd believe she had done just as he'd suggested, even if the dates were messed up.

The five hundred in her purse made her feel more at ease than she had in weeks. There was still the question of getting the necklace out of the pawnshop, but she had another week or so to reclaim it. Smiling to herself, she almost felt that her problems were behind her. Almost.

But Deirdre couldn't help but be haunted by her actions. She knew she had a serious obsession with the casino—even now while driving to Grammy's, all she could think about was taking the five hundred dollars and turning it into a thousand by properly betting it.

"There's Great-Grammy Mitchell!" Morgan called out, straining forward against her seat belt. "Oh, Mommy! Look at all her flowers!"

Morgan sounded positively awestruck, and Deirdre had to agree with her reaction. Gram had such a way with flowers. She could have grown roses out of clay in a snowstorm, she remembered Harry's mother saying when they'd all been quite young. Now as they neared the house, Deirdre could see why.

Grammy waved from her rose garden and gathered up a basket of newly clipped flowers. She had just reached the porch steps as Deirdre shut off the car.

"Hello, dearies," Mattie called out.

Morgan hurriedly threw aside her seat belt and jumped out of the car. "Grammy! I get to stay with you!" she squealed as if this might be news to Mattie.

"I know! I'm so excited," Mattie told her only great-grand-daughter. "We shall have lots of fun. Oh, and I have a surprise for you. My cat, Miss Kitty, had kittens earlier this spring and you'll have lots of fun playing with them."

"Oh boy!" Morgan said, clapping her hands. Then she noticed Mattie's basket. "You've got beautiful flowers," Morgan said, gingerly stroking one very pale pink petal.

"You can help me put these in water," Mattie told her. "Would you like that?"

"Oh yes!" Morgan exclaimed. "Can I carry them into the house?"

"Why, sure," Mattie said, handing her the basket. "That would be a very great help to me."

With a pride borne from knowing her task was important, Morgan jutted out her chin and secured the basket handle over her arm. "I get to carry the flowers, Mommy."

Deirdre smiled. "I know, sweetie. Why don't you go ahead and take them on in?"

Morgan didn't have to be told twice. She marched forward like a bride going to her groom. Mattie and Deirdre both stifled their giggles until the child was safely inside.

"She's priceless," Mattie told Deirdre. She slipped her arm around her granddaughter's waist and added, "but then, so are you."

Deirdre accepted Mattie's welcoming hug. "Before we get inside," she said, pulling away. "Dave wanted me to give you money for taking care of Morgan."

Mattie frowned. "You know better than that. I don't take pay for the pleasure of enjoying my great-grandchildren."

"I told him you wouldn't, but he insisted." Deirdre hoped she wouldn't overplay her hand. She had to present the situation in such a way that when it was all said and done, Mattie would agree to keep mum on the issue of money. "I don't suppose," Deirdre continued, "you could just do it this once?"

"Absolutely not. I'll talk to Dave myself—"

"No!" Deirdre said, grabbing hold of Mattie's arm. "Grammy, he's under such stress from this case and I think this would just burden him unduly. Maybe you could just say you took the money, or better yet, not say anything at all."

"That would be dishonest, Deirdre. If he asked me about it, I wouldn't want to lie."

Deirdre felt her stomach burning. "Well, what if you took the money and gave it back to me?"

"What do you mean?" Grammy asked seriously.

"I mean, just take the money and then offer it back to me as a gift for our trip. Dave would understand that. He'd feel at ease because he'd paid his debt to you, so to speak, and you would feel at ease because you wouldn't have to lie about it."

Mattie shook her head and grinned. "Will he really be that much of a stinker about it?"

Deirdre sighed. She was nearly home free. "He'll be the worst kind if he thinks we're leaving to have fun and you aren't properly compensated."

"All right," Mattie said with a nod. "Give me the money."

Deirdre felt her mouth go dry. What if Grammy had changed her mind? What if she actually did want the money? She reached into her purse and pulled out the five one-hundred-dollar bills. "Here."

"Five hundred?" Mattie questioned. "Goodness, he must have a supreme sense of duty in this matter."

Deirdre nodded, beginning to feel rather ill. She watched as Mattie folded the bills in half, then folded them again. Biting her lip, she waited to see what the older woman would do next.

"You know what, Deirdre," she said as if completely changing the subject. "I sure hope you and Dave have a great time on your trip to Hawaii."

"Me too," Deirdre said, forcing the words.

"I think I'd like for you to take this money and have an even better time," she said, pushing the folded bills back into her granddaughter's hands.

Deirdre felt an overwhelming sensation of relief wash over her. "Oh, Grammy. How sweet of you."

Mattie laughed and pulled Deirdre close. "There. Now you can satisfy that silly husband of yours and still have a wonderful time." She glanced up at the house. "We'd best get inside and see what Morgan's up to."

Deirdre nodded. "I need to get our things out of the trunk and then I'll be right in."

Mattie nodded and took off for the front door, while Deirdre pushed the money inside her purse. It was all going to work out just great. Morgan would stay with Mattie, and Deirdre would keep the money. Hopefully, Deirdre would have a chance to make up for her bad luck, and by the time she took off for her trip, everything would be back in its proper place. Afterward, Deirdre would be the one to come back for Morgan, and with any luck at all, Dave would never mention the money.

By the time Deirdre finished stashing their things in the upstairs bedroom, Mattie had sent Morgan off to play with Miss Kitty and her kittens.

"Now that you're back," Deirdre said, taking a seat at the small kitchen table, "how did you think Ashley was getting along?"

Mattie frowned and turned at the sink to wash her hands. "I think it'll be a long haul for both of them. The boys seemed to take it all very well. Of course, they didn't know about the baby and they can't understand Ashley's pain in never being able to have another child."

Deirdre nodded. "How about Jack?"

Mattie dried her hands and went to the refrigerator to retrieve a pitcher of tea. "Jack is taking this very hard. He feels somehow responsible for the entire matter, even though he has no reason to. I think it's the way of men. They feel it's their place to make certain their loved ones are protected, and when something happens to them—well, they just feel inadequate. He and Ashley were so happy about having another child, and to have that stripped away, along with the prospects of ever having any more children, has left Jack just as confused and out of step as it has Ashley."

Deirdre thought of her own mess and how distant Dave had become. It had started about the time she had started asking for more money. She grimaced when she thought of the correlation. She had insisted they landscape the yard, and since it was spring, it was the perfect time to get in there and do a good portion of the work. Then there was her own personal spending. A new wardrobe for Hawaii and summer clothes for Morgan. Not to mention the gambling.

"All in all, I think if they will just open up to each other," Mattie was saying, "they'll get through this. Honesty is always the best policy."

"I'm sure you're right," Deirdre murmured.

Mattie poured them both a glass of tea, then put the pitcher back in the fridge. "How about you? What have you been doing lately?"

Deirdre took the tea and shrugged. "Mainly getting the yard in shape and preparing for the trip to Hawaii." She felt guilty, thinking again of her desire to gamble. The strength of that need was something that Deirdre herself didn't understand, and she was deeply ashamed that she had somehow lost control.

"I imagine it's been hard on you having Dave so preoccupied by his court case," Mattie said with a sympathetic smile. "How's that going?"

"He's working himself to death," Deirdre answered honestly. "I've tried to get him to slow down, but it's almost like he's obsessed with this one case. He's been taken off of everything else and given completely over to this one project."

"Obsessions are dangerous," Mattie said thoughtfully.

Deirdre couldn't resist the urge to lay her problem before Mattie. She just wouldn't have to say that it was her own. "I've seen obsessions ruin the lives of some good friends," she finally confided.

"Oh, really? What are they obsessed with?" Mattie asked.

"Gambling," Deirdre replied. "They can't seem to stop and they spend more and more. They get it into their mind that they can recoup their losses, but it doesn't work that way."

"If it did," Mattie said with a look of patience, "the casinos would quickly go out of business."

"I suppose that's true," Deirdre admitted. "Still, sometimes they have good luck. Especially this one friend of mine. She really seems to get it all under control. She'll have a winning streak and do quite well, but I guess she just doesn't know when to quit."

Mattie nodded. "It's a dangerous situation to be in. Obsessions take hold of your life and pretty soon that one thing is running everything else. I suppose that's why I was worried when you mentioned that you were gambling with your friends. I know you felt that it would be harmless entertainment, but look at what you're faced with now."

Deirdre nearly choked on her tea. "What . . . what do you mean?"

"Well, your friend is in trouble. I know how you like to fix things and smooth out problems for people, but, Deirdre, I have to say, this is one of those things you can't fix for your friend. Don't even try. She has to want to stop gambling and she has to see the folly of her ways. No matter how much you tell her she's in danger, she won't believe you. Prayer is about the best weapon you have in this situation. Prayer and maybe your own love for your friend. Maybe you could get her involved in something else. Maybe you could suggest to the gang that you all do something completely different."

Deirdre nodded. She knew that Grammy spoke the truth. But it was hard to accept that she couldn't just go back to the casino and have her luck restored. After all, that's what luck was all about. Sometimes it was with you and sometimes it wasn't. Besides, along with the thrill of the game, Deirdre felt it was the only thing she had any real say over in her life. Dave made most of their decisions on how money would be spent, where they would go, and when. Dave had even been the one to decide on Morgan's private school rather than public school. And in most every case, the school issue included, Deirdre had wholeheartedly agreed with his choices. So why should she feel that she had so little say in her own life?

———————

After a restless night of sharing her bed with Morgan, Deirdre dressed for the day, then woke her child. "You'll miss the best part of being on the farm if you sleep through the morning," she told Morgan. This was something Grammy had said to them since they were old enough to remember. And Deirdre had to admit, it seemed right.

Mornings held a variety of shows. Some were crystal clear with brilliant blue skies and vivid colors. Some were shrouded in misty fog, muting the tones and blanketing the sounds. Still other days were frosty, showing icy drawings on the window glass and across the dried, dead grass.

Today was what Deirdre considered a soft morning. There wasn't the heaviness of fog, but a light haze rose up from the lake and gave everything a rather surreal look. The sun was a pale lemon yellow and the lighting reminded Deirdre of a Monet painting. Morgan, of course, had no such conceptions or appreciation. She was already rattling on and on about how Harry was supposed to come today and take her for a boat ride.

"Grammy talked to him on the telephone," Morgan said as she tied her sneakers. "And Harry said he would row over here and take me for a ride if it was okay with you."

"Yes, I know," Deirdre said with a laugh. "I was there when Grammy got the call."

Morgan's brow knit together for a brief moment, then relaxed as she continued. "I don't know how to row a boat, but Harry's going to show me."

"Morgan, you don't even know who Harry is," Deirdre said, grabbing her daughter's jacket.

"Grammy said he was the little boy who grew up next door. I like to play with little boys."

"Yes," Deirdre replied. "But you aren't listening to exactly what Grammy said. He was little, but he grew up. Harry is a grown man who's about the same age as your daddy."

"Oh," Morgan said sounding rather deflated. "Does he have a little girl?"

"No, Harry hasn't married yet, so he doesn't have a family."

"Will he like me?"

"I'm sure he will think you are positively charming," Deirdre said, helping her daughter into the jacket. "Now, why don't you go play in the back garden while Grammy and I fix breakfast. But don't pick her flowers."

Morgan nodded somberly and headed out the door. Deirdre

chuckled to herself, imagining that Morgan had figured she and some little boy were going to go boating on the lake. Kids!

Harry rowed in long, persistent strokes to cross the distance between his place and the Mitchell farm. He was glad to hear that Deirdre had brought Morgan to visit with Mattie for a spell. He hadn't thought Mattie to be herself since returning from Ashley's tragedy in Denver. Harry supposed that having to deal with Ashley's near-death experience couldn't help but steal some of Mattie's contentment and peace. After all, in spite of the physical distance, Mattie was still very close to all of her girls.

Harry tried not to think about Ashley and the accident. He had prayed fervently for her recovery, but he hadn't wanted to dwell on the details. He cared about what happened to her, but he cared more about how it affected Mattie. Sometimes the older woman seemed so strong, and other times she was very vulnerable—almost frail. Of course, Mattie would never have admitted it, but Harry had seen changes in her over the last year. Maybe age and time, heartaches and disappointments were taking their toll. He just didn't want to see her get old before her time.

Still, he couldn't worry about it. He was a firm believer that God had everything under control. Even the most minute detail was ordained by God, as far as Harry was concerned. Having a little girl around the farm would be just the ticket. Morgan would draw out Mattie's joy and help the older woman to regenerate her enthusiasm for life. It seemed preordained.

Up ahead he saw the wooden dock and waved at Deirdre and Morgan. Morgan seemed to be enthusiastically ready for her day as she jumped up and down on the wood planking. She was a precious little girl, Harry thought. Delicate and petite, with huge eyes that seemed to watch his every move. Hair the color of ripe wheat bounced in a ponytail fixed high atop her head. She was dressed appropriately in lavender jeans and a printed floral shirt, with a zippered jacket to ward off the chill.

"Grammy says to come have breakfast with us," Deirdre called, interrupting his assessment of Morgan.

"Are *you* Harry?" Morgan questioned.

"Yes," Harry replied, easing up alongside the dock. "You must be Morgan. I remember seeing you when you were just a couple of years old. You're half grown-up now."

"I'm five," she told him very seriously. "Five is old enough to go to school. I just granulated."

"Granulated?" Harry questioned.

"She means graduated," Deirdre offered. "They graduate from kindergarten now. They get a little cap to wear and receive a diploma that looks better than the one I got from college."

Harry laughed. "Well, congratulations, Miss Morgan." He tied off the boat, then climbed up onto the dock. "Why don't we go celebrate with breakfast."

Morgan seemed to approve of the plan and quickly put her hand in Harry's. "I thought you would be a little boy," she told him honestly, "but it's okay that you're a big boy."

Harry grinned and looked over at Deirdre. "It's okay, huh?"

"Yup," Morgan said sweetly. "I can live with it."

Harry was immediately charmed, and after breakfast he felt as if he'd spent a lifetime with the precocious child rather than a mere half hour. Morgan seemed completely at ease in his company, and in a way, she seemed to hold him in highest regard. Harry—the man with the boat!

They spent nearly two hours on the lake. Two hours that Harry really could have used to go over his equipment and work on making repairs to his hay shed. But somehow the time slipped away and it didn't really seem all that important that his chores were going undone. When they finally returned to Mattie's dock, Morgan slipped out of her life jacket and let Harry put her up on the dock.

"Don't run off," he told her. He laughed as she plopped down on the dock. "I want to show you how to tie some knots," he said, pulling the boat rope up to where he joined Morgan.

"Is it important?" Morgan asked, as though anything less than the most important of issues was beneath her taking time out to learn.

"It's very important," Harry replied. "And I've never shown another little girl. You will be the first one. Maybe even the only one."

Morgan nodded solemnly, the weight of this austere moment seeming to settle upon her shoulders like a queen's robe. "That *is* important."

"All the knots have secret names," Harry told her, "and only those people who have learned them know their names. This one is a clove hitch. You use it to tie up the boat." He showed her how to bring the rope around and draw it through.

Morgan immediately assessed the situation and understood. She took the rope from him and after two tries made a very decent knot for herself. "I did it!" she squealed.

"Yes, you did. Congratulations."

"Now I can tie up the boat."

"You certainly can," Harry said. "Maybe I'll let you tie up the boat tomorrow. That is, if you want to go on another ride?"

"Oh boy!" Morgan said, nodding enthusiastically. "Can I wear the life jacket again?"

"You always have to wear the life jacket when you go boating with me," Harry said seriously. "Boating can be very dangerous, and I wouldn't want anything to happen to you."

They rejoined Deirdre and Mattie, and Morgan told them, in her animated way, how she had helped to row the boat and had learned to tie a "clothes hitch."

"That's clove hitch," Deirdre told her daughter.

Morgan frowned. "You know about the secret name?"

Deirdre spied Harry, who was trying hard not to smile. "I heard about it from Daddy," she told Morgan, quickly trying to recover the moment. "You know how smart he is."

This satisfied Morgan, who, after eating her lunch and a dessert of milk and cookies, went begrudgingly to bed for an afternoon nap. Deirdre lifted her in her arms as they climbed the steps, and Harry could hear Deirdre comforting Morgan with the promise that her nap would not take very long at all.

Seeing them like that made Harry wish more than ever that he had a family. He loved children and had always wanted to have several of his own. He just didn't know that he wanted to have them with Sarah Hooper.

"You sure look down in the dumps all of a sudden," Mattie said as she cleared the table. "I have more cookies if that's what your frown is all about."

Harry shook his head. "I'd burst if I ate another thing. But you do make the best oatmeal chocolate chip cookies in the world."

Mattie laughed. "Well, you're welcome to the recipe." She finished putting the glasses in the sink, then asked, "Did you have a good time with Morgan? She seemed so taken with you."

"We had a wonderful time," Harry admitted. "She's quite the little charmer, although she did say something that made me wonder if there was a problem at home. I just wondered if Deirdre said anything."

"Such as?" Mattie came to the table and sat down beside Harry.

"Morgan said that her mommy and daddy were always yelling at each other and that her mommy seemed happier here on the farm. I just wondered if Deirdre was okay."

"She hasn't said anything to me," Mattie replied. "I know Dave is under a lot of pressure, so I'm sure Deirdre is as well. Hopefully this trip of theirs will help sort everything out. They leave next week."

"Does Deirdre plan to spend much time down here or is she hurrying right back to Kansas City?"

"She told me she'd stick around for the Memorial weekend picnic on Sunday. I guess after that she'll head home. I sure hope there's nothing seriously wrong. I'd hate to see another of my girls in pain."

Harry nodded. He'd hate to see Mattie caught up in yet another problem and almost chided himself for even having brought up the subject. "I'm sure you're right," he finally said. "I'll bet everything is just kind of going at full speed for Deirdre and her husband. Probably everything will iron itself out once they get away for a while."

Mattie's features seemed to relax. "Yes, of course. We all know how stressful planning can be. Why, just look at you, Harry. You're a ball of nerves, what with this wedding looming ever closer."

He swallowed hard and nodded. "I suppose so." But despite Mattie's accuracy when it came to pegging his own problems, Harry was in no mood to try to explain. "I guess I'll be getting on home. I promised Morgan we could take the boat out again tomorrow, so unless it's raining or Deirdre has other plans, I'll probably come by early like I did this morning."

"Plan to have breakfast with us again," Mattie encouraged. "I'll fix your favorite coffee cake."

He grinned. "It's a deal."

Chapter 20

To everyone's surprise, Erica and Connie showed up on Saturday. Each arrived in their own vehicle, having not told the other one that they were coming. It was so typical of the way they managed their lives.

"I thought you were sick," Mattie said as Connie gave her a big embrace.

"I think it must have just been food poisoning or something disagreeing with me," Connie replied. "I felt fine after a few hours, and I rested all day yesterday just to be sure. But I feel great and since I was looking forward to coming down here, I just thought I'd surprise you."

"And what about you?" Mattie questioned Erica, who was engaged in a quick exchange with Deirdre.

"My audition was yesterday and it went very well. I flew home last night with the assurance from the audition team that I'd hear something on Tuesday. I couldn't see myself just sitting around this weekend waiting for some word."

"What about Sean?" Deirdre questioned.

"Well, he's decided to take some time to pray and think about our future. He believes that we can surely find a way to work out both my love of the orchestra and our love for each other. I think the idea of us needing to move to a larger city has put him into a bit of a tailspin. So he's gone home to his folks in Springfield."

"Well, it's to my gain, then," Mattie declared. "We were just discussing having our own picnic tonight by the lake. Harry's going to build us a big bonfire down by the shoreline, and I plan to barbecue.

Doesn't that sound like fun?" Connie and Erica eagerly agreed.

Plans for the evening went through without a hitch. The mosquitoes were the biggest challenge to deal with, as they seemed to be everywhere at once and as big as June bugs.

"I had this area sprayed," Mattie said, swatting at the biting insects, "but it's been a couple of years. I guess it's time to do it again."

"Here, try this," Connie said, offering a bottle of lotion to Mattie. "I'm not getting bit at all."

"Can I use that on Morgan?" Deirdre questioned. "She'll be a mess of welts by morning if I don't do something quick."

"Sure," Connie replied. "It's safe for all ages."

Harry threw some more wood on the fire, then came to sit down on the blanket not far from Connie. "So how'd the school year play itself out?" he asked.

"We had several track meets in May and our school did exceptionally well. Our girls' team ended up placing second in our region, which was something no one expected."

"They must have had a good coach," Harry said, giving Connie a smile.

Seeing that Morgan was playing by herself along the water's edge, Mattie took a deep breath and decided now was as good a time as any to share the news Mavis Lane had given her only two days earlier.

"I had a call from Mavis," she began. "There's some further news about Rachelle's death, and since the three of you are here, I think it might be a good idea to tell you what she had to say."

"Why spoil such a lovely evening?" Deirdre questioned. "Is it really all that important?"

Mattie nodded. "I think it is. It seems that Rachelle's death was definitely a suicide. Mavis doesn't want everyone to know that and figured we wouldn't want everyone knowing it either. People already presume it was a suicide, but because there were no other indications that it was, most folks are content to call it accidental. After all, your mother was in the height of her popularity and demand."

"So it was a suicide," Erica commented. "She's still dead. Why does it matter one way or the other?"

"Well, it seems," Mattie said rather slowly, "that she left some letters. Apparently she wrote them on the trip to Alaska, knowing that she was going to end her life. She put them all in an envelope addressed to Mavis and slipped it into her luggage prior to taking the pills."

"What does that have to do with us, Grammy?" Connie questioned.

"The letters were to you girls. One for each of you and one for me."

The girls each looked at Mattie with such a stunned expression of disbelief that Mattie hurried to continue. "Mavis is sending the letters but is hopeful that we will keep the suicide issue to ourselves. She feels it will only add to the media frenzy and send a whole new onslaught of publicity our way. She knows I would rather avoid that, and I think you girls would rather avoid it as well."

"Rachelle wrote us a letter?" Deirdre questioned, shaking her head. "After all this time, she finally felt the need to say something personal to us?"

"Too little, too late, if you ask me," Erica said, crossing her arms. "I can't believe she did it."

"I can," Deirdre said, almost lost in thought. "She had to set things right."

"Don't you dare defend her," Connie said angrily. "She doesn't deserve it. She made her way in life and now she has to live with the consequences."

"Or die with them, in this case," Mattie said softly.

Across the fire she could see the black, glassy water of the lake. *How did things go so wrong?* she wondered. When she'd first come to live at the farm, life had loomed before her like a clean sheet of paper begging for her touch. What she wrote or painted or sketched on that sheet was entirely up to her. Now, sitting here so many years later, it seemed that the sheet had been gouged, trampled, burned at the edges, and scribbled on over and over.

"I've always tried to just think of her as dead," Erica admitted. "I know it sounds awful, but I even told someone that once when I was in college. I just didn't want to deal with the truth of it. It wasn't because I hated her, I just couldn't deal with my feelings on the matter."

"I think we were lucky that she had no part in our lives," Connie was saying, but Mattie hardly heard her. She was lost in her thoughts of Rachelle as her mind drifted back in time. She had been watching a television reporter some twenty years ago explain the overnight phenomenon of Rachelle Barrister.

"We're here today on the set of award-winning actress Rachelle Barrister. Rachelle's newest work is a historical intrigue set in Nazi-occupied France during World War II. Rachelle, we want to thank you for being with us today."

Zoom camera to Rachelle. She smiled and made eye contact with her public. Dressed in her costume for the film, she crossed her legs and extended her hand to the reporter. "It's simply wonderful to be here today."

Mattie watched with mixed emotions. The Rachelle on the screen was not the same woman or even girl whom Mattie had known and loved. This Rachelle seemed driven and hard. She said all the right things and gave the right gestures, but her eyes were empty of expression. Mattie thought them rather lifeless.

"Your current work deals with World War II. Do you find that a far stretch from the futuristic movie, *Devil's Sky*, that you made last year? The one for which we all remember you winning Best Actress?"

"It's not a far stretch at all," Rachelle told him. "Life is a big play and we all act out our parts. One movie is very similar to another. Someone directs. Someone takes care of the setting. Someone else arranges for the script. I simply put myself into the role, much as I have all my life—both on screen and off.

"However," she added with a mischievous grin, "that isn't to say that some roles aren't more important than others."

"What would you say have been your most important roles?" the reporter asked.

Mattie was glued to the set by this time. She longed to hear Rachelle say that the part she played as a member of Mattie's family had been her most important role. She longed to hear Rachelle tell him that the acting engulfed everything—everything but her relationship to her mother and children. But then she reasoned that perhaps she would feel better if Rachelle did admit that she had played her role in the lives of her children like a bad part. Mattie would have loved it even more had she voiced a demand for a new script.

The reporter was laughing at something Rachelle had said and Mattie realized that she'd just missed what her daughter had replied.

"Of course, my family died when I was very young," Rachelle said, sobering. "At least most of them did. It was very hard to go on. You can't imagine what that is like for a girl of twelve. To suddenly find myself so very alone—to lose the people you love—the ones who love you . . ." She let the words trail into silence as her eyes filled with tears.

Mattie hadn't heard Brook come into the house. She caught sight of the little girl's angry expression as she watched the television screen. Mattie would have given anything to have saved Brook from hearing those words. Rachelle had made it so clear that no one else existed for whom she could care about or love. She had relegated her children and even Mattie to a world of nonexistence.

"I hate her," Brook said angrily. "From now on I'm going to tell everyone that my mother is dead. I just wish it were true."

Mattie's heart had broken for her granddaughter then, just as it did now for the three who shared her company.

"Mattie." Harry spoke her name softly.

"Grammy? Are you feeling all right?" Erica questioned.

Mattie shook away the memories of Brook's hatred and Rachelle's indifference. It seemed like just yesterday those painful words had been issued.

"I'm fine," she said and looked at the bonfire to reacquaint herself with the present. "Harry, you made a dandy fire. We could just sit out here all night."

Nobody spoke for several minutes. It was almost as if they understood the thoughts Mattie had been thinking.

"Well, I know one person who can't sit out here all night," Deirdre replied, stroking Morgan's hair when she curled onto her lap. "I think it's someone's bedtime."

The little girl stifled a yawn. "I'm not tired."

They all laughed at this, which only furthered Morgan's resolve. "I'm not. I wish somebody would tell you adults to go to bed."

"Morgan!" Deirdre said sternly. "That was uncalled for."

Mattie chuckled. "Morgan, I wish quite often someone would tell me to go to bed or to go take a nap. Sometimes when you're all grown-up, you wish you had those things back from your childhood."

"Well, I don't like to sleep," Morgan said softly. "I get bad dreams."

Deirdre frowned. "Since when?"

Morgan shrugged. "I don't know. I just get them, and I don't like them."

Mattie nodded. "We all get bad dreams sometimes. When I have a bad dream, I pray and ask Jesus to help me think about something else. It always works for me."

Morgan seemed to think this a possibility. "I'll try it sometime."

"Why don't we get you to bed and you can try it tonight," Mattie suggested. She got up from her lawn chair and held out her hand. "How about if Grammy puts you to bed tonight? Would that be all right?"

Morgan jumped up and went eagerly to her great-grandmother. "Will you tell me a story?"

"Sure," Mattie agreed. "Is it okay with you, Deirdre? I guess I really should have asked first."

Deirdre laughed. "Absolutely. I remember your stories. Maybe I should have you tuck me in too."

They all chuckled at this as Mattie and Morgan made their way back to the house. It didn't take any time at all for Morgan to nod off to sleep. After listening to less than half of Mattie's story about Joseph being sold as a slave by his own brothers, Morgan gave up her fight. Mattie thought how precious she looked sleeping there in Deirdre's old bed. It definitely took Mattie back in time.

As she touched Morgan's forehead, it was like caressing a five-year-old Deirdre again. A tear trickled down Mattie's weathered cheek. Such innocence should never know despair and fear.

"Sometimes," she whispered, "I wish they could all be little again. I'd find a way to fix the things I did wrong. I'd find a way to make it all right."

Sighing, she wiped her cheek and turned on the night-light. At the door she paused, shut off the overhead light, and whispered a prayer of protection for Morgan before making her way back downstairs. She imagined the others were still down at the lake and thought she'd just stay in the house for the evening. She had no heart to listen to them talk about Rachelle. Besides, what if Morgan woke up and needed something? But then Mattie remembered she'd left a bag of piecework in the gazebo. She knew better than to leave it there all night and went to retrieve it before it collected too much moisture from the humid evening.

As she neared the gazebo, she could hear the voices of her granddaughters. Only instead of the civil, albeit painful, conversation she'd left them with earlier, they were now embroiled in a rather heated argument.

"Rachelle's entire life was a waste," Connie was saying. "There probably won't be a single cent left after her debts are paid. She gambled too much and lived too high on the hog."

This seemed to completely miff Deirdre, who snapped back, "It was her money to spend!"

Mattie figured her nerves were just a little too sensitive to the issue of gambling, especially since one of Deirdre's good friends was caught in a downward spiral from the activity.

"It was her life to spend as well," Erica commented. "She chose the fast lane—drugs, men . . . especially men. If you want to play the field like she did, you have to pay the price."

Connie was enraged. "You think just because someone lives their life to the fullest that they should die? Is that what you want for me? Why can't I live my life my way? At least I'm happy."

"Are you really?" Erica questioned. "You don't seem to be. Maybe you're just saying that to convince yourself—or better yet, to avoid dealing with the pain."

"Not everyone who dabbles in one vice or another has an obsession or addiction to those things. Rachelle just picked the things that made her happy. It doesn't mean she was right and we're wrong, it's just the choice she made for herself," Deirdre said, trying as always to be the peacemaker. "I think we should just calm down and wait until the letters come to Grammy before deciding that Rachelle was completely heartless where we were concerned. It's hardly fair for us to judge her motives."

"They don't sound too happy," Harry said, coming up from behind Mattie in the darkness of the garden.

"Oh, Harry," Mattie replied, shaking her head. "I figured you were right in the middle of that." She could barely make out his features in the moonlight.

"Nah. When things started to turn a bit heavy, I told them I needed to get the ax back into the shed. I cleared out of there before things got too ugly."

"They all seem so lost. So miserable. I was really hoping Rachelle's death might bring them closer."

"Maybe it will in the long run," Harry said. "I guess we just have to be patient."

Mattie nodded. "I suppose you're right, but it's so hard to listen to that and not react."

"You'll be happier if you stay out of it, Mattie. You've raised them right. You did everything you were supposed to do. They have to make their own choices now, and sometimes those choices aren't going to be what you want them to be."

Mattie knew he was right. The counsel he offered her was no different than that which she might have offered someone else under different circumstances.

"Well, I'll see you later, Harry," she replied. "I'm going back up to the house to be there in case Morgan wakes up."

"I'm going to row home," he replied. "I sure don't want to get in the middle of that ordeal and have one of them ask me for my opinion."

Mattie chuckled. "No, that would surely be a big mistake."

———————

Deirdre was still groggy the next morning when Dave surprised her by calling before anyone was even out of bed.

"Dave?" she questioned, her voice barely a whisper.

Without any words of greeting, Dave began. "Look, Deirdre, I'm sorry for this, but I need for you to come home. We have to cancel our trip."

Deirdre instantly woke up. "What do you mean?"

"The case isn't resolved yet. I can't leave. I thought we'd have finished up by now, but it didn't turn out that way. We can't go."

"That's ridiculous. We have reservations, plane tickets. Do you realize the money we'll be out?" Deirdre replied, trying hard to keep her voice down.

"The way you've been spending money over the last few months, it's probably not that big of a loss. We're going to have to tighten our belts anyway. Better that we give up a few deposits than get down there and spend more money."

"I can't believe you're doing this to me!" Deirdre declared. Her voice grew loud enough to wake Morgan.

"Are you fighting with Daddy again?" Morgan asked sleepily.

Deirdre ignored her child's question, as well as the guilt she felt that her daughter should have to witness something so ugly. "Dave, if you do this, I'll never forgive you. We need this trip. You need it. Our marriage is falling apart because of your job."

"Well, maybe if you would stop spending so much money, I wouldn't have to work so hard."

Another wave of guilt washed over Deirdre. He was right, of course. She had spent way too much money, and probably the only reason he had agreed to get caught up in such a monstrous case was because of her dreams and schemes.

"Look, Dave," she finally managed. "Things can't go on this way."

"You're telling me. Just pack up Morgan and come home. Help me get things under control. I don't know half of who we need to call in order to cancel this thing."

Deirdre hung up the telephone and bit her lip to keep from crying. This was all her fault. She never should have started gambling. Now she had all this debt to make up. But there was the money she was supposed to give Grammy. She could still use that. But what if Dave figured she'd get it back from Mattie since the trip was cancelled? Of course! That's exactly what he'd figure would happen. If she told him that Mattie had refused to give her back the money, it would not only be a lie, it would be unfair to Mattie. Dave would think her to be some sort of moneygrubber.

"Was Daddy mad again?" Morgan asked.

Deirdre looked at her daughter and felt an overwhelming sorrow. "He's just tired, honey," Deirdre told her. "He's working too hard."

She went to the closet and pulled out their suitcases. "I'm sorry, but you can't stay here with Grammy. Daddy wants us to come home."

"But I want to stay!" Morgan declared, crawling to the end of the bed. She was up on her knees, her little white nightgown bunched around her legs. "I don't want to leave." She started to cry.

Deirdre knew she'd reached her own breaking point. The last thing she needed to have to deal with was Morgan's temper tantrum. "I don't have a choice. Now get dressed." She tossed an outfit onto the bed and followed it with a pair of socks. "I'm going to pack the rest of this and then we're leaving."

Morgan continued to cry but did as she was told. Deirdre felt like some sort of monster as she made her way downstairs with Morgan still sobbing. She had just opened the door when Mattie came down the hall.

"What's wrong?" she asked, seeing Morgan's tears and the suitcases in Deirdre's hands.

"We're leaving. I suppose it's just as well. Dave had to cancel the trip and he wants us to come right home."

Mattie frowned as if sensing there was something more to the situation. "But what about Morgan? She can stay, can't she?" At this, Morgan wrapped herself around Mattie's waist and buried her face against Mattie's dress.

"No, she can't stay," Deirdre replied. "Dave said we were to both come home." She opened the door and marched out to the car. Morning dew caused the grass to glisten, and overhead gray billowy clouds suggested rain.

Mattie and Morgan walked out together and had just reached the car as Deirdre slammed the trunk closed. "Get in the car, Morgan."

"Can't I please stay?" she pleaded.

"Don't argue with me." Deirdre let the exasperation show in her tone. "I know you want to stay. I wish I could let you, but Daddy wants us home."

Morgan began to cry even harder and finally Mattie came to the rescue. "Say, how about I come visit you one of these days and maybe your daddy will let you come back to the farm with me?"

Morgan wiped at her eyes and sniffed. "Do you think so?"

"I don't know why not. We'll talk to him about it as soon as he can get his big case solved. Okay?" Mattie bent over to kiss Morgan's cheek.

This seemed to appease the child. "I love you, Grammy," she said, throwing her arms around Mattie's neck.

"I love you too, Morgan."

"Come on," Deirdre told her daughter. "We've got to get a move on."

She didn't know why she was in such a hurry. In fact, truth be told, she felt like not showing up at home for days—just to make Dave pay for the misery he'd heaped upon her. If it weren't for worrying Mattie, she'd do just that. She'd drive off in the opposite direction and disappear for days. Maybe even weeks.

"Don't you want to wait and say good-bye to your sisters?" Mattie questioned Deirdre.

"They don't care about anyone but themselves. Somehow we got to talking about your quilt last night and that made us just fight more. Even Erica managed to tick me off. I'm tired of their attitudes and it's probably best I just go. Otherwise I might say something I'll regret."

"Well, if you're sure that's what you need to do," Mattie said. "But you know how I feel about anger and arguments."

"Yes, I do," Deirdre replied sadly. "But it's too late. We let the sun go down on our anger, and we even slept on it. I think it will be with us for a long, long while."

Chapter 21

Connie soon followed her sister's footsteps. She was bounding down the steps just as Mattie came inside from telling Deirdre good-bye.

"I suppose you're leaving too?" Mattie questioned.

"I'm tired of always being picked on in this family. I can't do anything right by anyone. I thought about it last night and decided I'd rather go home to be alone than have to deal with Erica and Deirdre's snide comments."

"They only care about you."

Connie stopped and shifted her backpack. "I don't think they do, Grammy. I've tried to be more open to them, to see that they care, but all they want to do is show me how I'm living my life wrong and how I need to do things differently. They want me to be successful, but only if I honor their definition of the term."

"It doesn't have to matter," Mattie suggested. "They have to live their own lives and so do you. But, Connie . . ." Mattie let her words fall away. She eyed her granddaughter quite seriously. "I don't want you to be naïve. You don't have to live up to their standards, but there is a higher standard that you have been raised to follow."

"Not you too, Grammy," Connie said in complete exasperation. "Does everyone have to come down on me? I know I'm not perfect. I know I've made mistakes—that I will make more mistakes in the future. I'm trying to change—I'm trying to do better."

Mattie patted her arm gently. "I wasn't trying to come down on you. I just wanted you to know I care. I think that's all your sisters really wanted to say. Maybe they aren't using the right words, but I think the sentiment is there."

"I doubt that. They don't really care about me." Tears began to stream from Connie's eyes. "I've never felt like they wanted me in this family. I've never fit in."

"Maybe that's because you've never wanted to fit in," Erica said, coming down the stairs. "I'm so tired of hearing you play the outcast. It's like a Broadway play that's gone way past the point where it should have been closed down."

"Erica, that was hardly kind," Mattie said, turning to her youngest granddaughter.

"See what I mean, Grammy?" Connie asked, turning to frown at Erica.

Erica, hands pushed deep into her black jeans, shrugged her shoulders. "It's true, and everyone feels the same way. I may be the youngest, but even I know that a person's place in the family depends on what you've chosen for yourself. If you don't want to fit in—you won't."

Connie dried her eyes and sniffed loudly. "Wisdom from one so young. If you're so secure in your position, why are you having such trouble saying yes to your wonderful Christian boyfriend? Isn't marriage what you've always wanted? You condemn me for my actions outside of marriage, and maybe I have been wrong—"

"No maybe about it, you know what we've been taught."

Mattie quickly interceded. "Enough!" She shook her head at the two women. "I just listened to Deirdre go off angry, and now you two are at each other's throats. I don't know where it was that I missed the boat in raising you, but I thought that I'd instilled better values and principles."

"Sorry, Grammy," Connie said, turning to head for the door. "I know I've worn out my welcome. I'll just go."

"You're always wanted and welcomed here, Connie," Mattie said seriously. "You can tell yourself many things, but this farm is mine and I say who is and who isn't welcome."

"But it won't fit into her plan if somebody loves her for real,

Grammy," Erica said rather haughtily. "That's why she won't commit to a real relationship."

"Is that so?" Connie questioned. "Then what's your excuse?"

Mattie felt a supreme sense of frustration with both of them. "I said enough and I meant it! Now, either apologize or go your own way, but stop this bickering. You're saying things that are mean and spiteful—things you'll one day regret."

Connie nodded. "I'll call you later, Grammy." She kissed Mattie on the cheek, then headed to the door, ignoring Erica.

Mattie didn't try to stop her. Nor did she try to stop Erica half an hour later. Instead, she walked out onto the porch and watched the last of her granddaughters drive off. She stared out after the car, long after the dust had settled and the vehicle disappeared from sight. Finally, in complete dejection, she sat down on the front porch swing and tried to sort through her emotions.

"Lord, they are so lost and hurt," she murmured. "I just can't help them anymore. It's going to be up to you."

She smiled at that thought. She almost laughed out loud to imagine God's relief that she was putting Him in charge of something she'd been struggling with for years. But could she really just let it go? After a lifetime of giving herself over to her granddaughters, could she really just walk away from their suffering and allow God to work without her?

She rocked in the swing long past breakfast and was still rocking there when Harry's pickup came roaring down the drive. He caught sight of her on the porch and slowed considerably before stopping altogether.

"You okay?" he asked, bounding up the front porch stairs. "You weren't at church and I got worried."

"Oh, Harry, how sweet of you." He really was like a son to her. "I've just been sitting here wrestling with God."

Harry grinned. "Who's winning?"

Mattie laughed. "Who do you suppose?"

His grin broadened and he nodded. "I'm pretty sure I know."

He settled himself on the porch rail, seeming totally unconcerned for his dress slacks. Mattie thought to say something, then
decided against it. Maybe she just needed to stop trying to mother
the world.

"I see the cars are gone," he commented nonchalantly. "Did the
girls go home already?"

"Yes, I'm afraid so. Deirdre got a call from Dave. Seems he can't
leave work long enough to take their trip. He insisted that she and
Morgan come home immediately. Morgan was heartbroken and
cried and Deirdre just seemed hurt and angry. She was still mad at
her sisters, but madder at Dave. Connie decided she'd had her fill
and Erica quickly followed suit. And me, well . . . I was just sitting
here feeling sorry for myself and explaining to God how He should
take charge of this project."

Harry nodded. "Sometimes that's easier said than done."
He glanced at his watch and grimaced. "I've got to head out. I'm
supposed to have dinner with Sarah's folks."

"Don't sound so enthusiastic," Mattie teased.

Harry's face reddened just a bit and he looked rather sheepish.
"Sorry. Guess I let my guard down."

"You never need to be on your guard with me, Harry. I hope
you'll always remember that."

He nodded and got up, dusting his backside as he did. "I'm glad
you're all right, Mattie. And I'm sorry about the others."

"Thanks, Harry."

They looked at each other for a moment, their expressions
speaking volumes. Mattie knew she could count on Harry for just
about anything, and she was certain he knew the same of her. God
had put them together for a reason, and she cherished Harry's
loyalty.

"Try to have a good time, Harry."

He nodded and pushed back sandy brown hair. "I'll try."

After he'd gone, Mattie forced herself to get up and go into the
house. How very quiet it all seemed. She stood in the living room

for several minutes and shook her head. How much longer could she keep up with it all? How much longer did she want to try? The farm had long since become more work than pleasure, and even selling part of it off to Harry hadn't eased her burdens enough.

Every day of the week was devoted to cleaning two rooms of the house. Mattie usually kept a running pattern of cleaning one upstairs bedroom and one downstairs room. It worked rather well and still allowed her to take Sundays off. Still, it was getting to be too much. It hurt to climb up and down the stairs—her knees were starting to fail her. She frowned, wondering how much longer she'd be able to kneel down to tend to her flowers.

Deciding not to dwell on the seemingly hopeless thoughts, Mattie made her way to the sewing room. The shades were all drawn to keep the sunlight from fading the materials that she worked with. Flicking on the light switch, Mattie instantly caught sight of the prizewinning quilt. For a moment she just stood and gazed at it. She couldn't help but remember the loving pride she'd had in working the pieces together. Each circle appliqued with the utmost care to interlock with the next. She reached out and touched the square she'd devoted to Connie.

"Lord, this child is hurting. Her heart has a wall of stone around it and she's afraid to let anyone chisel it away. Please help her to see the truth. Please let her feel the love she so desperately needs."

Moving her hand to Ashley's square in the upper left corner, Mattie's heart ached. Her granddaughter was so broken—both in body and in spirit. "This child is wounded. Her body needs healing, but so too her heart. You alone know her pain—her misery. Oh, Lord, help her to reach out to you for comfort."

Brook's square adjoined Ashley's at the top right. "This child is worried for her future. She won't talk much about it with me, but I pray she's sharing it with you. Help her to see that she's loved just for being herself and not for her looks. Send someone to love her with a devotion that goes beyond her fame and beauty."

Her hand trailed down to the middle of the right-hand side.

Deirdre's square. "Lord, I don't know how to help this one. She's angry and hurt and facing a great deal of frustration in her marriage. She has so many responsibilities and so many concerns. She's always trying to fix things, and I'm just afraid this time she'll find the situation too big for one person to fix. Let her turn to you."

Finally, she touched Erica's piece. "There's so much hope in this one, Lord. She has big dreams and plans. I just ask that you would help her to figure out the right path. Let her find a way to keep both music and love in her life."

Mattie hadn't given the prayers much thought or preplanning, but it felt so right that she decided she would make it a part of her routine. However, before stepping away, she put her hand on the Mitchell square. "We're a family, Lord. Help us to join together as one. Let them see the common bonds—the love they have for one another. Enrich that love and change their lives for the better." She touched a circle made from the cloth of a dress that Rachelle had once worn. Tears came to her eyes. "Lord, I don't know where she is, but you do. I pray that she found salvation. I pray that she sought your forgiviness for her actions and came to know peace in her heart."

Going to the door, Mattie turned off the light and leaned against the jamb for a moment. It was hard watching them all hurt so much. There wasn't anything she wouldn't have done or have given to ease their pain and suffering. She couldn't help but think how much harder it must have been for God. He, too, watched His children suffer, knowing that He could interfere, but also knowing that it was better to allow them to make their own choices. Choices made of free will were always better than those forced upon you, Mattie reasoned.

She sighed and suddenly felt very tired and very old. Maybe a nap was in order. Her stomach growled loudly and suddenly she realized that she'd not eaten since the night before. Maybe lunch and then a nap, she reasoned, heading for the kitchen. No sense in going to bed hungry.

Chapter 22

Brook looked at her sparsely furnished apartment and wondered why she'd even bothered to keep the place at all. There was nothing here that couldn't easily be loaded into a small rental truck and driven away. Even her wardrobe was minimal. She supposed it was because she made her living wearing clothes that they held very little interest for her of late.

She looked at the empty walls and realized that she'd never really made this quiet sanctuary a home. She had never been one to collect mementos from her trips abroad, so there were no little personal knickknacks on the shelves. Even the few comforts of life that she had afforded herself—TV, VCR, stereo, and such—all seemed rather impersonal now.

Stretching out on the simple beige sofa, Brook gave serious thought as to what she should do with her life.

"I'm thirty years old," she reminded herself. As if anyone needed to remind her. The jobs were fewer than even two years ago and the glamour and excitement seemed to fade with each lengthy airline flight. "I miss simplicity," she decided aloud.

And it was true. She had longed for the quiet of the farm ever since she had gone home for Rachelle's funeral. Brook had felt a craving for the smell of the country, the peaceful visions of wheat waving in the breeze, of pastoral fields and wild flowers. Even now she could close her eyes and see those things clearly imprinted on her childhood memories.

The telephone rang, disturbing the gentle scene. Reaching over her head, she felt around for the phone and finally took hold of the receiver on the third ring.

"Hello?"

"Hi. It's Erica."

"What a pleasant surprise," Brook said, really meaning it.

"I thought I'd call and see how you were doing."

"I'm great. Just vegging out here on the couch and being extremely lazy."

"Me too."

"So how did your trip to Grammy's go? You were headed down there last week, weren't you?" Brook questioned. Erica didn't answer right away, and Brook immediately sensed the tension in her voice when she did speak.

"It was okay."

"Want to give me the real version?"

Again Erica hesitated. "Well, it's just that . . . things could have been better."

"How so?"

"Well, we kind of got into a fight."

"You and Grammy?"

Erica laughed. "No, silly. Me and Connie and Deirdre."

"Oh, you were all down there together?"

"Yes, but it didn't turn out so nice."

The next thing Brook knew, Erica was spilling the beans and telling her everything that had happened.

"Sounds kind of silly to me," Brook finally said. "Like when we were little kids and would fight over stupid issues."

"It wasn't silly," Erica said in a tone that suggested Brook had stepped on her toes.

"Well, you have to admit, three grown women fighting over who was living their life the right way seems rather foolish. I mean, you're all individual people. You're going to have your own interests and beliefs."

"What would you know about it?" Erica snapped in uncharacteristic anger. "You're never home long enough to know what anything's about."

The words hurt Brook deeply. "I guess I'm sorry I said anything."

"Well, you should be. Look, I've got to go," Erica said, suddenly seeming to be in a hurry.

"I really am sorry, Erica. I didn't mean to hurt your feelings."

"Don't worry about it. I'll talk to you later."

Brook hung up the phone feeling rather dejected. She hadn't meant to make Erica feel bad. She had only said what she had to help her sister see how pointless it was to argue over someone else's choice. Until they wanted to make changes for themselves, it really didn't matter what anyone else thought.

This gave Brook something to consider for herself as well. She had given ten years of her life to modeling, and not only was she worried about what the next ten years might hold, she was tired. Tired of being told what to do. Tired of having her entire life dictated to her by a woman whose main interest was how much money Brook could bring in.

"I miss my family," Brook muttered. "Especially Grammy and Ashley."

She sat up and picked up the telephone again. Dialing Grammy's number, she frowned as the busy signal tone pulsated against her ear. Refusing to give up, she hung up and then redialed. This time she called Ashley.

Jack answered in a rather preoccupied manner. "Dr. Issacs."

"Jack, it's Brook."

"Oh," he seemed to pause for a moment as if trying to remember who she was. "How are you?" he asked.

"Pretty good. Look, you sound busy. Did I call at a bad time?"

"Well, I'm not sure there's really any good time—not anymore."

"What do you mean?"

"Well, I've thought about calling you, but to tell you the truth, Ashley hasn't wanted me to."

"Why not?"

Jack lowered his voice as if to keep his words a complete secret. "She's extremely depressed."

"How long has this been going on?"

"Since the accident."

Brook shook her head. "I knew she was sad about the baby and the hysterectomy, but I thought she was getting over it. I mean, when I did talk to her last, she sounded so positive."

"It's all a show. I thought, given the way you two read each other like books, you'd have realized that."

Jack's words stung. Maybe if she hadn't been so busy with her career, she would have realized it. Maybe she had realized it but had pushed it aside, knowing it would cost her too much time and effort to acknowledge it and do something about it.

"Is there anything I can do? Can I talk to her now?"

"She won't come to the phone. She won't see anybody or do much of anything. I'm just glad the boys are off seeing my brother."

"What if I come out? I mean, if I'm there, she'll have to deal with me," Brook suggested.

"Do you have time to get away?"

"I'll make time."

"I think it might be the very thing she needs. You two could go up to the house in Estes and get away from everything. I had Ashley up there earlier and she seemed better there than here in Denver. Either way, she needs something, and I don't seem to be able to give it to her."

"Well, I'll just start packing and get the first flight out to Denver. Don't worry about picking me up or anything, I'll rent a car."

"Thanks, Brook. I think this is going to make a big difference for Ashley."

Brook hung up the phone and frowned. Why hadn't she sensed Ashley's dilemma? They were usually so aware of problems in each other's lives. Brook understood Ashley feeling bad about the baby. Brook, too, felt a sense of loss over the death of her unborn niece or nephew. She felt she could even understand Ashley's disappointment over the hysterectomy. After all, she knew how she'd feel if she couldn't have children.

Shaking her head, she grabbed her address book and quickly punched in the numbers for her regular airline. She booked a seat out on the afternoon flight and instantly went to work to pack the necessary items. Some time away in a Rocky Mountain cabin sounded like just the thing to give her some perspective on life.

She was nearly ready to walk out the door when she realized she hadn't called her manager. As if on cue, the telephone rang and Brook was surprised to hear Miriam's voice ring out on the other end.

"Brook, great news! That modeling job for Calvin Klein is yours. We leave tomorrow for Bermuda."

"I can't go," Brook said, hardly able to believe she was saying the words.

"I beg your pardon?"

"I said, I can't go. My sister needs me in Denver. I was just on my way out the door to catch my flight."

"Did you plan to tell me about this?" Miriam sounded completely miffed.

"Yes, as a matter of fact, I was just about to call you when the telephone rang."

"Well, you're going to have to cancel your plans. That's all there is to it."

"I can't. Ashley needs me."

"Brook, do I need to remind you how hard we've worked to get you this assignment? The image they're usually after isn't exactly what you have to offer. If you walk out on this deal, don't expect them to shed any tears over it. They'll simply have me reassign it to Kristy or Zoe, maybe even Sheila."

She had purposefully listed off Brook's strongest competition, and it really bothered Brook to realize Miriam was being intentionally mean. Her stomach churned.

"I'm sorry, Miriam. You'll have to give it to someone else. My sister is severely depressed and she needs me. I didn't insist on going when she had her accident, although I probably should have, but I'm insisting now."

"Well, have it your way. This is breech of contract as far as I'm concerned."

"I don't think so, Miriam," Brook replied, feeling her temper starting to kick in. "If you'll check that piece of paper again, it says that I get final say on all projects. Remember?"

Miriam was silent for several moments. "You know you aren't getting any younger. You can't hope to keep this up much longer. Maybe it's time for you to start thinking about what else you can do with your life."

Brook frowned. "Maybe so. Maybe that's what I'll think about when I'm in Colorado."

"Well, fine. Be kind enough to let me know when you get back. If it's not too much trouble."

Brook clenched her teeth and ignored the pain in her stomach. "I'll call you when I'm back."

She slammed the receiver down angrily, then stared at the phone for a moment before gathering her purse and suitcase and heading for the door. Maybe Colorado was the answer. Maybe she could make some difficult decisions while spending time with Ashley. She paused by the door, fighting a wave of nausea.

"I'm not going to give in to it," she told herself and opened the door. "I need to reclaim my life, and this is where I start."

Chapter 23

After nearly a week of receiving the silent treatment from Dave, Deirdre had changed her mind about turning the five hundred over to him. She'd argued with herself and decided that if he asked, she'd tell him that she was keeping it for something. Or she'd tell him it was extra money they had to pay out for canceling on the trip. She'd lie to him in whatever way she had to, because frankly, he was beginning to scare her.

Deirdre had never, in all her years of knowing Dave, seen him act in the manner he did now. He walked through his day like a zombie. At least when he was at home, in full view of her and Morgan, that was how he acted. Who knew what type of persona he took on at the office. He seemed so completely preoccupied with his case that no matter what anyone else said to him, it barely seemed to register. Deirdre even had to tell his mother, when she had called long distance from St. Louis, that Dave wasn't taking any calls. The woman had been hurt by her son's attitude, especially in light of the fact that she'd called in hopes of coordinating a get-together for Father's Day.

Deirdre had tried to smooth things over, reminding Julie Woodward that her son had canceled his own anniversary trip and suffered tremendous financial loss because of it. Her mother-in-law had been sympathetic but understandably hurt by Dave's rejection. Deirdre had ended the conversation by telling her that right now Dave wasn't the same person they knew and loved. This Dave belonged to the law firm and to the corporation he was defending, and to no one else.

By Thursday Deirdre had convinced herself that the necklace was no longer important to her. She had to use the five hundred to recoup some of the financial loss of the trip and ease Dave's burden. She reasoned that she was doing it for Dave, but in her heart she knew it was the hope that she could still win back the money that was driving her to this decision.

After watching Dave leave for work, Deirdre called a neighbor and arranged for Morgan to have a baby-sitter for the day. Morgan was excited because this meant she would get to play with her best friend, Susie. Happily humming and singing, Morgan packed her little traveling case with dolls and dresses and other mementos important to little girls her age and stood ready and waiting at the front door a full fifteen minutes before Deirdre herself was ready.

Deirdre dropped Morgan off with only a minor sense of guilt. She paid up front for the baby-sitting, subconsciously knowing the potential for danger if she kept the money with her. Driving to the casino, she actually argued with herself about what she was about to do.

"This could go very wrong," she said at the first stoplight.

"But it could go very right," she added as the light turned green.

And so the argument continued. Right up until she pulled into the parking lot and walked through the front doors to the casino.

"I won't spend anything more than the five hundred," she muttered under her breath. *The necklace meant nothing to me, so it's not like I pawned the family jewels.* But the necklace was an antique from Dave's side of the family. Morgan would have been entitled to own it one day, and perhaps she wouldn't have thought it to be so unattractive.

Deirdre cast the thoughts from her mind, determined not to let anything so negative ruin her chances at winning big. She decided her first order of business was to test the waters, so she sat down to the first dollar slot machine and gave it a try.

To her surprise and complete joy, three red sevens came up and her credits changed to show that she had won one hundred and sixty dollars. Smiling, she pressed the Cash Out button and took her silver dollars to trade for chips. Now she would move on to blackjack and make some serious money. This was all going to work out perfectly. God had surely heard her prayer.

"Deirdre, what a nice surprise," the dealer said with a winning smile.

"Hi, Jackie," Deirdre replied, instantly recognizing the young woman. "I've come to make my fortune."

"Well, I wish you the best," Jackie replied, and with that they began.

Deirdre gave no thought to the bets she made. She brazenly pushed the amount of her previously decided-upon limits and smiled when the money started rolling in. She was on top of the world. Everything was right. It didn't matter that Dave hadn't been himself in weeks. It didn't matter that she'd had to pay for a baby-sitter in order to sneak off to the casino. It was just too right to be wrong.

At least it was for the first half hour or so. As her chips began to accumulate, Deirdre began to get a little more risky. After all, big bets meant big payoffs.

"Hit me," she said, staring at the five of diamonds and the three of spades. Jackie's only visible card was a six. She dealt Deirdre the queen of hearts.

"I'll hold." Deirdre's tone was confident. She felt as though nothing could go wrong now. She would win back enough money to replace what they had lost on the trip and what she'd already gambled away, and Dave would surely feel better about everything.

Jackie finished dealing her own hand and went over. "You've sure done good for yourself today, Deirdre."

"I have, haven't I?" Deirdre said, pulling her winnings in.

"You want to increase your bet?" Jackie questioned. "I can't believe you'd waste luck like this on twenty- and thirty-dollar bets."

Deirdre nodded. "I think I've made enough of a cushion that we could safely increase it to fifty."

Jackie laughed. "I just hope you don't break the bank."

Deirdre laughed too. It felt so good to be winning.

But only two hands later, Deirdre's luck seemed to change. She lost fifty dollars and then another fifty. Feeling fearful—but not cautious—she placed a hundred-dollar bet in hopes of recouping her loss and coming back to where she'd started. She didn't have time to count the money on the table, but she knew she'd made up several hundred dollars, maybe even a thousand or more.

She felt her heart pounding as Jackie dealt her a jack of spades and a king of hearts. Jackie's single card showing was also a king—the king of diamonds. Her second card, however, was the ace of spades.

"Blackjack to the house."

Deirdre felt beads of perspiration form on her forehead. She wouldn't think about the money she'd just lost. She had to press on. And so she placed another bet and then another, and soon, instead of decreasing her bets, she increased them. But nothing was working.

With nerves that were raw from the constant anxiety of the game, Deirdre began to get a severe headache. *It's just a game,* she told herself. *You have to calm down.* But calming down was impossible when she realized she was down to twenty dollars. How could that have happened? Especially after having won one hundred and sixty right off the bat?

"I can't believe my change of luck," Deirdre said mournfully.

Jackie sympathized. "It happens to the best of us. But after so many bad hands, you're sure to start winning again."

And she did. Deirdre placed the bet and won.

"Look, I'm going to take a little break," she told Jackie. "I haven't eaten breakfast and I should get something in my stomach."

"You'll probably be in time for the lunch special," Jackie told her. "They stop that at two, but if you hurry you should make it."

Deirdre looked at her strangely. Hurry? She glanced at her watch. It was ten till two. She had lost all concept of time. Forgetting her desire for food, Deirdre made her way instead to the ladies' room and then to the ATM machine. She stood for a long time staring at the machine before making her decision to take out just a little bit of money to put with the forty she now had. But after inserting her card and punching in the code, Deirdre lost rational thought.

If I could just make one more really big win, she told herself. *Just put down one good-sized bet and walk out of here after one win.* She stared at the screen and saw the request for her to enter the amount of money she desired. The limit was three hundred dollars.

Biting her lip, Deirdre drew a deep breath and punched in the numbers. Three hundred dollars doubled would make back a little of her loss. But what if she took that six and doubled it again? Then she could make up for all the losses and come out ahead. Couldn't she?

Returning to the table, she beamed a smile at Jackie. "I feel lucky again. Let's give this a try."

Deirdre was lucky. She doubled the three hundred with a few quick flicks of Jackie's skillful wrist.

"See, I told you," Jackie encouraged.

"I know. I could feel it coming on," Deirdre replied. "Let's go one more, then I have to go home."

But two hours later and one more trip to the ATM, Deirdre had still not left the casino. She had lost it all and now felt that going home was the last thing she wanted to do. *How can I go home? I can't even remember how much money I've just lost.*

She wandered around the casino drinking the last of her soda and feeling as if she were in a daze. A bad dream. That was it! Maybe she was just dreaming.

But as she headed outside and felt the heavy humidity and saw the black, angry sky, she somehow knew that she'd not just dreamed it all. She wouldn't wake up from this nightmare until she confessed to Dave and everyone else that she was addicted to gambling.

"Deirdre! What are you doing out in this nasty weather?"

She looked up as she approached her car and saw Elaine Pruitt. Elaine was one of her former gambling buddies.

"Hi, Elaine. I just stopped by for a few quick hands of blackjack on my way home."

"Silly girl, don't you know we're in a tornado watch? They've already had a couple of touchdowns in Wyandotte County."

"Really?" Deirdre questioned, not having the faintest clue about the weather.

"Really," Elaine admitted. "I was coming to pick up Randy." Her son worked at the casino, which was one of the reasons Elaine had stopped coming with the gang. The other reason was her rather pompous announcement that she couldn't afford to spend the money anymore.

Deirdre glanced up at the sky and unlocked her car door. "Guess I'd better hurry home."

"You could just stick it out here," Elaine suggested.

"No, Morgan will be terrified. She's at the baby-sitter's."

"How is everyone?" Elaine asked, suddenly seeming to forget about the weather. "You look tired. Is everything okay?"

"I'm fine, Elaine. But obviously I haven't got time to wax nostalgic. Not with the storm bearing down on us."

Elaine appeared hurt by Deirdre's harsh words, but Deirdre didn't care. She couldn't deal with Elaine just now. Her mind could scarcely focus on what she knew she had to do.

"I'll talk to you later," she finally said and got into the car.

Racing against the storm, Deirdre dodged in and out of traffic and finally pulled into the neighbor's drive at four-thirty.

"I'm glad you came, Mommy," Morgan said fearfully. "Susie's mom said we might have to go to the basement."

Deirdre helped Morgan buckle up for the short ride home. "We might," she murmured, not bothering to try to comfort her child. How could she comfort Morgan when she was without such comfort for herself? She felt numb inside. Surely she hadn't really gambled away eleven hundred dollars. She mentally counted. She'd gone with five hundred, then took three hundred from the bank ATM and then another three hundred from her credit card. This just couldn't be happening.

She pulled into her driveway and hit the garage door opener. The door swung up, revealing Dave's car inside. She pulled in, surprised to find her husband home so early. What should she do now? Would she have to come right out and tell him about the money? Could she find a way to keep it from him?

Morgan hurried into the house, fearful of the weather and the possibility that the tornado sirens might go off at any moment. Deirdre followed at a slower pace, picking up the doll case Morgan had hastily forgotten.

"I won't say anything unless I have to," she said aloud. "Dave hasn't been talking much anyway, so hopefully he won't ask me where I've been."

She walked into the kitchen, where Morgan was being reassured by her father that everything would be all right.

"You're . . . ah . . . home early," Deirdre said in a hesitant manner.

"We won our case," Dave said, putting Morgan down. He smiled at her.

Deirdre felt her pulse quicken. He had actually smiled. Yet, even so, the emptiness remained in his eyes. "Have you heard any updates on the weather? The radio announcer made it sound like the storm is going around us," Deirdre asked.

"That's the way it looks too. They said on the television that once this clears out, that should be it for the night. They aren't expecting anything more."

Deirdre nodded. "That's good."

She turned away, unable to make real eye contact with her husband. "So what do you want to do for dinner?"

"Why don't we just have something delivered?" Dave suggested.

Deirdre swallowed hard. "I could just fix us something," she offered. "I have stuff on hand."

"Nah," Dave replied. "I've been too hard to live with and I'm trying to make amends. I know I've been griping about the money, but things are looking up."

Deirdre was awash in guilt. She could hardly stand the thought of what she'd just done. How could Dave ever forgive her, when she couldn't forgive herself? *Oh, God,* she prayed, *what have I done?*

Chapter 24

Ashley stared out the window absentmindedly. The barren flat-lands of eastern Colorado stretched out to the right of the inter-state. *Barren and empty, just like me,* she thought. "I don't know why you're bothering with me," she told her twin as they drove north on I-25.

Brook shrugged. "I figure it will do us both some good. Besides, you can't spend the rest of your life in bed."

"You try losing a child and having a hysterectomy and then tell me I shouldn't be depressed," Ashley snapped.

Brook winced and Ashley tried not to be affected by it. She couldn't figure out why Brook even cared. Ashley had been nothing but ugly and insensitive since her sister had flown in from New York three days ago. Worse still, she had no intention of changing.

"I know you're hurting, Ashley. I know that I can't begin to understand. But I love you and I care about you. I want you to get past this. I want you to remember the good things—the things you still have going for you," Brook said as she exited off the interstate.

"I wish Jack would have remembered to leave us the key," Ashley said, feeling strangely tense about stopping by the clinic.

"It won't take but a minute," Brook assured her.

They drove in silence to the clinic. Ashley felt a restlessness overcome her. Why was it that every time she was anywhere near the clinic, she felt herself coming undone? She hadn't even felt this way as they passed by the spot where the accident had been. Yet here she was, feeling almost panic-stricken.

"I won't be a minute," Brook said as she pulled into a parking place and shut off the engine to her rental car.

Ashley watched her sister's jean-clad figure disappear through the back door. Brook had put on a little bit of weight since the last time Ashley had seen her. Given the twenty pounds Ashley had dropped since her accident, she was now clearly the thinner of the two. There had been a time when that might have made Ashley smile, but now it really meant nothing at all. She would have gladly carried an extra fifty pounds if it meant that she could have her baby back safe and alive.

Movement at the far end of the parking lot caught her attention, and Ashley saw Gina Anderson walking toward a red sports car with a box in her arms. Gina had been one of Jack's nurses for about five years. The buxom redhead had always been a favorite of Ashley's. Friendly and sweet, the woman's gentle nature made her a wonderful nurse. But today, Ashley didn't want to deal with her or anyone else. People were always trying to encourage her, to offer her comfort and hope, but Ashley refused portions of either one. There was no comfort and certainly no hope.

As she watched Gina put the box in her car, Ashley could have sworn the woman was crying. For just a moment, Ashley flashed back in time. It was the day of the accident and she was standing inside the clinic, talking to Shelly. Then just as quickly as the image had come, it was gone.

"I was here," Ashley whispered to herself. "I just know I was here the day of the accident. But I don't remember it and Jack swears he didn't know about the baby until the surgeon told him I'd lost it." She tried to rationalize it all. "But if I had been here, I surely would have told Jack about the baby. We were both hoping to have more kids. He would have been happy."

She pressed her fingers to her forehead and closed her eyes. She tried to will the image to return to her mind, but as Gina drove out of the parking lot, Ashley's mind seemed to scramble. Against her better judgment, Ashley got out of the car and made her way up to the clinic door. She had a strange sense of this being important to her earlier image, but nothing would take hold in her mind.

Opening the door, Ashley made her way into the clinic. She stared around the room for a moment. Everything was pretty much as she remembered it. Mauve carpeting, coordinating wing-backed chairs. She'd helped to decorate this office, so it came as a very familiar scene to her. The walls held pastoral paintings and a delicate mauve pinstripe down cream-colored wallpaper. She remembered it all in detail. So why couldn't she remember the day of the accident?

"Ashley!" Shelly gasped as she rounded the corner and saw her for the first time since the accident.

"Shelly." Ashley spoke the name almost as if she were trying it out.

"How are you feeling? Jack has kept us updated, but we've all been so worried."

"I'm better. Thanks."

Shelly nodded and her expression was one of pure sympathy. "I'm so sorry about your loss."

"Everyone is," Ashley replied, not wanting to continue along that line of conversation. "One of my biggest frustrations, however, is not remembering the day of the accident. Maybe you could help me fill in some of the details."

"Me?" Shelly's voice almost sounded like a squeak as she continued. "I . . . I don't know what I could tell you."

Ashley frowned. The young woman was notably uncomfortable. But why? Why should it bother her to help Ashley better understand the minutes leading up to her accident?

"I remember that I came here," Ashley told her. "I thought maybe you could tell me more about what happened while I was here. How long was I here?" She pressed the question, knowing that if her bluff failed and she really hadn't been at the clinic, then Shelly might well believe her to be crazy.

"I don't remember," Shelly replied, the color draining from her face. "You weren't here very long."

So I was here! Ashley's mind began to whirl. She opened her mouth to ask Shelly something else, but Brook and Jack were coming down the hall laughing. Shelly seemed relieved and hurried back to her receptionist's desk as Jack noticed that Ashley had come into the building.

"Ashley, I'm so glad you decided to come in. I was just coming out to tell you good-bye and see you two ladies off to the mountains."

Ashley allowed his embrace, then stepped back. "Jack, I saw Gina leaving. She looked upset and she was carrying a box."

Jack cleared his throat nervously. "She resigned. She's taken a better position with another doctor. Nicci quit too, but we knew she'd be leaving once summer got here." He looked at Brook as if to explain. "Nicci's husband is an airline pilot and they relocated to California."

"That's too bad," Brook said before Ashley could comment. "I hope that doesn't leave you shorthanded."

Jack shook his head. "We use a temp service sometimes. They have a great pool of nurses and we've used several here at the clinic when things were tight. You know, like during the holidays and vacations."

Brook nodded. "Well, I suppose we'd best get on our way or we won't make it up to the house before dark."

"Let me walk you out," Jack said, pulling Ashley close. "You will call me when you get up there, right?"

Ashley nodded and watched her sister lead the way back out to the car. She longed to get away from Jack and everything, but at the same time she longed to ask him the question that was burning in her mind. Had she seen him the day of the accident? Now that she knew she'd been at the clinic, it made much more sense as to why she was heading south on the interstate.

Brook seemed completely happy to give Ashley and Jack a moment alone. She went and opened the trunk to pull out a jacket.

"Jack," Ashley said slowly, trying to think of the right words, "I think some of my memory is coming back."

His expression remained fixed, but instead of replying, he quickly kissed her. "In time it will come back or it won't. You don't have to worry or try to force it."

Ashley instantly felt as if something was wrong. Jack seemed very agitated by her announcement. She could swear she had felt him tremble. "I know I was here the day of the accident."

Jack laughed nervously. "No, you weren't here. I would know if you'd been here. It's probably just your imagination working over-time. Give it a rest. Go to the cabin and try to relax. You've been so depressed and discouraged—I'm sure this will be just the thing to help you recover."

He was talking ninety miles a minute and shifting from foot to foot as if the pavement had suddenly grown too hot. She knew this side of Jack. This was the Jack who had just been cornered to help with a project at the country club. This was the Jack who had to make small talk with the elders at church.

Ashley allowed him to walk her to the car and help her with the door. She knew something was terribly wrong. But what was it?

"You two have fun," Jack said as Ashley slowly pulled her seat belt across her body.

"We will, Jack," Brook replied and started the car. "We'll call when we get up there."

"Please don't forget."

He kissed Ashley again, then closed the door. Standing back away from the car, Jack waved and smiled broadly. *He's lying to me,* Ashley thought to herself. She gave a little wave, then turned away. *Why is he lying about my being here?*

Chapter 25

Estes Park was in the height of its tourist season. Memorial Day weekend always signaled the rush of travelers from as far away as Asia and Europe, and now as they entered the summer holidays, tourists packed into the little town like they were on a holy pilgrimage. The highway traffic barely moved as numerous vehicles competed for their coveted lanes. Everywhere they looked, people seemed to stream out from buildings and street corners, though most were oblivious to the growing numbers who joined their parade.

"Is it always this busy?" Brook questioned.

"Just in the summer," Ashley replied.

Brook nodded and smiled. "I can see why. This is gorgeous scenery. Just looking at those peaks makes me want to don hiking gear and take off on some great trek across the country."

Ashley said nothing and Brook began to worry. Her sister had barely said two words as they'd made their way up Highway 36. She had finally given up making one-sided conversation about the time they passed the town of Lyons.

"Do you want me to stop at the store first or just go on up to the cabin?" Brook asked.

"I don't feel up to going grocery shopping, if you don't mind," Ashley replied.

"That's fine. I can do the shopping. Jack told me how to get to your place, but I think I'm a little turned around," she said as she pulled up to a stoplight.

"Turn there," Ashley said, pointing. "Just follow that up and around and I'll tell you where to go once we get past the shopping center."

Brook nodded. At least Ashley was talking again. She maneuvered through the traffic and made her way just as Ashley had instructed. At Devil's Gulch Road, Ashley had her make a right turn.

"Oh, Ash, I can see why you love it up here. I feel so at home. What a wonderful place to live."

"I suppose so," Ashley replied, then said nothing more until they neared her driveway. "That's our place. Just turn in here."

Brook stared in stunned silence at the massive two-story home. "You call this a cabin?"

Ashley shrugged. "I suppose it is a bit big."

"I figured you had some little cracker-box place tucked into the hills. Ashley, this is a palace."

Brook got out of the car, completely awestruck. The view was incredible. In the west, the tallest snowy peaks in Rocky Mountain National Park glowed in the lingering sunlight as dusk descended on the area.

"I think I'm in love," Brook said softly, hoping Ashley hadn't heard her. Her sister had pretty much given up on life and there was no sense rubbing in her own joy at the setting. With a sigh, Brook went to open the trunk as Ashley finally got out of the car.

"I'll open up the house, then come back and help with the bags," Ashley told her.

"Nothing doing. Jack said you aren't to lift anything at all and no stairs. Doctor's orders."

Ashley shrugged. "That'll leave you doing all the work."

"I don't mind," Brook said, trying to reassure her sister. "I'm just so glad to have this break in my routine. Don't you understand? I need to spend this time with you."

Ashley's eyes met Brook's, and for the tiniest moment she felt as if she had finally connected to Ashley. But as wonderful as that would have normally been, the intensity of Ashley's pain seemed to come over Brook like an avalanche.

Ashley quickly turned away and walked up the path to the house while Brook wondered how in the world she could ever help her sister recover from this tragic time. Perhaps it was as Grammy had always said—there were some things folks couldn't fix. God was the one who would have to be their help.

Hours later, when the clock chimed ten and the shopping had been tended to and the call to Jack made, Brook and Ashley sat before a flickering fire drinking flavored coffee. Brook longed to say something to draw Ashley out, but she feared hurting her sister. It would be cruel to add to her pain by demanding answers. Wouldn't it?

But the more Brook tried to ignore her feelings, the more compelled she was to carry through with her thoughts.

"Ashley, I want you to stop this now," she said without even thinking about the words.

Ashley's head snapped up quickly and her expression betrayed her surprise. "Stop what?"

"Stop shutting me out," Brook said, putting her coffee mug down. "You've been shutting me out since the accident. I've tried to share in this with you, but you won't let me. Why is that? What have I done to make you push me away?"

Ashley paled and she looked back to the fire rather quickly. "I don't want to talk about it."

"Well, I do," Brook said, refusing to give up. "We used to share our thoughts constantly. We could practically read each other's minds. But now I know you're putting up barriers between us. I can sense it in more ways than one and I don't like it. I'm your twin sister. We agreed long ago that in spite of Grammy's love, we would be closer to each other than to anyone else on earth. You can't push me away without breaking that vow."

Ashley shook her head, and when she looked back to where Brook sat, she had tears in her eyes. "I don't want you to share this," she whispered in a barely audible voice. "It's too painful."

"Maybe so," Brook said, sliding off the couch to sit beside Ashley on the floor, "but you'd share my pain, wouldn't you? Won't you? I know it's probably unthinkable for me to ask that, but I had hoped to come here and take some answers home with me. Not just answers about you—but answers about me."

Ashley wiped at her tears. "I just can't do this anymore."

"Do what?"

"Bear this pain. Nothing is right."

Brook nodded. "The baby."

"The baby is only part of it," Ashley finally admitted. "I'm so very sad, Brook. If I let you be a part of that, you would be overwhelmed. I can't imagine anyone living through this."

"You're still alive, so there's proof that a person can survive."

"I'm not surviving, Brook. I'm only existing . . . and barely doing that." Ashley stared into the flames. "I thought I had everything. The perfect house. The perfect life. The perfect marriage."

"You'll feel that way again. You just have to give yourself time to heal."

"It's more than that," Ashley replied sadly. "I can't explain it, but it's more."

"Is it because you can't have more kids?"

"Partially," Ashley answered honestly. "But there's more."

"What is it?" Brook lightly touched her sister's shoulder. "Please tell me. You know I won't say anything to anyone else unless you want me to."

Ashley drew a ragged breath and a sob escaped her throat. "He lied to me," she barely uttered.

"Who lied?" Brook asked.

"Jack."

"Jack lied to you?" Brook shook her head in confusion. What could Jack have possibly done to Ashley at this point? "What did he lie about?"

Ashley shrugged and wiped furiously at her tears. "I'm not even totally sure." Her voice broke and she gave a harsh little laugh. "I can't remember."

Brook felt completely confused. "Then how do you know he's lying?"

"Because I caught him in part of it today."

"Part of it? What did he say today that was a lie?"

Ashley turned to look at Brook. "He told me I wasn't in the office on the day of the accident."

"And that was a lie? How can you be sure?" But even as Brook questioned her sister, she remembered Jack having said something to her shortly after the accident. Something about Ashley having been on her way home from seeing him at the clinic.

"Shelly told me I was there."

"I just remembered something," Brook said, knowing that she couldn't keep it from her sister. "Jack told me you were on your way home from seeing him at the clinic when the accident took place."

"See," Ashley said, her voice nearly pleading. "See, I told you. When we pulled into the parking lot at the clinic, I felt strongly that something had happened there. I just knew that I had been there the day of the accident. It's not the first time it's happened. Jack had me at the clinic once before. It was Memorial Day weekend and we were headed up here. I felt it then too."

"Do you ever actually remember anything? Anything specific?" Brook questioned, hoping that by talking about it, her sister might release some of her grief.

"No, not really," Ashley replied. "But now I'm troubled by more than not remembering. Now I know that Jack doesn't want me to remember for some reason, and that's what really scares me. What if I went there and told him about the baby and he wasn't happy? What if he said something mean and we argued?"

"I can't imagine Jack being that way, Ashley. After all, you told me he wanted another child."

"I thought he did, but maybe I misread him. Maybe he changed his mind, and when I came to tell him, we fought about it."

"But surely someone else would have overheard you fighting."

"Maybe they did. Shelly looked as though I'd just announced plans to bomb the place when I mentioned knowing that I'd been there on the day of the accident."

Brook shook her head. "You're absolutely sure that she was upset?"

"She lost the color in her face. She stammered and seemed *very* upset by the topic."

"Did she give you any real details?"

Ashley turned back to the fire. "No. You and Jack came down the hall about that time."

Brook remembered the moment. "She did seem upset."

Silently, Ashley nodded her head. "I know there is something more going on. I just can't figure out what it is and it's driving me insane. This sadness is threatening to eat me alive, and I have to find a way to exorcise myself of its control."

Brook closed the rest of the distance and embraced Ashley tenderly. "I'll help you figure it out. I promise to stay and help you as long as you want me here."

"I wish you never had to leave," Ashley said, putting her head on Brook's shoulder. "You're the only one I can trust to understand. The only one who won't think I'm crazy."

Brook hugged her tightly and knew in that moment that if Ashley needed her to stay forever, she would easily give up her career in New York. There had to be a way to break through the pain and veiled mystery of the accident. There had to be a way to release Ashley from the hold of her demons.

"I won't let you go through this alone," Brook whispered.

Chapter **26**

Mattie stared down at the packet of letters from Mavis. What secrets would be unleashed by this Pandora's box? What could Rachelle have finally decided needed to be said before she could die? The thought of opening each one and reading them before giving them over to the girls crossed Mattie's mind.

As she thought of the girls, Mattie felt overwhelmed with sorrow. She had never known such stubbornness in all of her life. When the girls were little, they had always been a handful. But now, as adults, they were almost impossible. Connie had closed her heart to her siblings, and everyone else seemed to accept it without challenge. Deirdre hardly acted like herself these days, and Mattie couldn't help but fear something was horribly wrong in her life. Maybe the problems in her marriage had escalated and she didn't want Mattie to know.

For nearly two days now, Mattie had tried to talk to Erica, Deirdre, and Connie by telephone. It was her hope to see the girls forgive one another and work through their problems, but now after talking to a decidedly bitter Erica, Mattie had reached her limit of tolerance. Erica felt it was Connie's place to apologize, then mentioned that she'd made the mistake of trying to explain the situation to Brook. When Mattie asked if Brook offered any suggestions, Erica had begrudgingly admitted that Brook thought the entire matter was nonsense. Without saying so, Mattie agreed. Enough was enough.

Mattie figured if that's the way they wanted it—if they couldn't see what they were doing to themselves—then maybe it was time she showed them. She threw the packet of letters onto the kitchen table and decided to get down to business.

With determination and purpose, Mattie decided to implement a plan she'd considered for some time. She headed first to the dining room, where she cleared the table of its ornate candlestick holders and brocade table runner. Then, taking out a plastic matting that she'd had cut for this table, Mattie covered the beautiful mahogany wood. Next, she pushed the chairs back against the wall and went to her sewing room.

Taking her rotary cutter, ruler, and pins, Mattie moved through the house with one goal. If the girls refused to see the situation for what it was, Mattie could think of only one way to prove her point.

Entering the sewing room, Mattie looked at the award-winning quilt and paused to pray. "Lord, I just want them to understand the importance of being together—of being whole. I think this is something you've been showing me for some time, and now I feel that the time has come for action. Please help them to see and understand. Please let them come back—if not to me, then to each other."

At eight-thirty that evening, it was still light enough to sit in the gazebo and work on her project. Mattie had turned on the light, nevertheless, knowing that her eyes didn't see quite as well as they used to. As the sun spilled into a hazy blend of colors on the horizon, Mattie worked with an inspired diligence. She finished the first side of her fourth wall hanging just as Harry came whistling down the walkway.

"Mattie? You down here?" he called.

"I'm in the gazebo," she replied. "I thought you might row over this evening. I guess you decided to drive instead."

Harry walked up the steps of the enclosure and took off his ball cap. "I was just too tired. It's been a busy week." He sat down opposite Mattie at the picnic table and motioned to her project. "That looks mighty familiar. Similar pattern to that quilt you won all those prizes with, isn't it?"

"It's not just similar, Harry. It is the quilt. I've cut it apart," she said, trying to keep her voice even.

Harry looked confused. "Why would you do that? I heard some-one offered you twenty thousand for that quilt."

"They did," Mattie said, putting her sewing down for a moment. She touched the piece fondly. "I'm doing this for the girls."

"I think it's pretty," he commented, seeming at a loss for words. "But I liked it better when it was all together."

"I did too," Mattie said with a smile. "And that's the point." She picked up the piece again, feeling no need to explain any further.

Harry seemed to sense Mattie's mood and stared off at the lake. June bugs buzzed at the bulb overhead, and off in the distance a choir of bullfrogs had begun their nightly chorus. Harry sighed and after the third time, Mattie couldn't help but ask him what was wrong.

"Wrong? I didn't say anything was wrong," Harry replied.

"You didn't have to." Mattie put the sewing down once again. "Don't you think after all these years that I know when you're upset about something? Do you want to come clean with me or do I need to play twenty questions?"

"No need for games," Harry answered. "I guess I'm just sort of rattled about the wedding plans."

"How so?"

He shrugged. "Just seems like a lot of fuss for a single event. And try as I might, I can't get excited about it."

Mattie heard the resignation in his voice—the same resignation that edged his conversation every time mention was made of his upcoming marriage to Sarah Hooper.

"Harry," she began, "this is a very important part of your future. Maybe the most important act you'll make as an adult."

"It doesn't feel that way to me," Harry said, shaking his head. "It just feels like a big . . ." His voice went silent.

"Mistake?" Mattie questioned.

He looked at her in stunned silence. Then finally, after what seemed to be an eternity, he nodded. "I guess it does."

"How long have you been feeling this way?" Mattie asked.

"I guess about the time Rachelle died," Harry admitted.

Mattie nodded. "About the same time the girls came home."

"I suppose."

"I think you more than suppose, Harry. Do your feelings have anything to do with seeing Ashley again? Are you still in love with her?"

"Nah, I don't think Ashley and I knew what love really was back then," Harry admitted. "I think I was already thinking about this long before they showed up. But after talking with . . ." His voice faded.

"Did one of them help you see things more clearly?" Mattie asked with a curious interest.

"I guess I'd have to say that Connie caught my attention."

"Connie?"

Harry grinned rather sheepishly. "I know what you're thinking. Leave it to me to be intrigued by the biggest challenge."

"You can't go after anyone until you deal with Sarah."

He nodded. "I know. And it's not fair for her to go on making plans for a wedding that shouldn't be taking place."

Mattie reached across the table. "Harry, you have to come clean with her right away. She'll be hurt, but it'll just get worse if you let this thing stretch on. The closer it gets to the wedding date, the harder it will be."

"It's just that I'm not sure what to do. How can I explain to her it's just not right for me?"

"Maybe you could start by telling her *why* it's not right. Tell her how you feel—or rather, don't feel. No woman should want to marry a man who doesn't love her."

Harry bowed his head. "I really tried to love her. I thought long and hard about it. I knew I wasn't getting any younger and I wanted to marry and have a family. I guess God just kept hounding me—showing me it wasn't right, that I didn't truly love her. She's a very nice woman, but she's too much like Ashley. She wants things I can't possibly give her."

"Then just tell her that," Mattie said softly. "She may not understand, but she'll be grateful in the long run."

"I guess you're right. It's been weighing on me for a long time. I just hope you know that Connie didn't cause any of this. I felt this way before she came back to the farm. It's just that when I saw her and talked with her, there was a spark of something that was clearly missing in my life with Sarah. I knew that I couldn't go ahead with the wedding."

Mattie carefully put away her sewing and got to her feet. "Go home, Harry. Go home and call Sarah. Tell her you need to talk to her. Don't put it off. And whatever you do, don't break the news to her over the phone, and don't take her anywhere. Just meet up with her at her house and sit and talk. That way, when you're done, you can leave and she will have the comfort of home."

Harry followed Mattie's example and stood. He looked long-ingly across the lake. "I wish it would just go away," he said, sound-ing very much like he had when his mother had taken sick.

"I know you do, Harry. But wishing won't make it so. Pray about it. Pray and then trust God to help you get through it. It won't be easy, but it will be for the best."

His head was bent, intent upon the ball cap he turned round and round in his hands. Finally he nodded. "Guess I'll be going."

"You call me if you want to talk," Mattie said as he moved past her.

He reached up to help her down the steps. "I will, Mattie. Thanks for understanding."

———————

Harry picked up the telephone and dialed Sarah's number. Mattie was right. He'd let this whole thing go on for far too long. Sarah deserved the truth, and Harry needed to be free from guilt—guilt of keeping Sarah hanging on when he knew he didn't love her, and guilt of caring for another woman and allowing her to consume his thoughts when he was engaged to Sarah.

"Sarah, it's Harry," he said when she answered the phone.

"I need to come over for a few minutes." Pause. "Yeah, I know it's getting late, but it's important that we talk now."

Chapter 27

"Are you sure you want to stay?" Brook asked Ashley.

"I can't go back to Denver. Not knowing that Jack is lying to me. Not remembering what really happened. Jack's already packed the boys off to church camp, and there's no reason for me to be there."

"No reason but your marriage," Brook replied.

Ashley hugged her arms, stroking her pink cashmere sweater. "I just can't go back yet."

Brook studied her for a moment, then nodded. At least Ashley was talking openly, which was more than she'd done in the beginning of their stay. Brook could honestly say that Ashley looked better physically during the week they'd spent together, and that she even sounded better mentally and emotionally. But there was still a hardness to her that frightened Brook.

"What about groceries and anything else you need? You won't even have a car here," Brook commented.

"The neighbors are good friends. They'll pitch in if I need something. Besides, once Jack knows I'm not coming back for a while, he'll no doubt hightail it up here. I'll decide then what I need. Who knows? Maybe I'll buy a new car since the other one was totaled."

Brook shook her head. "I still feel bad about just leaving you here."

"And I feel bad because we've hardly had time to discuss your problems," Ashley said, surprising Brook. "Why don't we talk about you while we still have a chance? You won't have to leave for the airport for at least another hour."

Brook smiled. "I came here to help you."

"I seem to remember you saying something about needing this trip to sort your own thoughts out. Were you able to?"

Brook walked to the window and looked out on the grandeur. For the first time she realized it was going to be very hard to leave it all behind. "I don't know if I sorted them out or if I just stacked them on a back burner. I've enjoyed the break, that's for sure."

"That's not a real answer," Ashley replied.

Brook turned and watched as Ashley made her way to the bed. Sitting down rather stiffly, Ashley folded her hands together. It was easy to recognize her sister's determination. "I don't suppose," Brook said lightly, "that you'd like to just let this drop?"

"Not a chance. I know I've been wrapped up inside myself. I know that I'll go back to being consumed with grief and misery and the struggle to regain my memory, but right now I want to help you."

Brook smiled. "I wish you could. But the one thing I need, you can't give."

"And what's that?"

"Time."

Ashley nodded. "You're right. I can't give you that."

"It's just not fair," Brook said, allowing herself to give in to Ashley's questioning. Maybe it would actually be good for Ashley to have something else to focus on for a while. Even for a short time.

She sat down in the window seat. "I have some very real choices to make, and it won't be much longer before I'll have to deal with them head on. Maybe even as early as my return to New York. My manager was furious with me for coming out here. I canceled on a big modeling assignment and she went ballistic."

"You did that for me?"

Brook heard the guilty tone in Ashley's voice. "I did it for both of us. I needed this and the thought of going back is probably one of the hardest things I've had to face since your accident. I don't want to go back."

"Then don't," Ashley said as though it were that simple.

Brook smiled. "You make it sound easy."

"Well, I guess I just don't see that it should be that hard." Ashley met her twin's gaze without so much as blinking. "The accident taught me that we have precious little time on this earth. What if you go back to New York and you're miserable and then someone comes along and kills you next week or you find out you're dying of some horrible disease? There you'd be. You would have wasted all this time doing something you hate."

Brook knew she was right. "But I don't know what else to do. I have no real skills—no one would hire me."

"So hire yourself," Ashley replied. "You've surely put aside a good nest egg. Buy yourself a business—something you like."

"A business?" Brook questioned. She'd never given any serious thought to such an idea. "What kind of business?"

Ashley shrugged. "What kind of business would make you happy? A restaurant? A florist shop? A clothing store? Just give it some thought."

"But even if I had something like that in mind," Brook replied, feeling a bit of excitement, "where would I do this? I can't stand New York."

"So come here or go back to Council Grove or Kansas City. The sky's the limit. Nobody says you have to settle in any particular place. Think of some place where you were truly happy and go there."

"I was happy on the farm with Grammy," Brook replied. "But I suppose thirty-year-olds aren't supposed to run away *to* home."

"Why not? If that makes you happy, I know Grammy would take you back in a heartbeat. Maybe you and Harry could fall in love."

Brook laughed and shook her head. "Harry and I would end up in abject despair. We are about as unsuited to each other as you two were. I see Harry as a big-brother type—nothing else."

"You see every man that way."

"That's not true," Brook replied. "I see every man as a threat."

Ashley smiled ever so slightly. It did Brook good to see this, even if the smile was in regard to something she'd said. "You don't believe me?" Brook questioned.

"Oh, I believe you," Ashley replied. "I just think we're finally getting to the bigger problem. You're lonely. You have no one to care for you. No one to know if you're late coming home. No one to meet you at the end of the day."

Brook felt her stomach tighten. She hadn't thrown up since she'd left New York, and she'd vowed she wasn't about to give in to those feelings of panic and anxiety. But Ashley's words had hit the nail squarely on the head.

"I *am* lonely. I can't begin to tell you how much I've enjoyed our time together simply from a selfish need for companionship."

Ashley nodded. "I know. I probably would never have agreed to come otherwise."

"Why do you say that?" Brook questioned.

"When you showed up on my doorstep with the idea of this ludicrous scheme to come to Estes, I know I dug my heels in and refused to come at first. But I could see in your eyes your confusion and pain, and I knew I couldn't allow you to return to New York without somehow first dealing with your problems. The only trouble was, I didn't expect the revelation of finding out that Jack is lying to me about the accident. I'm afraid that consumed more of my time than I had intended."

"I'm so sorry this has happened to you."

"Don't be," Ashley replied. "It'll all come together in due time. But I'm begging you for a promise. No, two promises."

Brook felt her mouth go dry. "Promises?"

"Yes."

"What kind of promises?"

"You know, the kind where I ask you to do something and you agree to do it."

Brook laughed nervously. "Are you playing on my sympathy? Do you think just because I nearly lost you that I'll be so grateful to have you safe and alive that I'll just up and agree to any old thing?"

Ashley smiled again and looked down at her hands. "Maybe I am being pushy in this instance, but I wouldn't do it if I didn't feel it was important."

Brook realized there would be no getting out of at least hearing Ashley's request. "Okay, so what are the promises you want me to make?"

"First of all, and we discussed this long ago at Grammy's, I want your word that the next time someone nice comes into your life, you'll give him a chance. Of course, I don't mean that you have to date someone you're genuinely turned off by, but neither do I want to hear about how you went running in the opposite direction when a stranger smiled at you from across the room."

"You don't ask for much," Brook replied softly. There were tears in her eyes, and it was hard to see her twin through the blur.

"I wouldn't ask if I didn't think it was important."

"I know. I just don't know if I can do what you ask. I'm afraid."

"I know you are," Ashley said, getting up and going to sit beside Brook. "I am too. But that leads me to the second promise. I want you to promise me that you'll be accountable to me in regard to your feelings. That you'll let me help you deal with the loneliness and the fear you have stashed up inside. In turn, I promise to make myself accountable to you. To allow you to help me deal with this painful journey of regaining my memory, and of letting go of that which I cannot change."

"You'd do that?" Brook asked, barely able to speak.

"Haven't we always done that in the past?" Ashley questioned. "We're two sides of the same coin. Both of us driven by so many of the same things. Rachelle influenced us more than we ever wanted to admit, but now that she's gone and now that I know how quickly life is stolen from us, I can let that part of my life go. At least I think I can. Maybe I'm just fooling myself, but I'd like to try."

Brook nodded. "Me too."

"So will you promise?"

Brook wiped her eyes with the back of her hand. "I'll try." She reached over to embrace Ashley. "I'll try my hardest."

Ashley held on tightly to Brook. "You'll always have a place wherever I am. Don't forget that. No matter what happens in New York—you're always welcome to stay with me."

"I appreciate that," Brook said, pulling back, "but I have to get my act together. Thirty seems a very appropriate age to stop blaming my miseries on my parents and to move ahead with a more meaningful life. My spirit is sorely empty, and Grammy would say I need to feed on the Word."

Ashley smiled. "Yes, she would. Maybe that's the only kind of food that will really help us now."

Mattie looked at the five brown paper parcels on the table. Inside each one was the individual quilted wall hanging from her and a letter from Rachelle. On the outside, each was addressed to one of her granddaughters.

She would mail them today. Five separate pieces going to five separate addresses. She had decided against putting any note inside with the hangings. She didn't feel the need to explain herself. Would they understand? Would they know what it meant—what she was trying to say to them?

She looked upward. "It's in your hands," she whispered. "There's nothing more I can do but pray that they will listen to the message in these pieces—better still, that they will listen to you, Lord. It's going to take a miracle—maybe five of them—to pull this family back together, Father, but that's the business you're in. I trust it's not too late."

Gathering up the packages, Mattie headed out of the house and climbed into the minivan. God was never too late nor too early, her mother used to say. And in all of her years of life, Mattie knew it to be true. Sometimes it seemed like God had forgotten or that He had let things go wrong for too long, but it always came together in perfect order, and Mattie was left to witness how the pieces fit back together like a jigsaw puzzle or a perfectly ordered quilt.

If anyone was in the business of mending broken hearts—hearts hanging by nothing more than a thread, it would be the loving Father who had created them. *Now,* Mattie thought with a smile, *if only I can remember to keep my hands off long enough to let God work it out.*

Chapter 28

Brook went home to a cold, empty apartment. The only living thing, a potted plant that she'd been given by her next-door neighbor, had wilted in her absence. It wasn't the first time she'd neglected the poor thing. Pushing her suitcases to one side, Brook juggled the armload of mail she'd picked up from the apartment superintendent. There wasn't too much to worry about. Some pieces of junk mail, a few bills, and a rather bulky package from Grammy.

Deciding to leave the best for last, Brook tossed the junk mail aside without a second glance and opened her bills. She owed the telephone company an exorbitant amount—nothing new about that. Then the thick white envelope beneath her credit card bill caught her attention. She pulled it out and noticed it was stamped with the address of her financial planner. Opening it, she was stunned. Her investments had paid off in a big way. Why hadn't she given this much thought before? She had always taken a good portion of her salary and invested it. She'd presumed with the market in such flux that she'd probably lost a good amount of her hard-earned money, but apparently her investor was wise enough to prevent a heavy loss. She'd have to give the man her thanks.

"This is incredible," she whispered and continued to double-check the figures to make certain she understood their meaning. With the amount reflected there, Brook quickly realized that she could probably take Ashley's advice and open a business of her own. Truth be told, with the totals she saw on the statement, she could probably retire. She wouldn't be able to stay in New York, but she could easily go back to Kansas and live on the interest of her investments. After all, what did she really need other than a roof over her head and food on the table?

The letter changed everything, and for a moment Brook felt some of her burden lift. Was this an answer to her prayers? She had spent most of the plane trip home feigning sleep and praying. It'd been such a long time since she'd really and truly made time to talk to God that she'd found the plane preparing to land before she'd run out of things to discuss. She'd asked for answers, for direction and purpose. She'd prayed for clearly marked paths and choices so evident that she'd have no chance of missing them.

"Well, Brook," she said aloud, "your biggest worry was financial and that seems to be under control."

So why didn't she feel better? Why did she still feel empty?

She looked around the room, letting the paper slip from her fingers. There was nothing here to keep her interest. Nothing of value, save a few precious pieces: the quilt on her quilt stand—a present from Grammy on her eighteenth birthday; several framed pictures of her sisters and Grammy; a porcelain vase given to her by Ashley. But besides these few things, Brook felt she could easily walk out the door and leave the rest behind.

Maybe that was the answer.

She spied Grammy's package and smiled. If she couldn't come home to someone she loved, then the next best thing had to be coming home to a package from Grammy. She pushed the papers aside and took up the parcel. Opening it slowly, Brook savored the moment. What would it be? What had Grammy designed this time? Perhaps it was a sewing project or even some of her homemade goodies. Grammy was known to do that from time to time.

Brook lifted the lid off the box and pushed aside the white tissue paper. Lovingly, she lifted the wall hanging and smiled. The piece looked familiar, however, and Brook tried to think where she'd seen the design before. Six perfectly positioned circles intertwined with each other to make the center piece. Of course! It was a replica of the quilt Grammy had made from their clothes. The one that someone had offered to buy for some outrageous amount of money.

Picking up the portable phone, Brook dialed Mattie to thank her for the piece. It felt good to have a reason to call her grandmother, and it helped to ease the loneliness of coming back to New York City.

"Grammy? It's Brook."

"Hello, sweetheart. How are you? Are you back home?"

"Yes. I flew out of Denver this afternoon."

"How did things go with your sister?"

Brook thought about her reply for a moment and moved to the window to look out on the lights of the city. "I think they went well. Ashley is still not herself, but she's better."

"It'll take time," Mattie encouraged.

"I know you're right, but I miss the old Ashley."

"What do you mean?"

"Ashley used to be so self-confident. I depended on that more than I realized. I guess, even though I knew she was the one with the tragedy in her life, I went to her hoping to draw from her strength."

"And you found that she had no strength to draw on?"

Brook nodded, even though she knew Mattie couldn't see her. "Yes. That's it exactly. It really made me think."

"About what?"

"About how I've wasted a good portion of my life. About how unhappy I am. My life just seems so meaningless."

"But it's not," Mattie told her.

Brook could imagine Mattie's worried expression and hurried to explain her statement. "I don't really think life is meaningless—it just seems the things I've chosen to involve myself in are rather meaningless."

"Then you should make some changes."

"My thought exactly," Brook replied. "I have lived my life so far outside of what you taught me was right. I've looked to things and people to make me happy, and somewhere along the way I relegated God to some faraway place. A place where I knew He'd be, but only if I really, really had to find Him."

"And has that time come?" Mattie questioned, and Brook could hear the hopefulness in Mattie's tone.

"I think so," Brook replied. "I really prayed for the first time in a long time while coming home on the plane."

"And did you come to any conclusions?"

Brook smiled. "Not clear-cut. Not yet. I guess one of the things I was so troubled over was that I made Ashley some promises. Promises that I have no idea of how to keep. In fact, I know that without help, I can't keep them."

Mattie laughed softly. "Reminds me of the time when you girls were about ten and we were having a surprise birthday party for Erica. Do you remember?"

"How could I forget?" Brook replied. "I'm the one who ruined the surprise."

"I made you all promise not to talk about the party—not even to each other. I gave you all special projects and—"

"And I decided it wouldn't hurt to talk things over with Ashley. After all, she was a part of the plan."

Mattie chuckled again. "Only problem was, Erica overheard you, which I knew would be the case if you talked amongst yourselves."

"Guess I've never been good with promises."

"Your guilt consumed you. You were miserable for days."

"I remember," Brook said, staring out at the city skyline without truly seeing it. Her mind flashed back to seeing herself sitting in complete dejection in her bedroom back on the farm. "I felt so horrible for having disappointed you. That was what bothered me the most. Erica still had fun at the party, but I'd let you down."

"So you do remember."

"I remember the only thing that made any sense was to go to you and beg for forgiveness. I knew that I had to set things right. Your forgiveness and the way you held me in your arms and told me that you still loved me . . . well, it was all that I needed. It set me free."

"Forgiveness is that way," Grammy said softly. "It takes the burden of responsibility from your shoulders and shares it with the one who does the forgiving. Then the weight isn't so heavy to bear. And with God, He doesn't even make you continue to carry the load. He takes it all and throws it as far as the east is from the west."

Brook smiled. "I remember asking you how far that was and you told me that it was so far that I could walk for all my life and never come to the place where the two came together."

"Forgiveness is often the only place you can start," Mattie told her granddaughter. "Even when the other person is dead wrong. Even when the pain is still fresh."

"Even when the past has scarred the future?" Brook questioned, already knowing the answer.

"Especially then."

Brook knew Mattie understood that her words were about Rachelle. Neither one had to say anything more. Walking back to the table, Brook spied the wall hanging.

"Oh, I almost forgot. I called because I got your present."

"My present?"

"The wall hanging. Grammy, it's so beautiful. You didn't put in a note, so I thought I would call and see what this is all about."

"I figured it spoke for itself."

"How so?"

"It's one-sixth of the Piece Work quilt. Your sisters each have a portion and I have the sixth piece."

"I see," Brook said. In the pit of her stomach she felt a nagging ache. She couldn't believe Mattie had torn the quilt apart.

"Oh, Brook," Mattie suddenly said, "Harry's just come to the door. I'm going to have to go for now. I love you, though, and I'm glad you called. By the way, there was something else in that package. The letter from your mother I told you about is in there as well."

"I didn't see a letter," Brook said, going back to the package wrapping. There in the bottom of the box was the envelope. "Oh, here it is."

"I'll talk to you more later, sweetheart."

"I love you, Grammy," Brook said, staring at the unopened

envelope. Her hand trembled ever so slightly as she hung up the phone.

She reached for the letter and opened it very slowly. Why had Rachelle chosen to speak to her now? What could she possibly say that would matter—that would make a difference for the future? Sitting down, Brook began to read.

> *To my daughter Brook,*
>
> *People always thought it strange that I had so many children when I didn't intend to be a mother to them. The truth is, I always intended to be a mother, but life got in the way. I realized very quickly that I couldn't be for you what you needed me to be. I felt inadequate to the task. People often ask me which movie role was the hardest, but the hardest role was never a part of any motion picture. It was being mother to five girls and knowing I had completely failed at the task.*
>
> *You may wonder why I'm writing this now—why I'm bothering you with details you no doubt care very little about. Well, the truth is, as you know by now, I intend to take my life. I can live no longer with the guilt I've carried all these years. The guilt of knowing I gave birth to five children and then walked away. But at the very center of my actions was a fear I could never overcome. To love you—to cling to you and need you—would have meant facing the possibility of losing you. Losing you like I had lost my father and brother—losing you like I lost your father. Brook, I could never have survived that pain. Call me a coward, for that is true enough, but try to understand that the idea of never loving someone again wasn't nearly as frightening as loving them only to lose them. So when you think of me—if you think of me—try to forgive my fears. They never protected me at all. I still loved you and it still hurts.*
>
> *Rachelle*

Erica returned to Kansas City from Baltimore, completely convinced that she'd just given the audition of her life. Her performance had been flawless, and unless the conductor and panel simply didn't care for her technique, she felt confident they would give her the job.

Whistling a tune she'd played at the audition, Erica picked up her mail and noticed the package from Grammy. Immediately she ripped away the brown paper and opened the gift. Pulling out the quilted wall hanging, Erica smiled. Grammy was always so thoughtful, spending her time and energy making them gifts. What a precious legacy she was leaving behind her.

The telephone rang, interrupting the silence. Reluctantly, she put down the piece and went to answer the phone.

"Hello?"

"Erica, it's Brook."

She felt an immediate sense of concern. The last conversation she'd had with Brook hadn't exactly gone very well. "Hello."

"I just got back from seeing Ashley in Denver."

"How is she?"

"Better physically, but still hurting emotionally."

"Well, life seems to do that to folks," Erica replied, instantly regretting her flippant response.

"Are you doing okay?" Brook questioned.

"Sure. Why do you ask?"

"You don't sound okay. You sound upset. Are you still mad at me?"

Erica felt her resolve give way. "I suppose I'm still smarting from the dressing down you gave me. But never mind that. I came home from having an audition in Baltimore and found the neatest present from Grammy."

"I know. I have one too."

"It looks just like that prizewinning quilt of hers," Erica said in rapid order. The last thing she wanted to do was get into a heavy discussion on feelings and problems with her older sister.

"It doesn't just look like it," Brook replied. "That wall hanging is your part of the original quilt."

"No way! That quilt was worth a small fortune. Besides, Grammy said she was going to keep it to remind her of her memories of us at home and the days gone by."

"I just talked to Grammy," Brook admitted. "She divided the quilt and sent us each one-sixth—our sixth."

Erica looked at the piece again and felt a tingling sensation run up her spine. "Well, so what if it is? Apparently she changed her mind about what she wanted to do with the piece. I think it's a wonderful present."

"I don't think it's intended to be a present," Brook replied. "Grammy didn't say it in so many words, but I think she's trying to show us something important here."

As Brook paused, Erica tried to think of what to say. She didn't like to think that Grammy had divided her beautiful quilt. The quilt's importance to Grammy had been very evident.

"Have you made amends with Connie and Deirdre yet?"

"That's none of your business," Erica snapped. "You thought it all childish anyway, so what do you care?"

"I care because I'm starting to see that maybe there's something more to all of this than just personal issues and inconveniences."

"Look, just stay out it," Erica replied, feeling angry that Brook would step in where she'd not been asked to come. "Dee and I always work things out and we're just fine. Connie can do what she pleases, just like she's always done in the past. I'm not going to be bothered by her melodramatics anymore."

Brook's voice took on a strange tone and Erica almost believed she was crying. "Listen to yourself," Brook said softly. "Do you really hear what you're saying?"

Erica was instantly consumed with guilt. She knew her harshness was born out of a culmination of problems and issues and not just because her sister had dared to speak her mind.

"What's happened to us?" Erica finally asked, her tone somber. "We didn't used to be like this."

"We've torn ourselves apart," Brook replied. "And I think we'll have to be the ones to find a way to put ourselves back together."

"Like Humpty Dumpty," Erica more stated than asked.

"Like six separate pieces of a beloved quilt," Brook replied, her voice cracking with emotion.

Erica felt tears come to her eyes. "I'm so sorry, Brook. I just never saw it that way."

"Have you read your letter yet?"

"What letter?" Erica asked curiously. She went back to the box and immediately spied the envelope.

"It's from Rachelle."

"Oh, that letter." Erica remembered Mattie mentioning that Mavis was sending missives for each of them. "Did you read yours?"

"Yes."

"And?"

"Read your letter," Brook said softly. "Then call me and we'll talk some more."

Long after they had concluded their call, Erica sat in a stupor and stared dry-eyed at Grammy's gift and Rachelle's letter.

How appropriate that they should come together in one package, Erica thought. She picked up the letter and read it again.

To my daughter Erica,

You were the last of my babies and probably the hardest to leave. For you see, I knew there would be no more after you. I had made such a desperate mess of my life and you were so unexpected. My one true love, your father, was dead before you were even born—dead from an overdose of the drugs he could never seem to beat. I never recovered from losing him. Every time I looked at you girls, you reminded me of him—of the love I'd lost.

By now you must know that I have taken my life. I hope you won't hate me, but then, I'm sure you probably already do. How could you not hate a mother who left you alone to be raised by a grandmother? How could you not despise me every day of my life? This letter seems a poor offering to tell you how much I wish I could take back the things I've done with my life. My acting and all the laurels that accompanied it are meaningless when I realize that the only thing that ever really mattered was the one thing I couldn't seem to get right. I'm sure it means nothing at all now, but I cannot leave without letting you know

*that I loved you. I know that if my mother had her way with you, you know all
about forgiving and loving. I'm sure she shared God and the Bible and all
those important things, and because of this, I can only hope that somehow—
someway—you might find it in your heart to forgive me. God knows I can't
forgive myself.*

Rachelle

Erica put the letter down and looked once again to the wall
hanging. "Six separate pieces," she whispered, knowing full well it
was exactly the kind of thing Grammy would do to prove a point.

She remembered Grammy saying, *"Sometimes when folks stop listening,
it's time to give them something more visual. Sometimes, you have to see what people are
saying rather than hear it."*

Today she was given new sight.

Chapter 29

Ashley couldn't say that she was happy to see Jack pull into the driveway. She knew he was furious with her choice to remain in Estes Park, but she had refused to deal with him over the telephone. She watched as he brought the Bronco to a stop and smiled as her boys bounded out from the backseat. She'd hardly seen them or talked to them since the accident, and now they were here, happy and healthy and exactly what she needed. It was easy to forgive Jack his intrusion as she watched the boys make a beeline for the front door.

"Mommy!" Zach called from the doorway. "Mommy, where are you?"

"I'm right here, Zachy," Ashley replied, coming into the room. "Goodness, but you look like you've grown at least a foot taller. Come give me a kiss and hug."

Zach ran at her and very nearly knocked her to the ground as he tackled her and wrapped his arms around her waist. "I missed you!"

"Zach! You can't crash into your mother that way," Jack called from the door.

Ashley looked up to meet her husband's brooding expression. "He didn't hurt me," she replied, wanting to add, "Not like *you* hurt me."

"Mom!" John called, scooting around his father's frame to run across the room.

She laughed at his tanned complexion and sun-bleached hair. "I guess you must have spent a lot of time at the beach in California."

"We went there every day," John replied, hugging her so tightly that it caused Ashley pain. She refused to acknowledge it, however.

These were her boys, and if they needed to connect to her in that way, she wouldn't refuse them for the world.

"So let's sit down and you can tell me everything you've been doing." She led them to the couch, not offering Jack so much as another word.

The boys rattled on about their trip to California and how nice the flight attendant had been to them. They gave her detailed accounts about going to the beach and practically living in Uncle Loren's swimming pool. Then they switched gears and told her about church camp and ran quickly to where Jack had left the bags by the door. Digging in, they each searched through their things until they found what they were looking for.

"I made this wooden cross for you," John said proudly. "We had to sand it and stain it and then polish it up. It's supposed to remind us of God's love."

Ashley held the piece in her hands and fought to keep the tears from coming. "It's very pretty, John. You did a nice job."

"Here's mine," Zach said, throwing himself on the couch beside her. For all of his time on earth, Zach had yet to simply sit down rather than fly through the air and take the furniture as if by attack. He put a leather heart in her hand.

Studying the piece, Ashley noted how the heart was actually two pieces lashed together at the sides by lacing rawhide through pre-punched holes. The top had been left open and there were pieces of paper inside the pocket.

"It's very nice, Zach. Did you sew the sides together?" Ashley asked.

"Yup. It's not sewed all the way," he said in his little-boy way. "That's so God can put His Word in your heart." He took the piece from her and spilled out the paper. "Those are my Bible verses. I memorized them at camp. Do you want to hear them?"

"I memorized some verses too!" John declared proudly. "I can tell you mine."

Ashley listened patiently as the boys recited their verses. They were very familiar verses—the kind that were taught to children. Easy-to-remember verses. Very important verses.

"'For God so loved the world,'" John began with the eloquence of a Shakespeare actor, "'that he gave his one and only Son.'" He paused and looked upward as if seeking guidance. He grinned and shrugged. "And if you believe in Him, you'll have eternal life."

"Very good," Ashley told her firstborn and hugged him tightly.

"I learned 'God is love.' It's really short," Zach said proudly. "It's on this paper if you don't believe me."

His simple words were arrows in her heart. *"God is love."* She could hear Grammy telling her that God's love was the kind that never failed. It was a love to be counted on.

"Boys, you need to give your mother a rest now. Why don't you go outside and play for a bit. You haven't been up here for a long time and there are probably lots of things you'll want to explore," Jack told his sons.

Ashley said nothing, knowing that Jack wanted to have time to speak with her in private. She had refused to give him any answers on the telephone and no doubt he felt entitled to some explanation for her delay in returning home.

"We'll find you some pretty rocks, Mommy," Zach told her as he threw himself into action.

"You do that, Zach," she told him and took up the pieces of Bible verses and replaced them in the pocket of the heart. "Thank you both for my presents. I feel so special that you would make these for me."

The boys hardly seemed to hear her, however, as they hurried outside. Their laughter warmed her heart. How she had missed them.

"So you want to tell me what this is all about?" Jack questioned.

Ashley looked at him. Really looked at him. He had dark circles under his eyes and his jaw was set in that tight sort of way that always revealed that he was upset. His normally tanned complexion, compliments of his Mediterranean ancestors, seemed almost pale and sallow. She wondered if he'd been sick but decided against asking.

"I'm sorry if I've upset you by staying here, but it wasn't the kind of thing I felt we should discuss on the telephone," Ashley replied softly.

"Well, what sort of thing is it?" he asked, coming to sit in the overstuffed chair opposite her.

"Jack, there are some things that we need to deal with. Things that I don't understand yet."

"If this is about your memory loss, stop worrying about it. You aren't missing anything but a few painful hours. Didn't you ever consider that this was God's way of helping you deal with the accident? If you had to sit around reliving the horror of what you went through in the wreck, it might well be too much for your mind."

Ashley bit her lip. How could she explain this to him without coming right out and accusing him of lying? Yet how long could she give him a chance to come through with the truth?

"I want to take the boys and go visit Grammy," she said, taking a different approach to the subject. "I need time to think, and I need time with them."

"I can't get off to go traipsing off to Kansas," Jack said, running his hands through his hair. "You know my schedule is pretty hectic. It was difficult just to get up here. There's no way I can go to Mattie's."

"I don't want you to go with us to Mattie's," Ashley said, trying as hard as she could not to sound bitter. "I need that time alone."

Jack stopped fidgeting and looked at her oddly. "What are you saying? You've had time alone up here. I thought I was being the understanding husband by giving you space, but I've reached my limit. I can't keep asking my mother to fill in doing the job that you should be in Denver doing."

Ashley felt her body tense. She wasn't going to let this turn into an ugly fight. She refused to give in to his baiting. "You won't have to worry about anything. I'll arrange for the housekeeper to be there to cook and clean and the boys will be with me."

"I think it's ridiculous," Jack said, getting up to pace. "You are barely a month out of the hospital. Granted, you've had an incredible recovery—"

"Yes, and I see my doctor on Tuesday. Unless she has some good reason for why I can't travel by car to Kansas, I'm going."

He turned and looked at her. Sheer panic and fear were etched in his expression. Ashley knew then that she'd been right all along. He was keeping a great deal from her. Her mind ran rampant. Had she told him about the baby only to hear his accusations and anger? Was that what she couldn't remember?

"I don't want you to go," he finally said. "There's no reason for it. Not any good reason."

She'd had enough. It was time to make herself understood. "Jack, I know I was at the clinic the day of the accident." There. It was a simple statement, and he could do with it whatever he chose.

He blanched. "Ashley, you're wrong. Your mind is playing tricks on you."

"And you're lying to me," Ashley stated evenly. She got up from the couch, clutching the gifts her children had given her. "I don't know why you're lying to me, but I do know that you are."

He began to pace again and the look on his face left Ashley no doubt that her suspicions were well-founded. Something was terribly wrong. And this was the heart of her fears and overwhelming sorrow. The key to her recovery was locked up somewhere in the events of that day—in the hours or minutes before the accident.

"Look what we found!" John declared as the boys burst into the house.

Jack exchanged a look with Ashley before he shook his head. "I can't talk to you when you're like this."

Ashley watched him walk off as the boys came to show her a bird's nest with its cracked shell remains. Now, more than ever, Ashley knew that she had to get away from Jack. He needed time to think and so did she. She also needed time with her boys. A week or two with Grammy would be just the thing to help her heal. She would go back to Denver with Jack, but she wouldn't stay any longer than it took to square everything away by getting a new car, or at least a rental.

Later that afternoon, Jack and the boys decided to drive into town for groceries. He was gone only a few minutes before he returned from the car with a package in his hands. "I forgot that this came for you. I guess I had my mind on other things."

Ashley took the package and noted the handwriting. "Grammy sent me a get-well gift, no doubt. She is so thoughtful."

Jack opened his mouth as if to reply, then closed it and went to the door. He looked back at her with an expression of longing that nearly broke Ashley's resolve to leave him for a time. She loved this man. Loved him dearly. Perhaps that's why it hurt so much to know he was keeping something from her.

"I'll be back in a few minutes," he said and then was gone.

Ashley took the small wrapped box to the table and opened it. She missed Grammy more than she could say and knew that she should call her. The few times she had taken Grammy's calls, Ashley knew her conversation had been less than satisfying. She felt miserable for putting her grandmother through such concern, but her emotions were raw and in order to protect herself, Ashley hadn't wanted to deal with anyone. Now, however, she felt the time had come. This gift would give her the perfect reason to call Grammy, and then she could announce her plans to go home. That would surely make up for some of the distance she'd put between them.

Lifting out the quilted piece, Ashley spread it open, then dropped it back on the table. She gasped in recognition, knowing full well where it had come from.

The perfectly embroidered *A* stared out at her from the center of intertwined circles—circles made from clothing that Ashley remembered quite well.

There was no doubt in her mind that Grammy had cut apart her quilt. There was also no doubt in Ashley's mind as to why her grandmother had gone to such a length. Somehow, Ashley knew instinctively that if she called her sisters, they, too, would have received a similar gift.

Tears came to her eyes and trailed down her cheeks. Her head began to hurt and she could feel her pulse beating at her temples.

"Oh, Grammy," she said, touching the quilt ever so gently. She traced the circles with her index finger and shook her head. "What have we done to you?"

She thought of the bitterness that had crept into their lives since Rachelle's funeral. She remembered all the ugly words they'd said and the fights and animosity they'd allowed between them. Prior to the accident, Ashley had given her sisters very little of her time or attention. After the accident, she had given them nothing. And with exception to Brook, she'd barely spoken to any of her family.

"Oh, forgive me, Grammy," she murmured and hugged the piece close. "You've torn it apart because you feel torn apart. Because we are torn apart." The message was powerfully clear to Ashley. But worse than that, she wondered if it was too late to make things right. Then she saw the envelope. A sense of dread and fear washed over her. Had Grammy written her further admonishments?

She put the wall hanging down and picked up the letter. Within seconds she had it open, only to stare at it in numb wonder as she found Rachelle's signature at the bottom of the letter.

To my daughter Ashley,

The first time I laid eyes on you, I knew you were someone special. Somehow I knew, even though you were the image of your sister Brook, that you were uniquely set apart. Then, as you grew up and I heard tales of your accomplishments, learned of your marriage and your family, I envied you. You were everything I should have been. And if I had been stronger, perhaps a better wife, maybe your father wouldn't have turned to drugs and maybe we could have been one big happy family.

You see, I never intended that my mother should raise you forever. I just knew that as a young mother of sixteen, I couldn't handle the job at hand. It was hard enough to face one baby, but two made me more frightened than I'd ever been. I know my choices were wrong, Ashley, but because you have children of your own, I want you to put yourself in my place. If you knew you would only cause them more harm and pain, would you force them to spend their life with you? I knew Mattie could care for you and love you in a way I didn't have to give.

I know I was wrong. I know I was selfish and foolish and that I never deserved you or your sisters. But I loved you. Believe it or not, now that I stand ready to end my life, it doesn't matter nearly as much that you believe it, as that I have a chance to say it. I wish I could have your forgiveness, and that is really all I want to ask for as I pass from this life. Again, think of your own boys, John and Zach. If you had disappointed them, hurt them because you were unable to deal with your own pain, wouldn't you hope beyond hope that they could somehow forgive you?

Rachelle

Ashley clutched the letter and felt the sorrow of all her losses wash over her in one big wave. "She knew their names," Ashley sobbed, rocking back and forth. *She knew my boys' names.*

———————————

Connie returned from jogging to find a small brown paper package leaning precariously on the ledge above the apartment mailboxes. Turning the key to the small box, she retrieved the rest of the mail, then took down the package. The return address was from Council Grove and even if it hadn't been, Connie would have recognized Mattie's handwriting.

Attempting to open the package as she made her way to her apartment, Connie nearly dropped her other mail. She found the key for her door and went inside, several letters falling from her grasp just as she stepped across the threshold. Pausing to pick these up, she hurried to the kitchen counter to see what Gram had sent.

As she pulled out the wall hanging, she stared at it for a moment, turning it first one way and then another. Connie then looked back inside the box for a letter that might explain the piece. The letter at the bottom of the box didn't look to have Grammy's handwriting, but Connie opened it nevertheless.

To my daughter Connie,

You came into this world in a hard way. The pregnancy was difficult and seemed to last forever—maybe because I knew I had wronged the husband I loved. Maybe because I knew I would never be able to deal with the consequences of my actions.

I wronged you, Connie. As much as I wronged Gary, I wronged you maybe even more. I denied you and fought against you even while carrying you. I thought perhaps if I didn't think of you there—inside me, growing every day—that somehow my indiscretion, my sin, would pass away. But you were there and you refused to go away. And now I'm so glad you didn't go away. You are special, Connie, and I see so much of myself in you. You are determined—a fighter—but you are not the coward I was. By now you probably know that I've taken my life. I make this choice because I can't live with the guilt of what I've done to you girls and to my mother.

Everyone has always seen me as strong, but I'm not strong. I never was. What I am is a good actress, and I made everyone believe what I wanted them to believe. I only wish now that could be true with you as you read this letter. I long for you to believe that I loved you. I long for you to forgive me, even though I don't deserve forgiveness. Someday you may know the need for forgiveness as well. You'll long for someone to have mercy—to take pity on you and sponge away the mistakes you've made . . . the hurt you've caused. Maybe then you'll know my longing in full. Maybe then you'll forgive me as well.

Rachelle

Connie put the letter aside and refused to think about the words on the paper. It was all a mistake. That had to be it. It was just a mistake—a joke. The quilt was Grammy's and the letter undoubtedly came from Mavis Lane, but the contents had to be forged. Rachelle would never have sent such a letter. Would she?

Connie picked up the quilted wall hanging and turned the piece in her hands. This was part of Grammy's quilt. She knew it was because she recognized the material in one of the circles. It was a sweet pale pink with fluffy white kittens in fields of lavender clover. This had been from a favorite dress Mattie had created for Connie when she was five.

Tracing the circles with her finger, Connie remembered how Grammy had said they were all connected to one another. Yet she had always felt isolated from her sisters—never a true part of the family. Erica said it was because she chose not to be a part of the family. Deirdre and Ashley had said as much on other occasions, and Connie was sure if she thought hard enough about it, that Brook had probably said something similar.

"But I never felt good enough to be a part of that circle," she whispered as she continued tracing the patterns in the wall hanging. Grammy's intricate quilting fascinated Connie. Such attention and focus had been given to the blank spaces in the quilt. More attention even than the colorful appliquéd circles and scrolling ribbon on the sides.

She kicked off her tennis shoes and sighed. "Maybe it was all my fault," she admitted to herself. "But it was hard not to feel that way. Especially after learning the truth."

The truth had come to her when she had been no more than ten. They were at church, and as usual, Grammy was helping to clean up things in the Sunday school class before they left for the day. With her sisters outside talking to their friends, Connie had come back to the classrooms to see if she could help Grammy.

"She looks completely different," one of Grammy's lady friends was saying. Connie couldn't remember who the woman was, but her words were forever etched in her memory. "It's easy to see she doesn't fit in—at least not by her looks."

Grammy hadn't seen Connie come into the room. Neither had her friend. "Connie has a different father," Grammy told the woman. "Rachelle was on the verge of a divorce and made some wrong choices. She never told me who Connie's father was, but when she went back to her husband, he wasn't inclined to want to raise another man's child."

Just then the woman noticed Connie. "Well, I suppose I should collect my kids and get on home. I'll see you at Wednesday night service."

Grammy had been surprised by the woman's reaction until she'd turned around and found the stunned Connie standing by the door.

"Are you all right?" Mattie asked Connie.

"I have a different father?"

Gram seemed surprised by this question. "You knew you had a different father."

Connie shook her head vehemently. "No, I didn't."

She remembered the look on Grammy's face. It was a mixture of pain and regret. "I thought you knew." Her voice was sincere. "Oh, Connie, I thought you knew."

Connie looked at the wall hanging and felt her eyes moisten. "I didn't know, Grammy. I knew I didn't fit in, but I didn't know why. I thought it was because Ashley and Brook were twins and Deirdre and Erica were so close in age. I didn't know it was because I was the result of a one-night stand."

She closed her eyes and pushed the images from her mind. Grammy had tried hard to handle the situation delicately. She had explained her mother's confusion and then tried to explain without going into the intimate details of what men and women did together, how Connie could have a different father. All while sitting there in the fourth grade Sunday school room on a hot, humid summer day.

It had stormed later that afternoon, and Connie had thought that God was mad at her. Mainly because she had ranted at God in her heart and was mad at Him. The storm had been fierce—ruining crops, downing power lines. It had even destroyed one of Grammy's outbuildings down by the old homestead. They had spent hours in the storm cave as one storm followed another and lashed the land unmercifully. Connie had felt sure that it was all her fault.

Shaking her head, Connie again looked at the letter. Her mother had asked for forgiveness. It was really all Connie wanted as well. Forgiveness for her own indiscretions. Forgiveness for the walls she'd erected as monuments to her own pain.

Someday you may know the need for forgiveness as well. You'll long for someone to have mercy—to take pity on you and sponge away the mistakes you've made . . . the hurt you've caused.

Connie remembered the words from the letter in vivid detail. No one could have known those feelings like Rachelle. The letter had to be authentic.

Tears came to her eyes. "I do know that need for forgiveness. So much of my pain has been my own fault," she whispered. "So much of my pain has been without need."

Chapter 30

Deirdre looked at the clouds overhead and decided to get in a bit of gardening before the predicted rain began to fall. Her nerves were raw from fighting with Dave. Fighting because he'd bounced two checks. Fighting because after arguing his position with the bank, he realized the reason for those bounced checks had to do with her withdrawals from the ATM.

She had listened to him rant and rave about her cavalier attitude toward finances. He had accused her of everything short of infidelity, then blamed her for the headache he'd been battling for the last eight hours. At one point he'd worked himself into such a dither that he stalked from the room—punching door frames and walls as he went. But when he'd calmed and returned, he wanted to know why she had taken the money and what she had done with it.

His expression revealed his fury and his eyes still suggested her betrayal. And because of this, Deirdre refused to tell him the truth. She couldn't have confessed her sin at that moment had a league of angels stood beside her for support. She had started to cry, and this in turn had upset Morgan, who had taken a bold and uncharacteristic stand for her mother.

"You made Mommy cry!" she had declared, throwing herself between Dave and Deirdre. "You aren't a nice daddy anymore."

This had infuriated Dave, but it had also wounded him more deeply than he would let on. Deirdre had seen the hurt register on his face. She had tried to call him back as he'd stormed out of the house, but it was to no avail. Her constricted throat wouldn't allow the words.

Kneeling in front of Morgan, Deirdre hugged her daughter for several minutes, then regained control of her own emotions and assured Morgan that Daddy was just tired.

"He's still a good daddy, Morgan. Sometimes grown-ups have problems that are hard for kids to understand, but it doesn't mean we don't love you as much as ever. Daddy loves you very much and so do I."

When things had calmed between them, Deirdre had talked Morgan into taking her afternoon nap, all hinging on the promise that they would go out for supper at one of the local kids-oriented pizza places.

Now Deirdre had time to herself. Time to think and time to make some very hard choices. She thought of the gift she'd received the day before. Grammy had sent her a wall hanging, only Deirdre knew instinctively that it wasn't just any hanging. Grammy had divided up her prized Piece Work and no doubt had sent each of her temperamental granddaughters a portion. Deirdre had wept when she saw the piece. She knew Grammy was telling them in her own way that the Mitchell girls had divided themselves in the same manner.

And then there was Rachelle's letter. Deirdre had practically memorized it.

To my daughter Deirdre,

You were the hope for a new start in my life. You were going to be the one responsibility I didn't shirk. I remember how happy I was when you were born, certainly more happy than I'd been when the others had come. Not because they weren't perfect and lovely and deserving of my happiness, but because my heart was different when you were conceived. You were going to help me make my life over. You were going to show Gary and me how to be parents, and maybe, just maybe, we would have found a way to bring the others back in our lives after we learned how to care for you.

I know none of this means much now. It doesn't matter that I loved you— that I loved your sisters. It only matters that I tell you the truth. By the time you read this, I'll be gone. I can't live anymore with the guilt and pain in my soul.

I long for peace, but there is none. I long for your forgiveness, but I suppose that is too much to ask for. I can only hope in time, you'll find a way to for-give me the past. You have your family, so you must understand how it feels to want them to forgive you when you hurt them. Think of this when you think of me.

Rachelle

Even now Deirdre felt tears come to her eyes. It was all so con-fusing. Her mother's words—Dave's anger—her own struggle with gambling. Not to mention the separation and bickering among her and her sisters. She knew she had been a disappointment to Mattie. She had always been the one to smooth things out, and Mattie often counted on her for that. But this time Deirdre had failed because she was too caught up in her own problems.

Picking up the gardening trowel, Deirdre knelt down and began attacking the soil around the flowers that bordered their backyard pri-vacy fence. She had artfully arranged a pattern of latticework and a suc-cessful garden of clematis. Grammy had told her that this was an extremely temperamental plant, but with Deirdre's patience, she could have a beautiful go of it. Deirdre had taken great pride in Grammy's confidence in her. Clematis had become a symbol of that confidence.

Orange, white, and purple blossoms with long, velvety petals that opened in a starlike pattern greeted Deirdre in a comforting way. She liked to work with her flowers. They reminded her of peaceful summer days in Kansas. Days when she'd been too young to be in any real trouble and life had a less serious slant to it.

"Oh, Grammy," she whispered, churning the dirt and pulling out the weeds wherever they dared to show themselves. "I wish I could tell you what I've done. You would think me so silly. Worse yet, I fear you would be disappointed in me."

She stretched to reach behind the lattice. One particularly stub-born weed refused to give in to her attempts to dislodge it. Finally working her fingers around it in a better hold, Deirdre pulled with all of her might and ended up falling backward when the dirt finally gave way. She sat on the grass for a moment, almost amused with herself.

What an effort I put into something so temporary as these flowers, and yet I avoid working out the details in my marriage and relationship with my sisters. I have a great deal of weeding to do, she thought solemnly.

Looking up at the back of the house, Deirdre thought of how Morgan slept soundly in the upstairs bedroom. She thought of the room across the hall from Morgan's and how it was to become a nursery for the next baby. A baby they might never have now that her relationship with Dave was so unsettled.

"You have no one to blame but yourself," Deirdre said aloud and got to her feet, dusting off her backside. "You won't tell him the truth."

She looked at her dirty hands and sighed. She, like Grammy, enjoyed the feel of the soil on her fingers. No dainty gardening gloves for this lady of the house. But still, after the gardening was done, Deirdre always longed to clean herself up. She loved the feel of coming clean. How she would love to come clean about her gambling.

How can I tell Dave I'm addicted to gambling? How can I explain to him that I've lost literally hundreds, even thousands of dollars—not to mention his mother's necklace— and all because of gambling?

"There's no way I can tell him." She shook her head to reinforce her words.

Yet if I don't, she reasoned with herself, *it'll just go on and on and on.*

"I have to come clean," she whispered.

She remembered when she'd first asked Jesus into her heart. She had been a young girl of eight, and Grammy had come to pray with her just before bedtime.

"I want Jesus in my heart, Grammy," she had said in her best grown-up, serious tone.

Grammy had beamed a smile of approval, and Deirdre had relished that smile every bit as much as the thought of saving her soul from the pits of everlasting fire.

"Do you understand what it means to ask Jesus into your heart, Deirdre?"

She had nodded. "My Sunday school teacher said it's like taking a bath."

"Taking a bath?"

"Yup, she said you ask Jesus to wash your sins away and it's like He comes and gives your heart a bath. You get all cleaned up so you can be with the King."

Grammy had nodded, assuring Deirdre that she had it right. "It feels good to get clean before God."

Raindrops now began to fall lightly upon Deirdre's cheeks, and she realized she had lifted her face upward. The memory was a sweet one. The tenderness of her grandmother leading her in prayer, the warmth of knowing she was doing something that met with not only her grandmother's approval but God's as well. It was important to Deirdre to have the approval of those she loved.

Maybe that was why it hurt so much to know that Dave was angry and hurting just now. She had shut him out and refused to be honest with him. And why? Because she was embarrassed and humiliated . . . and something inside of her still refused to admit the error of her actions.

Just then Deirdre heard the unmistakable sound of Dave's sports car pull into the drive. She imagined the garage door opening and Dave driving in to take his regular place. She pictured him getting out of the car and coming to find her. He would march across the yard and sweep her into his arms and assure her that nothing mattered more than that they work out their problems together. She could hear him telling her that no matter what she had done, he would forgive her and put the past behind them.

She smiled to herself and picked up her gardening tools. Maybe it wouldn't happen exactly like that, but she knew that she needed to be honest with him. No doubt he would be hurt—he'd never wanted her to go gambling with her girlfriends in the first place. They had argued about whether the wives of deacons in the church should be seen at places such as casinos. She knew he disapproved, but she had ignored his warning and had stepped out on her own. And now they would both pay the price for her mistake.

Deirdre washed off her tools at the outside faucet, then let the water wash away the dirt on her hands. *Come clean.* The message seemed instilled in everything she did. She lingered at the spigot, wishing that somehow she could go back in time and redo the last few weeks, even months.

Rain started to fall in earnest, and Deirdre knew she couldn't put off going into the house. She'd given Dave plenty of time to calm down and think about what he wanted to say to her. She would just go to him, and before he could issue a single word, she would confess her problem.

Deirdre knew that she would never know any greater peace than letting go of the past and of her addictive behavior. It wouldn't be easy. Even now she knew she could go to Dave with great resolve about her gambling, but come Monday, when Dave went back to work and she was left alone to contemplate their problems, what then? Would she have the strength to refuse?

She had just reached the back door when a blast sounded from somewhere above her and glass shattered and fell to the ground not ten feet from where she stood. Deirdre stared at the ground for a moment. What was it? What had happened? Had Dave thrown something through their window?

She backed up a step and looked up at their bedroom window. It didn't make sense. Then a feeling of dread—almost horror—overcame her. Deirdre felt her throat constrict and her pulse quicken. Without understanding why, she nearly tore the back screen door off its hinges, yanking it open and hurrying into the house.

"Dave!" she cried out in the silence.

She raced for the stairs and hurried to the second floor. Their bedroom door was closed, but down the hall, Morgan's was open. There was no sound coming from either room.

"Dave! Where are you?" Deirdre questioned in a voice that

sounded foreign in her own ears. She halted at their bedroom. Her hand shook violently as she reached for the doorknob.

"Dave?" The word was barely a whisper.

She knew she had to open the door, but fear gripped her heart like an iron band. Instinctively she knew what had happened, but to see it—to have it confirmed—Deirdre didn't know if she could stand it. Turning the handle, she took a deep breath and pushed the door open.

She opened her mouth to scream, but no sound came out. Blood splatters marred her beautiful white curtains and fell in awkward, unwelcome patterns against her pale rose wallpaper. These were the first things she allowed herself to see. The broken window, the blood on the curtains. But almost as if she had no choice in the matter, Deirdre found herself staring at the bleeding body of her husband.

The handgun he'd used was the one Deirdre had allowed him to purchase several years earlier when a rash of burglaries had made Dave apprehensive. It lay on the blood-soaked carpet not far from its owner.

When the initial shock froze her in place, Deirdre felt it also freeze time. This isn't happening, she told herself. *This is just a very, very bad dream.* She closed her eyes and opened them again.

It wasn't a dream.

Mechanically she backed out of the room and closed the door. Morgan could not be allowed to see what Deirdre had just witnessed. She went to her daughter's bedroom and looked inside. Morgan slept in blissful peace. How could she have not heard the gunshot that took her father's life? How could she have slept through Deirdre calling out for Dave? She shook her head and quickly closed the door. It didn't matter. Nothing else made sense. Why should this?

Uncertain what she should do, Deirdre finally collected her senses enough to realize she had to call for help. Maybe Dave wasn't dead! Maybe he needed a doctor!

This thought put sheer terror into her heart. Maybe she needed to be giving him CPR or mouth-to-mouth resuscitation. She hurried back to her bedroom and reentered with the sole purpose of trying to save her husband.

But what if I can't? she asked herself.

She moved closer to where Dave's body lay and only as she neared him could she see that there was no hope of him being alive. The back top of his head was completely blown away. She stepped backward and felt her whole body begin to tremble. Reaching for the telephone on her side of the bed, she quickly dialed 9-1-1.

———————

The events that unfolded in the hours that followed Dave's suicide were like something out of a strange foreign film. Deirdre knew that there were people in her house. Knew that they were supposed to be there, but nothing made any sense. She remembered a hysterical call to Mattie, even remembered Mattie's promise to come and be with her, but beyond that she failed to understand the questions being forced upon her.

"Mrs. Woodward," the detective in charge said in a soft-spoken tone, "we're going to have to ask you and your daughter to come with us to the station for some questioning."

"Questioning?" Deirdre looked up at the broad-shouldered man and shook her head. "I don't understand."

Morgan, who by this time had come to fully realize that her father was dead, had refused to be moved from her mother's lap and tightly wrapped her arms around Deirdre's neck, even as the detective spoke again.

"It's a simple matter of procedure. You have to come with us. While you're with us, my team will be taking care of things here."

"Taking care of things? Taking care of Dave?" she questioned. Her mind refused to think in a clear manner. "I should have taken care of him. I should have been honest with him."

"Honest with him about what?" the man asked, his tone a bit more demanding.

Deirdre shook her head. What was he talking about, anyway? What did he want to know now?

She held on to Morgan, feeling the child's trembling body and heart-wrenching sobs. She had to protect her child. She couldn't let Morgan see what she had seen.

"Daddy's gone away," she had told her daughter. "He's gone away and he can't come back to us."

Mattie felt nothing but overwhelming sorrow for her granddaughter. The call on that beautiful Saturday afternoon had been one of hysteria and utter terror. Mattie could still hear Deirdre's broken sentences.

"Grammy . . . please come. Dave's . . . Dave's dead. Gunshot . . . killed . . . himself."

Even now as Harry sped them ever faithfully toward Topeka, where they would pick up Connie before going to Kansas City, Mattie could hear those painful, horrible words.

"I don't know what to say to her, Harry," Mattie mumbled and stared out the window at the passing scenery.

"God will help you through this, Mattie."

"It's just so awful."

"Yeah, it is."

Mattie felt a horrible tightness in her chest. How could she comfort her granddaughter in such a time of need? And what of poor little Morgan? It was just too much to think about.

"How could this have happened? They were so happy."

"Apparently there's more than we know," Harry offered, keeping his gaze fixed on the road ahead. "It's hard to tell, Mattie. Who knows why a person decides that they can't go on?"

"But he'd just won his case. They had everything they needed," Mattie said, shaking her head. "Maybe it was the disappointment of canceling their trip. Maybe Dave felt really bad about it."

"That hardly seems like the kind of thing a person would kill

himself over. Seems a whole lot easier to just reschedule the trip."
Mattie looked at him and saw him grimace. "I didn't mean it to
sound so flippant," Harry added.

"Oh, Harry, I know you didn't." She felt her eyes fill up with
tears again. "I don't know what I'm going to do or say, but I'm so
grateful you were able to come with me. Harry, I hope you know what
you mean to me."

He nodded. "I think I do, Mattie, because you mean the same to
me."

Chapter 31

Morgan's shrill screams broke the otherwise silent room. She fought against the grasp of strangers while Deirdre, equally terrified, struggled to try to reach her daughter. So far Deirdre's experience with the local authorities was turning rather ugly. It was bad enough to have to come to the station to answer questions, but to be separated from Morgan in order for the officers to question her daughter in private was too much.

"I'm sorry, ma'am, but this is the way things are done," a black-haired police officer told Deirdre.

"You aren't taking my child away!" Deirdre screamed and reached out to take her hysterical daughter back into her arms. The policewoman holding her moved back a pace while two detectives physically restrained Deirdre, forcing her to sit in the chair they'd provided for her. "She's only a baby!"

"Mommy! Mommy!"

The terror in her voice was like nothing Deirdre had ever heard. "Let me go!" Deirdre screamed, trying again to get up.

One man leaned down and whispered in her ear, "This is already hard enough on your daughter. Your screaming isn't helping her any. Just cooperate and this will all be over in a short time."

Deirdre looked up at the man, the same man who'd been at her house. "Detective . . ." she paused, unable to remember his name.

"Stanford," he replied.

"Detective Stanford, this isn't going to be over for either one of us for a very, very long time. You can't just expect me to let you take my daughter off to be with strangers when her father has just died."

The tall, brown-haired man knelt beside her chair. "This is how it has to be," he stated sympathetically. "Resisting isn't going to change anything. Now, please make it easier on all of us and tell your daughter that it's okay. Either way, she's going into another room down the hall. You can send her there calmly and sensibly or continue being irrational."

Deirdre felt her cheeks grow hot. How dare he come to her with his mock sympathy and soft words. He was insane if he thought she'd let them take Morgan away. But then her eyes caught sight of Morgan. Her beautiful, golden-haired child was fighting for all she was worth, crying—sobbing hysterically—and reaching out for her at every chance. There was absolute terror in her expression, and Deirdre had never felt more helpless.

"Morgan." Her tone was calming, reassuring. "Morgan, look at Mommy."

Morgan, wild-eyed with fear, looked at Deirdre as though her only hope for rescue would come from her hand.

Deirdre drew a deep breath. "Go with them, Morgan. Go with them for a few minutes so that Mommy can talk to the police about Daddy."

Morgan said nothing, but she stilled in the arms of the policewoman who held her. The look on her face cut Deirdre to the heart. Betrayed! That was what her daughter's expression suggested. She had just been betrayed by the only trustworthy person left to her in all the world. The policewoman walked out the door talking softly to Morgan and promising her a can of soda.

Deirdre turned to the detective. "Are you satisfied? Is this how the law works? You terrify young children who've just lost their fathers? Is that what my tax dollars are paying for?"

"Mrs. Woodward, I understand how you feel," Stanford began, "but you have to understand how our procedures work."

"I don't care a hoot about your procedures," Deirdre replied coldly. "I only care about my child. Are you going to pay for her counseling bills when she's unable to get over this trauma? Her father is dead and you rip her from the arms of her mother in order to talk about funeral arrangements. How do you sleep nights?"

"We aren't here to question you about funeral arrangements," Stanford said, loosening his tie. "We need to know why your husband is dead."

"Offhand—and this is only a guess," Deirdre said snidely, "but I'd say it was the bullet in his head that killed him." Despite her anger, once her words were out, she could barely hold back her tears.

Stanford nodded solemnly. "I understand that you're upset. You have a right to be upset. God knows you've been through a lot in the past few hours. In fact, maybe some coffee would help. Simpson," he said to his partner, "why don't you go wrestle us up some coffee." The thirty-something woman smiled and nodded.

Deirdre couldn't believe the man's suggestion. Coffee? Why in the world did he imagine coffee would help anything? She said nothing, however, and leaned back into her chair and crossed her arms, looking at the stark room. The table she sat at was one of those cheap army-surplus-styled monstrosities, and other than two chairs, one of which she was sitting on, the room was empty. It reminded her of one of those late-night police shows. This was the kind of room where the murderer confessed to his crime. And now they wanted her to tell them why Dave was dead. What manner of nightmare had she fallen into?

When Detective Simpson had gone, Stanford sat down at the table opposite Deirdre and took out a pencil. Flipping open a notebook, he began to jot notes.

"I need to know what happened leading up to your husband's death."

Deirdre felt her mouth go dry. "Why?"

"We're investigating the death and we need all the facts."

"You found a suicide note. Doesn't that pretty much explain the facts?" she asked. Why were they doing this to her? She had answered question after question at the house. How long would she be treated like a criminal?

"Mrs. Woodward," he paused and gave her an apologetic look, "could I call you Deirdre?"

"Call me whatever it takes to get my daughter back," she said angrily.

"Deirdre, this is being treated like any other suspicious death. You have to understand. The facts are not always what they seem. Now, if you'll just cooperate with me, we'll have everything said and done as soon as possible."

Just then Detective Simpson returned. Deirdre was handed a cup of black steaming coffee, but the thought of drinking it turned her stomach. She put it down on the table and shuddered.

"Ask your questions and let me go to my child."

"Were you and your husband experiencing any marital difficulties?" he asked matter-of-factly.

"Yes," Deirdre answered without emotion. "Dave had been working too hard on a case at his law firm. I complained about his long hours, including the fact that he canceled a much-desired anniversary vacation we had planned to take to Hawaii." She paused, feeling her anger mount as he wrote in his notebook. "If I go too fast, just let me know."

"So you weren't getting along?"

"I didn't say that. I say there were difficulties. Dave settled his case, but he was unhappy because I had been spending a lot of money." Deirdre couldn't believe she was telling him this. "I had gone gambling several times and lost quite a bit. Dave wasn't happy about that and we argued about it this morning. Otherwise, we had a wonderful life. We were even planning to have another baby."

The questioning went on and on, and Deirdre began to think it would never end. She nearly tried to bolt from the room when they said her hands had to be tested to see if she'd recently fired a gun, but like an animal caught in a trap, she finally gave up and let them do whatever they wanted to her. She'd always assumed that the police would help her if something bad happened. Instead, she felt defiled and violated.

After two hours and no word about Morgan, Deirdre had reached her limits. She had answered every possible question, telling how she had found Dave, describing what she had done. Over and over again in intimate detail, she told them everything she knew about the last hours of Dave's life.

Finally it was too much. She had nothing left to give them. Breaking down, she began to sob. She couldn't stop the tears from coming, and soon she was crying so hard it was impossible to hear anything the detective was saying.

Why, Dave? Why did you have to do this? I know I shouldn't have spent the money. I know I shouldn't have lied, but why did you punish me like this? Why? Our daughter needed you. I needed you. You had no right to do this.

She felt someone touch her shoulders but had no idea who it was. She knew they were trying to comfort her, but there was no comfort.

Oh, God, she prayed, *help me. I can't do this alone.*

"Deirdre," Detective Stanford said, taking hold of her face. "You have to pull yourself together. I can't take you to your daughter like this."

"Morgan?" she managed to croak out between her sobs. Her ribs hurt from crying and her throat felt raw. Still, the thought of her daughter helped to calm her overwhelming emotions.

"You're free to go," he said softly and let go his hold.

She looked at him for a moment, the words not totally registering. "Go?"

"Your sister Erica has come and she's assured us that she'll take care of you both. Your husband's death seems quite clearly to be a suicide. Everything has checked out."

Deirdre's head was spinning, but she knew she had to collect herself. She had to get out of this place. She had to find Morgan.

"There's just one more thing," Stanford said sympathetically. "I thought you might want to have a copy of your husband's letter. It might help you to feel better about things." He reached over to the table and picked up a photocopied piece of paper. "You understand, the original, along with the gun, is being kept as evidence."

Deirdre could only nod and take the paper he offered her. As her thoughts settled and the pain in her head subsided a bit, she realized she was completely numb—stunned from the entire ordeal and exhausted beyond words.

She let them lead her out of the room and down the hall to where the police officer who'd taken Morgan sat trying to interest the child in some cookies. Deirdre walked calmly into the room and lifted her silent daughter into her arms and walked back out. She wanted nothing more than to leave this horrible place. But then an equally horrible thought came to mind. Where would they go? She certainly couldn't go back to the house. She never wanted to go back to that house again.

Morgan never said a word as they walked to where Erica waited. Deirdre met her sister's red-rimmed eyes and stunned expression. Poor Erica. She was hardly cut out for something of this magnitude.

"Dee, I'm so sorry. They wouldn't let me come back."

"It's all right," Deirdre replied. "Let's just get out of here."

Chapter 32

Harry knocked on Connie's door and waited impatiently. He felt jittery inside at the thought of seeing her again. He hadn't seen her since prior to confessing his interest in her to Mattie, and now, in spite of the trauma they faced, the thought of seeing her made him feel like a schoolboy again. Could there be some kind of future for them? He knew her life-style to be a vast contrast from what he thought acceptable, but it wasn't her life-style he was interested in—it was Connie herself who drew his attention.

He knocked again for lack of something better to do. All the way to Topeka he'd listened to Mattie talk about how impossible things had become. He listened to her speak tearfully of the family being ripped apart at the seams. Without ever making such a declaration, Harry knew that she was lonely. Lonely and tired and quickly losing her energy to deal with her responsibilities. Harry had hoped that her granddaughters would have seen this as well, but they seemed far too preoccupied with their own troubles to notice.

When Connie still hadn't appeared to answer his knock, Harry double-checked the number and reached up to try again. Before he could put his knuckles to the wood, however, Connie opened the door in a dazed stupor. Harry thought she looked small and vulnerable in her long, flowing sundress. The dress featured brilliant blues and pinks blended in patterns around white. It seemed to suit her very well—a bit unconventional, a little out of place. Just like Connie.

"Are you ready?" he asked softly.

"Ready?"

"Yeah," he said, uncertain what else he could say. "Mattie's in the van waiting."

She nodded, scarcely seeming to see him there. "I'll get my bag."

He followed her into the house. "Mattie's taking this pretty hard. Are you all right?" he asked.

"I'm fine. I just can't believe all that's happened."

He nodded. "Things like this are never easy to understand."

She looked at him for a moment, her dark eyes transferring a very real message of something akin to regret and sorrow. He wanted to reach out to her. She opened her mouth, then closed it and turned away from him. Harry felt certain that she had been about to say something important, but for some reason she didn't feel at ease enough to continue.

"Is there something else? Something you want to say before we join Mattie?"

She shook her head and went to collect her purse and bag. "No."

Instead, he glanced around the room. "Where's your room-mate? Does he know you're going?" Harry swallowed hard. "Does he want to ride with us?"

This seemed to bring her around a bit. "There is no room-mate," she replied, her voice taking on an edge of irritation. "We broke up a long time ago. I've turned over a new leaf, even before Grammy tore up her quilt. You did know she did that, didn't you?"

"Yes." It was all Harry could manage to say. Secretly he was glad she was alone and trying to change her life. But he could hardly tell her that. Nor could he be sharing the feelings he had for her on a day when they'd just learned about her brother-in-law's suicide.

"Why did you want to know about him?" Connie questioned in the awkwardness of the moment.

"You just seem more upset than I figured you'd be. I mean, this whole thing is a shock, but to tell you the truth, I thought you'd be a pillar of strength. I guess I was kind of counting on that for Mattie."

Connie's jaw tightened, and Harry thought she appeared to be battling within herself.

"I'll be as strong as I can be," she finally managed to say.

She stopped in front of the hall mirror and checked her appearance. Harry noted that her hair was acquiring some of its old color, her dark brown roots peeking out from under bleached layers. She barely had any makeup at all on her face.

Realizing he was staring at her, Harry shifted nervously. "We'd best get on our way," he said, leading the way back to the door. "Do you have a sweater in case the evenings turn cool?"

"I packed a jacket," she assured him and dug in her purse for her key.

Harry waited patiently while she locked her door, then walked in silence down the hall and out to Mattie's minivan.

Their hands touched as Harry took the bag from Connie. For just a moment their gazes met and Harry offered her a weak smile. "I'm here for you if you need me."

"Thank you, Harry," Connie replied, nodding. "I like knowing that."

Erica pulled into the driveway of Deirdre's house and shut off the engine. "I know you don't want to be here," she told her sister, "but Grammy's on her way and she won't know where to find us otherwise. Besides, you need to get some clothes and some things for Morgan, even if you just come stay at my place for a few days."

"I can't go back in there," Deirdre whispered from the backseat. Morgan hadn't spoken a word since leaving the police station, and now she slept rather peacefully against her mother.

"I suppose we could just sit here in the driveway and wait for Grammy," Erica reasoned aloud. She didn't know what to say to help Deirdre. Both her sister and Morgan seemed to be in such a state of shock that Erica was at a complete loss for words. How could anything she offered possibly help with the sorrow they were feeling?

Deirdre stared up at the house and shook her head. "I don't want to deal with it, Erica. I wish I could just make it all go away."

Erica turned in the seat and met Deirdre's stoic expression. "I wish that too. I feel so inadequate—I don't know how to help you through this. I want to say and do the right thing, but what is the right thing for a situation like this?"

"Grammy would say we had to cling to God's promises. She would tell us to trust even though things seem impossible."

"She would," Erica agreed.

Just then a silver minivan pulled into the drive behind them. Erica breathed a sigh of relief. Grammy was here. Grammy would know what to do and how to take care of the situation.

"It's Grammy," Erica said, craning her neck for a better look. "Connie and Harry are with her." Thoughts of Connie and their previous arguments made Erica feel rather uncomfortable. In light of Dave's death, Erica realized more than ever how fleeting life was. She thought of Mattie's wall hanging and what Brook had said about the piece. Somehow she had to swallow her pride and deal with Connie and the anger she felt toward her older sister. She knew she couldn't let any more sunsets pass by without making an effort at reconciliation.

Deirdre gently woke Morgan and stepped from the car just as Mattie approached her back door. Erica watched as Mattie embraced Deirdre and Morgan. Harry and Connie came to stand behind them, and Erica quietly walked to stand beside them.

"We got here as fast as we could," Harry said softly.

"I'm glad you're all here," Erica replied. "I'm not very good at these things."

"Not many folks would say they are," Harry answered.

Erica looked at Connie and smiled. "I'm sorry," she said and lightly touched Connie's bare arm. "I know this is a poor time to say so, but I am. This thing with Dave has really got me thinking."

Connie nodded with tears in her eyes. "Me too."

Mattie pulled back enough to lift Morgan into her arms. Erica worried that the five-year-old was too much weight for their grandmother, but Mattie acted as though Morgan weighed nothing more than a sack of flour. Morgan offered no protest in the transfer. Her eyes were blank, almost glazed over, and Erica couldn't help but worry about her niece.

"So what are you doing out here?" Mattie questioned, looking up at the house.

Deirdre shuddered. "I can't go back in there."

"I see," Grammy said, brushing back an errant strand of hair from Morgan's forehead. The child had nestled herself into Mattie's arms with her chin tucked tightly against her chest. Mattie seemed to consider the situation for several moments, then looked at Erica. "Have you called your sisters?"

"Yes," she answered, glad to have the subject changed. "I called Brook, and she promised to call Ashley."

"Good. Well, I suppose the only thing to do is collect some things for you both and stay elsewhere. I suppose I can't much blame you for not wanting to stay here."

"You can all come to my place, but there isn't much room," Erica offered.

"Why don't I take Deirdre and Morgan to a hotel," Mattie offered. "Connie can stay with you, and if Brook and Ashley are able to come back, we can worry about them when they get here."

"What about Harry?" Erica asked. She figured she could call Sean and get him to put Harry up for the night.

"I need to go back to the farm," Harry said before anyone could comment. "Mattie and I just finished discussing it. I'll take the van back down and return tomorrow or the next day at the latest."

Mattie nodded. "That way Harry can check on Miss Kitty and her kittens, as well as take care of his own needs. I know I'm presuming upon you and Deirdre for transportation, but I'm hoping you won't mind."

"Of course not," Erica replied, while Deirdre just stood there hugging her arms to her body. She looked so isolated, Erica longed to embrace her and shield her from the pain.

Mattie glanced at her watch. "Well, we can't make soup standing in the pasture." This was one of Mattie's favorite sayings to urge them into action when they were little. "Let's get your things, Deirdre, and then we can call for hotel availability."

"I can't go in there," Deirdre stated.

Mattie shifted Morgan and surprised them all by handing her to Harry. Morgan went willingly, as if she had no knowledge of being passed around. The fight had simply gone out of her.

Harry seemed glad for something physical to do. He held Morgan close, and Erica thought him very paternal as he patted the child's back. He would make a good father someday, she thought. Then she felt a tug on her own heartstrings. She longed for a child of her own. Usually she could fight the feeling, but at times like this when the whole world seemed to be falling apart, Erica thought a son or daughter would be a very nice addition to her life. So, too, would a husband. She sighed and realized that she longed to be with Sean. She wanted to curl beside him on the couch and have him wrap his arms around her. She wanted to hear him say that everything would be all right.

Mattie interrupted her thoughts. "Deirdre, you have to go inside and you have to get your things. You don't have to stay here tonight, but you have to do at least that much." Mattie looped her arm through Deirdre's. "However, I'll be with you every step of the way. I won't let you bear this alone. None of us will. Harry will sit on the couch with Morgan while Erica and Connie help us get you packed."

She had begun leading Deirdre up the path to the front door, all the while talking of what they would do once they were inside.

"Get your keys out," Mattie told her granddaughter gently, "and I'll unlock the door."

Erica was surprised that Deirdre offered no further protest. She did as she was told and allowed Mattie to take her back inside the house. Perhaps, Erica reasoned, she realized that Mattie would never willingly allow anything bad to happen to any of them. Perhaps she, like Morgan, was just too tired to fight.

Mattie snapped on the lights as dusk made for dark shadows inside the house. "Harry, you can sit in the living room with Morgan. I'll turn the television on for you and leave you with the remote." He nodded and took his seat in the middle of Deirdre's plush navy print couch. "Deirdre, where are your suitcases?"

Erica watched her sister as she seemed to ponder this for a moment. "I had them in our bedroom," Deirdre said as if struggling to remember. "But that was when we were going on the trip. They're not there now. I think I put them away."

Mattie nodded. "So where are they?"

"The storage room off the garage," Deirdre said automatically. "Yes, I remember now. That's where they are."

Mattie looked to Connie this time. "Do you think you could find them?"

Connie stood staring off into space and Mattie repeated herself. "Sure, Grammy. I'll get them," Connie finally answered and walked from the room without another word.

Erica watched Deirdre as she surveyed the room. There was very little to suggest that anything at all was amiss. Then her gaze went to the stairway and Erica could very nearly hear Deirdre's sharp intake of breath. This wasn't going to be easy for her.

"Erica, you come with Deirdre and me. We'll go upstairs and see what needs to be done."

"Grammy, you don't want to see that room," Deirdre said in a nearly hysterical tone. Then she seemed to catch sight of Morgan and turned away.

"It'll be all right," Grammy assured them, taking hold of Deirdre and heading for the stairs. "We'll do this together."

Erica followed behind, wondering for the first time exactly what kind of sight would be left for them. Dave had been removed from the house, but had the police or even the ambulance attendants bothered to clean up?

At the top of the stairs they moved down the hall in a pace that Mattie allowed Deirdre to set. When they finally stood outside of the master bedroom, Deirdre froze in place and looked at Mattie and then Erica with an expression of utter anguish.

"You don't know what's in there."

"You don't either," Mattie said softly. "They've taken Dave away, but chances are there's still a mess to be dealt with. We can clean up later, but for now you need to have clothes." Mattie's face expressed such gentleness that Erica thought she might be moved to tears. "I won't make you go in there if you're certain it's impossible for you, but I think it's better to face your fears head on. The worst has already happened," she told Deirdre. "Dave is gone and you were here for the horror of it all. Now it's just an empty room."

Deirdre bit her lower lip and Erica reached out to hold her hand. They exchanged a look and Deirdre nodded. "I'll go in."

Mattie nodded. "So will I."

"Me too," Erica assured and squeezed Deirdre's hand. She quickly realized that support and love was all she had to offer Deirdre. Words were of very little use, but action could definitely provide comfort. Maybe this was what Mattie had talked about when she said that offering family support was more important than anything else. Being there for one another in times of joy and sorrow, even when there was nothing to say or do that could change the circumstance.

Deirdre turned and pulled down the yellow tape the police had used to quarter off the room. Erica wondered for the first time if perhaps the police would object to Deirdre's invasion, but realized just as quickly that her sister wouldn't have cared if they did. She had clearly suffered at the hands of the detectives. They had yanked her from her home and treated her like some sort of suspect until they were satisfied that Dave's death had truly been a suicide. Erica wasn't even certain that the matter was yet resolved because when they'd left the station, Detective Stanford promised to be in touch.

Twisting the handle on the bedroom door, Deirdre stepped forward and turned on the light. Erica followed behind Mattie and immediately her gaze moved to the place where Dave had fallen dead.

A huge brownish red stain marred the rose-colored carpet. Around this, littered in a haphazard manner, were various wrappers and packaging from the emergency medical supplies used when the paramedics had arrived on the scene.

The bed had been pushed out of the way, along with Deirdre's quilt stand and free-standing mirror. Erica supposed this was done in order to give the paramedics more room in which to work. Either way, the room looked to have been completely trashed.

"Just get your things together," Mattie suggested. "Take whatever you think you'll need and if we have to come back later . . . well . . . we'll worry about it then."

Deirdre nodded, but it wasn't until Erica moved to push her in the direction of the closet that she actually turned away from the death scene.

"I can help if you'll just tell me what you want," Erica said, happy for a task that took her away from the ghastly sight.

"I don't know what to take," Deirdre replied. "I don't know what to do." She looked at Erica with mournful eyes and an expression that suggested she was about to break down.

Erica wrapped her arms around Deirdre and hugged her close. "I don't either, sis," she murmured. "Guess we'll figure it out together."

Chapter 33

Brook tied her long chestnut hair back into a ponytail, then tried Ashley's telephone in Estes Park for the fourth time. There was no answer. Even the answering machine refused to pick up. It was just as well, Brook reasoned, for she'd never leave a machine message telling of Dave's suicide. Especially since Ashley was alone.

Dave Woodward was dead. It was impossible to believe such a statement. Just like that—the snap of fingers, the blink of an eye—and a person she had known and cared about was gone.

Equally troubling was the fact that this death had come at his own hand. Brook sat down and tried to comprehend the situation. Why had Dave killed himself? Erica had given her very little information and none of it answered this question. Deirdre and Dave had seemed so happy. Of course, there was that issue of Dave canceling their anniversary trip, but even so, that wasn't related to the marriage so much as to Dave's job.

Brook shuddered. Death seemed to have a strong hold on their family. Within the last few months Rachelle had died, Ashley had lost a baby after defying her own death, and now Dave was gone.

"Life and death walk hand in hand," Grammy would say when they were young. Brook had never really understood it then. Yet she wasn't sure she was any better at understanding it now. Oh, it was easy to see that death was an unavoidable part of life, but to Brook it came as much more than that. She was afraid of dying. Especially of dying alone with no one to mourn her passing or be at her side when the end came.

She thought of Ashley and how much her sister loved her. In

spite of this, Ashley couldn't be expected to drop everything and give her life over to Brook. Ashley had told Brook she would always have a home with Ashley and her family, but Brook knew that was a less than perfect arrangement.

Thinking of Ashley, Brook wondered if she should try to call again. She'd not heard a single thing from her sister since returning to New York. Her own schedule had been nonstop since stepping off the plane, but Brook had made numerous attempts to reach Ashley. It bothered Brook a great deal that her sister was back to making herself unavailable. At least that's what it appeared she was doing. There didn't seem to be any other logical explanation.

Brook thought of how troubled Ashley was by Jack's lying. It seemed to come as a final blow to her sister, and Brook couldn't help but worry that Ashley and Jack might be headed toward a separation— maybe even a divorce. This thought seemed to rear up to contradict her earlier concerns about isolationism and dying alone. A person could find a wonderful mate, only to lose them like Deirdre had. Then what?

Brook shook her head, unable to fathom what Deirdre must be going through. She longed to be with her. To be with all of them and know the comfort of family. Thoughts of things her sisters had said about Brook's tendency to keep herself confined in New York came back to haunt her.

"If you came around more often . . ."

"If you lived closer . . ."

"If you really wanted to spend time with us . . ."

Brook put her hand to her temples and rubbed the throbbing pain with her fingertips. Her life was like a pyramid turned upside down. Family was at the base, but the base was small and minute compared to the top portion—her career. Family and its responsibility was smaller than every other aspect of her life. It was no wonder that at times like this Brook felt the pyramid was about to crash to one side or the other.

Going to her desk, she pulled out the top drawer and took out her address book. She'd given little thought to what she was to do in regard to Dave's funeral. She knew she needed to be there, but she had also agreed to film a television commercial. Getting out of it would be impossible. They were already into their second day and the crew and sponsors were all rather cranky that things had taken so long on day one.

Brook stared at the telephone number for the airline. She didn't even know when the funeral would be, but if she judged it by other funerals, then it would probably be set up to give everyone enough time to come from far away. Perhaps they'd set it at two or three days at the most. She could always reserve a seat and pray that the filming would conclude within that time. Maybe if she explained the situation, the sponsor would find a way to step up the production—at the very least perhaps he could arrange for the rest of her filming to be concluded first. She'd never pulled the prima donna act on anyone in all the time she'd been modeling. Maybe now was the time to pull out the stops and demand a few rights for herself.

She picked up the receiver and dialed the airline. Explaining the situation, she booked a ticket out of New York for the day after tomorrow. And then, without really thinking as to why she was doing what she was doing, Brook dialed Ashley's home in Denver. Maybe Jack would go and break the news to her sister in person. After all, telling someone that their brother-in-law had just committed suicide wasn't exactly the kind of thing that suited a phone call. Ashley would need someone to be with her when she learned the truth.

Brook waited impatiently as the phone rang once, then twice, and finally three times. She was about to hang up when Jack's voice sounded on the other end.

"Hello, Dr. Issacs here."

"Jack, it's Brook."

"Oh, Brook. How are you?"

"Not so good. Something has happened and I need to get ahold of Ashley."

"What's wrong?"

"This is hard to believe, but Deirdre's husband killed himself," Brook replied matter-of-factly.

"What!" Jack's voice boomed out the question.

"I had the same reaction," Brook admitted. "I don't know many of the details, but I got a call from Erica. I guess he shot himself earlier this afternoon."

"I don't believe it."

"I know. I can hardly believe it myself. I don't know when the funeral is planned, but it will probably be in Kansas City. I'm hoping to go and figured I'd call and coordinate things with Ashley."

"She's not here."

"Is she still up at the house in Estes? I tried calling her but there was no response."

Jack issued an audible sigh. "She's not up there. She came back to Denver with me, but she's making plans to take off. She wants to go to Mattie's."

Brook felt an uneasiness settle over her. "By herself?"

He didn't answer right away and Brook was instantly sorry that she'd questioned the situation.

"No, she wants to take the boys. She plans to go see Mattie and enjoy some time with the boys before school starts up."

"Will she fly?" Brook questioned, wanting to know whatever details Jack could give her.

"No, at least I don't think so. She had me go with her to pick out a new car to replace the one she wrecked. She's off finalizing the purchase right now."

"Would you have her call me when she gets back?"

"Sure. Do you want me to break the news to her about Dave?"

"That would probably be the best thing," Brook said, chickening out of her obligation. After all, she could scarcely believe she'd gotten through the announcement to Jack without feeling that old sensation of queasiness creep up on her. No sense in pushing it.

"I'll tell her and then have her call you," Jack promised.

Brook thought of what Ashley had told her about Jack lying and wished she could say something to help matters. Instead, she mumbled a hasty good-bye, then sat staring at the phone feeling completely foolish for not having confronted Jack with the truth. After all, he'd been the one to tell her that Ashley was on her way home from seeing him at the clinic when the accident happened. Whatever his reasons for lying to Ashley, he couldn't have the same thought when it came to Brook.

She reached for the telephone, determined to call Jack back, then stopped and shook her head. "I'm not very good at confrontations and relationships," Brook muttered. "I keep telling people this, but no one seems inclined to listen to me. If I call back, I'll probably just make matters worse."

Steeped in feelings of remorse, Brook realized the one person she still had to deal with was Miriam. If she waited until tomorrow to explain the situation, there would be too great a price to pay. Dialing the number of her pager, Brook left her number and waited for her manager to return the call.

"God, you have to show me how to handle this," Brook prayed aloud, eyes open and fixed on the silent telephone. "I don't know where you're leading me or what I'm supposed to do, but I need you to be in charge of the details."

The telephone rang.

Brook shuddered and looked away. "And I need for you to protect me from Miriam's wrath."

———————

It was Mattie who made the call to Dave's parents in St. Louis. She talked first to Julie Woodward and then to Mike, Dave's father. Both were stunned silent for several moments and then both began to cry and ask questions. Concluding that call was one of the hardest things Mattie had ever done. She knew what it was to lose a son. She knew the need for a lifeline to someone who could help—someone who would listen or, better yet, give some answers.

But there was too much yet to be done. She had managed to get

Deirdre packed, and after a few calls to area hotels, she had settled on a reliable hotel chain near to where Erica lived. Morgan and Deirdre had followed her lead like silent soldiers heading off to battle. Their expressions were fixed, their stares were glassy-eyed and empty. They were shell-shocked in a sense. They'd seen too much—endured too much.

To Mattie's relief, the hotel had a small suite with a sitting room and adjoining bedroom. In the bedroom was a king-sized bed and in the sitting room the couch pulled into a queen-sized sleeper. Mattie had encouraged Deirdre to take the bedroom with Morgan, while she would make her bed on the couch. Deirdre had argued with her only briefly. It had taken nothing more than Mattie explaining that certain calls had to be made and arrangements decided upon for Deirdre to see the sensibility in the suggestion.

The room itself was rather comforting. The colors were rich and the decor appeared to be English Victorian. Thick swag drapery dressed the windows in deep forest green, while the wallpaper held the same dark green against pinstripes of burgundy and gold. Mattie felt a certain comfort in the room. The dark tones and richly polished woods seemed to warm the room—if not physically, then certainly emotionally.

However, as Mattie stared at the clock, she couldn't help but wonder what the night ahead had in store for them. A comfortable room would hardly resolve their problems. "Eight-thirty," she said aloud, then yawned. It felt more like midnight.

"She's asleep," Deirdre said, coming out from the adjoining room. "I left the light on, but I'll close the door so we can talk."

Mattie smiled and nodded. Deirdre seemed a little more like herself now that she'd put the horrors of the house and the earlier events of the day behind her. Mattie patted the sofa. "I guess we have plenty to talk about."

Deirdre had changed into a comfortable-looking nightshirt and shorts. She sat down on the couch and tucked her legs up under her before meeting Mattie's gaze. "This is all my fault, Grammy. I might as well tell you that up front."

Mattie gazed at her granddaughter. "How do you see this as your fault?"

Deirdre took a deep breath and looked away. "Remember when I told you about my friend? The one with the gambling addiction?"

"Yes," Mattie replied. "I remember."

"There was no friend, Grammy. That was me. I was talking about myself." She looked back at Mattie, and the pain in Deirdre's eyes nearly made Mattie wince. "I couldn't tell you it was me because I didn't want to face your disappointment or your lectures. But it got away from me. I took a great deal of money out of our checking account, and I even pawned an antique necklace Dave's mother had given me. But I lost it all. I lost every cent and then some."

"I'm so sorry, Dee," Mattie said, praying she'd say the right thing.

"Dave found out about the money, but I couldn't bring myself to tell him about the gambling. He wanted to know where the money had gone, but I just couldn't confess it to him. I was too ashamed. I couldn't believe I'd fallen victim to something I clearly knew was a danger."

"It happens to everyone at some time in their life," Mattie gently told her granddaughter.

"But this particular problem should never have happened. I knew gambling could be a problem, and even when I saw early on that there was one, I thought I could control it. I just kept thinking that if I could only get one more win, then I'd have enough money to pay back the money I'd taken. But I could never get enough."

"But that's no reason for Dave to kill himself," Mattie stated seriously. "I know he loved you a great deal. There had to be something else."

"That's what he said in his note," Deirdre replied. "He said I wouldn't understand until later, but that I wasn't the problem. He told me he didn't really care where the money had gone or what I'd used it for, but that there were things in his life that he had done and now he couldn't live with his own guilt." She shook her head and stared at the blank black screen of the television. "Imagine him thinking that there was something he couldn't live with."

"He didn't say what it was?"

Deirdre pulled her legs up and rested her head on her knees. "No, and the police kept asking me if I had any idea what he was talking about. They suggested an affair, but, Grammy, I just don't think Dave was cheating on me."

"No, I don't think he was either," Mattie agreed quickly. The last thing Deirdre needed to worry about was whether or not her husband was being faithful. "It was more likely something to do with his job. He probably felt he'd made some poor choices. You know how seriously he took being a lawyer. He wanted justice for all. Maybe when he couldn't get justice for all, he felt he'd failed."

"I suppose you're right. That would be just like him," Deirdre admitted.

"I guess the really important question is—where do you go from here?"

"Well, it won't be back to a casino, I can tell you that much."

Mattie nodded. "I hope not, for your sake."

"No, it's not for my sake. I don't deserve any consideration at all. It's for Morgan's sake. She hasn't spoken a word since I told her that Dave was dead. She was traumatized at the police station and now I'm worried that it might cause some permanent trauma for her."

"Give her time, Deirdre," Mattie suggested. "This can't be easy for her. Maybe there's a bereavement counselor who can help. Maybe after the funeral you can look someone up."

"Maybe," Deirdre replied.

"Speaking of the funeral, you're going to have to make plans. After all, Julie and Mike are leaving tomorrow morning to come here."

"I know. Too bad Mavis can't handle the details like she did for Rachelle's funeral."

Mattie smiled. "I suppose we could all use a Mavis in our lives from time to time."

"I don't have the first idea of where to start."

Mattie nodded and reached out her hand to touch Deirdre's cheek. "I do."

Deirdre scooted across the couch and leaned against Mattie just as she had done when she was a child. Mattie held her close and stroked her arm ever so gently.

"This can't be happening. Dave can't be gone, Grammy. I need him too much. I love him—I'll always love him."

"I know," Mattie said, remembering a time when she had felt those same things. "And it hurts down deep inside," Mattie whispered, "in a place where no one but God can reach."

Deirdre nodded, tears running down her cheeks. "Why did this happen? If God loves me like you've taught me to believe, then why did this happen? I know I did a bad thing, but this punishment is too much to bear."

"Deirdre, Dave's death is not God's punishment for your addiction to gambling. I don't believe that for one moment. You have a great many responsibilities in life, but Dave's choice to take his own life was just that. *His* choice. You aren't responsible for his action and neither is his action a punishment for yours. You need to get your life together. You need to see what is real and what is important.

"Morgan needs you now, more than ever. She needs you to be strong because it's your witness and example that will show her that everything will be all right. She's going to be an emotionally scarred child for a long time. She'll probably carry some portion of this with her throughout her life. She may even blame herself for what happened. After all, you told me that she'd interceded on your behalf and told Dave he wasn't . . . what was it she said?"

"That he wasn't a nice daddy anymore." Deirdre was barely able to speak the words.

"See what I mean?" Mattie questioned, knowing that Deirdre would quickly understand if she allowed herself the chance.

Deirdre wiped at her eyes. "This isn't Morgan's fault. There is no portion of this that is her fault."

"But you may not be able to convince her of that unless you find a way to convince yourself. Dave had a problem—obviously a very serious one. None of us realized the extent of that problem, but by your own admission he'd been troubled for some time. You tried to be supportive and loving and you did the very best you could. You can't go back and relive those days, and you can't bury yourself alive in 'What If's.' Morgan needs to see you act in a way that assures her that you will survive this and that you will trust God to see you through, despite the fact that it makes no sense."

"I just don't know if I'm strong enough," Deirdre said, looking up at Mattie.

"That's why you have your family," Mattie replied. "God put us here for a reason, but we can only help you if you let us. The days to come are going to be hard. There's no doubt about that. But if you shut us out, we can't do a single thing."

"It seems too much to ask. Too much too expect."

"Love is never too much to expect," Mattie replied, taking hold of Deirdre's hand. "And love is the rock on which you rebuild your life—and Morgan's life. When everything else fades away, love is all that endures."

"Love wasn't enough to keep Dave alive. It wasn't enough for him," Deirdre said, seeking Mattie's face with eyes that seemed to plead for her to prove Deirdre wrong.

"Sweetheart, do you remember your old Bible verses? 'God is love.' And God is enough. He is sufficient even when we think He's somehow forgotten us. Love was enough for Dave, but somewhere along the way he decided otherwise. We can't know what Dave was thinking—not really. But love was there for him all along. He simply made another choice. And now all the choices are yours."

"I don't want the responsibility," Deirdre answered, her voice raw with emotion. "I just don't know what to do."

Mattie hugged her close again. "When the way is darkest, even the tiniest point of light can be seen as a beacon. Let your family be

Chapter 34

Connie woke up in Erica's guest bedroom, and for a very few moments she couldn't remember where she was or why she was there. Then, like an unwelcome intruder, the memories flooded her conscious thoughts and Connie longed for sleep to overcome her once again.

Slipping out from the comforting warmth of one of Grammy's log cabin quilts, Connie pulled on a borrowed robe and padded down the hall to the living room. Seeing that Erica was nowhere in sight, Connie went to the sliding glass door and quietly opened it.

The humid day greeted her without offering any comfort. Connie sighed and leaned against the balcony rail, wishing against all hope that she could find a way to make things different. Was it wrong to plead with God for mercy in your hour of need? Especially when you hadn't given Him much consideration when things were going okay?

"I've done this to myself," she murmured. "I let myself get away from God. I put a wall between us and now it's time to tear it back down."

"I thought I heard you get up," Erica said, joining her sister on the balcony. "Did you sleep okay?"

Connie nodded and smiled. "Considering everything, I slept very well. Thanks."

Erica quickly left the pretense of chitchat behind. "I still can't believe that Dave is dead."

"Me either."

"I probably knew him better than you or the others. After all, I lived close enough to see them two or three times a week, if I had the time," Erica said, running her fingers through tangled auburn curls. "I thought he was such a great guy and now he's gone. It just doesn't seem real.

"This whole thing got me thinking about Rachelle again," Erica continued. "I suppose it's silly."

"How so?"

Erica turned and gave Connie a brief smile. "When I was little, I used to pretend that Rachelle really wanted to be my mother, but that she only wanted me and not everyone else." She lowered her gaze to the floor. "I know that sounds awful, but that was how I rationalized her absence. I told myself that she couldn't be my mother without explaining to the rest of you that she didn't want to be your mother. And in my mind, I was just positive that she was too kind to hurt you all that way. And I loved all of you too much to tell you my theory on her absence. It was sort of like bearing some awful burden alone because you knew it would cause those you love too much pain if you shared it."

Connie felt a sensation akin to an electrical current run through her body. Erica could have been talking about her. Wasn't that exactly what she was feeling just now?

Erica moved away from Connie and plopped down on a plastic lawn chair. "I suppose we all rationalize things in a way that makes sense to us. At nine years old, that scenario made sense to me. At twenty-five, it sounds ludicrous."

"No, it doesn't. I used to pretend things like that too," Connie admitted. "Only I pretended that she really loved my father and that she had run away with him and one day would send for me to join them. Then we would be a family."

Erica looked rather shocked. "You too?"

Connie shrugged. "Guess it was just a good way to deal with the pain of being deserted. It was hard to admit that your own mother left you by choice."

Erica nodded. "But you know, with Rachelle's death, I felt a sense of closure. I didn't feel sad or empty. I didn't want to cry and mourn her. I just felt that finally I knew the truth. Finally I knew she was never going to call and ask me to join her. She was never coming home to declare what a horrible mistake it had been to leave us all. It was simply over and done with."

Connie couldn't have put it better had she tried. She had felt that same sense of completion. It was as if Rachelle's death had stamped the words *The End* on a page of Connie's life.

"But then her letter came," Erica said softly. She stared out across the landscape. "That letter was something I never expected. I never, ever would have thought Rachelle would need to clear her conscience that way."

"No," Connie admitted. "Me either." She thought of her own letter and the way it had touched her frozen heart. Connie, who had vowed her mother would never have any power over her, had broken down at the idea that her mother shared the same sense of longing and desire for forgiveness that Connie had for herself.

"I guess the letter really settled things. It's the only thing Rachelle has left to us of herself."

"Grammy would say you're wrong on that account," Connie replied. "Grammy would say Rachelle left us one another and that through each other, we have a part of Rachelle that the world can never have."

"But we've never seen it that way—never considered having anything of Rachelle."

"No," Connie admitted. "We were just angry and bitter and hard and unforgiving. And all the while Grammy had given us her life and love. How it must hurt her to see us fight and bicker when she's given her all."

Erica's eyes filled with tears. "Connie, I know I haven't been a good sister to you. But I really want to be. I want to stop being so selfish and I want to be there for each of you. We must stay strong— together."

"I agree," Connie said, opening her arms to embrace her

younger sister. "I'm so sorry for my attitude." They held each other close, crying and then laughing at their reunion.

"Please just tell me that you forgive me," Connie finally said, breaking away. "I need that more than ever. I've sought it from God and really tried hard to clean up my life. But now, especially in the wake of Dave's death, I need your forgiveness as well."

"Of course you have my forgiveness," Erica said, wiping her tears. "I hope I can count on the same thing from you. I feel so stupid—so undeserving."

Connie nodded. "Me too. Gram would say that none of us deserve to be forgiven, but that's what makes it so sweet. Mercy is a rare and precious thing and forgiveness is like a cold drink on a hot day." And for the first time in her life, Connie knew exactly what Grammy had meant.

Chapter 35

"Boys, I want you to bring in every bit of trash," Ashley instructed as she stepped out of her new burgundy minivan. She had purchased lunch for the boys at one of the fast-food stops on the way home and knew that if she didn't instruct them to clean up after themselves, they would conveniently forget.

She leaned across the driver's seat and retrieved a sack of groceries. It didn't constitute much in the way of supplies for the household, but that was because she planned to leave first thing in the morning. While they were gone, Jack would probably eat out most of the time.

She followed the boys into the house and was rather surprised when Jack met her at the door. He took up the sack and it was then that Ashley noticed the somber look on his face.

"We need to talk," he told her.

"I need to get the dry cleaning out of the van," she replied and turned to walk back out.

"Ashley, it will keep," Jack said and the tone of his voice left her little doubt that something was very wrong.

"All right," she said softly. "What about the boys?"

"I've sent them next door to play. I told them just as they came in the front door. I've already talked to Mary," he said, mentioning their next-door neighbor.

Ashley knew that if Jack had gone to all the trouble to arrange someone's help in keeping their boys occupied, the topic must indeed be important. She followed him into the kitchen and waited until he put the sack down on the counter before stepping anywhere near him. Sadly she found a great deal of her affection for him was lost in the wake of his lie. Yet she still loved him—maybe that's what hurt the most. If she could only convince herself not to care, things might be so much easier. Her biggest fear, however, was that he would expect her to be intimate with him, and she simply couldn't allow that with this unresolved issue between them. She wanted nothing to do with anything that might be misconstrued as interest in something physical.

Jack seemed to understand this as well because he backed off and leaned against the counter while Ashley put the perishable things in the refrigerator.

"So what merits this moment of privacy?" she asked nonchalantly after stacking a package of steak and a container of pasta sauce atop a sealed plastic bowl.

"Something really bad has happened. Brook called to tell you, but you weren't in Estes and so she called here."

"Is it Grammy?" Ashley questioned, feeling a nervous sensation in her stomach.

"No."

"So what's happened?" She closed the refrigerator door and leaned against it as if for strength.

"Dave is dead," Jack said, his tone somber.

Ashley looked at her husband as though he'd suddenly started speaking a foreign language. *Dead? Dave?* She shook her head. "How?"

"Suicide," Jack replied. "He shot himself."

Ashley felt her nerves fire up. A tingling sensation started in her lower spine and worked its way up her back and into the base of her neck. "But why?"

"That I can't tell you. Brook didn't know much. She wanted you to know about it and said that most everyone was gathering in Kansas City. I guess Mattie is already there. Connie too."

"I guess we'll head there instead of Council Grove," Ashley said, rather overwhelmed by the information. "I suppose the boys and I can leave tonight instead of tomorrow."

"Or you could fly," Jack said softly. "And leave the boys here."

She shook her head. "No. I had this visit planned anyway. I'll just drive to Kansas City. If we leave tonight, I can stop in Limon or even push to Goodland. That way we can be there tomorrow night."

"You have no business going that far by yourself. Look, the funeral hasn't even been planned yet. Why don't you talk to your grandmother first?"

"I'll talk to Grammy before leaving—that is, if I can locate her," Ashley said. "I suppose calling Deirdre's house or Erica's would be the best bet."

She moved away from the refrigerator and headed for the telephone, but Jack stopped her. "Come sit with me," he said, pulling her to the small alcove where they usually ate breakfast. He put his hands on her shoulders and pressed lightly to get Ashley to take a seat at the table. "I have something else to say."

Ashley studied his serious expression. Was there something more to Dave's death? Something he wasn't telling her? Had something happened to Deirdre?

"Is Deirdre all right? Morgan?"

"They're okay," Jack said, sitting down beside her. "It's just that this whole situation left me completely stripped of my resolve."

"I don't understand," Ashley said, shaking her head. "What resolve?"

"I did lie to you," Jack began, continuing despite the gasp Ashley couldn't quite conceal. "You've been right all along. I know it was wrong, but I was afraid."

"Afraid of what?" she asked, almost terrified of the answer. If she could have just remembered it all for herself, it might not seem so horrible.

"I was afraid of losing you." His voice cracked emotionally. "You did come to the office on the day of the accident. But you never told me about the baby. You didn't get the chance."

Ashley felt her breathing quicken and her heart race. The

moment of truth was before her and she wasn't exactly sure she wanted it exposed. "Why are you telling me this now?"

Jack bit his lower lip and looked down at the table. "I guess it was hearing about Dave. It was the reality of his suicide that made me realize that I wasn't so very far from such thoughts myself."

"What!" Ashley declared louder than she'd intended. The idea that her husband had contemplated taking his life was more than she could fathom. "Why in the world would you say such a thing?"

Jack looked up at her, his eyes were damp with tears and his expression betrayed abject pain. "I deserve to die after what I did to you."

"I don't understand."

"You came to the office to tell me about the baby. And instead, you opened the door and found me . . . you saw me . . ." his voice trailed off. He coughed and choked back his tears. "You saw me with Gina."

"Gina?" Ashley still couldn't remember it. She saw herself walking down the hall to Jack's office, felt her hand on the door, but opening the door revealed nothing but blackness.

"I was kissing Gina."

"Kissing her?" Ashley felt that somewhere in the back of her mind this statement had support in her memories. She visualized her husband and the redheaded nurse. She forced herself to think of them passionately kissing.

"I didn't mean to let it happen, Ashley," Jack continued. "I can't think of anything I've ever done that was more stupid than having an affair with Gina."

"An affair?" Ashley echoed in a whisper. "You had an affair?"

"Yes. That's what I'm trying to tell you. You saw us together and you freaked out. I can't blame you, but I also couldn't stop you. You ran for the car and took off in a blind fury. I came after you, but by the time I caught up . . . well, the accident had already taken place."

"I see," Ashley said, forcing her tone to be even. "How long have you been having this affair?"

"It's over now, but it was going on for about two months," Jack said and got up to pace the room. "I don't care anything about her. I don't love her. You have to know that."

"Then why did you cheat on me with her?" Ashley asked. It was almost impossible to digest all the information he'd just given her.

Jack stopped and shook his head. "I don't know. It was just one of those very stupid mistakes. She'd been coming on to me for several months and I just kept putting her off. Then one evening when you'd called to say you weren't going to be home until late and I decided to stay on at the clinic and get some extra work done . . . well, Gina convinced me that I was being rather neglected."

"Neglected?"

"I know it sounds lame, but she appealed to something inside of me. She made me feel young and important. She esteemed my knowledge and fed my ego. I know it was wrong, but I was lonely and you were always busy."

"And do you think that excuses your behavior?" Ashley questioned, starting to get angry.

"No," Jack said, coming back to the table. "I know it doesn't excuse anything. I don't want to be excused—just forgiven. I don't want to lose you, Ashley. I couldn't live like that. I know too many divorced people—we both do. You know how awful that life is for them and for their kids."

"But even knowing that, and knowing that I'd have very little tolerance for such a thing, you went ahead and slept with your nurse. Why should I forgive you?"

Jack slumped to the chair. "You shouldn't, but I'm praying that you will. I'm trying to make amends and set things right. I asked Gina to resign."

"So you punished Gina for your indiscretion?"

"I didn't punish her. I talked to some of my colleagues. She has another job—a better job. And I asked her to forgive me. She's consumed with guilt, Ashley. She knows the part she had to play in this whole thing. She feels every bit as responsible for your accident as I do."

"We lost our baby," Ashley stated, swallowing hard to keep her composure. "I had to have a hysterectomy, and all because you allowed Gina to make you feel nineteen again? I'm supposed to understand that and just up and forgive you?"

Jack said nothing. He didn't have to. Tears were streaming down his cheeks. It was only the second time Ashley had ever seen him cry. The first time was at his father's funeral.

Overwhelmed by this news, Ashley got up from the table. "I can't think about this here. I'm going forward with my plans. I'll leave tonight."

"Please let me go with you," Jack said, getting up. He reached out to her only to have Ashley recoil.

"Don't touch me, and please don't think that this matter is resolved. Confession may have been good for your soul, but you've just ripped mine to shreds." She tried not to think of the full impact of what Jack had told her. "I'm taking the boys and going to Kansas City. Then after the funeral we're going to spend the rest of the summer with Mattie. I'll cancel all of their other activities, so don't worry about having to do a single thing."

"Please don't go off like this. What if something happens?"

"Something has already happened, and I don't want to talk to you about this anymore."

She turned and walked out of the room, wishing she could once again feel the numbness that had sustained her after the accident. Instead, a brilliant white-hot pain seemed to sear her heart. Ashley imagined the scene in Jack's office. She could very nearly remember it. How could he do this to her? How could he have betrayed his family that way?

She walked to the minivan and opened the back to retrieve her dry cleaning. Her husband had cheated on her. She was now no different than most of the country club wives. Rhonda would say, "Welcome to the club, sweetie." Willa would good-naturedly offer to drive them all to the nearest bar where they could drown their sorrows. But this wasn't something Ashley wanted anyone to know. Not even her best friends. Not even Brook.

She took up the dry cleaning, most of which were Jack's dress shirts and slacks, and closed the hatch. Leaning against the car, she stared back up at the house. *Our dream house,* she thought. The house they had spent months looking for. It was a perfect house to raise children in. A perfect house for entertaining. It should have been everything that she had wanted out of life. But it wasn't. Her life was a sham.

Grammy would chide her for placing her sights on things below. Ashley could remember nights in front of the fire when Grammy had reminded them that houses didn't make homes—people did. That possessions were irrelevant in matters of the heart, and that love could grow anywhere so long as it found fertile, willing soil.

"I don't love her. You have to know that," Jack had said, his voice thick with emotion.

Down deep inside, Ashley knew it was true, but it didn't matter, and maybe in some ways it only made things worse.

"You don't love me either, Jack. Because if you did, you couldn't have done this horrible thing."

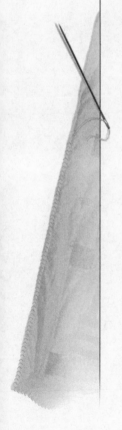

PART THREE

a time to sew

Chapter 36

"You're all wasting my time," Miriam Wells stated, then paused to take a long drag off her cigarette. "I'm busting myself to keep you in the top-paying modeling jobs and what thanks do I get? Kristy announces that she's pregnant." She pointed the cigarette at the rail-thin blonde at the end of the table. "Sisi gets busted for her little heroin addiction, and you," she said, turning to Brook, "are no longer taking your job seriously."

"I take it as seriously as it needs to be taken," Brook said, tired of being browbeaten by her manager.

"Well, that's not how I see it. You're thirty years old and your days of playing the youthful fun-girl are over. You can't get the same modeling jobs you used to because your age is starting to show. No one wants to peddle to a young market by using an old has-been."

Brook stood up and smoothed the lines of her black skirt. She'd taken all she was going to take. She'd tried to talk reasonably to Miriam—not only the day before, but also this morning before their production meeting—and nothing phased the woman. She wouldn't have cared if all of Brook's family had just dropped dead, and she wasn't about to allow Brook to take off again and risk spoiling yet another good job.

"Well, this old has-been is going to make it official," Brook announced, looking at her colleagues. "I quit. I've taken your cutthroat way of doing business long enough." She took up a cardigan that matched the shell she was wearing and grabbed her purse off the back of her chair.

Miriam stood speechless at the end of the table. Her eyes were wide in stunned surprise, but no more so than the other eight girls who sat around the table. Brook had tried to find a way to make friends with them all, but realized now how little she knew about any of them. Short of sharing their gripes and complaints about Miriam and their jobs, they rarely ever shared anything personal.

Brook had thought to simply stalk out of the room riding high on her own determination, but instead she stopped and shook her head. "I'm sick to death of the pretenses and falsehoods this city seems to perpetuate. I'm tired of being held up as valuable only for my looks and my ability to wear clothes. I'm bored and frustrated by a world where no one ever talks to each other except to lie about who they were last seen partying with or what prince or king they plan to vacation with. I'm tired of parties where I'm endlessly paraded around to clients as though I were nothing more than this week's produce."

She looked hard at Miriam. "But perhaps most of all, I've had more than I'm going to take of listening to you suggest that I'm selfish and foolish for putting my family ahead of my career. After all, you've been telling me for months, even years, that my career is the same as over. Why should it bother either one of us if I walk away?"

"You have . . . you have a contract!" Miriam declared.

"Yes, I suppose I do. You can discuss that issue with my lawyers," Brook said calmly. "But I fail to see why you would want an 'old has-been' under contract."

"You tell her, Brook," Kristy chimed in. "We're all sick and tired of your attitude, Miriam. We're people, not cattle. You can push us around and send us from one location to another, but we have very real needs in our lives and I, for one, salute Brook for having the guts to tell you."

Miriam took this salvo without so much as flinching. "In a few short months, you aren't going to find anyone who's so much as willing to look at your portfolio, much less hire you for modeling."

Kristy shrugged. "It won't be your concern, Miriam. My contract is up next week, as you well know. I think I've just ended our negotiations with regard to renewing."

Several of the girls gasped in surprise, but Brook fixed her gaze on Miriam and realized what a sad example of womanhood she'd become. Brook remembered her manager years earlier when she'd seemed vibrant and full of life and concern for mankind. But after a rather ugly divorce from a man she'd been married to for fifteen years, Miriam had never recovered. It made Brook sad to realize that she was only causing the woman more grief, but she also realized there was a tremendous liberty in being the one to say "enough."

"I wish I could have known you all a little better," Brook said, taking her gaze from Miriam's still-stunned expression to the table of her co-workers. "We might have made life a little better for one another. I feel like I don't know much about any of you, and I'm sure you know very little about me. But this morning I woke up and realized that I needed to make some tough choices, because frankly, we all know Miriam is right. Our looks will fade. Our popularity is determined by the sales of products and magazines, but ultimately it's settled by public opinion. And quite honestly, I don't like having to keep up with what someone else thinks of me. I figure God has a purpose for me, and it isn't focusing on myself."

She moved to the door of the conference room and paused as she opened the door. "If you're ever in Council Grove, Kansas, come look me up. I don't know that I'll still be there, but I do know that wherever I am, I'll be a whole lot happier than I was here."

She pulled on her cardigan and stepped out of the room. Freedom! That was the only word for it. She had obtained her freedom. Oh, she knew it would cost her something in breaching her contract and ending it ahead of time, but she didn't care. She had enough money invested. She could afford the loss. Especially given that she would soon sell her apartment and move from New York altogether.

The cab ride back to her apartment gave her time to reflect on her years in New York. Ashley was right. She had spent her time running from love and commitment, all because her mother had failed to live up to their expectations. She had denied herself the chance at real happiness in order to settle the score with a woman who never even realized how much she'd hurt Brook.

The cabby pulled up in front of her apartment, and Brook quickly paid him and hurried inside just as the first drops of rain began to fall. Even a summer downpour wasn't going to dampen her spirits.

Two hours later, Brook cinched herself into a first-class seat on a plane bound for Kansas City. In spite of the fact that the rain had refused to move on out into the Atlantic, Brook maintained her spirit of enthusiasm. She almost felt guilty for her lighthearted manner. After all, she was headed home for a funeral. But even Dave's death couldn't bind her in the chains that had held her captive for years and years. God had given her the strength to move forward.

I trust you, Lord, she prayed, *and I know you'll show me the next step.*

————————

Deirdre listened patiently to her in-laws as they questioned her for every detail of Dave's last days. She knew they longed for a connection—something that would help them to put closure on the situation. They asked her about a suicide note, and Deirdre said that while there was a note, the police had kept it. She didn't tell them that she had a copy. She didn't see the need in sharing it with them. It said nothing about them, and she feared it would have reflected poorly on Dave. He believed himself to have done something bad enough to die for. His parents would only be wounded by that.

"I don't understand them keeping the note," Mike Woodward said, his hand still clinging tightly to his wife's.

"It's evidence. They kept it along with the gun," Deirdre said calmly.

About that time, Morgan emerged from the suite's bedroom. She carried her favorite doll close to her body. Her protective manner made Deirdre think of how she longed to shield Morgan from the pain they were all experiencing.

"Poor baby," Julie said softly. "Has she been like this since . . . since . . ."

Deirdre knew it was impossible for her to finish the sentence, so she answered very simply, "Yes."

Morgan didn't even seem to notice that they were talking about her. She climbed over the arm of the wing-backed chair where Deirdre sat and snuggled herself tightly against her mother.

"Morgan, Grandma and Grandpa Woodward are going to take care of you while Grammy and Mommy run to town and take care of some things. I'll bring you back something to eat, but I want you to be good for your grandparents. Okay?"

Morgan said nothing. She started sucking on her thumb and drew the doll up under her chin. Deirdre gently stroked her head and turned back to Julie and Mike. "I appreciate your help. I want to take care of things so that after the funeral, Morgan and I can immediately go to Council Grove."

"You know, you could come back to St. Louis with us," Julie said, glancing at her husband. "We'd love to have you there."

Deirdre nodded. "I know you would and I appreciate that. But I have to have time to think, and the farm has always been healing for me."

They seemed to understand, but Deirdre knew they were grasping at straws. Anything was better than nothing, and anything connected to their son meant just one more way in which to reach him.

Mattie came from the back room, gathering up her things. "Are you ready, Deirdre? Erica and Connie will probably be here any minute."

Deirdre eased her way off the chair and out of Morgan's reach. "I won't be gone long, sweetie," she told her daughter. It would be the first time since the police station nightmare that they had been separated.

Morgan scarcely even glanced up at her. It was almost as if the child had simply resolved that life and its disappointments could only hurt you if you paid attention to them. She seemed to drift in and out of her own world, making no declarations or requests, seeming not to notice anything or anyone.

Deirdre knew she was going to have to do something for the child, but it seemed senseless to start that in Kansas City. They were, after all, going to Mattie's for an extended stay. She'd find someone in Council Grove who could help. Maybe by that time Morgan would have snapped out of her silence and returned to being the sweet, chatty little girl Deirdre had always loved.

Mattie and Deirdre walked in silence to the hotel lobby. Deirdre appreciated that Mattie could understand what she was going through. She wouldn't have wished the experience on anyone, but it helped to know that someone else knew what it was like to lose her husband.

"There's Erica," Mattie commented as they came through the hotel's entry doors.

Erica waited with Connie in the parking lot just off the office entrance. Deirdre slipped into the backseat and Mattie did likewise.

"If you'd rather sit up here," Connie said softly, "I can move."

Deirdre knew that everyone was treating her with kid gloves. It was like they watched her for clues, then calculated what their actions should be.

"Look, everybody, I'm better now. I'm not happy, nor do I understand why this has happened, but you don't have to worry that I'm going to go off the deep end. Just treat me normally. Ask your questions and talk to me like you used to."

"Well, I don't have a question," Erica said, maneuvering the car into traffic, "but I would like to say something."

"Go right ahead," Deirdre encouraged.

"Connie and I have been talking and we both agree that Dave's death has caused us to realize how limited our time on earth can be. We don't want our final words to each other to be words of anger."

"That's right," Connie joined in from the front passenger seat. "I know I've been a miserable sister to you both, but I'm hoping to do better."

Deirdre nodded and noted the tears that seemed to instantly form in Mattie's eyes. Her grandmother said nothing but looked out the window as if preoccupied by the passing scenery.

"We all need to do better," Deirdre said simply.

At the bank, Deirdre took up the death certificates she'd been given by the funeral home and went in to close out Dave's private accounts and to consolidate everything into one new account. An account that would bear only one name—hers.

She tried to be calm about the whole thing, but she felt unsure of what she had to do. This was the beginning of putting Dave out of her life, she thought. Then she shook her head and knew that she'd never be able to put Dave out of her life, no matter how hard she tried.

"I need to close out two accounts," she told the teller, then added, "and start up a completely new one."

The woman directed her to take a seat at a desk in the middle of the lobby. Within a few minutes a suit-clad businessman joined her.

"I'm Ralph Warner," he stated and extended his hand for her to shake.

Deirdre did so and nodded. "I'm Deirdre Woodward. I have, or I should say, my husband and I have two accounts with your bank. I'd like to close those out and start another account."

"May I ask why?" he questioned, taking his seat in the richly upholstered leather chair.

"My husband passed away last weekend. I'm the executor of his estate and have the papers and death certificates with me today. I need to put my business in order prior to leaving town." She put the death certificate on the desk, then added the checkbook for their joint account. "I don't have Dave's checkbook with me, but here's the number for the account. You'll find I'm the beneficiary on the account." She pushed a piece of paper across the desk to join the other articles.

"I'm sorry to hear about your husband, Mrs. Woodward. I can't say that I knew him personally, but I would still like to extend my condolences."

"Thank you. I appreciate that."

He took up the certificate and Deirdre watched as he glanced over the details. She saw him raise his gaze to her for the tiniest moment. No doubt he had come to the place that listed the cause of death as a self-inflicted gunshot wound.

The man nodded and turned to his computer. "Just let me pull up all of the pertinent information."

Deirdre sat back in the chair and watched as he worked. He wouldn't find all that much of interest. Dave had a private account for tax purposes, and this was where he put all of his money. Afterward, he would cut her a check for their shared account and it was with this that she would run the household and pay all of the other bills.

"And you say you want to put everything into one account?" he questioned.

"Yes, a new account with just my name," Deirdre replied. "I've talked with the life insurance company and there may or may not be insurance money coming our way. If a large sum is issued, however, I might want to open up a savings account as well. It'll just depend."

"So you want the entire thirty-five thousand in checking?" he asked seriously. "You could earn better interest if you put most of it into a certificate of deposit. Unless, of course, you need the money right away."

"Thirty-five thousand? What are you talking about?" Deirdre questioned, leaning forward again.

"Your husband's private account shows a deposit a few days ago of thirty thousand dollars. I take it you didn't know."

"Absolutely not," she said, shaking her head. "Are you sure about this?"

He checked the information given. "Looks to be accurate. Oh, and there's a safety deposit box. He opened that on the same day that he made the deposit. Did you want to check the contents of that today?"

"I don't have the key with me," Deirdre replied, not wanting to admit to the man that she hadn't realized there was such a box in Dave's name.

"Well, just come back with the key and we can take care of that then."

Deirdre listened as he explained all the various ways that she could put her money into their care. Before it was all done she had acquired a headache and longed for nothing more than a dark room where she could sleep it off.

Here I thought money was a problem. Dave had thirty thousand dollars and never told me. Where could the money have come from? She flashed back to the police station interrogation and the suicide note.

"It says here that your husband has done something he's not proud of," the detective had said. *"Something he can't live with. You have any ideas what that might be?"*

Of course, Deirdre had no clues about Dave's actions at the time. He had always been aboveboard on everything. Why, he was the kind of man who would return to a grocery store if he realized the clerk had given him too much change. That was one of the reasons she hated herself so much for lying to him about gambling. He would have been very hurt had he realized her problem.

She decided while Mr. Warner was typing up information on the computer that she had to figure out what it all meant. Maybe finding the safety deposit box key would help. Of course, that meant going back to the house. *Can I do that? It's just a house—just the place where he died.* Her thoughts began to take her in a direction she didn't want to go. *I know I can do this. Grammy will come with me. The key might hold the answer to where this money has come from. It might even hold the answer as to why Dave is dead.* She summoned her courage.

"Why don't I go home and get the key," she said, glancing at her watch. "I can be back here in an hour and then we can just conclude everything at once."

"That's fine by me," the man replied. "It'll give me time to put together your paper work."

Deirdre nodded and got to her feet. "I'll be back."

She only explained that there was a missing safety deposit box key and never told her sisters or Mattie anything more. There had to be something going on. Something big that had weighed Dave down with guilt. Deirdre had to know what it was.

"I tell you what," she said, reaching into her purse for her keys, "Erica, just drop Grammy and me off at the house. We can get my car and go back to the bank."

"It's no trouble to drive you around," Erica replied.

"I know. I just thought it might be better to do things this way." She didn't want to hurt Erica's feelings and so she added, "It would be a great help if you two wanted to go get something for everybody to eat at the hotel. I promised Morgan I'd bring her back some lunch." She pulled twenty dollars out of her purse and handed it to Connie. "If it costs more than this—"

"We'll pay the balance ourselves," Erica said, turning onto Deirdre's street. "We can easily do that much."

Deirdre watched as her house came into view. She had once loved the very sight of her home, but now it filled her with apprehension and regret. Had they pushed too hard too soon to have the best in life? Had Dave felt that in order to keep up with her needs he had to do something illegal? The thoughts raced inside her head. At least with her mind preoccupied with this, she felt more confident about returning to the scene of Dave's death.

"Are you absolutely sure you want us to go on?" Erica questioned. "We can come inside with you—if you need us."

Deirdre smiled and reached a hand up to touch Erica's shoulder. "Thank you. I know you would do this for me, but I'll be okay." Then, almost as an afterthought, she reached over and touched Connie. "Thank you too. I appreciate that you're here for me."

She got out of the car and waited for Mattie before heading up to the front door. "I've used the front door more this last week than I have since moving in," she said, trying hard to sound nonchalant. "Usually we went in through the garage."

Mattie seemed to understand. "Your flowers are absolutely gorgeous. You've done a good job with them."

Deirdre smiled sadly at the begonias and petunias that vied for space in the containers by her door. Who would care for her flowers while she and Morgan were in Council Grove? Was there some service she could hire to come and watch over her house? These were questions she'd not even considered before deciding to go to Mattie's.

"Do you suppose there's some way I could find a gardener to come and take care of things while I'm gone?" she asked as she slipped the key into the front door.

"I would think so," Mattie replied. "You'd certainly hate to let all your hard work go to waste."

The house smelled rather musty from the hot, humid days. Deirdre wrinkled her nose and went to the thermostat. "I guess I had the air conditioning turned off," she muttered and played with the adjustments.

"So what do we do now?" Mattie asked, tossing her purse onto the nearest chair.

"Well, I need to find that safety deposit box key," Deirdre replied, forgetting about the air conditioning. She came clean with Mattie. "I didn't even know he had a safety deposit box."

"Well, perhaps it dealt only with his work and he felt it unnecessary to let you know anything more."

"Well, he also neglected to tell me that he'd just come into thirty thousand dollars," Deirdre replied.

"What?" Mattie questioned.

She shook her head. "The bank says that shortly before Dave's death, he deposited thirty thousand dollars. Grammy, I figured money was a real problem for us, given my abuse of it. I mean, it wasn't like I thought we'd lose the house or miss a car payment, but I thought I'd probably cost us a good chunk of our savings money. Then, too, we lost a lot of money in deposits on the trip. But with this kind of balance in his private account, I don't know what to think. You're the only one I've told about the suicide note. You know that Dave felt he'd done some things he couldn't live with."

"And you think the money might have something to do with it?"

Mattie asked.

Deirdre glanced up the stairs. "It might. I just don't know. I'm hoping maybe the safety deposit box will give us the information."

"But it may not, Deirdre. You have to accept the fact that you may never learn the truth."

Deirdre had never allowed herself to believe that. She had to have answers as to why her life was suddenly turned upside down. "I suppose you're right," she finally said, though unwilling to admit defeat. "I guess we'd better get to looking."

"Where should we start?"

Deirdre looked back to the stairs. "I guess the bedroom."

Fear gripped Deirdre's heart. Could she go back into that room? Could she see his blood on the rug and the walls and not fall to pieces? She took a hesitant step and then another. Then without giving it another thought, she was halfway up the stairs with Mattie close behind.

When they reached the bedroom, Deirdre took a deep breath and plunged right in. There was no sense in delaying the inevitable. She immediately noticed that Mattie or someone else had duct taped a thin piece of plywood over the broken portion of window. The curtains were also missing and the wall had been scrubbed clean. On the floor, the blood-soaked carpet had been cleaned, but a brown stain still remained to remind her of where her husband had lain.

Deirdre began to tremble. "Did you do this?" she asked Mattie softly.

"The girls and I did," Mattie replied. "Remember when I left you and Morgan with Julie and Mike yesterday?"

Deirdre nodded. "But how did you get in?"

"Erica had a key."

Deirdre nodded again. Yes, that was right. She had given Erica a key to manage the house while they were in Hawaii. When they'd canceled the trip, she'd forgotten to get the key back. "Thank you."

"I know it doesn't take care of everything and it certainly won't block the image you have of what happened here, but I didn't want you coming back here to find the mess."

Deirdre began to cry. Her whole body was shaking. "Oh, Grammy. You're so good to me. How many more of my messes are you going to have to clean up?"

Mattie opened her arms to her granddaughter and held her tightly. "As many as I need to. That's what family is for. Someday you'll no doubt be helping me with my messes."

"I thought I could do this. I thought I'd put this behind me."

Mattie pulled back and looked Deirdre in the eye. "It's not even been a full week, child. You can't expect to put something like this behind you for a good long while. Look, you tell me where Dave kept his things and I'll look. You go downstairs and see if you can't find the number for a good gardener."

Deirdre didn't even bother to protest. She was simply too emotionally raw to try to do otherwise. "Dave's chest of drawers is the one over there by the window. If that key is here in the house, it will either be there or in his desk in the den. I can check the desk."

"Good. See, we'll share the work load. Now, you go on back downstairs, and I'll get to work here."

It wasn't long before Mattie appeared downstairs with the key in hand. It had been in Dave's top drawer, carefully hidden in an old cigar box with a bunch of old coins he had been collecting for fun.

Mattie volunteered to drive them back to the bank, even though she chuckled when they'd pulled into the street. "I haven't a clue which way to go," she admitted.

Deirdre even laughed at this. "We're quite the pair, aren't we?"

She gave her grandmother directions to the bank, then mustered her courage to do what had to be done.

Inside, Mr. Warner was ready and waiting for her. He took her to the vault where the safety deposit boxes were kept. "I'll leave you alone to go over the contents," he told her after they'd taken the box to a table and unlocked it.

Deirdre nodded and just sat staring at her husband's secret. The box was probably no more than eight by ten inches, but for reasons that she couldn't understand, Dave had felt the need to conceal this part of his life from her.

Dear God, please let this answer my questions, she prayed and lifted up the lid to the box.

Inside there was a white envelope addressed with her name on it. The only other contents was a manila envelope with no markings on the outside. It clearly contained quite a few papers, for the envelope was thick and forcibly folded in half. What could it be? She looked at both and chose the one intended for her eyes. Her hand shook fiercely as she opened the white envelope.

"'My dearest wife,'" she murmured. "'If you are reading this, then I am dead.'"

By the time Deirdre finished the letter, she not only knew why her husband was dead, but by leaving her this final missive, Dave had also left her a way to see that his life had not been in vain. Wiping the tears from her eyes, she folded the letter and put it in her purse before taking up the manila envelope. This envelope held all the information she needed to set Dave's memory back in order.

"Oh, Dave," she whispered. "I would have understood. We could have fixed this together."

Chapter **37**

After living in Denver most of her adult life, Ashley was hardly intimidated by the maddening pace of Kansas City traffic. She managed the minivan through more than one bottleneck and only had to recheck the map once in order to find her way to Erica's apartment complex.

"Are we at Aunt Erica's yet?" Zach asked in complete exasperation.

Ashley smiled and shook her head. "No, not yet. But if you close your eyes and count to one hundred, I'm thinking we'll probably be there."

This seemed to be just the challenge that Zach needed. He began to count. "One, two, three, four—"

"Zach, I meant for you to count to yourself."

"I am counting to myself."

"No, I mean count it in your head without counting out loud."

She glanced at him via the rearview mirror, saw his brow knit tightly as he considered this, then watched him close his eyes and start his task once again.

Ashley shifted a bit to catch sight of John. He seemed strangely silent and she wondered if he was worried about the events to come. He had never gone to a funeral. When his Grandpa Issacs had passed on, John had been very small and so Ashley had left him with a sitter. And becaus and Jack had opted not to tell the boys about Rachelle's death, the miscarriages, or the loss of the baby in the accident, this was the first time either one had been called upon to face death.

As if reading his mother's mind, John called from the back, "Will we have to look at Uncle Dave's dead body?"

The question caught Ashley by surprise, but as a parent she was used to these kinds of uncomfortable questions. "No, sweetie. You don't have to look at Uncle Dave's body." She didn't even know if they were having an open casket service, but she would see to it that John didn't have to view the body if that helped to still his own concerns about the funeral.

"Are there going to be a lot of people?" John asked.

"I don't know," Ashley replied. "Since we didn't hang around with Uncle Dave, it's hard to tell if he had a lot of friends. His family will be there and all of our family will probably be there. I don't know for sure if your aunt Brook can come, but the rest will."

This seemed to satisfy John for the moment, and it was a good thing. Ashley recognized Erica's apartment complex from the only other time she'd been there nearly two years before.

"One hundred!" Zach called out.

"See," his mother said, "we're here."

The boys gave a little cheer and Ashley felt like joining them. Her body ached from having driven over six hundred miles. It would feel good to relax in Erica's apartment while they figured out what they should do for accommodations.

Ashley watched the numbers on the building and finally spotted her sister's car in one of the parking spots. She pulled in beside it and sighed. They were finally here.

Their search for Erica's apartment was quickly concluded when John sited her number on a metallic strip over the door. Zach helped the expedition by pounding his fists against the door as though he were trying to knock it down rather than get the attention of the occupants.

Erica opened the door and beamed a smile at the trio. "I'm so glad you're here!"

Ashley hugged her baby sister and then waited patiently while John and Zach allowed their aunt to fawn over them.

"Come on in. Connie's here and she'll be so happy to see you all. And I have another surprise," Erica said, pulling Ashley inside. "Look who else is here!"

Ashley came around the corner into the kitchen. "Brook?" She welcomed her twin with open arms, then caught sight of Connie and did the same. "I can't believe we're all here."

"Isn't it great?" Erica replied. "We've been sitting here talking and hoping you'd make it before much longer. Connie was thinking of going out to bring us some food."

"Well, the boys ate about half an hour ago, but I'm starved. What are we getting?" Ashley questioned.

The plans were quickly made to retrieve Chinese takeout and Connie suggested the boys go along to help.

"I'll even buy you some ice cream while we're out, if it's okay with your mom," she said, eyeing Ashley.

"That would be fine by me," Ashley answered, "but stay with Aunt Connie. You don't know anyone else in this city and I don't need you getting lost."

The boys cheered and danced excitedly in the hall while Connie collected her purse and borrowed Erica's car keys. "We'll be back before you know it."

After they had gone, Erica, Brook, and Ashley relaxed in the living room. "I can't believe this has happened," Ashley finally said, breaking the silence. "Does anyone know why?"

Erica shook her head. "There doesn't seem to be much in the way of answers. I know Deirdre feels guilty. She thinks she pushed Dave too hard, but other than that, I haven't a clue. She's really not talking that much to me."

"That must be hard on you," Brook said softly. "I know how I feel when Ash doesn't talk to me."

Ashley looked up, a sense of guilt washing over her. "Like what you went through last week?"

Brook nodded. "I thought we were past that."

Ashley sighed. "It isn't your fault, so please don't blame yourself.

A lot has happened. Some good. Some bad. We can all talk about me at a later date. Right now we need to think about Deirdre. How can we best help her through this?"

Erica shrugged. "I don't have a clue. She plans to go to the farm after the funeral."

"Me too," Ashley said. "I hope all the extra company won't be too much of a burden on Grammy."

Brook shook her head. "You know better. We could all move back in lock, stock, and barrel and Grammy would dance a jig in downtown Council Grove."

They laughed at the thought. "She would," Ashley replied, knowing it to be true.

"Morgan hasn't said a word since Dave's suicide," Erica said, sobering all of a sudden. "I think Deirdre's going to have a big problem on her hands in that area. Maybe being with the boys will help Morgan. She'll have some kids close to her own age to play with, and maybe that way she won't feel quite so isolated. I get the impression that she's completely lost inside her own little world."

"Poor baby," Ashley said, thinking how hard it would be on her own boys if they were to lose their father. Of course, that thought triggered memories of her own problems. Hadn't she contemplated taking her boys away from their father? It wasn't a death situation, but it would no doubt be just as devastating. Not only that, but Jack had mentioned understanding the idea of suicide. Was he contemplating his own death because of what he'd done to Ashley—to their family?

"So where did Dave kill himself?" Brook questioned.

"Their bedroom," Erica replied. "It was just awful. Connie and I helped Grammy clean up the mess, but it was pretty hideous."

"You had to clean up after that?" Ashley questioned.

"Nobody else would," Erica said. "It isn't the job of the police, and the paramedics certainly had better things to do with their time."

"How awful. I had no idea. I just presumed the police had some sort of detail that took care of the worst parts of it." Ashley couldn't imagine having to deal with the grotesque aftermath of a suicide.

"Deirdre doesn't even want to go back to the house. She says she's going to sell it and never spend another night there. Grammy's trying to get her to take things slow and give herself time before making rash decisions."

"That would be best," Ashley said thoughtfully. "She might get down the road and realize that the house is all she has to remind her of the good times as well as the bad times. It's best not to make decisions based on emotions." She pushed aside thoughts of her own problems, knowing that the same advice was true for her situation.

The sisters talked companionably for nearly half an hour before Connie returned. After that the four sisters ate and talked and enjoyed the evening in spite of the sorrowful event that had brought them all together. Ashley couldn't remember when they'd had a better time together. They were far more open and less hostile than they'd ever been.

She thought of their childhood days and the pain they shared because of Rachelle. What a contrast to see them together sharing the pain of Dave's death. This ordeal seemed to knit them together, whereas anything associated with Rachelle only seemed to pull them apart.

"So how's Grammy holding up?" Ashley questioned as the evening wore on. She glanced over to find her boys sound asleep on the floor in front of Erica's television.

"Gram's doing pretty well," Connie answered. "She's had to deal with so much, but she has such strength."

Ashley thought she denoted a softness to Connie that had never been there before. Her sister seemed so reserved, almost demure. It just wasn't Connie's personality at all, but it was rather nice.

"I suppose it would be good to give her a call. If someone can direct me to the hotel where they're all staying, I'll collect my boys and head on over."

"You don't have to do that," Erica said. "I mean, I know we're limited on room here, but I kind of like having the extra company."

"Besides, the bed in the guest room is a queen," Connie pointed out. "You and Brook could share it and we could pull out the sleeper sofa for the boys, and I'll sleep in the recliner."

"Oh no, you won't," Erica protested. "You can sleep with me. My bed is queen-sized too. If Brook and Ashley can share a bed, surely you and I can. We are, after all, sisters."

Ashley sighed in her exhaustion as her sister continued to decide the arrangements. It felt so good to be with family. She had worried about having to keep up her guard the entire time she was in Kansas City, but now something told her she was wrong. Something had changed.

Maybe holding back from her siblings had allotted her only grief and isolation. Maybe it was time to let go of the past and the painful events they held one another accountable for. Maybe it was time to let go of Rachelle and the competition that so clearly drove each of them off in different directions.

She closed her eyes and tried to pray. Ashley wanted nothing more than to leave her problems with God, but Grammy always said that even though God would bear the burden of their problems, He would still expect them to work in faith to do His good will. What if that good will meant that she was supposed to forgive Jack and stay in her marriage? What if that good will meant that she would never be avenged for the wrong done her, but instead, that life could be put back together for a wonderful future? Could she let go of her heartache and forgive?

Ashley opened her eyes and looked at her sleeping sons. Forgiveness was a high price to expect of her . . . but was it too much to pay for her children's sake?

Chapter 38

Dave's funeral drew nearly two hundred and fifty people. Deirdre hadn't known what to expect and found herself pleasantly surprised to find her husband so well admired and esteemed. It meant a great deal to her that she would have this support. But even more so, it meant the world to her that her entire family had come to stand by her side in this horrible experience.

Later, after everyone—with the exception of Harry and the family—had gone and Deirdre's arms were aching from having carried Morgan most of the day, Mattie announced that she had arranged a private dinner with Deirdre's church. To say she was surprised was only partially true. Nothing Grammy ever did truly surprised Deirdre. But this time she was touched at the extra effort that must have gone into setting up this arrangement. Mattie knew no one else in Kansas City, yet somehow she had coordinated with the church to provide dinner after the late-afternoon funeral.

Deirdre had worried terribly about Dave's parents, but Mattie had this under control as well. They had announced that they were heading back to St. Louis rather than going to the family dinner. Their eyes were red-rimmed from crying, and after the crowds had gone, Deirdre had honored their wish to have the casket opened one last time for a private viewing. She herself had no desire to see Dave again—not that way. She was working too hard to remember the good times—the times when they had been full of hope about the future and refused to allow anything to come between them.

When Mike and Julie announced their decision to leave, Deirdre had wanted to reach out to them, but she found she had no strength left. She was drawing from an empty bucket.

Fortunately, Mattie knew what was needed. Deirdre felt an over-whelming sense of relief as Mattie took charge of the situation. She watched her grandmother take Julie and Mike by the arm and talk very softly to them, with an occasional backward glance at Deirdre and Morgan. Deirdre pretended to be absorbed in something else, as it seemed Mattie wasn't really trying to draw her attention. Before long, Mattie returned to say that Julie and Mike would meet them at the church.

But it wasn't until that evening, after her sisters had gone back to Erica's apartment and Morgan had fallen asleep for the night, that Deirdre was able to thank Mattie for all she had done.

"I know I couldn't have made it through this day without you," she said softly, stretching her legs out to rest atop the suite's coffee table.

Mattie smiled and seemed to relax a bit in the wing-backed chair. "It was a hard day, but we faced it together, all of us—together with God."

Deirdre nodded. "I know that now. I know that God has been with me all along. It won't be easy, though. Even knowing that."

Mattie nodded. "No, it isn't easy. You loved Dave very much. Just as I loved Edgar."

"He was my whole world," Deirdre replied, then shook her head. "No, he was a good portion of it. I'm going to be so empty without him." For the first time that day she allowed her tears to flow. She had tried so hard to be brave for Morgan's sake. "What am I going to do without him, Grammy? I loved him so much."

"You'll do what you have to do," Mattie replied. She sighed. "It's funny the way life works. We can stand back and look at the events other people endure and say, 'I could never make it through something like that.' Then before long we find ourselves up against some of the very same things and realize that we're doing what had once seemed impossible."

"Yes," Deirdre agreed. "It's just like that. I would have told you last week that I would have crumpled up and died if anything like this were to happen. Now here I am, taking each moment as it comes—living through it."

"But that's the secret. You're taking each moment as it comes. You can't live in the future or the past, you must live for the here and now. Remember, Jesus said to take up your cross daily and follow Him. He knew it was all we could manage. And sometimes, quite frankly, I have to take up my cross a whole lot more frequently than daily because I put it down a great many times along the way. Sometimes I put it down to nurse my wounds, sometimes to hurl stones at those who are attacking me—but when it's all said and done, there it sits, waiting for me to pick it back up and follow Him."

Deirdre sniffed back tears and let her head rest on the back of the couch. "Just tell me this, Grammy. When will it stop hurting so much?"

Mattie said nothing for several moments, causing Deirdre to lift her head. "Grammy?"

"I was just thinking about your question. In some ways, I'm sorry to say, it still hurts. But in other ways, God has filled those empty places with such warmth and love. He gave me you girls and that made my life so much more worth living. But He also gave me His peace and assurance that He would never forsake me. And that, more than anything, is what I continue to cling to. You must find your strength in Him. Just be open to whatever manner He chooses to provide it. Whether it's from the Bible or your family or even a complete stranger. God works in mysterious ways. Sometimes in ways that seem perfectly logical to us, and sometimes in ways that seem so convoluted and foreign that we wonder if we have somehow miscommunicated the situation to Him. As if He didn't already know our need."

Deirdre found solace in Grammy's words. "I just wish this had never happened. Not only for me, but for Morgan. She's hurting so much, and although I've tried to talk to her, to reassure her, she doesn't even seem to hear me."

Mattie nodded. "Then let your actions reassure her. She's just lost half of the stability she had known in her life. Not only that, but she said something harsh to Dave, and in her child's mind she probably believes it impossible to be forgiven."

"I only wish Dave would have addressed that in his letter to me," Deirdre said rather absentmindedly. Then with a start, she jumped up from the couch and pulled the white envelope from her suitcase. She glanced over the letter for what must have been the twentieth time and smiled. "Of course," she murmured, then looked to Mattie. "He did address it. He says right here, 'I will always love you and Morgan.' It's the last thing he says in the letter. It may not deal with the words exchanged on that day, but maybe it will be enough to give Morgan encouragement and the understanding that she was forgiven."

Mattie nodded. "There's a great healing in forgiveness."

Deirdre clutched the letter close. "This whole family could use a heavy dose of forgiveness. We desperately need to heal."

"I think the healing has already begun, Deirdre," Mattie told her granddaughter with a content, peaceful look on her face.

Deirdre realized she was probably right. She had seen the way her sisters had come together on her behalf. She had listened to their words and feelings and knew that something was greatly different from the last time they'd come together. Rachelle's funeral had been a time of tearing down, of rending the hearts and souls of those she had betrayed and left behind. Dave's funeral, however, had brought them together in a loving way of support. Perhaps the time of rending had concluded. Perhaps now was the time to put the pieces back together.

Chapter 39

Weeds had taken hold in Mattie's flower gardens. It was amazing how much damage could be done in such a short time. She knelt on the ground, pulling at the strangling vines until she'd freed her flowers. It reminded her of the girls and the hold bitterness had taken in their lives. They were all experiencing a weeding of sorts, and she could see that the results were varied. Just like her flower bed.

She glanced heavenward for a moment. The only constant in her life had been her heavenly Father. Mattie had to admit that, in all honesty, she didn't understand why things had happened the way they had, but her love for God had never wavered. He had seen her through too many storms and had repaired her lovingly after each and every battle. Her faith told her implicitly that He would continue to be worthy of her trust.

Returning her attention to her flowers, Mattie delighted in her gardening. Like God, it was one of the constants in her life. She took joy in her flowers like she did in nothing else. While the vegetable gardens provided food and nourishment for the body, her flowers provided food for the soul. She delighted in their delicate artistry.

She was delighted, too, that some of her girls were home again. Ashley and her boys were staying for the rest of the summer, and while Mattie knew there was a deep, secret hurt in Ashley's life, she also felt confident that sooner or later Ashley would share her heart.

Deirdre and Morgan seemed right at home. Morgan still refused to speak, which was a constant concern to Mattie, but Deirdre didn't want to rush the child and refused to seek counsel.

Mattie prayed constantly for them, hoping she could somehow find a way to help Morgan release her hurt. Ultimately, however, she knew they were both in God's hands.

When her knees would no longer take the pressure, Mattie decided she'd worked long enough. Mattie remembered when she would have literally worked from sunup to sundown on her various gardens. Now she was lucky to spend more than an hour at a time. Her life was beginning to come to a close, and while that didn't worry her in the sense of what awaited her beyond this world, she felt a concern that she'd not yet accomplished all that she'd been called to do. Until her girls were settled and drawing their strength from God, how could Mattie even think of leaving them to find their own ways?

Still, they belonged to God. She had committed each one to Him long ago. She had trusted God to help her raise them properly, and she had to let go and trust that He could handle their futures as well. She sighed and put away her tools. The aching in her knees and now in her lower back reminded her that she could only do so much.

Climbing wearily up the garden path, Mattie couldn't help but wonder how many years she had left on earth. It was kind of funny. Sometimes she never thought about her life coming to an end, and other times she almost longed for it—like homesickness. She never said this to anyone, fearing they might misunderstand. But in truth, it was nothing more than a desire to let go of the bonds that earthly life had given and be in perfect harmony with God. It was the desire to sit at His feet and labor no more.

"Silly old woman," she chided herself and smiled. It would come in God's timing, and as her own grandmother used to say, *"If a body is still walkin' the earth, it must be there for a reason."* Usually she'd add that the reason indicated that God still had something special for you to do. Apparently, He still had plans for Mattie as well.

Inside, the house was pleasantly cool, compliments of the hard-working central air system she'd had installed nearly twenty years earlier. Kansas summers could be pleasant or blistering, and air conditioning seemed to be a luxury that quickly became a necessity. It was amazing how much longer her curtains and draperies lasted now that they were protected from the humidity and dusty winds of summer days. The interior paint seemed to fare better as well, and Mattie had never had to replace the wallpaper, except by choice, since the air conditioning had been installed. It was amazing how modern conveniences intended for one purpose could also help in others.

Washing the dirt from her hands, Mattie decided a tall glass of iced tea was in order. She rummaged through the refrigerator, poured herself a glass of tea, and went to check on her family. There had been mention of taking an afternoon swim in the lake, and Harry had even commented on the possibility of coming by to spend the evening with them. Mattie thought it all sounded rather pleasant.

Finding no one in the living room, Mattie checked around the other rooms before making her way upstairs. The silence in the house assured her that Ashley's boys had found some other place to occupy themselves. My, but those two could be a handful. Mattie nearly laughed out loud as she remembered them capturing a snake and two bullfrogs and having no understanding of why she didn't want to allow them residency in her house.

"Is anyone here?" Mattie called out.

"I'm in here, Grammy," Ashley replied. "Folding clothes."

Mattie made her way to Ashley's room and smiled. "I've just come in from weeding and thought I would see what else was going on."

"I finished a load of wash," Ashley answered. "Harry called a few minutes ago to say he'd be over shortly to take the boys swimming. The boys ran with the speed of wild horses to await his arrival on the front porch."

Mattie drank her tea and studied her eldest granddaughter. *How can I make you talk to me?* she questioned, pondering the pain she saw in Ashley's eyes. Mattie knew Ashley hadn't been the same since the accident. Her personality had changed so drastically from the motivated and driven young woman Ashley used to be, and it was this that really worried Mattie. Her body seemed to be healing fine, but her spirit seemed fragile.

Mattie made a decision to just jump in and deal with her concerns. "Well, with the boys occupied, and Deirdre and Morgan apparently busying themselves elsewhere, would you like to talk to me about the real reason you came home?"

Ashley's face paled ever so slightly. Her thick brown hair was pulled back into a braid, leaving her face looking rather gaunt—her cheeks almost hollow. She sighed audibly and seemed to give up whatever battle had been going on within her. Sitting down on the edge of the bed, Ashley rested a pair of jeans upon her lap. She looked to be considering Mattie's suggestion.

"You don't have to talk if you don't feel like it."

"I don't suppose I'll ever *feel* like it," Ashley replied. "I keep wishing my emotions would heal as fast as my body has. Honestly, I've planned all along to talk to you when the time was right. I suppose this time is as right as any."

Mattie sipped at the tea and waited for her granddaughter to continue. She didn't want to do anything that might appear too forceful or demanding.

"You might as well sit down," Ashley told her softly. "This might take a few minutes."

"That's fine," Mattie said, pulling up the rocking chair. "I have my chores done for the time being."

Ashley nodded. "I came home because I needed to rediscover who I am—or at least to find a way back to what I once knew to be true. I thought I had it all under control. I had my faith in God, faith you established in me. I had a great home, good friends, my family . . . my whole life seemed charmed. I thought I must surely be living exactly as God wanted me to because everything was so perfect."

"Then the accident happened?" Mattie questioned.

"Something happened before the accident, only I couldn't remember what it was. In fact, I still don't remember much about it, but Jack has filled in the missing pieces."

"I see."

Ashley sighed. "I wish I did." She turned to better face Mattie. "I was running away the day of the accident."

"I don't understand."

"That makes two of us. I went to tell Jack about the baby, but instead I found something so horrible that I ran." Ashley stopped and lowered her gaze to the floor. "Jack had an affair with his nurse. I . . . I came in on them and my reaction was to simply run."

"Oh my," Mattie whispered the words. Never had she imagined Ashley would tell her something of this magnitude. She had anticipated Ashley talking about being depressed over losing the baby or the fact that she couldn't have other children. But the fact that Jack had had an affair . . . why, the thought had never entered Mattie's mind for a moment. She had always adored Jack and thought him perfectly suited to Ashley.

"He ended it. Said she meant nothing to him. Apparently she had boosted his ailing ego and made him feel young and important. She resigned her position at Jack's request and he helped her get a job with a colleague. He says it's over and will never happen again."

"And do you believe him?" Mattie questioned.

Ashley raised her gaze to meet Mattie's eyes. "I want to."

"Do you still love him?"

"Yes. That's what makes this so hard. I want to put it behind us, but at the same time I feel like I'm the wounded party and no matter what I do, nothing can bring back what I've lost. I can't have justice in this."

"Justice or revenge?"

Ashley shook her head. "I suppose I'd take either one."

"But as you said, nothing can bring back what you've lost," Mattie replied.

"I know that. It's just that I feel so torn. Dave's funeral made me realize just how much I do love Jack, even if he's betrayed that love. I don't really want a divorce. . . ."

"Then don't get one," Mattie stated simply.

"But what do I do?"

"Do you want to hold this marriage together?"

Ashley nodded. "I really think I do, but I don't know if I can put it behind me. Jack's actions cost me so much. I lost my child and the possibility of ever having any more children. I nearly lost my life."

"I'm not suggesting that your losses aren't great," Mattie began, "but I would suggest you weigh the possibilities and decide if you are willing to lose even more than you already have."

"What do you mean?"

"If you don't go back to Jack, if you get a divorce or separate from him, then you lose even more. The boys lose a father and you lose a husband and companion. You probably will lose the financial security you've come to depend on, and frankly, I think you would lose more than a small portion of your happiness."

"But I've already lost a big portion of that," Ashley protested.

"I know, but it would only get worse."

"So I just go back to him and let bygones be bygones? Forgive and forget—is that it?"

"What more should there be?"

"I don't know, some kind of justice?" Ashley said, sounding very much like a spoiled child.

"And who would decide what justice is in this case?"

"You aren't making this easy on me, Grammy."

Mattie smiled. "Was I supposed to?"

Ashley had to grin at this. "You always have a way of cutting through the weeds to get to the flowers—or in this case, the thorns."

"If you came here for pity, Ashley, you know better. Pity has never helped anyone. It cripples and maims in the worst sort of way. I won't give you pity, but I will give you support and love, no matter what you choose. I'm just asking you not to counter Jack's mistake with one of your own."

"So you think I should just put this behind me and go back home?"

Mattie drew a deep breath and let it out in a rather heavy sigh. "I'm saying that like so many other things in life, there comes a time to make hard choices, and that most of the really difficult choices are ones that we have to make alone."

"But you've always said that we're never really alone. You've always told me that I could take everything to God in prayer and that He would give me answers. You said that no matter how difficult . . ." She fell silent and Mattie smiled, knowing that she'd suddenly become very aware of her words.

"I don't want to add to the problem," Ashley finally admitted, walking to the window.

Mattie followed her and saw that Harry had the boys out on the dock. He was showing them how to get into the water safely. Not far from where they played, Morgan and Deirdre watched in apparent silence.

"Can you forgive Jack?" Mattie suddenly asked. "Really forgive him? I know as a human being you can't forget very easily, but can you forgive him?"

Ashley continued to watch her boys. "I've asked myself that so many times. I just want to put the pieces back together."

"Then you'll have to work with them one at a time and carefully stitch them back into place."

Ashley turned at this comment and smiled. She went to her armoire and opened one of the drawers. "Can you put this back together as well?" She held up the wall hanging and gave Mattie a sad smile. Mattie's vision blurred for just a moment as tears came to her eyes and Ashley continued. "I don't want the quilt to be torn apart any more than I want my family torn apart. I know you did what you did because of the way I was acting—the way we were all acting. I think we all see that now. The question is, how can we make things right? How can we piece our lives back together, along with this quilt?"

Mattie reached out to touch Ashley's cheek. "Piecework is never easy. It requires diligence and patience and above all else, dedication and hard work."

"And forgiveness?" Ashley asked softly.

"It's always best to learn from our mistakes and move forward," Mattie replied. "Otherwise we have a tendency to keep coming back around to the same place again and again. Never moving on. Never completing our work."

Ashley nodded and looked at her quilt piece for a moment. "I want to put things back together, and I'd like to start with this." She handed Mattie the wall hanging. "I know you have the sixth piece. You can at least join *them* back together."

Mattie was touched by Ashley's need. She longed to give her granddaughter the hope that mending her future might be as simple a task. But there was no way she could guarantee that for Ashley . . . no way she could promise her a perfect life.

Chapter 40

"Surprise!" Brook announced, walking into Mattie's farmhouse without knocking. A week had passed since they'd been together, but it was as if no time at all had separated them.

"Brook!" Mattie declared, coming across the room to embrace her granddaughter. "Why didn't you let us know you were coming? Are you here for Fourth of July celebrations?"

"I'm here for that and more," Brook replied. It was nearly six-thirty in the evening and to her surprise, everyone was assembled rather casually in the living room. She beamed a smile. "I sold everything in New York and I've decided to come back to Kansas for a time. I'm not sure where I'll land—it might be here for a time or Kansas City. Erica told me I could stay with her while I decided."

"Well, come on in and just leave your bags by the stairs. We'll help get you settled later. We were just trying to decide about an evening swim. With the days staying light until nine or so, it seems like we have so much more time for fun and games after our work is done."

"A swim sounds like fun," Brook admitted. How long had it been since she'd had a chance to go swimming in the lake? She spotted her twin and smiled. "How about it, Ash? Going swimming?"

Ashley smiled. "I've been thinking about wading. I'm not sure I'm up to actual swimming yet, but the boys, as you can see, are already dressed for it."

Brook looked across the room to where the boys played checkers by the floor-to-ceiling windows. They were wearing swim trunks and T-shirts and had nothing more than plastic sandals on their feet. "I guess they are. What about you, Deirdre? You and Morgan going to take a swim?"

"I don't know," Deirdre replied. "I need to check on Morgan and see if she's interested." She got up and closed the book she'd been reading. "It's really good to have you home, Brook."

"It's good to be here too. How are you doing?"

Deirdre shrugged. "It's hard. I miss Dave a great deal. It still doesn't seem real. The worst part of it is Morgan. She still isn't talking."

"Have you taken her to see someone?" Brook questioned. She noted immediately that Mattie and Ashley exchanged looks. Apparently she had touched on a tender subject.

"I don't want to rush her," Deirdre replied. "She's healthy otherwise."

"Yes, but you can't just leave her locked up inside herself. You need to get her with a grief counselor."

"She's *my* daughter, Brook! If you want to make the decisions, have your own kids!" Deirdre declared, completely out of character. She stormed from the room and Mattie instantly went after her.

"I didn't mean to hurt her," Brook said, shaking her head. "Me and my big mouth."

"No, don't take it so hard," Ashley said, coming to give Brook a hug. "We've all tried to talk to her about it. She refuses to listen. I can't figure out what has her so afraid of letting Morgan talk to someone else. Maybe it's just that she wants to be the one to fix Morgan's hurts. I just don't know."

"What about you?" Brook questioned. "Am I going to tick you off by asking how things are going for you?" She smiled gently and watched Ashley's face for some sign that she'd overstepped her bounds.

Ashley just grinned. "Nah, come on out into the garden with me. I don't want to talk in front of the boys."

Brook followed her sister out into the balmy evening. Shadows touched the vivid green landscape as sunlight filtered through the trees, sending veiled streams to the ground below. It was the time of day that Brook liked best. Not quite evening, but not the harsh heat of the afternoon. The sun seemed to just hang in the west like an iced yellow cookie. The blue of the Kansas summer sky was fading, promising a beautiful sunset to come later. It was simply perfect.

Brook smiled at the glorious aroma of Mattie's flower gardens. *Honeysuckle and roses*, she thought, remembering childhood games of hide-and-seek in Grammy's landscaped yard. She had a favorite hiding place near an old well where Grammy had planted several lilac bushes to discourage the kids from playing atop the uncertain foundation. It never discouraged Brook from hiding there, however, and in May the sweetness of the lilacs would draw her in for more than hiding games.

"I've been meaning to call you," Ashley suddenly began. "I've wanted to get something off my chest for a while, but I'm glad we can talk face-to-face. I really prefer it to talking on the phone."

"Me too," Brook replied. "You seem better somehow. I think I sensed that even in New York. I just kept praying for you and then all of a sudden I had this peace about it. Is it time or being away from Colorado that's helped to heal your heart?"

"It's facing the truth and letting the truth set me free," Ashley said as she gazed out across the rose bed.

"And what is that truth?" Brook questioned.

"Jack had an affair. That's what I learned the day of the accident—the part I couldn't remember."

Brook listened angrily as Ashley explained her husband's infidelity. How could she act so nonchalant about the very deed that had changed her life forever? How could Jack have done this to her?

"I don't know if I could be so forgiving," Brook said when Ashley finally concluded.

"I wasn't sure I could live with the alternative."

Of course she was right, Brook realized, but her own initial anger at Jack's insensitive actions gave her little sympathy or forgiveness for the man.

"In and of myself, I know I don't have it in me to do," Ashley continued. "I've pretty much given up on the idea of doing it on my own. But Grammy and I talked and I realized that I don't want to live without Jack. He's genuinely sorry for what happened. He's been completely devastated at losing the baby, and the reason he lied to me about being in his office was because he knew that if I remembered him with Gina, he'd lose me too."

"But not now?"

Ashley sighed and looked at her twin. "No. I still need to think through some of this, but it's time to heal and put the family back together. I can face that there will be no more children. I can face that somewhere along the way, Jack was human and made this awful mistake. And now I have to find a way to let it go. I can't go back until I let God work this out in my heart."

"I admire you," Brook said softly. And she did. Her sister was such a pillar of strength considering everything she'd been through.

"Don't," Ashley said shaking her head. "My first reactions were just like yours. I guess one of the things God reminded me of was what it was like to grow up without a father. I can't do that to the boys. Jack adores them and they worship the ground he walks on. I can't lose my family just because of pride."

"But how can you be sure he won't do this again?" Brook questioned, feeling guilty for bringing up the issue.

"I can't be sure of anything," Ashley said seriously. "But that's where faith comes in. All I can do is accept his apology and forgive him, then trust that it won't happen again. I have to have faith or there's no sense in even trying."

Brook nodded. "I know you're right. I'd hate for the boys to grow up like we did."

"It wasn't that Grammy didn't do a good job, but she was only one person. She shouldn't have had to be our mother."

"No, but she did a fine job. She did what was asked of her and she never let us down."

"Even now," Ashley said, "after all the years and heartaches, she's still working to put us back together. I even brought my wall hanging from Colorado and asked Grammy to piece it back with her part. I can't bear for her to think of us all divided up like that."

Brook laughed and Ashley frowned. "What's so funny?"

Brook shook her head. "I brought my piece along with me from New York. I was hoping for the same thing. Every time I looked at it, all I could think of was that Grammy had gone to such lengths to show us our errors."

"Me too. I guess great minds think alike," Ashley said, grinning. "It wouldn't be the first time we both came up with the same thought."

Brook nodded. "I think we're both moving ahead."

"Here's to forgetting the past and looking forward," Ashley said as though making a toast.

"And to that slender thread that keeps us tied together through thick and thin," Brook added with a peaceful sigh.

Chapter *41*

Erica paused her car at the end of the lane to Grammy's farm. She wanted to soak up the ambiance for several moments before plunging into the business of reuniting with her family. She loved this farm with all of her heart and felt a warm sense of belonging whenever she came back to this place. She was loved here. A warmth of happiness washed over her. She had agreed only two nights ago to marry Sean. They had talked long into the evening and worked out all of their concerns related to careers and the future. Erica felt that the entire world had been set right. She loved Sean and knew that he loved her.

Grammy would be pleased. Grammy always told them that marriage should be a lifelong commitment. *"No sense in marrying with the idea that you can run at the first sign of trouble,"* she would say. Erica cherished and respected her wisdom with new appreciation.

Life here had been very simple. They had worked hard together and played hard, but they always knew that Grammy would be there for them no matter what. Grammy held their hands when they were afraid and Grammy dried their tears. She was everything to them, and Erica suddenly wondered why they should have ever cared to have Rachelle in their lives. Thoughts of Rachelle reminded Erica of the stop she'd made just before coming out to the farm. She'd actually turned into the cemetery drive before even realizing what she was doing. Once there, it seemed silly not to at least see the grave.

Surprisingly enough, it was nothing like she had expected. A simple gray headstone marked the spot. Edgar and Robert Mitchell were buried on one side and a wide open field splayed out from the other. As the field gradually rose to the north, the local country club could be seen atop the hill. It all seemed very fitting.

"I forgive you, Mother," Erica had said, standing before the stone. *"I wish things could have been different."* And it was true. Erica did forgive her mother for the choices she had made.

Shaking away the memory, Erica turned her car down the lane and headed for Mattie's house. She pulled beside Brook's new red Camaro and waited for the dust to settle before getting out. She smiled at the fancy sports car. She'd helped Brook pick it out and couldn't help but remember her sister's sheer delight in buying her first vehicle. In New York, Brook told her, she never had much need for a car and therefore hadn't even considered buying one. Now that New York was behind her, Brook felt it was time to do the deed. Erica got out of her own car and remembered the verse from Ecclesiastes. *"To everything there is a season, a time for every purpose under heaven."* She smiled thinking of how her own life was changing.

"Erica!" Mattie called out as she came around the corner of the house. "What a wonderful surprise. I'm so glad you could make it for the Fourth of July."

"Me too," Erica said, crossing the drive to give her grandmother a bear hug. She dropped her hold and gave Mattie a huge smile. "I'm so glad to be home."

"Well, I'm mighty glad to have you home," Mattie said, dusting off her apron. "I came outside to get a couple of onions for dinner, and a few well-placed weeds attracted my attention."

Erica laughed. "I can just imagine. You were always getting side-tracked by one thing or another. So is everyone going to be here for the Fourth?"

"I'm not sure about Connie. I've called and left messages, but she hasn't responded one way or the other. I imagine she's pretty busy. Otherwise, everyone else is already here."

Erica could clearly hear the disappointment in Mattie's voice. "Well, Connie still has a couple of days until the Fourth, right? We have to have hope."

Mattie smiled and nodded. "We always must have hope."

"I have something to show you," Erica said, grinning. She held up her left hand to show Mattie the engagement ring. "Sean and I talked through all our troubles and concerns just like you advised. We're getting married!"

Mattie assessed the ring and then wrapped Erica in her embrace. "What wonderful news! Your sisters will be delighted for you."

———————————

Supper turned into a celebration for Erica. Each of the girls contributed something, creating a wonderful assortment of dishes. Ashley fried chicken. Brook tossed a salad. Deirdre made a raspberry pie with berries from Grammy's own bushes, and Erica surprised even herself by making twice-baked potatoes. Mattie declared that they had taken all the responsibility from her and that she had nothing to do, but the girls quickly requested her creamed peas and pearl onions and Mattie eagerly complied.

Sitting around the table, chatting about everything under the sun, Erica had never felt more content. There was nothing elaborate or special about the setting, but for once in a very long time, Erica felt as though her sisters were allowing their past differences to be set aside. They seemed to genuinely enjoy each other's company, and to care what each one had to say.

"Just think of the wonderful wedding shower we can throw for Erica," Brook said between bites. "I'm already getting ideas for a theme."

"A stroll down Fifth Avenue?" suggested Deirdre.

They all laughed as Brook scrunched up her nose in distaste. "I was thinking something more along the lines of a musical theme. I'm thinking of opening a catering business and I could get started by practicing on family first."

The conversation was soon filled with exclamations and questions as the sisters discussed Brook's announcement. When everyone had eaten their fill, Ashley began to clear away the leftovers.

Erica loved the happy chatter. It was as if each of her sisters had somehow suddenly found their rightful place—the place where they fit the best.

After the table was cleared and the dishwasher loaded, they were called into the living room by Deirdre. This came as a surprise to everyone, and even Erica felt a bit uneasy. Supper had been so peaceful and pleasant, but Deirdre's expression clearly revealed the need to get serious. Erica couldn't help but wonder what she had on her mind. They had always been close, but since Dave's death, she felt Deirdre had changed.

"I have something important to tell all of you. In fact, I've sent the boys to play in the garden with Morgan because I didn't want us to be disturbed. I hope that's okay with you, Ashley," Deirdre said softly.

"It's fine, but what's this all about?" Ashley questioned as Erica joined her and Brook on the sofa.

Erica watched Deirdre closely. She looked so composed and at peace. Erica could only pray that Deirdre was somehow mending from the horror of Dave's death.

"I wanted to talk to you about several things. First of all, I need to tell you something very important about myself. I would never have shared this problem had Dave not died. In fact, I thought my problem was the reason Dave committed suicide."

Erica frowned and waited for Deirdre to continue. How could anyone suppose another person's choice to die was their fault?

"I have a gambling addiction," Deirdre stated rather nonchalantly. The intensity in her expression, however, told everyone that the issue was far from casual in their sister's mind. She looked rather awkward standing before them, and Erica wondered if she was losing her nerve. Deirdre gave a quick glance at Mattie, who smiled reassuringly.

"I had taken a great deal of money from our account and had lost it. I had even pawned an antique necklace that Dave's mother had given me. Dave was irritable and unhappy and I figured it had to do with the fact that he saw me spending all this money and never accounting for it. As he became more and more moody, I became more consumed by my guilt." She paused and drew a deep breath. "I knew I was doing wrong, but I kept thinking that I could somehow make it right. I kept thinking that if I could just play one more hand of blackjack or play one more slot machine, then I could win it all back and Dave need never know about my problem. Now he'll never know about my problem—because he had a problem of his own."

Erica felt completely drawn into her sister's story. It played like one of the movies in which Rachelle might have had the starring role.

"Dave's problem was not me, it was his job. He had been assigned to a very big case involving a man who had been in a car accident. Dave's firm represented the car manufacturer, and the man was claiming that the vehicle equipment had been at fault for causing the accident. Worse still, this man lost his wife and two daughters in the accident. And he will be in a wheelchair for the rest of his life.

"The legal firm put Dave on the job, and naturally Dave went to work in his usual one-hundred-fifty-percent manner. He spent long nights digging deep into the issues in order to prove the man wrong. But instead, he found that the man was right. The man had his suspicions and nothing more. But Dave had proof that would nail the responsibility to the door of the manufacturer. Dave went to his boss and met with the manufacturer and it was decided that Dave should bury the information he'd found. No one at the manufacturer was going to say anything because they didn't want to lose their jobs. So it was up to Dave."

"How did you find this out?" Brook questioned.

Deirdre nodded as if anticipating the question. She glanced at Mattie, who sat quietly contemplating everything from her favorite chair.

"I went to the bank to close out the old bank accounts and open a new one. While I was there the bank officer told me that Dave had made a recent deposit of thirty thousand dollars. He'd also rented out a safety deposit box. I had no idea of either transaction. Frankly, I was stunned. I thought we had money problems and that Dave couldn't deal with the pressure anymore. I was certain that my gambling had caused him to take his life, but here this man was telling me that money wasn't an issue. Once I went through the safety deposit box, I found out the reasons for the money and for Dave's death."

She paused and walked to the fireplace. The weather had been far too warm for any type of fire, yet Deirdre stared into the hearth as if she could see the flickering flames from days gone by. Erica longed to comfort her sister but knew she needed to hold her tongue and stay put. Deirdre obviously needed to work through this herself.

"Dave moved forward with his case and he won it. The man walked away with nothing, not even payment for the funerals or his own medical expenses. Dave, in turn, walked away with his thirty pieces of silver. That's exactly how he put it to me in the last letter he ever wrote me." She turned. "That letter, as well as the evidence against the manufacturer, was inside the safety deposit box."

"What will you do?" Erica asked, unable to contain herself.

"I've already done it," Deirdre said, meeting her gaze. The moment seemed to be shared solely between the two of them, and Erica felt the connection she had been missing since her brother-in-law's death.

"Dave asked me to get in touch with the man and his lawyer and to turn the evidence over to them with his sincere apology. I did this and also gave the man the thirty thousand Dave had earned as a bonus. I told the man what had been happening. I told him about Dave's guilt and his suicide. I apologized on Dave's behalf and asked the man to forgive Dave. And you know what? This man, who had suffered such loss, told me that he forgave Dave the moment he stood against him in court. He told me that God had always been the most important part of his life and that even though he'd lost everything dear to him, that, like Job, he would go on trusting in God."

Deirdre shook her head, and for the first time that evening took a seat. "I can't tell you how humbling that was. But now it's in the hands of the lawyers and I can get on with my life." She looked at each of them and added, "Which brings me to another reason I asked you here. I'm selling the house in Kansas City. I hired a team of professionals who will see to everything. They will pack our belongings, ship them to storage, clean the house, replace the carpet in our bedroom, and repair the window. Then they will put the place on the market and conduct all of the business without my needing to ever return to that place. You may think me silly or emotional or even stupid for my actions, but I've prayed about this and I know that for Morgan and for me, it's the best choice. Neither of us are up to facing that kind of pain for some time to come."

"Where will you go? Will you live here with Grammy?" Erica asked.

"For a time. Grammy has agreed to let Morgan and me stay with her as long as we need. I hope that isn't a problem for anyone here."

"Why should it be?" Brook questioned.

Deirdre shrugged. "I wouldn't want anyone offended by my returning home. I'll pull my weight and pay for our needs. Grammy won't be taken advantage of in any way."

"No one would ever believe you'd do that," Mattie chimed in. "They know only too well that I'd have you all here in a heartbeat if I could."

"Well, I just want to make it clear so that no one feels they have to question the details behind my back. I want our communications to be wide open, and I want everyone to feel free to ask any questions they have."

Erica admired Deirdre for her strength. This was so uncharacteristic of the sister she had known and loved for so many years. The old Deirdre wouldn't have just announced her plans, the old Deirdre would have asked permission first. She would have worried about how everyone else felt and whether it would cause any hard feelings. *I suppose we've all found strength to deal with the issues of the past. I let go of thinking it had to be music or love, but never both. Brook has let go of competing against Rachelle's image, and now Deirdre is taking a stand for her own best interest and that of Morgan. Good for her.*

"I know it won't be easy to get over Dave's death. Maybe I'll never get over it, but I have to think of the future and I have to think of Morgan. You'll be happy to know that I have an appointment for her to see a local pediatrician on Monday. He'll give her a complete physical and then suggest who we should go to in order to help Morgan deal with her grief."

Erica saw tears form in Deirdre's eyes. She knew how difficult it was for her sister to see her child in pain. Erica bit her lip and fought back her own tears. Healing was often just as painful as the infliction of the original wound.

Brook got to her feet and went to hug Deirdre. "I'm glad you're going to do this. Would you like me to go with you? You know, just for moral support?"

Deirdre smiled through her tears. "I'd like that very much."

Erica felt a twinge of guilt for not having thought of it first, then felt jealous for not being the one Deirdre was turning to. But even as the feelings touched her heart, Erica knew that this was the start of a new beginning. It was a bonding between Brook and Deirdre that needed to happen. It was time for them to let go of clinging to one or the other. They were family, and they needed to find strength in their numbers.

Chapter 42

Harry pulled his pickup into the left-hand lane in order to pass a carload of old ladies who appeared to be out for an evening drive. They seemed in no hurry and certainly weren't about to go the allowed seventy miles per hour on the interstate.

Harry glanced at his watch. Seven o'clock. What kind of madness had taken him? He was nearly to Topeka and he still couldn't explain his driven need to talk to Connie.

Maybe it was because Mattie had commented three times on how she'd tried unsuccessfully to get ahold of Connie. Or maybe it was because everyone at Mattie's had been making big preparations for the Fourth of July and wanted Connie to be a part of the plans. Whatever the reason, Harry had finished his chores, eaten an early dinner at his favorite restaurant in Council Grove, then instead of heading the pickup back to the farm, had turned onto Highway 177 to make his way up to Interstate 70 and then to Topeka.

To say he had thought a lot about Connie since Dave's funeral would be the understatement of the year. His mind had been on little else. How could it be that he had managed to lose his heart to this wild card of a woman?

Connie was everything he had chosen to avoid in life. She did whatever she wanted, whenever she wanted, without regard to the rules. Anyone's rules. She was a constant source of concern for Mattie with her mountain climbing, sky diving, bungee jumping, or whatever else she wanted to try. And the knowledge that she had taken several lovers by her own admission deeply tore at Harry's heart.

She wasn't anything like the type of woman he ideally would have chosen for himself. Yet somehow, some way, Connie had worked her way into his heart and now Harry was hard-pressed to know what to do about it.

I didn't figure it this way, Lord, he prayed. *I thought I knew exactly how things were going to be, and yet here I am with the wheelbarrow upset and my life dumped out around me.* He shook his head. It just didn't make sense.

Heading off the Gage Street exit, Harry made his way through town, retracing the streets he'd taken when he'd come with Mattie to pick up Connie after Dave's death. He didn't have any trouble navigating his way. As Connie's apartment complex came into sight, Harry thought for a split second about turning back around and heading toward the highway. *Am I doing the right thing?*

As he headed into the apartment complex, Harry literally felt his heartbeat pick up the pace. It had to be the right thing. Finally he stood at her door, knocking, and the worries he felt no longer mattered.

To his relief, Connie opened the door immediately. Harry let his gaze travel over her to take in the entire picture before settling on her face. She had dyed her hair back to its natural color and Harry liked the way it had grown out just a bit to frame her face. Her eyes were wide with surprise and her mouth had fallen open in obvious shock, but to Harry, she was radiant and beautiful.

"Hi," he said, feeling rather sheepish about the whole affair.

"Hello." She glanced down at herself and shrugged. "I wasn't expecting company."

Harry presumed she was apologizing for the cutoffs and University of Kansas T-shirt. "No problem," he said softly. "I wasn't expecting to be company tonight. It just sort of happened."

She nodded. "Come on in." She led the way into the kitchen, then motioned for him to take a seat at the table. "Would you like some coffee? I just made a fresh pot."

"Sure," Harry said, pulling off his cap and tossing it atop the table. "Coffee sounds good. I'll need it to keep me awake for the trip back."

He watched her fuss around the tiny but orderly kitchen, taking down blue glass mugs and filling them to the brim with the steaming liquid. She placed a mug in front of Harry, then went back to retrieve her own, as well as a couple of napkins. She reminded him in many ways of Mattie.

"There's sugar and creamer on the table if you want them."

"Black's fine." Harry lifted the mug to his lips as if to prove his point. The coffee was strong. Almost too strong. But he liked the nutty flavor and presumed it must have been one of those fancy gourmet coffees that he always saw in the store but never bought. "It's good."

"Glad you like it. I made it kind of strong," she admitted. "But I figured on being up late tonight. I have a lot to do."

"And then I came along and interrupted. I'm sorry," Harry said, uncertain as to what he should do next.

Connie shook her head. "That's okay. I'll get to everything."

She seemed a bit uncomfortable, so Harry asked her how school was going. "Aren't you teaching summer school?"

"No, I helped with some weight lifting classes earlier, and then I was supposed to help with the girls' softball, but my principal relieved me of the responsibility."

"How come?" He tried to keep the feel of the conversation light, but Connie remained tense.

"I guess I was just too depressed about Dave and it showed enough to make a difference in my work. But enough about me. How's the farm? How's Grammy and my sisters? I guess everyone is down there but me."

"That's true. Mattie is still hoping you'll come down for the Fourth of July. We're planning quite a celebration. I'm in charge of fireworks and everyone else is doing food and anything else we need. Are you coming?"

Connie lowered her gaze to her coffee. "I'd like to. I'm going to try. But . . . well . . ."

Harry put down his mug. "Connie, I know there's something bothering you. Something more than Dave. At least that's what I suspect."

She snapped up, fixing her gaze on him with determination. "I'm fine," she said in a brusque manner.

"You don't sound like it. You aren't returning Mattie's calls and you look like you've lost your best friend. By your own admission, you didn't even know Dave all that well. After all, it wasn't like you were spending much time with anyone in the family, much less Dave and Deirdre." Harry hated the fact that he didn't sound very compassionate, but the words seemed to have a will of their own.

Instead of getting offended as Harry had presumed she might do, Connie looked at him rather uneasily, then returned her gaze to her coffee. "I guess some of it has to do with life catching up with me. Dave's death made me put things into perspective. I don't like myself very much, Harry. I don't like the choices I've made, and try as I might to seek God's forgiveness, I know I don't deserve it."

"None of us do," Harry reasoned. "That's what makes it so special. We get a gift we certainly don't deserve."

"This is more than just simple mistakes, Harry. This is my entire life. All of my choices have been direct rebellions against what I knew was right to do. It's almost like I looked at what was right and wrong and deliberately chose to do wrong every time. I left home feeling smothered in rules and regulations, and so I sought to find a way to dispel what I thought was a myth—that godly living equals happiness.

"In college I did what I pleased, partying and drinking and going out with anybody and everybody. I never gave any thought to what it would all mean later on, and now it's caught up with me."

A million thoughts raced through Harry's mind, but one made its way to the surface and came out of his mouth before he could put it into check. "You aren't pregnant, are you?"

"No, I'm not pregnant, Harry. It's just that my actions have isolated me. I feel as though I'm on a deserted island with no one but myself for company. Not that I can blame anyone. Who would want to keep company with me?"

"I can think of a few folks. You have a family who loves you very much. Mattie is beside herself worrying about you. She knows that things are wrong. She always does. She can read people like a book, my mother used to say. Your sisters love you, and I even overhead them saying how much they're worried about you. They feel like you've pushed them away. I know you've already taken the first step in working things out. Erica mentioned to me at the funeral that you were all realizing the harm you'd done each other. Don't you think it's time to put the past to rest and come home?"

"But what if they don't want me?" Connie said, tears streaming down her cheeks. "What if God doesn't want me back either? I've done such horrible things." Her cheeks flushed red as she met his gaze. "Horrible things, Harry."

Harry felt that she was trying in her own way to tell him what he was up against. But for reasons beyond Harry's understanding, he didn't care. He smiled gently. "So you've slept with the pigs. You aren't the first one. Remember, the Prodigal Son had the same problem and his father welcomed him back with open arms—even killed the fatted calf. I'll bet Mattie would rustle up one if she thought the family could finally be put back together."

Connie looked at the wall where Mattie's quilted square hung. "I just don't know if we can put it back together," she whispered.

Harry followed her gaze. "I'm thinking some things are impossible without the Master's touch. Why don't you just give your life back over to God, and maybe Mattie can see to putting the quilt back to one piece."

"You make it sound so easy," Connie said, turning to Harry.

He had to fight the urge to reach out to her, for he wanted nothing more than to hold her, to assure her that it wasn't nearly as hard as she wanted to make it. But something held him back. He knew Connie had to come to her own conclusion. She couldn't seek forgiveness and start a new life based on his desire to set her straight.

He shrugged and gently touched her cheek. "All I know," he said softly, "is that things generally go a whole lot easier when you give them over to someone who knows what they're doing."

Chapter 43

The clock chimed ten and Mattie rubbed her eyes and yawned. "I had no idea it was getting that late," she murmured.

"Me either," Ashley said, looking up from her book. "Once the boys go to bed, I tend to lose all track of time." Erica nodded and turned another page in the magazine she was glancing through.

Deirdre looked up from her sewing. "I know what you mean. With Morgan sleeping, it just seems like time does its own thing. Sometimes it seems to linger and other times it whizzes right by."

"It's so different in Kansas, compared to a city like New York where things never close down," Brook commented as she stretched. She'd been busy jotting a letter and seemed quite content in the silence of the evening.

Mattie nodded and closed her eyes. Leaning her head against the back of the chair, she thought of how blessed she was. God had shown her many things in life and given her much to be grateful for. In spite of the trials and sorrows of the last few months, she could see how God had creatively orchestrated every move to bring about a more positive result.

The sound of vehicles coming up the drive surprised everyone. Ashley and Erica made it to the window first, but Mattie was close behind.

"Looks like Harry's truck," she murmured. "But I don't know who else is out there. I hope nothing's wrong. Harry isn't usually one to make late-night visits."

Mattie went to the door and switched on the porch light. She unlocked the door just as she heard footsteps on the porch. Opening it, she found Connie reaching out for the screen door. Harry was a few paces behind her.

"Connie!" Mattie smiled and opened her arms to hug her granddaughter. "Oh, I'm so glad you're here."

Connie broke into tears and nearly collapsed in Mattie's arms. Her sobs caused everyone to exchange a questioning glance, but Mattie's eyes sought Harry. His expression reassured her.

"I'm so sorry, Grammy," Connie said, barely able to speak the words. "I'm . . . so . . . sorry."

"What's this all about, Connie?" Mattie questioned, all the while stroking Connie's short tresses.

"I've been so stupid. I've lived so foolishly. Please just tell me you forgive me," Connie said, pushing away. "Please."

Upon hearing the desperate, pleading tone in Connie's voice, Mattie felt her own eyes fill with tears and choked back a sob. "Connie, you know there's never anything so bad that I wouldn't forgive you. But this time I'm not at all sure what you're even talking about. Why don't you come in and explain."

Connie nodded and Mattie pulled her close and drew her into the house. The others had already gone back to the living room and were assembled in a rather tight-knit group, silently questioning each other and murmuring about this newest event. Mattie turned to encourage Harry to join them, but he slipped Connie's bags inside the door and then closed it quietly behind him.

Mattie waited until Connie calmed down, then sat beside her on the couch and listened as the sound of Harry's truck faded into the distance. Finally, she turned to Connie, gripping her hand tightly and asked, "What's this all about, Connie?"

Connie looked at her sisters and then to Mattie. "I've been so awful to all of you. I know you've probably given up on me. I didn't want to need any of you. I didn't want to care because I was afraid if I cared, I would get hurt worse than ever. You all seemed so much a part of each other, and I never felt right about my place in this family." She sniffed back tears and looked at Ashley and Brook. "You were twins and you had each other, and I envied that bond. Then you grew up and had wonderful lives and I envied that as well."

Mattie watched as Ashley and Brook exchanged a knowing glance, then returned their attention to Connie. Their lives were certainly less than perfect, but Connie didn't need to hear that just now.

"I envied Deirdre with her beautiful family, and I'm so sorry that Dave is gone." Connie barely got the words out before tears overpowered her. She cried quietly against Mattie's shoulder. "I envied Erica and her sweetness and her musical talent. I envied you all, and I know it was wrong. I know, too, that it drove me away from the family. I couldn't bear to deal with any of you. When I looked at you, it was like seeing a reflection of everything I couldn't have.

"I tried an outlandish life-style. I disregarded the rules and thumbed my nose at God," Connie said, her pain terribly obvious. "I thought I could find the love I was looking for in other relationships, but that never happened. Now I realize the emptiness was my own creation. I know that I need to fill that spot with God. Harry helped me see that tonight, but I knew I couldn't go to God without coming to each of you first," Connie said, giving a serious glance at each of her sisters. She returned her gaze to Mattie. "Please tell me I'm not too late. Please tell me you still care about me—that you wouldn't rather I be dead like Rachelle."

Before her teary-eyed sisters could make a move from where they stood, Morgan appeared in the room. She padded across the floor in dainty pink ballet-style slippers. Her little white gown swayed gracefully back and forth as she made her way to where Connie sat beside Mattie.

Everyone seemed to hold their breath for a moment. No one had expected Morgan, and Mattie could see that Deirdre wanted very much to reach out and pull Morgan away so as not to bother Connie in her grief. But something stopped Deirdre from interfering.

Without a word, the golden-haired child climbed up on Connie's lap and began to wipe away the tears on her aunt's face. Her pudgy fingers moved slowly and methodically on Connie's cheeks, and every so often she would stop and pat the cheek ever so gently.

"My daddy died," she told Connie, speaking for the first time in weeks.

A sob erupted from Deirdre, and Mattie watched as Brook and Ashley came to her side to support her. Erica's gaze was locked on Morgan in tearful fascination.

"I don't want you to die, Aunt Connie," Morgan said softly. "When you die you go away like my daddy, and I wish he hadn't gone away 'cause I want to play with him."

Connie sniffed and nodded. "I know how you feel," she said. "My daddy went away when I was little too. And I never got to play with him."

"You can play with me," Morgan said, stroking Connie's face.

"I would like that very much," Connie said, pulling Morgan against her.

Mattie felt like singing and laughing and crying all at the same time. Her prayers were answered and she felt a spirit of peace wash over them all. It wasn't too late. It was never too late, as long as the heart was willing to open itself to love.

Deirdre knelt beside Connie and Morgan and placed her hand atop Connie's. "I love you, Connie. Welcome back to the family."

"I love you too," Erica said, slipping onto the sofa beside Connie.

"That goes for me as well," Brook and Ashley both said, moving to stand behind the sofa. They gently touched Connie's shoulder, and the final barriers broke away.

─────────

That night, with all of her living family under one roof, Mattie stood before a portrait of Rachelle and smiled. "You did a good thing by bringing them all into the world. You could have chosen differently, and few would have faulted you. But I thank you."

Mattie then looked down at the letter Rachelle had written shortly before her death.

Mom,

Words cannot begin to express how sorry I am for the pain I've caused you.
Seems pain is what I do best. When Daddy and Robbie died, I wanted to die
too. I knew if it hadn't been for my silly play practice, Daddy would have been
safely at home. I guess that's why I felt I had to become the best actress that I
could be. I had to do this so that Daddy's death wouldn't be in vain.

I used to mourn that I couldn't give the girls the kind of life they deserved,
but then I realized that's exactly what I did in giving them to you. I was so silly
and headstrong. So ridiculously stupid. I know you forgive me, without even
having to ask. I can see you standing there—your loving smile, your gracious
manner. But, Mom, I can't forgive myself. And if I can't forgive myself, how
can God forgive me? I don't really want to die, but I just want the pain to go
away. I'm sorry that I'm not strong like you. I've always loved that about
you—I've always loved you. Please don't blame yourself for my choices. As I
was selfish in life, I'm selfish in death. I'm doing this for me.

Rachelle

Crawling between crisp, cold sheets, Mattie settled into her bed.
The letter was still in her hands and Mattie contemplated the words
for a long time before praying.

"Father, she was so lost. If only I could pray her into heaven . . . ."

But Mattie knew she couldn't do that. And to focus on the sorrow of Rachelle's lost soul would take away from the wonder of Connie coming back to God and her family. Mattie refused to be
sad—refused to bathe herself in regret. She couldn't help Rachelle
anymore, but she could help Rachelle's daughters.

Connie sat comfortably in the gazebo watching the sun rise
over the horizon in brilliant magenta hues. The skyline turned
crimson, spreading painted fingers upward into the darker blues
of predawn.

"*Red sky in morning, sailors take warning,*" Grammy would often say, and
sure enough, a storm usually brewed up by evening.

Connie couldn't help but think of the storm from the night before. A storm of spirits and wills and broken hearts that had festered in their wounds. But then the healing came with the calm of the night, and long after her sisters had drifted off to their various rooms in the house, Connie had felt their love keeping her warm. In their love she had been renewed. In God's love she was a new woman. It was like nothing she had ever known. She felt forgiven, and she felt blessed in having been released from her past.

"I see you're up early."

Connie startled from her thoughts to find Harry standing at the bottom of the gazebo steps. She smiled. "I didn't hear you come up. Did you row across the lake?"

He nodded. "I knew you'd be here and thought I'd come over to speak my mind."

"You saw me from clear across the lake?" Connie questioned. "That's impossible."

"I didn't say I saw you," he said with a grin. "I just knew you'd be here—somewhere. And that was all that mattered."

Connie felt her cheeks grow hot and she looked away as Harry joined her under the canopy. How was it that with just one look, he seemed to reach beyond her walls and see into the depths of her heart?

"If you'd rather me not be here, I don't have to stay," he said softly.

But Connie knew that the last thing she wanted him to do was go. "I'm glad you're here," she replied. "I wanted to thank you for helping me find my way home, both to God and to Mattie and my sisters."

Harry said nothing for a minute, and when Connie looked back she found his gaze fixed on her as if he were memorizing her every feature. "Did you hear what I said?"

He nodded. "I'm glad you feel that way. Did everything work out okay? Did you talk to them?"

"Yes," Connie said, smiling. "I apologized and told them everything. Then the most wonderful thing happened. In the midst of realizing that I was truly accepted and forgiven, Morgan appeared and told me she didn't want me to die like her daddy."

"Morgan talked?" Harry said, his excitement evident in his voice.

Connie shared his feeling of joy. "Yes. And that was the very best part. Because when Morgan spoke and told me she loved me, it was almost like hearing it from God himself."

Harry coughed and looked away and Connie was certain he had been moved to tears. He had such a gentle heart and sweet spirit. She had never met a more remarkable man . . . and to think he had been there, just across the lake, all of her life.

"So how would you feel if I told you the same thing?" he finally questioned, looking back to meet her study of him.

"What are you saying?" Connie felt a tugging in her heart—a hopefulness that began to diminish as her fears crowded in.

"I'm saying that I care deeply for you. If I ever had any doubt about it," Harry continued, "I realized last night that it was true."

"But, Harry . . . look at me and what I've done. You deserve much better than me . . . after all my past—"

"Has been forgiven," he said before she could say anything more.

"I know that, but even if my soul is renewed, the rest of me is still damaged goods. I don't deserve—"

Before the sentence was out of her mouth, Harry was at her side, pulling her to her feet. "Don't you understand? I don't care. I love you, Connie."

Connie bit at her lip to keep from crying again. She felt Harry's hands, warm and gentle, as they grasped hers. He had given her everything she had ever hoped for—an unconditional love that came fully aware of the possibility of trials and sorrows. Harry was a man that a woman could count on, and Connie knew that she wanted very much to be that woman.

"Thank you, Harry," she whispered, leaning into his embrace.

She heard the rapid beat of his heart as his arms tightened around her shoulders. It was enough, she thought. The empty places were finally filled, and peace flooded her soul like a clear mountain river that promised to wash everything clean.

Chapter 44

Ashley and Brook sat on the front porch snapping green beans for Mattie. It was an old task birthed somewhere way back in their childhood and Ashley thought it a very pleasant job. *Pinch the ends and snap the middle,* she thought, remembering Grammy's instructions.

She laughed to herself, causing Brook to look over in question. Ashley shrugged. "I just thought about that time when I asked Grammy why we had to snap the beans."

Brook nodded and laughed. "Because they can't snap themselves."

Ashley nodded. "We had a fun time of it, in spite of our complaints."

"We were more fortunate than we realized."

"Our parents may have been absent, but seeing the things that are out there today, I know that many children have parents in residence who are just as absent from their lives." Brook nodded. "And," Ashley continued, "I think that would be the worst of all."

They glanced up at the sound of a vehicle coming up the long, narrow lane. Ashley immediately recognized the Bronco.

"Jack." She whispered his name. "I can't believe he's come here."

"What are you going to tell him?" Brook asked, gathering up the sack of beans. She took the bowl from Ashley and placed it atop her own.

"That depends on what he's here to say," Ashley said thoughtfully. "I want to believe that I can trust him, that we can start over."

"That will require a great deal of faith on your part," Brook said, glancing down the drive.

"I know, and that's the hard part. It's going to take a lot of effort not to let the past come between us."

"If it were simple and clear-cut, Ashley, it wouldn't be faith. Faith requires trust and effort . . . but you have to make the choice to believe."

Ashley nodded and barely heard the screen door slam as Brook made her way inside. Looking down at her jeans, Ashley brushed off the bits of bean stems and got to her feet. She almost wished she could go inside and change her clothes, but Jack was already getting out of the car and it wouldn't be right to make him wait after he'd come all this way.

He approached her cautiously, his face filled with a look of complete misery. There were dark circles under his eyes and his once confident, almost arrogant look of self-assurance was gone.

"Look, I know you wanted some time alone," Jack began. "I wanted to give you as much as you needed, but I can't bear it anymore. I know I did wrong, Ashley. I know I don't deserve your forgiveness, but I'm begging for it just the same. I need you and I love you and home just isn't home without you."

Ashley recognized his sincerity—after all, she'd lived with this man for ten years. They had come through joys and sorrows together. They had hurdled tremendous ordeals as a couple and had found ways to ease each other's pain when no one else could help.

"Please, Ash," Jack said softly, "I know I can't undo what I've done, but I swear it will never happen again. I'll go to counseling or therapy or whatever else you think I need, but please say that you'll take me back. That we can be a family again."

Ashley knew all too well the need for forgiveness. She'd known it herself and she'd seen it so clearly displayed in Connie only the night before.

"I've thought about a lot of things, Jack," she began. "I know I allowed things to come between us. I know I sometimes put you last on my list. I've renewed my heart and my faith, and I know God has a plan for our future." She paused and opened her arms as she added, "Together."

Jack rushed up the stairs and pulled her into his arms. He held her so tightly that Ashley could scarcely breathe.

"Oh, I'm sorry," he said, pulling away. "I forgot about your incision. How are you feeling?"

"A little tender now," she said with a smile, "but otherwise unscathed and rapidly coming back to normal."

He took her in his arms again, this time gently. "I've missed you so much. I couldn't bear to think that I might lose you. Every time I looked at your side of the bed, all empty and untouched, I thought to myself that this was like a death of its own. I killed your faith in me, but, Ashley, I'll do everything in my power to give life to it again."

She nodded just as his lips closed over hers. With a sigh, Ashley knew that she'd done the right thing. He couldn't promise her that their marriage would be easy. Nor could he even guarantee that there wouldn't be times when they'd want to walk away from it all. But it was a start, and that was all they needed.

Brook smiled as she watched Jack and Ashley move off the porch and walk down the winding garden path. She knew her sister had longed for nothing more than this reconciliation, and she felt in her heart the kind of bonded peace that they shared when things went well. Ashley's joy had been restored.

Brook couldn't help but think of the Piece Work quilt. She had given Grammy her part of the quilt, hoping, as Ashley had, that the quilt could be rejoined. Now her sister's life would know the same kind of repair.

"You are a very wise woman, Mattie Mitchell," she whispered, thinking of her grandmother's tactics. "You knew the way to touch our hearts—not only when we were children, but even now when we are sometimes childish."

Deirdre hung up the telephone just as Morgan came into the kitchen. Mattie stood over the stove, adjusting the lid on her pressure cooker, but glanced over her shoulder at Morgan's announcement that she had to talk to her mother.

Deirdre lifted her daughter and smacked her lips against Morgan's neck, making her laugh. "And what is so important that you must interrupt the canning of beans?" Deirdre asked her teasingly.

"I want to live here, Mommy. I don't want you to buy another house. I like living with Grammy Mitchell."

Mattie laughed and dried her hands on her apron. "And I like having you living with me," she said as she came to stand beside the duo. "I like it very much."

Gratitude flooded Deirdre's heart at the sound of her daughter's voice. The words were like music to her ears and she would have granted Morgan any wish she desired. "Hmm . . . well, I suppose we could stay for a while at least."

Morgan clapped her hands. "Then I can plant flowers with Grammy and listen to the birds sing. 'Sides, Grammy promised to teach me to sew on her quilts."

"That's right, I did," Mattie said in mock seriousness. "It's a very special job, as you can well remember, Deirdre."

Deirdre put her daughter down and nodded. "I do remember. In fact, I have something that needs your attention."

Leaving her daughter and Mattie in the kitchen, Deirdre hurried upstairs to retrieve her wall hanging. When they'd made plans to come to Council Grove, it was the one thing from the house that Deirdre couldn't bear to leave behind.

Coming down the stairs, she listened as Mattie and Morgan moved down the hall toward the living room. She followed the sounds, smiling all the way. She could never love any woman more than she loved her grandmother. What a privilege and joy it was that her daughter could know this very special person.

"Here," Deirdre announced, thrusting the wall hanging into Mattie's hands. "I heard you were collecting these." She saw Mattie glance at the piece, then raise her face to Deirdre. "As parts, they are beautiful, but as a whole they are far more than pretty. Together they are useful and have a real purpose. I want you to put them back together, just like you put our family back together."

Erica and Connie came into the room, seconding the motion.

"We have our pieces too," Connie declared.

"Well," Mattie said, looking at the girls and then rubbing the top of Morgan's head. "I'd say we have our work cut out for us."

Chapter 45

Mattie gathered her sewing supplies and went into the dining room. She took up her special covering for the dining room table and spread out the pieces her granddaughters had brought to her. Then smiling, she began to call her girls to come.

"Ashley Kay! Brook Ann!" she called as she used to when they were little. "Constance Marie, where are you?" She smiled to herself and continued. "Deirdre Sue! Erica Lynn! I want to see you all in the dining room."

The girls came nearly at a full run. They hadn't heard this kind of calling in some years and each one bound into the room with a look that seemed to be a cross between urgency and concern.

"What's wrong?" Ashley questioned, Jack and the boys not far behind her.

"Yeah, Grammy, what gives?" Connie joined in.

Brook and Erica arrived together and Deirdre and Morgan brought up the rear.

Mattie looked at them all and laughed. "Today is the Fourth of July, or have you forgotten?"

They all shook their heads collectively.

"Well, you know the rules around here. Chores get done *before* fireworks and picnics take place."

They all nodded in unison.

Mattie laughed and pointed to the table, where she had laid out each of the wall hangings. "We have some work to do, girls."

"She said girls, so that means we can still go down to the lake and go fishing, right, Dad?"

Jack looked to Mattie and she nodded. "That's part of your chores. We're going to want fresh fish for our barbecue tonight."

"Oh boy!" John declared, tugging at his father's arm. "I'm gonna catch the biggest one ever." He looked up at his dad and seemed to feel sorry for the man. "We can show you how to fish, if you don't know how, Dad. Harry showed us."

"Harry?" He looked at Ashley with a questioning glance. "Your Harry?"

"Not hardly," Connie interjected. "He's my Harry now."

They all looked at her with open mouths of surprise. Laughter filled the room as Ashley rolled her eyes and scooted her brood out of the room. "Go on with you, now, I have to hear about Connie's new boyfriend."

"Can I sew too, Grammy?" Morgan asked softly.

"Absolutely," Mattie declared. "This is a family project." She went to her basket and took out a package of needles and several spools of thread. "A family kind of peace work, as well as a quilting piecework." They all nodded in understanding.

"I think she means business," Brook said, taking a seat at the table. "I'll give it a shot, but you may not like what I can do. I haven't sewn a stitch since you taught me to embroider."

"You think you have problems," Connie said, taking a seat beside Brook. "I can't even hold a needle. I'll be lucky to know which end gets the thread."

Ashley and Deirdre rolled their eyes heavenward and took seats on the opposite side of the table. "If you had kids," Deirdre said, "you'd learn quick enough how to hold a needle."

"Well, maybe if and when I do have kids," Connie said, smiling at her sister, "you can come over and show me how to sew for them."

"It's a deal," Deirdre replied, laughing.

Erica picked up the challenge eagerly and began threading a needle. "I think I can still manage," she told the others. "Even if I haven't had the practice mending kids' clothes that you've had. Besides, I need to get good at this."

The chatter continued happily as Mattie threaded a needle for Morgan. She drew the child to her lap so that she could better reach the pieces.

This is all I ever wanted, God, Mattie prayed silently. *I wanted to give them an understanding of you, but I also wanted them to desire the love of family and be close to one another. I wanted them to count on each other when times got bad and to know that the strongest thing in all the world is love.*

Everyone laughed at something Brook had said, and Mattie smiled and nodded as if she had heard every word. But she didn't need to hear the words to know that she understood their hearts. Her girls were home and the pieces of their lives were finally being fitted together for His purpose.

And, oh, Mattie thought, *what a wondrous work it will be when it's finished and presented to the Master.*